BENEATH THE BISHOP'S BONES
A VATICAN ARCHIVES THRILLER, VOL. 2

By

E. R. Barr

This book is a work of fiction. Names, characters, places and incidents are either the product of the author's imagination or are used fictitiously. Any resemblance to actual persons, living or dead, or to actual events or locales is entirely coincidental.

BENEATH THE BISHOP'S BONES: A Vatican Archives Thriller, Volume 2
Copyright © 2022 by E. R. BARR. All rights reserved, including the right to reproduce this book, or portions thereof, in any form. No part of this text may be reproduced, transmitted, downloaded, decompiled, reverse engineered, or stored in or introduced into any information storage and retrieval system, in any form or by any means, whether electronic or mechanical without the express written permission of the author. The scanning, uploading, and distribution of this book via the Internet or via any other means without the permission of the publisher is illegal and punishable by law. Please purchase only authorized electronic editions and do not participate in or encourage electronic piracy of copyrighted materials.

The publisher does not have any control over and does not assume any responsibility for author or third-party websites or their content.

Cover and title page art by Howard David Johnson
Cover and title page art designed by Howard David Johnson

Said Judas to Mary, music and lyrics by Sydney Carton
The Rare 'Ould Times, music and lyrics by Pete St. John
Into the Fire, The Scarlet Pimpernel Musical, music by Frank Wildhorn/lyrics by Nan Knighton
Secret Agent Man, music and lyrics by P. F. Sloan and Steve Barri
Exorcisms and Related Supplications, USCCB, 2017
Gaelic Music,*The Selected Poetry of Jessica Powers*, Jessica Powers

Publishing Services by Telemachus Press, LLC
7652 Sawmill Road
Suite 304
Dublin, Ohio 43016
http://www.telemachuspress.com

Visit the author website:
www.talesofconorarcher.com

Categories: Fiction / Thrillers / Historical

ISBN: 978-1-956867-41-1 (eBook)
ISBN: 978-1-956867-42-8 (Paperback)

Version 2022.08.15

REVIEWS OF THE FIRST BOOK IN THE VATICAN ARCHIVES SERIES: *GODS IN THE RUINS*

Action-packed, intense, and thematically profound, this is a conspiracy thriller done right ... Barr crafts an absorbing plot around history, religion, myth, archeology, and secrets long buried in his engrossing latest in The Vatican Archives series, featuring Vatican archeologist Fr. Daniel Azar and his best friend, Swiss Guard Luca Rohner ... Heavily shadowed with fantasy and myth, the novel is given weight by its focus on religion, terrorism, the mood of a war-trodden land engulfed in chaos, and the characters' interpersonal dynamics. Meticulously researched and intelligently crafted, the novel has a swift pace. Along the way, Barr captures the war-laden cultural milieu of Iraq with compelling detail. The result is a rich, vivid, and addictive book filled with deeply realized characters and settings. Meticulously researched and brilliantly crafted, this swiftly paced, action-packed tale is a treat for lovers of conspiracy thrillers.
—*The Prairies Book Review*

Move over, Indiana Jones! There's another swashbuckling hero in town! *Gods In The Ruins: A Vatican Archives Thriller* by E. R. Barr is the fantastic debut to a genre-blending new series. The protagonist, Fr. Daniel Azar, is not your average priest. He's also a trained archeologist and the godson of the current pope.

I was thoroughly impressed by the diversity of the characters and their distinctive personality traits. I cannot overstate how much I enjoyed this book! It could be adapted into a great blockbuster film. Monsignor Barr has an exceptional gift for storytelling. He seamlessly combines fact with fiction to create an unforgettable story that is impossible to put down. I was blown away by the creativity, the unexpected moments, and the accuracy of the archeological details! The narrative is written so that readers are privy to the secret motives of supporting characters and left wondering when the truth will be revealed in the plot.

It is a perfect blend of action and humor that has rekindled my love of archeology. Therefore, I am pleased to award *Gods In The Ruins: A Vatican Archives Thriller* by E. R. Barr a rating of four out of four stars. Fans of the Indiana Jones series and The Mummy franchise will relish this novel. I certainly did! Now I'm waiting with bated breath for the sequel.

—*OnlineBookClub.org*

DEDICATION

This novel is dedicated to Reverend Michael Kurz, devout and dedicated priest whose silent heroism represents the best of a vocation that seeks to give all to Christ and humanity.

TABLE OF CONTENTS

Cast of Characters	i
The End Times Tablet	ix
Prologue	xv
A Cry From The Dark	3
Nightmare	8
Veritas Comes Together	13
The Tunicle	20
A Puppet On A String	29
A Canterbury Tale	34
A Last Supper	42
Dem Bones, Dem Bones, Dem Dry, Dry Bones	51
There Was This Guy	64
A Babylonian Interlude	69
Miss Jenny Wren	75
The Poor Of The World	79
What The Fawkes Is Going On?	83
Blood In The Water	89
What's This Guy Doing?	94

Better To Reign In Hell Than Serve In Heaven	98
The Cats Of Caracalla	103
One Jewel To Rule Them All	115
Eleanora Regina Anglorum, Salus Et Vita	124
An Abbey Without A Soul	131
Masquerade	137
The Blood Is Life	149
Betrayers	155
A Superpower Flexes	160
A Quick Trip To Rome	166
A Sunday Brunch At The Vatican	171
Interlude	176
Into The Thick Of It	183
Putting On The Ritz	187
The Streets Of New York	192
Book Of Daniel Chapter 7	197
Meeting The Allies	203
Prelude To The Apocalypse	211
The Gallu	222
Why Guy?	232
An Infestation Grows	244
The Encircling Gloom	253
The Nest	260

The Grief Of The Good	266
Miracle In Canterbury	270
A Revelation Of Some Secrets	278
Into Fire, Into Hell	286
Disinfection	289
Considerations	305
A Time For Miracles	309
End Notes	317
Other Books By E. R. Barr	327
About The Author	329

BENEATH THE BISHOP'S BONES
A VATICAN ARCHIVES THRILLER, VOL. 2

CAST OF CHARACTERS

THE AMERICANS

Aunt Rue: President Putnam's aunt.

Tom Bentley: CIA attaché at USA Embassy, Rome.

Bart Finch: Techno Geek for Antiquities Division CIA.

Leslie Richardson: Director of the CIA.

John Nance: Wealthy philanthropist to the Vatican.

Rebecca Perez: Mossad-trained agent transferred to CIA, naturalized U. S. citizen.

Antoine Petrie: New York City fisherman.

Oliver Sebastian Putnam: President of the United States.

Harriet Putnam: First Lady of the United States.

Isaac Weiss: Mossad-trained agent transferred to CIA, naturalized U. S. citizen.

THE BRITISH

St. Thomas Becket (1120–1170): Chancellor of England (1155–1162), Archbishop of Canterbury (1162–1170). Murdered by soldiers of King Henry II. Venerated as martyr and saint.

Sandra Blessing: reporter from the BBC.

Sister Cecelia Campbell: Deacon, Canterbury Cathedral.

Edward Grim (?–1189): clerk who defended St. Thomas Becket during assassination, wrote account of the martyrdom.

Eleanor of Aquitaine (1122–1204): Queen of France (1137–1152), Queen of England (1154–1189), Duchess of Aquitaine (1137–1204). Most powerful woman of the Medieval Era, buried at Fontevraud Abbey.

Guy Fawkes (1560–1606): Catholic leader of the Gunpowder Plot (1605), a terrorist plan to kill the Protestant king and place a Catholic on the throne. Fawkes's persona is appropriated by Enki as a disguise.

Isabella of Angouleme (1188–1247): Queen of England (1200–1228), wife of King John Plantagenet, buried at Fontevraud Abbey.

Henry II Plantagenet (1133–1189): King of England and Lord of Angevin Empire (1154–1189), buried at Fontevraud Abbey.

Richard I Plantagenet, the Lionheart (1157–1199): King of England and Lord of Angevin Empire (1189–1199), buried at Fontevraud Abbey.

Rosamund (1140–1176): mistress of Henry II.

Henry VIII Tudor (1491–1547): King of England (1509–1547).

Elizabeth I Tudor: (1533–1603), Queen of England and Ireland (1558–1603).

Henry IX Windsor: King of Great Britain.

John Johnson: *nom de plume* of Guy Fawkes. Also appropriated by Enki as a disguise.

Stephen Langton (1150–1228): Cardinal Archbishop of Canterbury (1207–1228).

Lionel Mergen: a reporter from Sky News.

Reginald Pole (1500–1558): last Plantagenet heir to the throne, Cardinal Archbishop of Canterbury (1556–1558). Last Catholic to hold that position.

Peter Pomeroy: Archbishop of Canterbury.

Michael Throckmorton (1153–1558): special agent and spy for Cardinal Pole.

Vincent Traling: Cardinal Archbishop of Westminster.

THE CHINESE

Sung Kai: Vice President of People's Republic of China.

THE FRENCH

Louis VII (1120–1180): King of France (1132–1180). Protector of Thomas Becket.

Louis XIV (1638–1715): King of France (1643–1715). Known as the Sun King.

Gabrielle de Rochechouart (1645–1704): Abbess of Fontevraud Abbey (1640–1707). Known for her wisdom and piety, she was especially revered by Louis XIV. Rebecca disguises herself as the abbess at the evening costume party in Fontevraud Abbey.

THE IRAQIS

Dr. Frances Azar: wife of Markoz and mother of Monsignor Daniel Azar, world-famous archeologist.

Dr. Markoz Azar: husband of Frances and father of Monsignor Daniel Azar, world-famous archeologist.

Walid Badawi, the Bedouin: chief assassin in Babylon, killed by Abednego, one of the Three Brothers, amidst the Babylon ruins.

THE VATICAN/ITALIANS

Alexander III (1105–1181): Pope (1159–1181), considered an exceptional pope, protector of St. Thomas Becket. Daniel Azar takes his disguise for the evening costume party at Fontevraud.

St. Anthony of Padua (1195–1231), born in Portugal and died in Italy, Anthony was one of the first Franciscans and known as a stunning preacher and miracle worker. He possessed a Star Sapphire which passed to the Vatican Archives where it lay undiscovered until found by Pope Patrick.

Monsignor Daniel Azar: Son of Drs. Azar, Roman Catholic Chaldean priest, stationed at the Vatican, head of VERITAS.

Antonio Bigetti: pilot, Vatican Air Fleet.

John VIII, Pope (872–882): considered one of the best popes of the 9th century, he created a naval fleet to successfully defeat the Islamic Saracens who were invading Italy.

Michelangelo Buonaratti (1475–1564): artist and friend of Cardinal Pole.

Benjamin Capito: one of the transient poor of Rome.

Dr. Abigail Duchon: Sindonologist (expert on Shroud of Turin), Nobel Prize Chemist, member of VERITAS.

Nicky Farrell: Clerk at Irish College, Vatican/Rome.

Maria Franco: Girlfriend of young Daniel Azar.

Grigio: Mysterious dog companion of Monsignor Azar.

Josiah Hindermas: Corporal in the Vatican Swiss Guard, member of VERITAS.

Mattias Kurz: Corporal in the Vatican Swiss Guard, member of VERITAS.

Colonel Mario Minitti: Head of the Vatican Swiss Guard.

Liam Murphy/Pope Patrick: First Irish pope.

Benito Mussolini (1883–1945): Il Duce, fascist leader of the Italian State (1922–1943). Made a treaty with the Vatican in 1929 whereby Vatican City was guaranteed its existence as an independent state.

Dr. Bartholomew Rappini: physician at Gemelli Hospital, Rome.

Fr. Salvatore Rovere: priest aide to Pope Patrick, member of VERITAS.

Luca Rohner: Captain of the Vatican Swiss Guard, best friend of Daniel Azar, member of VERITAS.

Rupert (last name unknown): leader of the thugs in the tunnels of the Baths of Caracalla.

Luigi Stefan: Cardinal Secretary of State of Vatican.

Franco Salamone: Pilot, Vatican Air Fleet.

Tia (last name unknown): a witch who is part of the gang of thugs in the Baths of Caracalla, possibly a Babylonian entity.

Gemma Tortelli: Nursing Supervisor, Gemelli Hospital, Rome.

Miss Jenny Wren: one of the transient poor of Rome.

THE SYRIANS

Dr. Nabil Kasser: Islamic scholar and imam, founder and head of the 'Islamic Studies Worldwide Initiative' (ISWI), based in Washington, D. C. Acknowledged by some as the Mahdi, the prophesied leader of the Islamic peoples.

TERRORIST GROUPS

Memento Mori: Terrorist Group founded by John Nance. In English, its name means 'Remember Your Death.' Nance assigned the group to assist Enki.

UNITED NATIONS ORGANIZATION

Rabindranath Basu: Secretary-General of the United Nations.

James McCoy: President of the General Assembly of the United Nations.

THE ANCIENTS

Anunnaki: the ancient gods of the Fertile Crescent (Babylon, et. al.). The word means 'those who from the heavens came.' Conspiracy theories and ancient astronaut theories have arisen during modern times concerning these beings. Most are ridiculous in their details, but all seem to enshrine the ancient idea that there were beings on this planet who helped civilize humans. It seems to be a notion not easily expunged from humanity's memory.

Caracalla (188–217): Roman emperor (198–217), builder of Baths of Caracalla.

Marduk: Chief pagan god of ancient Fertile Crescent (Babylon, et. al.).

Mithras: Pagan god whose cult and persona were inspired by Iranian worship of the Zoroastrian divinity Mithra. The Roman Mithras is different in many respects, however an so should be seen as derivative. The mysteries were popular among the Imperial Roman army from about 50–350 CE. Worship took place in a *Mithraeum*, an underground temple.

Enki: Pagan god of water and mischief of the ancient Fertile Crescent (Babylon, et. al.).

Nebuchadnezzar II: (630–562 BCE \, reigned 605–562 BCE) Greatest king of Babylon.

Shadrach, Meshach, and Abednego: the three mysterious strangers, all brothers, discovered in stasis in the tomb uncovered by Daniel and the Drs. Azar. They claim to be from the time of King Nebuchadnezzar and have great knowledge and wisdom.

Tarhuan (c. 9000 BCE): King of Gobelki Tepe, reputed to have reigned over 500 years.

Tiamat: the pagan mother goddess of the ancient Fertile Crescent (Babylon, et. al.), possibly manifesting in the Baths of Caracalla disguised as a witch.

THE AVATAR

Ranbir Singh: CIA Antiquities Division cybernetic hologram created by Bart Finch.

THE ARTIFACTS

The End Times Tablet: discovered by the Drs. Azar in Babylon on top of an ancient tomb, it prophesies a coming apocalypse on November 1.

The Esagila: the ancient Temple of Marduk in Babylon where the End Times Tablet was found along with the Tomb of the Three Brothers.

Gobelki Tepe: a Neolithic archeological site in Southeastern Anatolia, Turkey. Dated between 9500 and 8000 BCE Its discovery upended archeology since large, obviously, urban structures should not have been possible before agriculture developed. Conspiracy theorists posit it as influenced or built by the Anunnaki.

'Oumuamua: a cylindrical asteroid that in this story has a huge part to play in the coming apocalypse of November 1.

The Regale of France: A large ruby cabochon given by King Louis VII of France to the Shrine of St. Thomas Becket in the hopes that his donation and prayers would help lead to the healing of his son, Phillip. In fact, the boy recovered from a deadly illness at the time Louis was in Canterbury. The jewel disappeared after the destruction of the shrine by King Henry VIII in 1538. In the story, the jewel is known to have great healing powers.

Shroud of Turin: the supposed blood-stained burial cloth that wrapped the crucified body of Jesus Christ.

Star Sapphire Rings: Six rings each with a central star sapphire surrounded by six diamonds. The rings enhance the bearers and serve as weapons of power and force with some healing properties. One is lost, but five are known to exist. The Pope, Daniel, and the three brothers possess these.

The Tunicle: blood-stained white vestment (surplice) that is part of the liturgical vesture of deacon, priest, or bishop. An authenticated relic worn by Thomas Becket as he was martyred in his cathedral.

THE END TIMES TABLET

Translated from Akkadian Script by Monsignor Daniel Azar

By the rivers of Babylon
We dreamed the dream—
The night visions of terrible power.

A Beast from shadows between the stars—
Whose mouth is fire,
Whose breath is death,
Whose will is woe—

Has risen in our minds,
And devoured our hearts.
So, we sleep,
In the arms of the nether world.

But our brother from long ago walks again.
He walks beyond the veil.
He has seen the Beast—

Whose mouth is fire,
Whose breath is death,
Whose will is woe.

He tells us to wait,
To wait the passing of years.
For a time to come,
When the Dreamer returns.

The earth shall shake;
The tomb shall open;
Blood shall flow;

Darkness shall seep
Into the Land Between the Rivers,
Where war has waged
From age to age.

Armies ride the Beast—
Whose mouth is fire,
Whose breath is death,
Whose will is woe.

The Dreamer and the Guided One
Shall unite against it.

War and bloodshed break out—
The fire from its mouth.

Pestilence and famine descend—
The death from its breath.

Panic and chaos erupt—
The woe from its will.

The pillars of the earth shake,
In the year of the Lord
November First,
When the mark of the Beast
Traverses the heavens.

OLDE ENGLAND 1170–1179 CE

PROLOGUE

i

Tuesday, December 29, 1170 CE. Evening, Canterbury Cathedral, Canterbury, England

CLOUDS OF INCENSE spiraled heavenward as the procession made its way up the cathedral's center aisle. The thurifer knew his role well, swinging the censor far forward and backward so as not to be smothered in the exotic smoke. The cross-bearer, immediately behind, held high the processional cross which shimmered gold in the candlelight from tapers clutched by the monks and laity who had gathered for Vespers here on the fifth day of Christmas 1170 CE.

He was here. Oh, they knew that God was present but that wasn't the "He" they waited for. The Archbishop of Canterbury, Thomas Becket, was here, walking at the end of the procession behind the monks of the cathedral priory. Tall and noble of bearing, despite his merchant background, Thomas looked at peace, though he was the only one to appear so. The people weren't sure he would appear, as a death sentence seemed to be shadowing him.

The last monk in the procession, just before the archbishop, looked back at the prelate and gave a nervous smile.

"It will all be right, Brother Edward," said Thomas as they walked. "Whatever happens will be for God's glory and honor." He took his hand and placed an object in Edward's palm, saying, "Hide this well, and if I do not survive, take it to Louis in France. He will know what to do with it."

Brother Edward Grim wasn't so sure things would be all right. Whatever the archbishop had given him—it felt the size of a hen's egg—he placed it in his pocket. How did he deserve such a charge? He had just made it to Canterbury hours before and had introduced himself to the archbishop, indeed, was presenting his credentials, when the door to the palace banged open and four knights in their grubby surcoats had plunged in and accosted them. At least, thought Edward, they had the decency to leave their swords and armor outside.

The knights had come from King Henry II's Christmas court in France and sailed the Channel because they had heard and saw Henry smash his wine goblet down at a banquet and yell at the top of his voice, "Will no one rid me of this meddlesome priest?"

King Henry, Lord of England and much of France, was known for his quick temper. The knights recognized it was Becket Henry was speaking of, for the two formerly best friends had been at odds for years. And so, the knights, fresh from their sailing and galloping towards Canterbury, screamed at Thomas Becket, accusing him of infidelity to King Henry, his lord and liege, and demanded that he lift the excommunications of the king's retainers.

Thomas refused, and in a rage, the knights stormed out. All the monks feared further violence, but the archbishop insisted on celebrating Vespers, the Evening Prayer of the Church. Those in attendance intoned Psalm 115, *Non nobis, Domine, non nobis, sed nomini tuo da Gloriam.* "Not to us, O Lord, not to us, but to your name be the glory!" A perfect psalm to encapsulate Thomas's wholehearted fidelity to uphold the honor of God, regardless of what the king, his former best friend wished.

Becket made it up the first few steps of the sanctuary when the Cathedral doors burst open and the four knights along with a renegade monk supporting them shouted for Thomas to show himself. Thomas turned to a side altar and faced the oncoming soldiers.

"Where is Thomas Becket, traitor to the king and kingdom?" shouted the knights, their voices echoing in the cathedral. "Where is the archbishop?"

"Here I am!" said the archbishop. "Not a traitor to the king, but a priest! I am prepared to die for my Lord!"

Seeing him, they rushed him. He took hold of a pillar so as not to be removed from the church, but one of the knights raised his sword to bring it down on Thomas's head.

Then was the moment, Edward Grim, a monk not known for his courage, raised his arm and partially blocked the strike. The sword nearly severed his arm while striking a glancing blow to Thomas's head. Thomas fell into the wounded arms of Edward. A second blow from a sword cut Thomas more severely, and he knelt and raised his hands to God. Then came the third blow to the head, which exposed the archbishop's brain, but Thomas was still able to say, "For the name of Jesus and the protection of the Church, I am ready to embrace death." A fourth knight struck the head of the archbishop again, and so powerful was the stroke of the sword that it clove through Thomas's head and shattered into pieces of steel on the stone of the cathedral floor. Then a fifth villain, an evil monk who hated Thomas, took a dagger and spread the blood and brains out upon the stone pavement saying to the knights, "Let us go. He shall not rise from here again."

As the knights and clerk ran from the cathedral, screaming broke out throughout the church and the monks fled. Only Brother Edward Grim remained, cradling the fallen archbishop, Becket's blood soaking into his holy vestments. Grim marveled that the face of Becket was unmarked, just a thin line of blood from his left cheek to his right temple hinted at the devastation of his body, a horror all too present when the monks crept back to hurriedly bury their archbishop.

Grim was tended by the monk's infirmarian who now had little else to do. The monk didn't think he could save Grim's arm and left him to rest in the infirmary. The wounded monk pulled out the object Becket had given him. It was slippery with all the blood, much of it the archbishop's, but much also of Grim's. As he wiped it clean on his robe, he saw that it was a massive jewel, a ruby actually mounted in a black oculus. It was amazingly beautiful, and Grim knew it was worth a king's ransom. It felt warm to the touch, and as Grim prayed for the dead archbishop, he felt a warmth come over his body, as a shadow fell across his face. He looked and knew a presence was there, though the form was indistinct. Into his ear whispered the words, "Be healed little monk for the good you have done. Go to King Louis in France and go now!" The ruby brightened, and Grim's damaged arm suddenly felt on fire. Then, the pain was gone, and so was the wound. To Grim's amazement, the wounded arm was whole again. Becket had worked his first miracle.

ii

August, 1179 CE. Canterbury Cathedral, Canterbury, England

KING LOUIS VII of France looked at the immense Cathedral of Canterbury looming above him as he clutched The Regale of France, the beautiful ruby cabochon pendant around his neck. So many years ago, a young brother monk had returned it to him, the blood of Becket dried upon it.

The King had given the pendant to Thomas when the fugitive bishop had returned to Canterbury nearly a decade ago. He told Thomas, "Wear this pendant always, and God will protect you from harm. The Regale of France is an ancient jewel that once healed the great Charlemagne." Why Thomas took it off that Christmas night so long ago and gave it to the monk, Louis could not fathom. It healed the monk's wound but condemned Thomas to the death heard round the world.

Now, it had failed even the King of France, for his son Phillip lay dying in his fevered bed back in Paris. Louis had done everything—laid the jewel on the boy's chest, had the lad drink water the gem was boiled in, even wrapped it in linen said to be part of the swaddling clothes of Christ and bound it around the child's head. All to no avail.

But then came the dream. Thomas Becket appeared to the King of France and told him to go to Canterbury on pilgrimage with The Regale, and all would be well. One thing every subject of the king said without reservation is that Louis was a pious man. If the now most popular saint in Christendom appeared to him in a dream, then he must do what the vision commanded. And so, Louis found himself outside the cathedral doors.

But he was not alone. King Henry II, Lord of the Angevin Empire, sat beside the worried king on horseback. Henry had long since made peace with the murder he admitted he was partially responsible for. He had done hard penance for the death of his friend and foe, beaten with whips by the monks of the abbey, a solitary penitent day and night before the archbishop's newly constructed tomb, both his penance and the tomb wonders to behold.

"My lord," said Henry to Louis, for though Henry was far more powerful than the King of France, Louis outranked him and was owed fealty. "You have come then to pray for your son."

"Indeed," said Louis. "Thomas required me to come."

"No doubt," muttered Henry, "he can be most insistent, even in death." But even the king of England was humbled before the shrine. Thousands of miracles had already been wrought over the years at this tomb inside the cathedral. Who was Henry to deny an aging father's wish for the recovery of his sickened son? Becket had been a busy bishop in life; Henry wondered where the sainted archbishop found the time in heaven to do all the many miracles that drew tens of thousands of pilgrims to the shrine each year.

He followed his liege lord into the cathedral and watched as Louis knelt before the magnificent shrine of the saint. It was huge, covered in gold, with apertures along the sides where pilgrims could touch the tomb, making their heartfelt petitions. The opulence of the shrine was tremendous, but it was not the result of the Church enriching it. Pilgrims from throughout Christendom had come through the years leaving objects of wealth to honor the saint. Thus, it was no surprise when the prior of the abbey stepped forward and whispered the words to the king of France that all clergymen were familiar with: "If you find it in your heart, O Majesty, to donate to the shrine, we can continue the upkeep of this most beautiful memorial to the saint and place of light for all who seek to banish the darkness within themselves."

Ever the pious Catholic, King Louis VII of France immediately, and rather absent-mindedly, promised thousands of florins to the shrine. Then he prayed for the healing of his son. He took off the pendant around his neck and wrapped the chain around his thumb, placing the shining Regale of France as if it were a ring on his hand. His heart burst with sorrow with the thought that his only male heir might pass into eternity while he was on pilgrimage here in this godforsaken, cold and wet country.

Even Henry, hardened as he was to life's verities—his three sons rebelled against him, after all—was touched by Louis' evident love for his child. Both monarchs wept; indeed, all the pilgrims present wept as well. That's when it happened.

Louis felt a tugging on his hand. The Regale was moving. The jewel mounted in the black oculus of some unknown mineral was trying to separate itself from Louis' hand. Everyone saw it. There was a flash of clear light, bright as a diamond, a loud snap as the chain was broken, and The Regale of France leaped from Louis's hand and flew several yards till with a loud pop it affixed itself to the upper side of the gold-plated tomb. Now it swirled red and cast a warm glow upon the pilgrims, as the Cathedral bells somehow found it prudent to chime in glorious praise of God. Henry and Louis looked at the pulsating jewel, an emperor among the diamonds and emeralds and gold honoring the saint.

"My lord," said the prior.

"Of course, the shrine may keep The Regale," said Louis, still marveling at the sight. "It is a sign from St. Thomas that my son will heal. And," said the king, waving his hand sans Regale, "you may also keep the florins I promised. This is a pilgrimage worth a king's ransom."

King Louis departed home shortly thereafter, having been sent the news that his son was recovering. Spurred on by miracles such as this, the shrine continued to grow in popularity. Everyone noted the presence of The Regale. Like a lighthouse upon the darkling sea, it shone in the cathedral as a sign of hope and the presence of the saint. King Henry even had one of his jewelers fashion an angel of gold set at the base of the tomb, pointing towards The Regale. To the pilgrims who came and saw, its beauty trumpeted the power of the saint to dispense the mercy of Christ.

Rome was more magnificent in size, but nothing was as beautiful as the jewel that welcomed the pilgrims to the shrine of St. Thomas of Canterbury. It was a place of healing and hope for nearly four hundred years until another king came and wiped it from the face of the earth, and The Regale disappeared.

PRESENT DAY

A CRY FROM THE DARK

Wednesday, March 17, Present Day, Noon, Rome, St. Peter's Square

BLUE SKIES AND a warm sun fell on the Eternal City. Pope Patricius, known as Pope Patrick in English-speaking countries, decided to celebrate his patronal feast day with the usual Wednesday audience, but on this beautiful spring day, held outside instead of the modern audience hall. Weather forecasters had long promised a warm week and crowds were out to the max, tourists, and locals, as much to enjoy the weather as to see the pope.

Pope Patrick, who had been Liam Murphy, the Cardinal Archbishop of Armagh, Ireland before his election as the youngest pontiff in recent memory, loved the crowds and the excitement. He was only fifty years of age, tall with a handsome, craggy face with black curling hair and grey eyes that could turn the color of steel when angry or shine warmly blue when life was fine.

"Do not be afraid!" he exhorted the crowd during his brief address. "We live in a world where war and rumors of war, plague and violent destruction, famine and anxiety tear our hearts with worry and concern. Do not be afraid! For there is One who has conquered all and promised to be with us to the end of time—Christ himself—and he will not leave us abandoned and adrift on seas of darkness."

Everyone knew what he was talking about. Less than a month ago, archeologists from Iraq including their son, Monsignor Daniel Azar, adopted nephew of the pope and a rising star in archeology himself, had translated an ancient Babylonian tablet that foretold terrible times to come on November 1 of this very year, times of suffering and perhaps even the end of the world.

That didn't go over very well across the globe. There were a few riots but much more consternation. World and religious leaders found themselves riding the waves of emotion cast by their citizens and followers. Only a concerted and united front presented by the United Nations, the United States and Russia, Israel, the Vatican, and several powerful Islamic imams kept the anxiety from exploding. China tended to dismiss the warning but tamped down even more strongly on its internal media. Not since the pandemic years earlier had the globe been so on edge.

But it was St. Patrick's Day, the first one ever really celebrated at the Vatican, and the pope was determined to make it a joyous experience. He was taking a spin around St. Peter's square in the popemobile to greet the people when it happened. He had just passed the marble marker on the pavement that denoted the exact spot where one of his predecessors, St. John Paul the Great, had been shot and nearly killed decades ago. Pope Patrick was dressed in his white cassock with a beautiful red cape thrown around his shoulders, and a white zucchetto on top of the thick black curls of his head. Heavy as it was, the cape billowed in the wind as the popemobile carried him through the crowds. Everyone could see the joy on his face and responded in kind.

He saw her first, climbing up one of the short barricades that separated the crowds and allowed the pontiff to drive through safely. The pope noted she was dressed in the colorful rags that the poor of

Rome sometimes wore, a mismatched wardrobe of crushing poverty. The young woman was screaming something which couldn't be heard above the cheering of the crowd. But then, she started to leap with amazing dexterity from barricade to barricade toward the approaching pope. Like a rag doll puppet on invisible strings, she bounced along, never slipping or falling, twirling in a mystic dance all her own.

Fortunately, the pope was not the only one who saw. Captain Luca Rohner, of the Swiss Guard, was on ceremonial duty out in the midst of the crowd. Wearing the blue and gold garments designed for the Guard centuries before and a silver helmet glinting in the spring sunlight, he looked like a statue. He also carried a halberd, not just another decorative spear but amazing in its ability to control a crowd in the hands of an experienced wielder. Luca was such a one.

The lady on the barricades lurched and jumped towards the pope, and Luca moved rapidly to intercept. Seeing she was somewhat handicapped—one shoulder was higher than another—he didn't want to hurt her. Luca was close enough to hear what she was screaming. "The Beast is coming!" she shrieked over and over again.

But that was not what horrified Luca. Out of her filthy garments, she dragged a knife of huge proportions and launched herself in the air toward the pontiff. So small, she should not have been able to make the leap, but she seemed possessed of extraordinary strength. Luca swung the halberd, expertly disarming the woman, knocking the knife away. But he could not stop her from crashing into Pope Patrick.

There were definite advantages to having a younger, stronger pope. As the popemobile came to a stop, the pope caught the woman when she smashed into him. He held her shoulders as she started to scream again. Then, he looked into her eyes and saw the chaos there—a parasitic darkness that did not belong to this poor soul swam in the murk and cloudiness of her eyes. Luca was climbing into the popemobile to assist the pontiff when he suddenly looked at him and said, "Stay away. This is no ordinary assassin."

She couldn't have weighed much, and the pope was able to lift her up onto the seat of the vehicle. Moving his hands to the sides of her head, he looked into her despairing eyes, breathed on her, and said, "Leave her!" Putting his face close to hers, he said clearly, "The power of Christ commands you!" Above the crowd, a wailing was heard ending in a thunderclap, which some thought was gunfire. But no, the pope stood straight and tall, red cloak billowing around him, shielding both him and the woman, and caught her as she collapsed into his arms. He noted her eyes were now clear, yet she was confused.

"Where am I?" she asked.

"Someplace safe," said the pontiff. "What is your name, little one?"

"I don't know," she said. "Once I did, but now ..."

The pope gestured to Luca telling him to take her to the hospital to make sure she was physically all right. For a moment, the Pope watched in silence as Luca gently led the woman away. Then the Popemobile lurched forward and the crowds cheered wildly. It wasn't every day one got to witness a miracle.

This wasn't the first exorcism performed in St. Peter's Square. Pope Patrick's three immediate predecessors were rumored to have done similar ones during their time as successors of St. Peter. Technology wasn't as fine-tuned in their day. Their deeds were only rumors. Cameras now were everywhere as were microphones, and the attack and Pope Patrick's response were clearly filmed up close and personal and headlined that night's evening news. It was like a scene from the old movie, *The Exorcist*, only real and immediate this time. Depending on the paper and individual media, the headlines screamed or desultorily proclaimed the news:

POPE MEETS BEAST BEFORE WORLD'S END!

POPE 1, SATAN 0

CAPED CRUSADER BATTLES POSSESSED WOMAN

POSSESSED WOMAN AT VATICAN? POPE SNATCHES PR OPPORTUNITY

POPE AT VATICAN: DIFFICULT TIMES NEED STRONG SPIRITUAL MEDICINE

NIGHTMARE

Wednesday Afternoon, March 17, Rome, Irish College

WHILE THE POPE held his Wednesday audience at St. Peter's, Monsignor Daniel Azar, his adopted nephew and godson, was grabbing a quick nap at his apartment in the Irish College.

The last weeks since he had returned from Babylon had been filled with frenetic activity. He was trying to get used to his new title of 'monsignor'. "The head of VERITAS has to have a little status," said the pope.

However, that promotion was the least exciting thing on his plate. His father and mother, Drs. Markoz and Frannie Azar, world-famous Iraqi archeologists, had fulfilled their promise and revealed to the world what the newly discovered tomb in the ancient city held. Well, mostly revealed. There was an engraved tablet, and then there were the bodies in the tomb. Like Daniel, they kept the existence of the stasis-revived Shadrach, Meshach, and Abednego a secret. These three young men, if that is what they truly were, apparently had survived for millennia in some type of suspended animation. They seemed to be the young men talked about in the biblical Book of

Daniel and had survived to help this modern era endure and defeat a time of darkness and woe.

The message everyone was excited about was written about on an engraved golden panel on top of their sarcophagus. Called the 'End Times Tablet', it revealed that a type of heavenly phenomenon, a comet or asteroid, was coming back after an absence of thousands of years to wreak havoc on the earth this coming November 1. Its purpose was to release some kind of beast to torment humanity. When this had happened to humanity before, terrible destruction had occurred, sending the human race back into barbarism. Or so the three young men had said.

Daniel, an esteemed Vatican archeologist in his own right, and his parents, found themselves partnering with the American CIA to get to the bottom of this mystery of the End Times Tablet. If what the tablet said was true, mass panic and world upheaval were sure to result, not to mention the paralysis that would set in as nations vied to come up with a solution to what seemed to be a growing apocalyptic situation.

What Daniel and the team on the ground in Babylon discovered was much more than the dust and ashes from a long-vanished civilization. On his hand, he wore an ancient ring, given to him by a crazed Saddam Hussein on the night Americans visited Shock and Awe upon the tyrant so many years ago.

Daniel was just a child then, but the ring had molded itself to his finger and remained dormant for years, only to suddenly activate when Daniel's life was threatened. It revealed itself to be the ancient Star Sapphire Ring, rumored to have been passed down to certain humans from the time of King Nebuchadnezzar of Babylon.

Daniel discovered, after two attempts on his life, that his enemies were aware of the ring and wanted it. Even the Arab who might be the prophesied Mahdi, or Savior of the Islamic people, tried to take it when he met Daniel in Babylon.

Those things Daniel could understand, strange as they were. Since the time of the fruit on the Tree of the Knowledge of Good and Evil in Eden, human beings were greedy for power and knowledge. But what blew his mind was that something else in the wastelands outside of Babylon sought the ring as well, an ancient godlike being named Marduk, who had at his command, the *sirrusha* dragons of Babylonian myth. As Luca Rohner, his best friend, said so graphically, "They were a true pain in the *kiester*."

Death followed death in the archeologists' camp, culminating in a battle between ISIS and Iraqi forces for possession of the tomb, its contents, and the ring. When Daniel and his friends discovered three young men, alive and well in the tomb, also wearing Star Sapphire Rings, they were further smacked with the revelation that these three beings believed the priest to be, if not the reincarnation of their friend, the biblical prophet Daniel, then the genetic duplicate of him. They called themselves Shadrach, Meshach, and Abednego.

Lucky for Daniel and friends, the good guys won, and the priest brought the three strangers back to Rome without the faintest understanding of what he was going to do with them. Pope Patrick and the papacy were further wrapped up in the mystery when the pontiff revealed that he had discovered another one of the rings in the Vatican Archives. An assassination attempt occurred at the Apostolic Palace in what turned out to be a failed effort to procure the rings.

Meanwhile, Daniel's parents held the press conference of the century in Babylon, telling the world of the danger that was coming but also revealing the wonders of the tomb. The crypt held vast quantities of Babylonian records primarily on medicine and astronomy, documents never seen before which promised new discoveries that could help humanity.

But so far, there was nothing in the tomb to indicate how the coming apocalypse was to be averted. That was what preoccupied

Daniel the past few weeks. He had his mother and father forward copies of the astronomical observations to the Jesuit astronomers at the pope's observatory at Mt. Graham in Arizona. The location always surprised people, even those who knew of the vibrant science programs the Vatican supported. They thought the observatory was at Castle Gandolfo, the summer residence of the papacy. No longer. Urban light pollution made the pope build a new research facility in the U.S.A. The pope's astronomers were making fast progress doing their Jesuit thing on the knowledge being revealed, hoping to find a hint at fighting the coming celestial calamity.

In fact, Dr. Markoz Azar and his wife, Frannie, were farming out the knowledge found in the tomb to scientists around the world as fast as they could. Their sleepless nights were shared by their son who was trying to make sense of all the things out of legend and time that had been discovered in the past month.

And that's why Daniel was taking a nap while his uncle was fending off an evil attack in St. Peter's Square. His sleep was a peaceful one until he started dreaming. Lately, his dreams, like his namesake's, had become prophetic, forecasting future events, and this one was no different.

He found himself in the papal observatory at Mt. Graham, talking to Fr. Peter Rinaldi, famed Jesuit astronomer who was a comet specialist and discoverer of extra-planetary objects within the solar system. Next to Daniel sat Grigio, the wolf-dog who haunted his dreams and appeared in real life as his sometime bodyguard. Fr. Rinaldi absently petted Grigio's head.

"You see, Msgr. Azar," said the renowned scientist, "it is my contention that the only object that fits the description found in the End Times Tablet is 'Oumuamua, that oblong piece of rock that hurtled into our solar system a few years ago and exited just as quickly. I've plotted its course and it's definitely coming back this autumn. It could be the celestial object foretold. Even though it

has an unpredictable orbit, I believe it has visited us before, thousands of years ago. Currently, it is not on a path to strike us."

"Then what's the problem?" asked Daniel.

The scientist whipped off his glasses and leveled a piercing gaze at the priest. "Some of my colleagues believe that the rock is not natural, that it is in fact of alien nature, and, if so, could easily change direction. Either way, it is going to make a close pass at us."

Then as dreams do, the scene morphed, and Daniel found himself among the stars out beyond the solar system where darkness reigned and lost things remained forgotten in the void.

There, he saw it, 'Oumuamua, named 'The Messenger' in Hawaiian. He estimated it was about 5000 feet long and 2000 feet wide, and it sure looked alien to him.

The closer he got; the more fear gripped his gut. He sensed a malevolent presence there—it wasn't a dead piece of rock. As he studied it, an otherness began to probe him. There was a consciousness present—searching, knowing that something was looking at it. Though Daniel knew he was dreaming, he didn't feel safe. In the sci-fi movies he often watched, this was about the time grappling hooks, or transporter beams, or shuttle crafts or maybe just destroying phasers would be deployed to deal with him, the unwelcome guest. But nothing that drastic happened. Instead, he heard Grigio barking a warning, and felt the presence searching for his mind through the millions of miles of space. As the tentacles of questing evil touched his consciousness, he began to scream as his body convulsed.

His eyes flew open to see Nicky Farrell, the clerk of the Irish college standing over his bed, shaking him awake. Sweat pouring off his face, Daniel grabbed Nicky's arms.

"Wake up, Msgr. Azar!" said Nicky. "There's been an incident at the Vatican!"

VERITAS COMES TOGETHER

Wednesday, March 17, late afternoon, papal apartments, Apostolic Palace, Vatican City

"ARE YOU OKAY, Uncle Liam?" said a frazzled Daniel Azar as he burst breathlessly into the pontiff's sitting room in the papal apartments. He tripped a little on his new cassock with the red buttons, scarlet piping, and magenta sash. This ceremonial stuff was going to take some getting used to. He looked around for a moment. The room was looking less formal every day. The pope favored rocking chairs, and he was currently sitting relaxed in one of the several that furnished the room.

"I'm just fine, Dani," smiled the pope, "though like everyone else I was caught by surprise. I hadn't seen anything like that since I did my mission work in the Republic of the Congo, years ago."

"You think she was really possessed?" said Daniel.

"I do," said the pope. "It was the most palpable sense of evil that I had felt in a long time. She was clearly distressed and under control by something malevolent, beyond her ability to fight. We're going to keep tabs on her and make sure she's truly healed."

"Won't convince the secular media," groused Fr. Salvatore Rovere, elderly secretary to the pontiff. "Already some are saying it was a set-up, a hoax to get His Holiness more clout when he goes before the United Nations next week to talk about the crisis that infernal End Times Tablet has put us in."

"I don't expect to be believed instantly by a world that long ago forgot its Creator," said the pope. "It's a fine line the Church will have to tread. There is little middle ground, and, by that, I mean only a small number will support the Church at least at the beginning.

"There are two large groups that will do everything to oppose us. The first is the secular world which sees the threat against us as simply the ravings of a dead civilization long passed into dust.

"The second, and growing group, are the survivalists, conspiracy theorists, and, basically, those who refuse to educate themselves as to how this coming event should be interpreted and what exactly we should do about it. The Church will have to convince the secularists to 'follow the science'. That object in space is going to encounter us. And, of course, the conspiracy theorists are going to have to trust that someone has it together enough to fight any evil that oppresses us from this event. The Church is uniquely situated to do just that."

On a couch tucked into one of the corners of the room sat three large men, dressed in modern clothes but possessing a bearing from ancient times. Their steel grey eyes suggested great age and experience though they seemed not more than three decades old. Shadrach, Meshach, and Abednego—the strangers found in the newly discovered tomb in Babylon—had done a massive job of trying to fit in, but several weeks into the process they still stuck out like sore thumbs. They continued to insist they were the three young men talked about in the biblical Book of Daniel who navigated the burning, fiery furnace King Nebuchadnezzar cast them into over two and a half millennia ago.

Of course, they also claimed that Daniel Azar, while not exactly the reincarnation of the prophet Daniel, somehow possessed the prophet's DNA and prophetic abilities. Obviously, given what they might say to an unsuspecting populace, the pontiff was not allowing them to be seen in public, while Luca and Daniel strove mightily to bring them up to date on current customs.

Shadrach, who sported a black close-cropped beard and wore wire-rim glasses, spoke out for the first time: "Regardless of what people believe, a destructive force will hit this planet on November 1, causing a catastrophe unparalleled in human existence."

Meshach, the largest of the three, heavily muscled and clean-shaven with wavy black hair, said, "Assuredly so, though we do not know what form that destruction will take. The comet or heavenly object is on a collision course despite what the astronomers say. Its first encounter with earth seems to have been some eleven thousand years ago, an encounter that devastated the civilizations that existed then. We have only rumors and hints of rumors to go on as to what actually happened."

"The fragmented records," said Shadrach, "were found recently at Gobelki Tepe in your modern-day country of Turkey. They matched some obscure references that we also have in our possession. There was an advanced civilization there in 9000 BCE. Our records say a king named Tarhuan ruled at this time. He was a once-in-a-thousand-year king, a superb ruler, and a top-notch warrior. The early cuneiform carvings at Gobelki Tepe and our records in Babylon also indicate that he was 512 years old when he confronted, the 'thing from the sky'. The object Tarhuan encountered was 'Oumuamua, the space projectile or asteroid, if you will, of your day and age. Back then, when it landed upon earth, its first contact was with Tarhuan and his kingdom. It was a first contact with terrible results."

"You've got to be kidding—512 years old?" scoffed Fr. Salvatore. "Obviously myth."

"Really?" said Shadrach. "Does this mean I'm not getting a 2600-year-old birthday party this year?"

Daniel burst out laughing, "My God, he made a joke! Shadrach, that's got to be a first!"

The pope frowned at his nephew and said to the brothers, "Go on."

"It seems," added Abednego, the quiet one but the most athletic among the three brothers, "that the destruction 'Oumuamua caused was both physical and cultural. The populace at the time was decimated, but the survivors, led by Tarhuan, seemed to resist and ultimately proved successful in defeating the attempt to extinguish them, though at a great cost. We are not sure how they were victorious."

"Well, then," said Fr. Salvatore, as he whisked across the room in his black cassock to get something to drink from the bar, "we should have no trouble. We are technologically superior to the ancients, right?"

"Perhaps so," said the pontiff, "but this will not be simply a technological battle. It will be a spiritual one as well, and I think our mysterious three visitors would agree that the spirituality of ancient times was far stronger than our atheism of today. Pagan they may have been, but they believed.

"Physical strength will not be enough. Technology will not be enough. Terror and despair can grip the heart and destroy a person as easily as bullets shot from a gun. Just look at the fear that woman caused at the audience today. She was the unknown, her malady not understood. She could do things that ordinary humans could not. Everyone there just froze in horror."

"You didn't," said a new voice coming into the apartment. Luca Rohner, Captain of the Swiss Guard, had taken off his uniform for more casual attire. Walking in with him were two other Swiss Guard who Daniel recognized as Corporal Josiah Kern and Corporal Mattias Kurz. Seeing the pontiff wave them to the bar to get something to drink, Luca said, "Holy Father, you showed not only strength of character but religious power when you encountered our Miss Jenny Wren. She didn't give her name so I named her after one of Charles Dickens's characters. She kind of looks like her."

The pope smiled, "Always the Anglophile—at least she has a literary name and not one of your favorite TV characters. But I have to tell you, you did well also. That trick with the halberd that so easily disarmed her saved my life. It was worthy of the best of the Irish stick fighters with a little bit of kung fu added in. Had the abbot of the Shaolin Temple come visiting, he would have admired the hint of martial arts present in your swing. Thanks again."

Luca blushed and nodded.

Daniel smiled at his friend's embarrassment and said to the pope, "Now, he'll be impossible to deal with for days."

"Be careful little grasshopper," said Luca referencing the old *Kung Fu* series, "I'll have to humble you in our training tomorrow."

Daniel, at the pontiff's request, had taken up training with the Swiss Guard. He loved extreme sports, but the pope wanted him to have more skill at fighting any enemy that might present itself. These were dangerous times Pope Patrick pointed out, and Daniel already was grateful for the lessons since they had helped him while he was recently in Iraq.

Josiah, who was shorter than his companion, and Mattias said nothing and just gulped their drinks, surprised at how informal everyone was.

"Uncle Liam," said Daniel, "is this what you are going to try to do at the UN: have the nations recognize that this will not simply be a technological struggle but a spiritual one as well? Do you think that will work?"

"I'm not sure," said the pope. "But we must move heaven and earth to try. Attempting to convince skeptical nations and a superstitious populace will be difficult, but we will have allies, few though they may be. Besides, I'm forming a plan that will involve you, Daniel, and your VERITAS team."

"Uncle Liam," said Daniel with exasperation, "there's only five of us on the team, three of us who know nothing of this time or place—sorry guys," he smiled at the three on the couch, "no offense."

"Well," said the pope, "you have three more. Fr. Salvatore is now part of your group as are Josiah and Mattias."

Josiah smiled as the always ramrod straight Mattias almost silently kicked his boots together.

The old priest gasped. This was news to him. "I can't possibly," he said, "I mean, I am too old to go gallivanting around the world looking for trouble, supernatural or otherwise."

"No," smiled the pontiff, "you can't. But I need this group to be very mobile, and its leader, Daniel, will be on point most of the time. You will have to hold the fort here and be their liaison with me except for one little upcoming trip—no, no; don't ask. It will be an open secret shortly.

"Luca, I know you vetted these two candidates from the Swiss Guard that I picked weeks ago and have assured me they would mesh with the team. You two, Josiah and Mattias, were noted computer programmers in your previous life before you joined us and have conducted yourselves as superior soldiers here. I need your brains, not only your brawn. The three Swiss Guard will stay with me in the papal apartments. I've already selected rooms for you. Despite what the world thinks, the Apostolic Palace is no lap of luxury, but the rooms will be adequate. Besides, you won't be spending much time here."

"The Guard will talk about this, wondering what it all means," said Luca.

"Not after tomorrow," said the pontiff. "Tomorrow, I announce the expansion of the Swiss Guard. As we saw recently, the Vatican is more vulnerable than ever, particularly to terrorism. We need more protection and more investigative ability. We will look to number 500 of the Guard, something which has never been seen before, but we will slowly increase to that goal over two years. I've already notified the Catholic cantons of Switzerland to be prepared for higher recruitment. That news will keep the Vatican gossip hens busy."

"Now," said the pope, "I have several more surprises for you. First, we're going to the Archives. I want to show you something that came in yesterday. It bears directly on our next move to prepare for whatever the forces of darkness are planning to throw at us this November."

THE TUNICLE

Wednesday Afternoon, March 17, The Vatican Archives, Vatican City

THE ARCHIVES WERE deserted. The pope had already planned this visit, and he made sure the staff was scarce. Daniel marveled at the energy of the man. He heard that the entire populace of Vatican City was constantly out of breath just watching him operate.

The pope strode to a new elevator inside the Archives. "Going down," he said pleasantly.

"But Holy Father," said Luca, "nothing's lower than this floor."

"That you know about," smiled the pope. "But I and others have been busy while you were doing your Swiss Guard duty and out saving the world with my nephew. Actually, plans for this have been going along for some time. You are about to see your new offices."

They all piled into the large elevator which quickly descended.

"This is a long way down, Uncle Liam," said Daniel.

"'Tis indeed," said the pontiff, who laughed and broke out in a cheerful whistle of 'It's a long way to Tipperary.'

Luca laughed thinking it would be a long time till the Vatican took the Irish out of this guy.

"Seriously, though," said the pope, stopping his brief entertainment, "we had to go down one hundred feet so we would miss all the archeological ruins that we figure lie under the Vatican. Your father and mother, Dani, would never forgive me if we run roughshod over their next excavation site."

"You're right about that, but to dig that far—was it really necessary?"

"You tell me," said Pope Patrick as the doors opened to a magnificent sight.

No one present but the pope had seen this before, so they all gaped. The room was two hundred by two hundred feet square with a vaulted, wooden beamed ceiling. Some office cubicles were already roughed out, but much of the space was beginning to be filled with computer equipment and laboratory necessities. On two facing walls, there were windows that looked out to grottoes, already planted and flourishing under artificial lighting.

Seeing their eyes flash to the greenery, the pope said, "We thought you ought to have some space to walk and reflect, so we have for your spiritual and mental health two grottoes of live plants and trees to refresh the soul and mind as well as a beautiful chapel where you can pray."

"How could the Church afford this?" asked Daniel. "I mean the annual collection worldwide is called 'Peter's Pence' not 'Peter's Millions'." He didn't know whether to be amazed or horrified.

"The Church didn't pay for it, Dani," said the pope softly.

"Don't tell me," said Daniel. "It was another John Nance gift?" John Nance was the richest man in the world and a most generous Catholic benefactor to the Church.

"It was his money, yes, but not his gift," said the pope. "He knows nothing of this space." Seeing the looks on the team's faces, the pontiff further explained. "When I became pope, John Nance and my predecessor had already concluded the deal for the air fleet which has proven to be necessary and welcome. Nance asked for nothing in return. He then offered the pope an extraordinary amount of money to help lift the Vatican from the nineteenth century to the twenty-first. He suggested it go to infrastructure. 'Like it or not,' he said,' the Vatican is a major world power and it is about time it started acting like it.' My predecessor agreed.

"But you know as well as I that money is never freely given. John Nance and my predecessor had an arrangement, and I do not know what it was. I am not … as close to Mr. Nance as he was. The Vatican had already accepted the gift. To return it to the richest man in the world would cause an international incident and make the Church look like it was playing politics over and above what it should be doing."

"But that's exactly what was being done," said Daniel.

"Yes, but what's done is done, and the money will go to what I believe the Church needs, and this complex was part of my wish list. Mr. Nance is due to have an audience with me tomorrow, and I'm sure he will want to talk about money. But this you all need to know about me. I do not trust John Nance, and though he has been very generous to the Church, seemingly with no visible strings attached, my trust will not be given to him. It can't be, no matter how virtuous he fancies himself to be. He is far too powerful to be a partner with the pope."

Signaling that the discussion was over, he turned to Daniel and said, "It will be up to you, Dani, to rearrange the main space as you would have it. This is the first surprise. The second is near the far wall."

Nobody had noticed yet that a table was set up on the opposite side of the room and a person, a woman, was seated before some large boxlike object. The pontiff escorted the team down the center aisle. Hearing them approach the woman stood up and faced them with a smile.

She was young, in her early thirties, thought Daniel. She was wearing a white lab coat, so, he thought, probably a doctor or some scientist. She wore her blond hair short which made her look full of energy. Looking around her, Daniel saw that it wasn't a box on the table but a reliquary, gold with glass sides. Inside the reliquary looked to be an article of clothing.

"May I present to you, Doctor Abigail Duchon," said the pope. "She is the newest member of VERITAS, and she is a Sindonologist, an expert on the Shroud of Turin, the burial cloth of Jesus Christ. Doctor Duchon was the one who vanquished the skeptics last year who thought the shroud was a medieval forgery. So convincing was her research and her arguments that she won the Nobel Prize in Chemistry."

The pontiff introduced the scientist to everyone present. "Call me, Abby," she said, but Daniel barely heard. He couldn't keep his eyes off the reliquary.

"Uncle Liam," said Daniel, "why is there a reliquary here? What's in it?"

There was a gasp from behind as Fr. Salvatore pushed himself forward, staring intently at the golden miniature shrine.

"It just came today from Canterbury Cathedral to whom we loaned it," said the pope in a low voice.

"Becket!" said the priest throwing his hands up to his face in excitement.

"Indeed," said the pope, "what we have left of him. We loaned it to England for their commemoration of the 850th anniversary of his death."

"But I don't understand," said Daniel, "it's a cloth in there, not part of the remains of Thomas Becket. In fact, didn't King Henry VIII destroy Becket's body during the Reformation?" And then it dawned on him, why the pope would invite a Sindonologist to be on the team. "Doctor Duchon, Abby, you're going to prove something about this cloth too, right?"

She smiled but it was the pope who spoke. "Gloves please. Fr. Salvatore, grab the cloth ones over there. I want our three friends from Babylon, Dani, and I to wear them as we take the cloth out and spread it on this sanitized table."

The pope reached in and gently pulled out the ancient fabric. "It's the Tunicle of Thomas Becket," he said, "though we might be more comfortable calling it a surplice, a white garment worn under the embroidered cope an archbishop might be wearing at the time he prayed vespers."

As the five gently unfolded and spread out the garment on the table, everyone could see huge stains and spatters of a dried, dark liquid on the front. As they turned it over, the same could be seen on the back. There was more than one involuntary wince as thoughts of the violence that could have caused this entered their minds.

Why they did it they never said, but Shadrach, Meshach, and Abednego glanced at one another and took their gloves off, placing their hands directly on the Tunicle.

"No! You mustn't!" cried Abby, but she was too late. No one could have stopped them, and the moment they touched the garment a huge crack like thunder rippled through the underground room and a blue light blazed up and enveloped both the garment and the three men. It was clear they were in pain, but no one dared touch them.

"Dani," said the pope quietly, "take your gloves off. I'll do the same. We have to see what they are seeing. Their rings enable them to merge with the garment. Ours should do the same."

Both the pope and Daniel were wearing the Star Sapphire Rings which had been revealed as rings of power at the tomb in Babylon. There were six rings; the three men from Babylon each wore one as did Dani and the pope. The sixth was still missing.

The rings were made of solid meteorite, dark blue, almost black, and no one had noticed them. They seemed to have the ability to mask their presence when on a person. Now, even the six diamonds around each star sapphire jewel could be seen clearly. The pope kept his hidden under his pontifical ring. Still not sure what they represented, both the pope and priest knew that they were part of whatever or whoever the three strangers really were. So, with a bit of hesitancy on both their roles, they extended their rings into the blue dome and touched the garment.

Immediately, their rings flared like the others. Daniel, and, he presumed the pope, were enveloped in darkness. Then, to Daniel's perception, a red hue began to brighten the darkness, and, suddenly, he was suffused with terrible pain, all over his body. He felt himself pushed down upon stone pavement, and a crushing blow, blocked somewhat by someone else, smashed on his head, and he fell into the arms of a monk who himself was screaming in pain. The monk's arm was almost severed as he tried to shield Daniel, and the priest felt warm blood all over him. Another blow to the head, and he heard himself saying, "I die now for the honor of God. I die as a priest of Jesus Christ." As soon as Daniel felt himself say that, another blow struck his head, and he felt his spirit flee. He caught an emotion of triumph of someone outfoxing his murderers.

Daniel woke and found himself on the floor of the VERITAS office gasping for breath, the pope helping to lift him up. The pope nodded and said, "I felt it too but not as bad as you." They looked to the three young men who still maintained their touch on the fabric. Slowly their eyes opened and they withdrew their hands as the blue glow faded away.

Shadrach looked at Daniel and the pontiff. "I am sorry you had to experience that. You are ill-prepared for such events."

"Experience what?" said Fr. Salvatore.

"Fr. Salvatore," said Daniel, "I, we, those of us touching the Tunicle, we experienced Becket's death. It was horrible."

"It was terrible," said the pope, "but I think our three friends experienced more. Tell us, please, if you will."

"First of all," said Meshach turning his huge figure to Dr. Duchon, "you who are called Abby need not worry. No harm was done to the garment. You intend to test the blood spatter, for that indeed is what it is, and you will estimate the age of the cloth. Your tests will be confirmation that the cloth and blood can be dated to 1170 CE. After what we saw and experienced, we can confirm that Thomas Becket wore this garment, and his blood was shed upon it. As Daniel has said, it was a most brutal murder."

Luca had taken over ministering to Daniel, and they both looked at each other. "Luca, it made that 'Game Of Thrones' show look like Disney World. No death in that series ever approached this horror."

Abednego now spoke pushing his glasses higher on his nose, "There is another fact that even took us unaware. This saint of yours, this Thomas Beckett, is one of us."

No one spoke for a moment and then Luca said, "You mean he wielded a Star Sapphire?"

"That is yet to be determined," continued Abednego, "but his blood is of our type." Turning to Dr. Duchon once again, he explained, "The blood of my brothers and I has many divergences from the normal human type. We suspect, but you, doctor, have the ability to confirm that Daniel's and the pontiff's blood were modified much more recently and bear the same markers. If Thomas Beckett was in possession of a ring, then he, too, was one of the old ones like ourselves, and he should not have died, and he should have healed of his wounds. Did he have such a ring, and if not, why not?"

Fr. Salvatore spoke up, "Maybe I was included in your group because I am a Becket scholar, but I assure you, there was nothing strange or particularly noteworthy about the archbishop's ring, which I presume was handed on to his successor since that was the custom of the time.

"However, there has always been a rumor that Becket gave something to Brother Edward Grim, a companion of his, just before his death. It is notable because the grievous wound that Grim received from the first sword cut on Becket should have killed him too, but he healed miraculously. Grim went over the Channel to meet with King Louis VII and give him this personal item on the express wishes of Becket. Apparently, the king had loaned it to Becket. During the archbishop's exile in France, Louis and he had formed a firm friendship. The jewel seemed to strengthen Louis who was in ill health, and the king hoped it would help protect Becket.

"It was at the same time that Brother Edward appeared at court that the French Crown began to exhibit publicly what has become known as The Regale of France, a huge, almost the size of a hen's egg, cabochon mounted in a black-rimmed oculus suspended on a pendant. Nobody knew what the metal was and as for the jewel—some said it was a ruby, some a sapphire, some a diamond. It appeared differently to whoever saw it. All said it was magnificent.

"Stunningly beautiful," continued Fr. Salvatore, "the jewel was kept in Louis's possession at all times until 1179 CE when he went on pilgrimage to Canterbury to pray for the healing of his son. There, it was as if The Regale had a mind of its own. Witnesses said the jewel broke free of its chains, leapt off the king's hand, and adhered to the newly built shrine of Thomas Becket. It stayed there nearly 400 years, and, with its addition, increased the healing power of the saint. When the shrine was destroyed by King Henry VIII, during the Reformation centuries later, the jewel disappeared, never to be seen again."

"You are wise, old one," said Shadrach to Fr. Salvatore. "Though it was not a ring, The Regale obviously had similar powers to the others. It was mounted in an oculus of black-colored metal, perhaps also of meteorite origin. Why Becket gave it away just before his murder is a mystery. It surely would have protected him."

"Well, then," said the pope. "It seems we have another surprise for this day that even I was not expecting. If Becket was more than history thought, why he released this gem and suffered martyrdom is a mystery worth puzzling over.

"There is little left of Becket; King Henry burnt his bones so they say. The small relic fragments of his body that remain throughout the world in churches of his name, pale in comparison to this Tunicle, worn by the blessed man and obviously still a conduit to that terrible time. But something else occurs to me. The fact that The Regale has never been found, sounds like a search clearly made for VERITAS, a task I now give to you all. Beckett has a mystery for us to solve; namely, how does The Regale help us fight the doom that is coming upon us? Perhaps it was meant to be found and joined with the rings to help defeat the darkness that descends upon us.

"Dani," said the pope, "I want you and the members of VERITAS to go to Canterbury and meet with the Anglican archbishop there, Peter Pomeroy, and see if you can enlist his cooperation in this matter. He wants to talk about the End Times Tablet, but we need to know more about these Becket issues. St. Thomas Becket was a force of nature when he was alive and a healing saint after death. Perhaps now we know a little more exactly why. Good hunting to you all."

Pope Patrick turned on the heels of his dark burgundy shoes, and with head bowed in thought walked out the room, leaving a stunned VERITAS team to plan how to achieve their goal.

A PUPPET ON A STRING

Thursday Morning, March 18, Vatican reception room, Apostolic Palace, Vatican City.

POPE PATRICK FOUND himself surprisingly ill at ease as he greeted dignitaries on this fine spring day. Ambassadors were usually friendly and their wives or husbands charming, and he enjoyed handing out the Vatican rosaries which were the signature gift of the pontiff. But he was nervous. It was coming close to the last greeting before noon, and knew he would have to end the morning's meet and greet with a private audience given to John Nance.

As he smiled and exchanged pleasantries with the ambassadors, Pope Patrick's mind swirled with thoughts and bits of info about the richest man in the world. John Nance had been a friend of the previous pope, childhood friends who had grown up together. They were thick as thieves, and whatever ultimate purpose all that money was going to was nipped in the bud by the untimely death of the pontiff from a late-stage variant of the Covid-19 infection.

The new pope had met Nance several times over the first year of his pontificate, but this would be a new thing—a private audience. The pontiff was determined to get some answers.

"Your Holiness," smiled the trillionaire, "you do me a great honor with this meeting." Nance was as tall as the pope but there the resemblance ended. His hair was silver, and his black, penetrating eyes missed nothing. A faint British accent leant an aristocratic air to his bearing.

The two men were walking from the reception hall to the pope's study. As they kibbitzed lightly, chairs were pulled out for them, and an aide softly closed the doors on them. They were alone.

The pope said, "I too have looked forward to this meeting. I can't believe we've just exchanged pleasantries for the past year. I apologize. It's not the best way to thank the chief benefactor of the Church."

"Think nothing of it. You've been busy charming the world with your youth and energy."

The pope smiled at the flattery. "Actually, I was establishing an attitude, if you will, for the Church, that will reshape the way it interacts with the world. For too long, we Catholics have lived a schizophrenic existence, living in the world without really demonstrating our values, and saving our spiritual experience for the confines of our churches. That has to change. I want the Church to be a light of learning and faith to the whole world once again. Another Renaissance as it were. Don't you agree, Mr. Nance?"

Nance sipped his coffee in order to reflect a moment. "Indeed, I do," he finally said. "It's one of the reasons I bequeathed such a large sum of money to the Church under your predecessor. I, too, want to see the Church be more active in the affairs of the world. We have 2000 years of experience that we should be willingly sharing, yet, in the past two centuries, despite our best efforts, we continue to withdraw from society. We've almost become simply a quaint culture, albeit a huge one, on the sidelines of human activity."

"I couldn't have said it better myself," replied the pope, "but I must tell you, there are no documents to demonstrate the purpose of the gift you gave the Church. Why did my predecessor and you not outline the way this money was to be spent, who or what it was to benefit? In other words, what its purpose was and if you placed any restrictions on it?"

"Well, that is blunt and to the point. I've been told you don't waste time with diplomatic niceties."

"You're a busy man and so am I. You're wondering if I will have a similar mindset as my predecessor. You are probably as concerned about this meeting as I have been." Pope Patrick gave John Nance his most charming smile.

"I've made no secret of my friendship with the previous pope," said Nance. "He and I grew up together. He was French and I was British but we attended the same schools and were close friends. I wanted to modernize the Vatican, and he agreed and was grateful for it. No strings were attached."

"Well, that is good to hear," said the pontiff, "but I can't believe you two did not have some plan together."

"Only that he would allow me to advise him on matters to which large sums of the grant were to be spent. I didn't want to be involved picking out carpet for the Apostolic Palace, but I did express my wish to help guide him on the best use of the money. Strictly advisory of course. I would never think to usurp any pontiff's final decision-making authority."

"Well, I must say the Vatican air fleet was a touch of genius," said the pope. "That alone will help us easily reach places far more efficiently than before."

Nance shifted uneasily in his seat recalling that just last month, he had almost shot down the plane carrying the pontiff's nephew. He was concerned that the Vatican was controlling the narrative of the End Times Tablet too strictly and wanted to make a point without revealing his identity.

"You certainly have added life and enthusiasm to the See of Peter," said Nance. "I've noticed that world leaders I have spoken to are amazed at your energy and your willingness to follow your agenda. It's not completely popular though."

"Yes," said the pontiff, "so I experienced last month."

Nance again shifted uncomfortably. He also had been the one to send the assassin to kill the pope as worries mounted among his own friends that the pope was becoming too powerful during the growing apocalyptic crisis. The sudden decision to do away with the spiritual head of 1.5 billion Catholics was not his usual *modus operandi*. He still felt somewhat guilty about sending the Bedouin to do the job, but his gut feelings rarely led him wrong. One could always get another, hopefully, more pliable, pope. One could always find another way to get rid of the Church.

It even seemed strange to Nance, that he had to save the Church in order to destroy it. The modern Church was in danger of becoming an anachronism, and the world really wouldn't care if the Church disappeared. Nance knew better. The Church had already resurrected itself from the pit of destruction more times than Jesus Christ. If Nance was going to kill off the Church, he had to raise it to a level where its fall would be spectacular and much missed.

The pontiff seemed not to notice Nance's uneasiness. "I'm afraid that the assassination attempt in February and the one yesterday will not be the last."

"How will you protect yourself?" asked Nance, eager, at least, to get some inside information.

"Not many know it, yet, but I will be increasing the size of the Swiss Guard contingent here at the Vatican. Terrorism and random violence are increasingly setting their sights on religious institutions. I'm not so worried for myself as I am for the many pilgrims that come each day to the Vatican and the churches around Rome to experience our ancient faith."

"Sounds like a plan, and I would expect you to use some of the funds I have given to help achieve that goal."

"No doubt, that will happen, but I must caution you, Mr. Nance. Your contribution is most generous, but I will apply the most stringent rules and regs to keep your involvement with those funds at a minimum. The Church has had too many issues with fiscal mismanagement in the past few years, and I do not want a breath of scandal to ever touch your generous gift."

Bastard! thought Nance. And an ungrateful one at that. Nance had truly liked his friend, the previous pope, but that pontiff was a pushover, and Nance knew in his heart that he, himself, would easily control where that money went. Seriously, he thought, it was billions and billions of dollars. Even the secular governments would have a fiduciary stroke if they knew how much he had given. And he would be damned if he let this upstart Irish prick of a pope stop his ambitions of controlling much of the Church. He knew his history. In times past, the rich benefactors of the Church often ran the institution, and if a pesky pope popped his head above the status quo, then that said pontiff had a very short reign. Nance smiled as he walked out of the papal offices. History could definitely repeat itself again. Obviously, this pope had not been frightened by the two attempts on his life. Nance would have to think of something more diabolically effective.

A CANTERBURY TALE

Thursday Morning, March 18, Canterbury Cathedral, England

DANIEL, AFTER CONSULTING with Luca, decided to take the whole VERITAS team with him with the exception of Mattias and Josiah. Their job would be to put a security apparatus into place around VERITAS headquarters so the compound could stay as secret and protected as possible. They would also continue the investigation into Miss Jenny Wren's attack on the pope.

The only thing that troubled Daniel was his three newfound friends from Babylon. They were acclimating swiftly to the culture. Though they were traveling with him, he had enjoined them to be a background presence rather than taking part in any conversations that would happen in Canterbury.

The Archbishop of Canterbury planned to meet them at the airport. Daniel was surprised, yet pleased with this development. He had heard only good things about the head of the worldwide Anglican Communion, the branch of the Church that Henry VIII had separated from Catholicism.

Peter Pomeroy, affectionately known in British circles as 'Peter, Peter Pumpkin Eater' because of his massive size, was the first

Canterbury archbishop in years to get kudos from the worldwide press for being smart, savvy, and a great leader all at once.

The Dassault 900 LX, made swift work of the flight to London Heathrow Airport, and sure, enough, the archbishop was there on the tarmac with a large limo van and accompanying security vehicles, ready to take the group the ninety miles to Canterbury.

"You picked a good day to come," laughed the cleric enclosing his meaty hand around Daniel's. "I had several days of meetings with the king, and was on my way home anyway. Here now, introduce me to your friends, hop in the van, and let's get going."

The ride was swift and time passed with the archbishop pointing out landmarks with their history and sometimes bloody background, the team nodding and agreeing along the way as was appropriate. After arriving in the episcopal town, the archbishop had the driver give a short tour of the tiny city, and then they pulled up to the Old Palace where the cleric lived, next to the cathedral.

"Listen," said the archbishop, "the pontiff told me you wanted to see the places Thomas Becket was most associated with here in the area. The cathedral is the first place to start. He said you wished additional first-hand information as you plan to make the Tunicle we just returned a more public artifact. No doubt that's why you brought Dr. Abigail, the charming Sindonologist with you. It's amazing what an old cloth tinged with blood can tell us now since your profession has done such wonders with the Shroud of Turin."

Abby smiled and said, "First of all, the Tunicle is such a precious relic However, I believe it has more tales to tell, and I wanted to get the ambiance of the place where it was created."

"We promise not to get in the way of the tourists or staff of the cathedral," said Daniel. "Our task won't take us more than two days."

"Well, then," said the archbishop, "I'll let you get right to it, and hope you will join me for dinner, around 8 PM, this evening."

"We would be honored," said Daniel.

The rotund archbishop laughed and said, "Oh you will enjoy the feast. The chef is fantastic and his meals are how I keep my svelte figure." Like a modern-day Friar Tuck, he patted his stomach with gusto. Laughing to himself, he took his leave of the group, after depositing them at the entrance to the church.

Luca looked up at the vast building and said, "It's not St. Peter's but it sure is beautiful. Like the Vatican, it has so many stories to tell."

Talking to the group, Daniel agreed but added, "I can't believe the topic of The Regale didn't come up. The archbishop must know we are interested."

"If I may," said Shadrach, speaking softly with the first words he had uttered since the trip began. "While the story of The Regale is well known, its disappearance is also clearly documented. No one seriously believes it can be found."

"Too true," said Fr. Salvatore. "Some think that King Henry VIII had it set in a thumb ring, but The Regale was really too big for that. Most have just accepted that it disappeared out of history."

One of the doors at the cathedral entrance opened and a nun, dressed in a black Benedictine habit looked out. She was good-looking with skin like mocha, tall and ramrod straight in physique, hair hidden beneath a modified habit headgear. She smiled and said in a beautiful Jamaican accent with an English burr, "Ah, the Vatican contingent. I'm Sister Cecilia Campbell of the Canterbury Benedictine Sisters. I'm also Archdeacon of the Cathedral and the archbishop has tasked me with being your tour guide and all-around helper for your stay here." Laugh lines crinkled around her eyes softening her severe bearing and Daniel liked her instantly. She seemed no-nonsense and very welcoming.

As she walked them to the front of the cathedral, she pointed out the architectural wonders but then turned right and stopped by a small altar above which hung two swords and a twisted cross reproduced in a menacing artistic display.

"This is the place," she said in a low voice, "where Archbishop Thomas Becket was struck down so many centuries ago. It was the most famous and compelling murder of the Middle Ages. It nearly brought down a king and a kingdom, and it certainly captured the imagination of the medieval peasants and intelligentsia."

"But why?" said Luca. "I know St. Thomas Becket is famous, but a murder is a murder. What makes this one so special?"

"Good question," said Sr. Cecilia. "You have to remember how violent the death was. In our day of AR-15s, handguns, and various other weapons, swords and daggers may seem archaic, but the death of Thomas Becket shows how truly horrendous such a violent act of murder upon a famous archbishop actually was. I know this is ghastly, but after piercing the head of the saint, one of the swords shattered on the pavement. Think of the force that took, and the amount of blood and brains—sorry for the graphic nature of this—was horrific. After the death, the peasants came and soaked up the blood and brain matter with cloths, keeping them as relics to be dipped in water for a tea or drink for those who were ill."

"That's truly disgusting," said Luca who in his young life had already seen enough blood and terror to satiate any curiosity he had.

"Maybe," said Sr. Cecilia, "but Captain Luca, in your Catholic tradition, you have a place for rather gory relics as well. After all, the Tunicle of Becket you possess with its ancient blood spatters, would have disturbed people who saw it on the bishop's body. In fact, many cures in the days after the assassination were attributed to the efforts of the peasants to preserve the blood of the martyr."

"Point taken," said Luca with a grimace.

"How did the Tunicle escape being used in this fashion?" asked Abby.

"It was the monks," said the Anglican nun. "They finally found their courage, came back and rescued the body from relic hunters including the clothes the slaughtered archbishop was wearing."

"All the more reason, Dr. Abigail," said Abednego, stepping somewhat forward, "that you submit the blood on the Tunicle to your scientific tests looking for any anomalies or properties not normally present in human blood. It may be the only relic that still has actual samples of Becket's blood."

"Good point," said Abby. "We have found, archdeacon, that the blood of the Shroud of Turin has some peculiarities due to a high energy burst given to the Shroud at some time, and of course, we believe that time was at the moment of the resurrection. Those peculiarities have stymied the most rabid of our critics. Now, I have heard it said that hundreds and hundreds of miracles occurred almost immediately after the saint's martyrdom. Perhaps something similar occurred with the archbishop's vestments."

"True," said Sr. Cecilia, "but the miracles were not simply close in time with the martyrdom. For nearly 400 years, until King Henry VIII destroyed the shrine, many miracles were done. However, I must say that your study of the Tunicle and the blood on it will most likely lead nowhere. Faith was the bridge between the gathered blood of the martyr and the sick who came into contact with it."

"You are probably right," said Abby, "but it's worth a try. But there may be more to this cathedral than the simple resting place of the saint. We Catholics believe that the power of the martyrs rests in their ability to bring heaven and earth together at the moment of their violent deaths and that the power may reside there afterward, for years perhaps. The place where a martyr died and the very body of the martyr became a locus, a portal, between heaven and earth for people to meet God. I'm thinking the most famous martyred saint of the Middle Ages may have some secrets he might wish to share."

That might be, thought Daniel, but even at this exact place of the murder committed so long ago, he felt nothing like he did when he touched the Tunicle. He saw that Shadrach, Meshach, and Abednego were not affected either. Good enough, he thought. He hadn't wanted to explain strange blue lights to the archdeacon.

Sr. Cecelia said, "Come with me now, down into the crypt. I'd like to show you where Becket was first buried before his fabulous shrine was constructed."

It took the group a while to traipse down into the lower crypt which unlike the soaring Gothic upper cathedral, was Romanesque in design. It was quiet down there, shadows flickering in candlelight cast against the arches of the ceiling. Daniel wondered why no tourists were present.

Seeing his surprise, Sr. Cecelia said, "I had Hospitality clear the areas you would visit for the time you were present. I wanted you to see the ancient grandeur without the selfies being taken and pictures being snapped."

"We appreciate your kindness," said Fr. Salvatore. "Could you refresh my memory on the original burial?"

"Of course," said the archdeacon. "The monks were afraid that the murdering knights would return to steal the body of Becket so they hastily buried him in the crypt in this spot, a burial that would last forty years until the massive shrine was completed. However, when King Henry VIII destroyed the shrine in 1538, he supposedly had the bones burnt or destroyed.

"Yet, rumors persist that the monks of that time spirited them away and reburied them just to the east of here but still within the crypt."

"Could we see the other possible resting place for St. Thomas?" asked Daniel.

"Yes, of course," said Sr. Cecelia. She took them over to the Magdalene Chapel where a red light burned. "One of the deans of the cathedral in the 1920s felt so sure of this place that he had the red light installed representing martyrdom. His view has not been shared by history, yet the lamp remains." Nonetheless, the archdeacon showed the pavers underneath the lamp where a forgotten tomb supposedly rested.

Daniel drew close to the overlooked burial. The archdeacon thought he was reverencing the once inhabited grave, but he was not. He placed his hand on the stone and immediately felt an electric charge go through his right hand and into his ring finger. Quickly placing his left hand over the glowing ring, he stood and backed away, making sure that no one saw the light and that the three brothers stayed far back. Unlike in the upper cathedral, something was here that attracted his ring.

Their tour concluded, Sr. Cecilia walked them over to the Canterbury Cathedral Lodge in the precincts of the cathedral and left them to get settled in their rooms.

Daniel decreed an afternoon tea meeting in the library. Later, when they had gathered, Daniel said, "Impressions? Comments?"

"Well," said Fr. Salvatore in his crusty voice, "your uncle, the Holy Father, has some competition in the charisma department with this Archbishop of Canterbury."

"He does seem like a good fellow," said Daniel, "but I'd like to take a closer read of him at dinner tonight. I want to see if we can get his cooperation to do a little deeper looking around in the crypt."

"Why?" said Abby. "Did you see something there the rest of us missed?"

"More like felt something you might have missed. My ring began to react at that tomb by the Magdalene Chapel just like it did back home. No visions this time, but you might have noticed me backing the three brothers off from any close inspection. Something's there, and I don't know what it means."

"I've done some investigation on the excavation of that supposed burial," said Fr. Salvatore. "It was sloppily done, and I don't understand why. Maybe it was basic Anglican ambiguous feelings about finding that the saint's mortal remains might not have been destroyed."

"Would it make any difference if the bones were there?" asked Luca. "I mean would people really care?"

"I did some checking too," said Abby. "I walked the archdeacon out of the hotel and asked her if many miracles had happened since the dissolution of the shrine up to modern times. She said no, but indicated the occasional rumor that a miracle had occurred. When you think of it, this is really startling because the number of miracles associated with this shrine before its dissolution was immense. There was clearly a connection between the bones of Thomas Becket, The Regale of France, and the faith of the people. They formed a triumvirate of healing. Once those connections were broken, the miracles fell precipitously in number. And this is a faithless age. I doubt we will see an increase soon."

"Unless we re-establish connections," said Daniel. "You know as well as I that it would be amazing if his bones are still here. Yet we do have fragments of his bones that escaped the destruction because they were sent to other churches throughout the world. And if we found The Regale and returned it, perhaps the faith of the people could be tapped into, and a shrine, once the hope of all Europe, could be re-energized to help this troubled world and help us in our time of need when disaster impinges upon us."

And that's why he's my friend, thought Luca. Always the optimist, always looking for possible solutions. Let's hope his hope is not misplaced.

A LAST SUPPER

Thursday Evening, March 18, The Old Palace, Canterbury, England

THE WARM WEATHER had continued throughout Europe, so the VERITAS team walked through the cathedral grounds to the Old Palace, the local residence of the Archbishop of Canterbury when he was in town.

A butler greeted them at the doorway and led them to a sitting room where the archbishop and Sr. Cecilia were already enjoying drinks and conversation.

"Friends!" greeted the archbishop, "welcome to the Old Palace. Not as grand I'm afraid as my residence in Lambeth Palace in London, but, actually, more to my liking. I've only been archbishop a few years, but lately I have found myself more and more obsessed, as it were, with this lovely cathedral and the history it contains."

"What exactly do you mean, Your Grace?" asked Daniel.

"Daniel, please," smiled the archbishop. "Tonight, let's all be on a first-name basis. Call me Peter, I insist." The archbishop's face grew grave. "No doubt, you wonder why I agreed to this meeting so readily, why I met you at the airport, why I'm staying here while you are here. It's not because I wish to make serious forward progress in ecumenical relations, though that would be nice. Nor because I want to spy. It's because of you, Daniel. Of what you found in the desert. Of what your father and mother unearthed and you translated, and, may I be frank, set us all down an unknown course to disaster or change. I fear that after November 1, humanity will have passed a Rubicon that will see it transformed forever."

Daniel grimaced, "I think you are right, Your Grace, I mean Peter. Something is coming and governments and religions are going to have to unite in order to face it with all humanity's strength. Governments are going to have to take seriously what beliefs are in the hearts and souls of their people, and faith itself will have to find the courage to act openly in the world once again secure in its ability to help all humanity find meaning and purpose."

"Spoken like your uncle, the pope," said the archbishop somberly. "I want to help you find what you are looking for. I realize this is not just a pro-forma visit. You think there is something here, in Canterbury, that can be of help in humanity's facing this apocalyptic event. Am I right?"

"Seriously," said Daniel, "I'm not sure. But I sense there may be something."

"Then let's get ourselves into the dining room and fortify our bodies. I always find a good meal helps bring perspective to whatever we are working on." The archbishop stood and led everyone to what turned out to be a fabulous repast.

The dining room was fashionably ornate, and when the archbishop had seated everyone, he had wine poured—a deep red cabernet. He stood, raised his glass, and said, "My friends, God's blessings to you, to your health, to the king and to the people of this blessed land. A toast as well to the benefactor who will enable us to restore the Shrine of St. Thomas Becket to its original glory."

There was a collective gasp around the room, as restoration of the shrine was totally unexpected news. From the look on the archdeacon's face, this was the first she had heard of it.

"Let me guess," said Daniel, "would the benefactor happen to be John Nance?"

"Yes, indeed," spoke the archbishop, "a fine fellow who has chosen to use his trillion-dollar net worth to lift up the beauty of religion, its architecture and traditions, as well as accentuate its gifts to civilization."

Daniel asked, "It's totally inappropriate for me to inquire, but it's important, archbishop. Did he have any *quid pro quo* attached to the gift?"

"None, whatsoever. He seems committed to helping any reasonable religious cause. He approached me around the time your uncle was elected pope over a year ago. In consultation with the king, I have the authority to approve such a project. The king gave his full support, and as John Nance was footing the bill, I did not have to consult with anyone else to spend the money. The king has a marvelous art studio outside of Edinburgh. Anglican and Catholic artists have worked hard this past year to duplicate what they could of the old shrine and add some modern touches as well. The work has progressed swiftly, even more so since your team's discovery in Babylon. The shrine will be a bulwark against the fear of the coming darkness and bring healing to many. There was a time when the shrine was the most popular of saints' pilgrimages. May it be so again. That is my hope and prayer at least." The archbishop beamed at his assembled guests.

"Other than to the king and Nance, I spoke of my project only to Pope Patrick on his ascension to the papal throne. I knew him before his elevation and of his hopes to make the faith far more central to culture again. Apart from king, pope, benefactor and artists, you are the first to know of this. How fortuitous that is—

Anglicans and Catholics united once again over what once tore us apart. From your faces, I know you are shocked, but this event is worthy of a toast. Now raise your glasses and let us praise the Becket Initiative!"

A tinkle of glass was heard behind them, by the room's bay window, and its complimentary sound echoed from the archbishop's wine goblet which shattered into a thousand pieces. He looked puzzled as he gazed over his guests. Then, a rivulet of blood trickled from his mouth, and he took a sudden gasp of breath.

"He's been shot!" cried Luca. "Everyone down!" He pushed Daniel to the floor and grabbed the arm of Sr. Cecilia to his right, pulling her down as well. The archbishop fell forward, still as the crown pork roast that sat in the center of the table. For a moment, no one moved from their place on the floor, but Luca quickly stood up once it seemed that no more shots would be fired. He looked through the window and saw no one. He ran to the archbishop and felt for a pulse.

The brothers from Babylon made a move toward the fallen prelate but Daniel shook his head. The dead could not be revived even by a Star Sapphire Ring.

"Is he ... is he gone from us?" asked Fr. Salvatore, making a swift blessing over the body.

"I'm afraid so," said Luca. "He was shot in the heart. The bullet exited his back. He died instantly." Wiping his bloody hands on a crisp linen napkin, he said, "Let me check the grounds for the assassin."

"No need for that," said a voice, as the dining room door opened. A masked man stood there, with a silenced Sig Sauer in his hand, casually waving it at the group. "I am here." He laughed a bit as if he had made some sort of joke.

"What do you want?" said Daniel, anger forcing him to grit his teeth.

"Well," said the man, "my boss wanted the archbishop dead, and now that is done. That leaves just one thing left to do."

"You won't have time to do it," said Sr. Cecilia. "I'm sure the butler will have called the authorities."

"Not likely," said the man. "I thanked him in a most special way for letting me into the palace. I'll be leaving shortly, though, as soon as I take care of the one Vatican dignitary who matters to me—you, Msgr. Daniel Azar."

As the assassin lifted up the gun and pointed it at Daniel's head, a tinkling of glass was heard once again from the windows and a bright red flower bloomed on the forehead of the masked man. Two more bullets tore into his chest and the dead assassin crumpled to the floor. A gun barrel swept the loose panes of glass in the window away, and a woman dressed in a dark blue pantsuit stuck her head in and said, "It's over. He was by himself."

"Rebecca!" shouted Luca. "You show up at the just the right time!"

Rebecca Perez of the CIA frowned and said, "Not quite. Too late to keep death coming for the archbishop. I tracked this slime all day, but in the last few minutes he eluded me. I'm so sorry I was not able to be here sooner to save Archbishop Peter." Sweeping more glass from the window, she was able to climb through.

Sr. Cecilia had already dialed for the ambulance and police and sirens could be heard. The palace was about to become inundated with the authorities.

"Luca," said Rebecca, "check that man's right hand. See if there's anything on it, a tattoo, a mark, whatever."

Luca moved around the table, grabbing the gloved hand of the dead man. Pulling off the glove, he immediately noted a small tattoo between the thumb and forefinger.

"He's got one," he said. "It looks like the outline of a waterfowl with the letters JJ on the breast. That is really weird."

"I was worried about that," said Rebecca. Turning to Daniel, she said, "The CIA has been tracking various terrorist groups that have been getting more active in the past few weeks. They're jumping on the apocalyptic hype that has everybody having anxiety attacks. This particular group is new to us, but we received a tip a few days ago that a terrorist group would target the religious and royal symbols of Britain. As of now, they're known by this bizarre tattoo on their right hand. They're called *Memento Mori*—which translates as 'Remember Death,' particularly, 'Remember Your Death.'

"Your boss, Pope Patrick, called mine and asked for a favor; namely, that both the CIA and MI5 cast its eyes and ears around Canterbury, in an abundance of caution. MI5 also has more agents surrounding the king. The Director of the CIA, Leslie Richardson, thought this was a case for the Antiquities Division, so I'm thankful for the help they sent. I ran into the shooter earlier today. Stupid spy; he wasn't wearing his gloves, and I caught a glimpse of his tattoo. It was just a hunch, but I followed him. I warned MI5 of the problem. They still thought the archbishop was at Lambeth Palace. That means there was a deliberate breakdown in security. I'm just sorry I couldn't get here sooner."

"You saved us," said Daniel, "and we are grateful. But why this man felt he needed to execute the archbishop is a mystery to me. The archbishop mentioned the reconstruction of Becket's Shrine. That sounds like a major undertaking with political and religious repercussions attached. Could that have anything to do with this?"

"I must confess," said Sr. Cecilia, "that the rebuilding of the shrine is news to me, and I should have known about it. I don't understand why the archbishop did not trust me with his plans. I knew he was meeting with someone last night, and it was to be a very private meeting. Looks like this wasn't a cobbled-together wonky idea, but a well-planned project that he and Nance just put the finishing touches on. It seems the king was in on it as well."

"Nance moves swiftly, and the shrine would cost millions to reconstruct it back to its original state," said Daniel. "However, Nance has money to throw around. Still, the question presents itself. How would a terrorist group even know the two planned something like this, and what would they gain by killing the archbishop?"

"Chaos," said Rebecca, "upheaval in the Anglican Church. Am I right, Sr. Cecilia, that reconstruction of such an ornate tomb will turn liberals and conservatives upon each other and rip open old ecclesiastical wounds?"

"Yes," said the archdeacon with a frown on her face, "it would pit those who want a faith without miracles against those who would like the more Catholic view of things. But it would be even more than that. With the crisis that is coming November 1, it's possible such a religious rumble could destabilize the government and even the monarchy. Strange things are happening throughout the country in the light of the End Times Event."

Fr. Salvatore grumbled, "Other than the Islamic enclaves, there's little faith left in Great Britain. I'm sure the rebuilding of a shrine that last existed when England was Roman Catholic would cause a lot of comment, but hardly a change in the European abandonment of religion."

"What many forget," said Daniel, "is that apocalyptic moments in history bring out the worst in people along with a redoubling of religious fervor, both good and bad. Conspiracy theorists, who are usually dismissed, are lauded as sage seers and wisdom figures. The criminal element, always looking for an opening, seizes upon peoples' fears to terrorize and victimize them. But then, there are the planners, the one's behind the scenes. In America, we used to call them the Deep State, government figures who use the unstable moment to change the course of history."

"We found that out last month in Babylon," said Luca. "It was amazing how fast the governments and terrorist organizations perceived the danger the tomb and The End Times Tablet brought." (For a moment, he paused, deciding not to mention what would happen if the world knew that the real Shadrach, Meshach, and Abednego—the three young men in King Nebuchadnezzar's burning, fiery furnace—were the inhabitants of the tomb). "Look at the Mahdi," he continued. "It didn't take long for Nabil Kasser to walk out of Babylon a lot more convinced he's the Promised One. You've all seen his new speeches around the Middle East. Our erstwhile professor has put at least part of the apocalyptic shawl around his shoulders. He's awfully close to declaring himself."

"You would think," said Rebecca, "that this new terrorist group had just put the kibosh on any upheaval in the religious or political realm. The Shrine of Thomas Becket seems a dead issue."

"Quite the contrary," said Daniel. "The archbishop said the shrine is almost completed. He saw it as the international place of healing it was half a millennium ago and a testament of hope in a world going mad. Word of the shrine would have leaked out of the archbishop's and Nance's meeting eventually, right Sr. Cecelia? That's why he told us tonight."

The archdeacon nodded her assent.

"But now, within just a few hours, this plan hatched by a popular archbishop and the world's most famous philanthropist will be all over the news being studied and picked apart." Daniel smiled ruefully. "Don't forget, the Reformation was only 500 years ago. That's a blink of an eye to the Vatican and Lambeth Palace. The wounds still run deep, and I have a hunch that Canterbury Cathedral will become an even more important part of the Christian faith in the months to come."

They all heard the emergency and police vehicles skid into the Old Palace roundabout and knew the questioning was about to begin.

Daniel pulled Sr. Cecelia over and whispered to her. "Please come see me when the interrogation is finished. We have more work to do tonight."

DEM BONES, DEM BONES, DEM DRY, DRY BONES

Thursday Night, March 18, Canterbury Cathedral

"ALL RIGHT, SR. CECELIA, fess up," said Daniel. He and Luca were hosting the impromptu meeting he had asked of the archdeacon in his hotel room. "Are the bones of Becket still in the cathedral? Because just rebuilding the shrine is not enough without its saint. You spouted off the current theories that say they have been burnt to dust, but you didn't say it convincingly. I happen to know other theories have rattled around for years. What about the archeologists that dug up that supposed bishop's grave in 1888 in the crypt where Thomas was originally buried?"

"They were inept," she snapped. "And I don't like you questioning my veracity. It's bad enough that the archbishop is dead and we were just subjected to the most humiliating questioning."

"I know," said Daniel, filling his voice with a little more sympathy. "But something is different here. The plan of the archbishop for the shrine—it's the biggest thing the Church of England has ever undertaken. Its intricacy and detail and importance will outshine St. Paul's Cathedral in London. Why would he do that if he didn't know something else that would tilt his plan toward success?—like the fact that Becket's bones may not be burnt to a crisp."

Sr. Cecelia glared at him. "I admit there are rumors, and, as I said, some of the previous archdeacons had their own thoughts about the whereabouts of Thomas' body. The only strange thing that continues to be seen is that red lamp or candle above the supposed grave found in 1920."

"And you aren't curious?" said Luca. "Don't you think that's a good enough reason to check the tomb again more thoroughly?"

"Perhaps with a more modern archeologist, like me?" said Daniel with a smile.

"No!" she frowned. "Finding his bones will just upset things, particularly now when everyone is so distressed. They'd be expecting miracles. We'd be swamped with superstitious believers and ridiculed in the press and by the government. Despite the archbishop's obvious love for the place, I didn't want to push him towards that kind of decision. He is, or was, too good of a man to be made a mockery."

"Nonetheless," said Daniel, "there is something down there in that crypt that has a presence. I felt it this afternoon when we walked by that old tomb. I'd like to look at it, tonight if possible."

The archdeacon gasped. "You can't be serious. The authorities will still be combing the Old Palace; the archbishop's body isn't even cold yet."

"Yet, we must look. Others will be coming in the days and weeks ahead. We must find whatever can be found."

"But the amount of work ... how can we do this in a single night?" she asked.

"The three brothers we brought have certain capabilities that will make our work much easier," said Daniel. Noting that she had included herself in the excavation, he said, "All we need is the permission of someone high up in the cathedral governance to take a quick look-see."

"I could be fired for this," muttered the archdeacon. "The last time it was opened all hell broke loose."

"Something is coming," said Luca, "that will make hell look like Disney world."

"You should know that the pope has tasked us with certain projects that might be of help in delivering this world from disaster," said Daniel. "I'm not sure this is one of them, but I'd hate to miss the opportunity. What do you say?"

She sighed. "When do you want to do this?"

"Now," said Daniel. "I can't think of a better time."

Luca roused the team and, together with Sr. Cecelia, they casually walked over to the locked cathedral. Law officers still present on the grounds recognized them and supposed they were going over to pray for the archbishop.

However, the team quickly descended into the crypt. There were several candles lit, but the light was dim, so Daniel and Luca flipped on the flashlights they always carried since the Babylon event.

"Take us to the tomb by the Magdalene Chapel. Please, Sr. Cecilia," said Daniel.

She walked quietly over to a part of the crypt that was in darkness except for the faint glow of a red presence candle hanging from an arch. Daniel shone his flashlight on the stone floor, and everyone immediately saw the slab of stone, sunk into the stone pavers. It was only four feet by four feet, so Daniel figured that, if any bones were present, the skeletal remains would be in a smaller coffin. There were no markings on the stone.

Daniel looked at the brothers and asked them, "What do you sense or see?"

All three knelt down and touched the stone. They were quiet only for a moment and then said, "Like you this afternoon, we sense something now, though we don't know what it is. It is deeper than whatever lies directly under the stone."

Daniel remembered his research. When this grave was opened last, in the early 1920s, the bones were simply laying on the ground, reverently placed. At first glance, they appeared to be Becket's because of the height and the wounds, but later, the investigators thought they had discovered enough anomalies to kill that theory. Amazingly, they did not go more deeply into the tomb, because the cathedral records show that there could be other archbishops buried there. Daniel was sure their lack of curiosity could reflect on their research ability as well.

"Shadrach, Meshach, Abednego, raise this stone," said Daniel.

"We have no tools. Now just how do you think they're going to do that?" said the archdeacon.

Daniel smiled and said, "The brothers have unique skills. Watch and see."

Standing by the stone slab, they raised their hands over the supposed grave. The rings on their fingers glowed a soft blue, and as they moved their arms, the grout around the stone cracked and the stone lifted several inches. They were able to slide it to the right.

"Who are you people?" asked the archdeacon. "How did they do that?"

No one answered her, for all eyes were on the uncovered tomb. Scattered bones greeted them, presented haphazardly on a dirt floor.

Fr. Salvatore, the closest thing they had to a Becket scholar, raised his hands into the air. A haunted look crossed his face as he said with the words of an ancient biographer, "'The tyrant king unshrined the saint, and burnt, at last, the holy bones!'"

"I don't think so," said Daniel. He reverently removed the bones and began to sweep away the dirt with a small brush he carried in his pocket for just such a need. It took a while, but, then, the red presence lamp revealed an almost ethereal glow across his surprised face. At first, the rest saw nothing new in the grave. A few more sweeps of the brush revealed a burlap blanket, darkened with age, lying the length and breadth of the tomb. Daniel knelt down and carefully folded it back to uncover another, much more beautiful blanket of wool. Opening this as well, Daniel, along with everyone else, gasped because there lay the remains of a very tall man. However, the gasp was not for what was found but for what was missing. The bones were missing a head.

"This is not what the records say should be here," said the archdeacon. "Those 20th-century amateur archeologists described an almost intact body."

"So why would they lie?" said Rebecca, returning to the group after doing the rounds of the crypt making sure they were alone.

"Perhaps," said Fr. Salvatore, "they didn't want to say what they had really found."

"What could be more important than the bones of Becket?" said the archdeacon.

"Well," said Fr. Salvatore, "there were many reports through the centuries that Becket's head was kept separate from his body and placed in the Corona chapel. It was covered with a silver mask and was quite lifelike. If these are the remains of the sainted archbishop, then where is the head?"

"Perhaps," said Daniel, "the answer lies further down below. Sr. Cecilia, may we?"

The archdeacon looked at him and nodded, not really knowing what to do next.

Gently, Daniel and the three brothers lifted the remains out of the ground, set them aside, and then gazed within the tomb again. More stone looked up at them.

"Now we know why the amateur archs didn't go further," said Daniel. "This stone looks quite heavy."

Without saying a word, the three brothers approached again, and using their rings, lifted this slab as well, setting it to the side. When the flashlights illuminated the interior, they could see a small vault in the center. Daniel easily lifted the top off and a leather bag, well preserved, revealed itself. Everyone knew something remarkable was kept in this vault. Carefully, Daniel reached down and raised the bag with both hands, setting it on the crypt floor. Gently, he undid the string and found that a linen cloth covered the contents.

"Don't touch that cloth," said Abby. "See the marks on it, how random they look? I believe that's blood. If we're careful with it, we can test the blood and see if it matches with that of the Tunicle. That will help confirm the provenance of whatever the cloth covers."

"Let's see," said Daniel. He fished in his pocket for tweezers, found it, and gently removed the cloth, placing it on top of a piece of clean plastic he had retrieved from his pocket. Everyone gasped at what they saw.

Glittering before them was a human skull, the front gilded in silver, and the back, holding part of the shattered bones together, was a silver mold as well. It was not macabre, but rather a loving restoration of a face broken in death. Death masks had been common back in the days of Thomas, only they seldom contained the actual skull. This one did, and there could be no doubt—this was the head of St. Thomas Becket. It bore the characteristic wounds of his martyrdom.

But that's not what caused the team to gasp. All had read that the night Thomas died, his followers crept into the church and tried to put back the contents of Thomas's head as best they could. But time is an implacable thing, and those remains were long gone. Instead, as the rumors once whispered, the skull was filled with gold and precious stones. Obviously, King Henry VIII who sent his men to despoil the shrine missed a few pieces. The monks had been busy the afternoon the despoilers came.

Daniel looked up at the three brothers and said, "As magnificent a find as this is, this was not what I was sensing this afternoon."

"Nor we," answered the brothers, "yet whatever presence we are aware of is connected to this relic. Perhaps it rests further inside the skull."

"Gently," said Fr. Salvatore, "empty it gently. The bishop deserves that mercy."

Using tweezers rather than his fingers, Daniel deftly pulled each precious jewel and piece of gold from the skull. Suddenly his ring began pulsing, and he found his hand stretched out over the relic. He noted that the three brothers were doing the same.

"What's happening?" he said to them.

"We expect that whatever we sensed is now aware of our presence. Behold! It comes."

A red light began to show at the base of the skull and rising up out of the remains came something like an oval black locket. It seemed to grow as it rose to the size of a hen's egg, and then it paused, fire like sparks coming off it, sprinkling in the dark, the source of its own light.

"I was hoping it would be The Regale of France," said Daniel. "But I guess that was too much to wish for."

The locket began to pulse and then it moved until it floated over Daniel's upraised hand. He turned his palm face up and the light in the pendant winked out as the large locket dropped into his palm.

"Extraordinary!" exclaimed Sr. Cecilia, not looking at the ornament, but at the men who seemed to have conjured it out of the sainted archbishop's shattered head. "These three men, these members of your team, and you as well, I suppose, are gifted with miraculous power. You lift these ancient slabs and raise up evidence of a forgotten jewel as if you did this every day."

"It's a lot to take in, I know," said Daniel. "But …"

"Things happened in Babylon that changed everything," broke in Luca. "These three brothers were in the tomb with the End Times Tablet. They don't look like it at the moment, but they used to play on King Nebuchadnezzar's basketball team. They are part of the mystery we found, and as you have seen, they can do things."

The three brothers looked enigmatically upon the archdeacon.

"Then, there's the locket," she said, "rescued from a grave nobody suspected. I may not be from Babylon, but I know the provenance of this piece. Look at it. The ancient writers described The Regale as 'the size of a hen's egg,' and this pendant is easily that. Look, too, at how it shifts in the light, sometimes black, sometimes red, sometimes dazzlingly white, mimicking what was said of the jewel—so brilliant that some thought it was a diamond, not a ruby. Everyone in Thomas's time knew The Regale was no ordinary gem. It was enclosed in a black oculus."

She looked more carefully. "In fact, it was probably made for the gem to nest right in there. Do you know the legend of the jewel? First, it belonged to France, then King Louis loaned it to Thomas and, then, with his dying breath, the archbishop mysteriously sent it back to King Louis, presumably for safekeeping. And Louis brought it back here. Like it was said before, The Regale jumped from his hand and affixed itself on the gold-plated tomb. It had healing properties of its own but was somehow connected to Thomas. King Louis had to come here to pray for a cure for his sick son, a cure that was granted."

"It is an otherworldly thing, belonging to no one," said Shadrach. "The pendant, or locket as you say, is made of the same metal as our tomb and the rings we wear. Not just the jewel, but the metal itself has a power in it. It is meteorite in origin and there is no mineral on earth that compares to it."

"Perhaps," said Abby, "Archbishop Peter suspected some of this, and that is why he was so eager to re-establish this place of prayer and healing."

Nobody spoke for a long moment. Then Daniel said, "I'd like to go up to the Trinity Chapel where the shrine was built. Sr. Cecelia's comment about the connection between the gem and St. Thomas gives me a thought. Bring the saint's head and I'll carry the oculus. I have a hunch I want to check out."

Softly and quietly, they walked up the stairs and through the cathedral where hundreds of thousands had walked centuries ago to pay their respects and place their petitions to the saint. At a place near the top of Trinity Chapel's Quire, Daniel knelt and placed the skull on the floor and put the locket back inside. The others knelt as well.

"I think it won't be long," said Daniel.

In fact, they could hear a whispering noise far up in the cathedral roof. It was not the scraping hiss of bat's wings, but more of an ethereal fabric touching the ragged stones. They all looked up, but Daniel and the three brothers watched the locket which once again floated in the air. As the almost transparent veil continued to drop down from the heights of the cathedral ceiling, the little group began to feel a sense of awe and hear vaguely in their ears or minds, a soft chanting of sadness and woe, pierced with pain and mourning. But that was not all they heard, for woven within the soft sounds was another theme—of aching longing, of honor besmirched, of victory snatched from a violent end. Finally, the only real words the listeners understood—quiet alleluias bringing the descending veil down around them.

The music did not stop nor did the gossamer wisps of transparent veil cease moving. It was like a fabric from heaven floated down to earth, and, suddenly, they were in the midst of it and not alone. For walking along these strands of memory—of suffering and strife, of victory won and salvation assured—came a cloaked and hooded figure who moved towards Daniel and the three young men. The vision bowed to Daniel and as it did, a drop of blood fell from his cowled face onto the priest's hands. Then the hooded figure plucked the oculus from the air and placed it in Daniel's hand without a word. It then walked to the three brothers, raised its arms, and embraced them in silence, except for the gasp that escaped their mouths. Then the figure lifted up and, with a graceful movement of his hands, blessed the team, and quite remarkably, folded into the gossamer veil and disappeared into the darkness of the cathedral ceiling.

"It was Thomas," said Daniel in a whisper, as he watched the drop of blood melt into the pendant which, perhaps, once held The Regale.

"Yes, but something more, we think," said Shadrach. "If it be Thomas or someone else, whoever it was is one of us, of our blood, of our kind. And that fact changes everything. Most importantly, that we are not alone in our defense of what is to come, but at the same time, we are much more vulnerable, for there is apparently more happening here than we first surmised."

"What do you mean?" asked Fr. Salvatore.

"At first," answered Abednego, "we brothers thought we were preserved through time to be a resource to all of you, to help you as that horrible heavenly body visits this world again. But our meeting with this shade tonight means that what happened here so long ago is connected with what will be. There is the tomb in Babylon; now, there is a gem and a saint linked to a healing power that might be found and reactivated. What else shall come to connect us all?"

"And if I may," said Shadrach. "When the cowled figure embraced us, we also felt terrible sadness. Whoever this shade might have been, it is trapped here and cannot fulfill its function. It is missing something and needs to be released, but how that should happen, I do not know."

"What could it be missing?" asked Fr. Salvatore.

Just then a click was heard, and Daniel felt the locket move as a small, black panel popped open from the back. "What is this?" he said. Carefully, he pried apart the halves of the panel. "There's a tiny rolled scroll tucked in here."

"Careful," said Abby, "it looks old and could be fragile."

"It's made of vellum," said Daniel, "so I think it's strong enough to unroll."

He walked over to a side altar and spread the tiny document open. Everyone crowded around to see the faint but beautiful writing upon it.

"It's in English, Shakespearean English, I think," said Daniel, "and here's what it says:

> *Three lions rampant on the red,*
> *Lead you to the mournful dead,*
> *Pluck the jewel from where it lays,*
> *Bring it to its proper place.*

"Well, that's the first side," said Daniel. "There's more on the back. It says:

> *Then the one who weeps in shade,*
> *Shall place the jewel in pendant made,*
> *Purpose fulfilled, peace shall come,*
> *Thus, the healing of the world begun.*

"At the very bottom, hardly legible are three letters, *RCP*. Must be the initials of the one who wrote this. Whatever the specifics of this message are, it's clear that what we just felt here in the cathedral, that intense sadness, will not dissipate till we find The Regale, which, I believe, originally rested in this pendant. If that's so, the reports of the jewel being very large must be true. I just can't imagine how it has survived undiscovered for so many centuries."

"I think, Sr. Cecilia," continued Daniel, "that Archbishop Peter's meeting with John Nance was merely part of a much bigger plan and not just the thought of a renewed shrine. He was in charge, not Nance, and for some reason convinced Nance to use his funds to help the cathedral and the world. Archbishop Peter was the master designer of this strategy, not Nance. If only we could get into his personal computer we could see what his real intentions were, but I suppose the authorities have confiscated it."

"They did," said the archdeacon, "but he backs everything up into the Cloud of which I have access to. Let's go over to my office and see what he was thinking."

Whatever Archbishop Peter was, he was certainly not cut out to be a man of many secrets. His files on the restoration of the shrine were there for all to see, as was a note that Nance was coming to visit him. Even here, the archbishop showed himself no fool. He was concerned about Nance's interest but also in need of a benefactor with deep pockets. He noted, however, that Nance would be the first confidant he would entrust with his ideas outside of the king and pope.

Daniel pointed out to Sr. Cecilia, "There is one file not labeled. Let's see what it is."

When she opened it, the archdeacon could see it was private notes concerning the possible shrine, but one entry caught her eye. "Look at this," she said.

Whenever I walk through the crypt, my mind bursts forth with fantastic ideas for a possible reconstruction of Becket's shrine. There is something present here that feeds my imagination, as if someone, maybe the saint himself, is calling from beyond demanding that amends be made. And maybe they should be made to bring a healing balm back to our land. The world is in need of such signs.

"Do you think," said the archdeacon, "that he was in touch with what we saw and felt tonight?"

"We'll never know," said Daniel, "but I think we've seen enough to realize that the restored shrine was not just a whim of the archbishop's imagination. He saw it as something that would truly make a difference, not just in the religious realm but in the world at large. And something from beyond was urging him to complete the task."

It was late and Daniel dismissed his team to their hotel rooms. After he said goodnight to the archdeacon, he and Luca walked the paths around Canterbury Cathedral.

THERE WAS THIS GUY

Thursday, March 18, 11 PM, Canterbury Castle Grounds

THEY LEFT BY the front door of the cathedral, just as the bells began to strike midnight. No one was around but the glow of flashing lights showed the authorities still had business at the Old Palace.

Luca and Daniel walked together silently down one of the paths, stopping for a moment by a bench next to a statue of Steven Langton, one of Becket's successors.

Daniel looked back in the direction of the Old Palace. "Archbishop Pomeroy was a good man who certainly didn't deserve this," he said.

"He was a fool," said a voice behind the statue. Daniel and Luca started. Turning toward the bronze memorial, they saw a face in some kind of clownish mask appear. "A fool I say, and so should you if you value your lives."

Luca reached for his gun, but the stranger was far faster. An arm now appeared with a Ruger Max 9 in hand. "No, no, no," said the figure. "Don't tempt me yet. Reach for it again and your friend dies."

"Who are you?" said Luca, enraged at yet another possible violent attack.

"Calm down, Swissy," said the mask. "Don't you recognize me? You're the movie and media expert, so I hear."

Daniel caught his breath first, but it was Luca who spoke, "'V for Vendetta'," he said. "A Guy Fawkes mask."

"Head of the Gunpowder Plot, 1605 that almost blew up Parliament. A Catholic terrorist," said Daniel.

"Well, I wasn't really the head, just the most famous of the merry band of bombers."

"Who are you really?" said Luca.

"Mind if I sit? It's such a long story." The man moved out from behind the statue and approached the bench. The two men backed up. "Don't go running away now," he said as he waved the gun at them.

"Out with it," gritted Luca between clenched teeth. "You can't be Fawkes. He's dead. Who are you?"

"I am as you see me. Fawkes in the flesh. At least as far as you're concerned. After what you've seen in the past two months, nothing should surprise you."

"What do you want with us?" asked Daniel.

"Your death," said Fawkes, matter-of-factly. "I really don't care what happens to the Swiss chard over there." He raised an eyebrow of dismissal at Luca.

A wolf's howl sounded in the dark. Fawkes snapped his head around. "There can't be wolves here in Canterbury, nor anywhere in southern England. Not in this day and age."

Daniel hitched his breath in hope and tried to distract his soon-to-be murderer.

"Your minion missed his chance at me earlier," said Daniel, "so you are here to bat clean-up?"

"Something like that. I'm a closer of loose ends. The death of the archbishop was most important. He had …" and here the man spun his gun lazily in the air, "ideas that had come too close to a reality my employer simply could not permit." Fawkes stood up from the bench and walked around it. "Do you know that he actually thought he could capture the secular world again with his benighted fantasy of a restored Becket Shrine that would bring Catholic, Protestant, and even atheist together here in a gooey, smarmy, kumba-yah movement of art, religion, and healing? He thought he could unite merry olde England once again. He was a fool."

"But a fool you were afraid of," said Daniel.

"Yes!" snapped Fawkes. "What was it the saintly Pope John Paul II said, 'The weakness of secularism is not that it has rejected God, but it has nothing to replace him with.' Britain as well as the rest of Europe is searching for something, hasn't found it, and my employer worries that the archbishop's folly has just enough cachet to catch on with the masses. He was funded, by my employer no less, who likes to play both sides of the issue. But the archbishop was supremely talented; more than we thought. He was going to make it happen. He had to go."

"So, you killed him," snarled Daniel.

"Without remorse, as I'm about to do to you. You see, you represent the pontiff's ideas which are no different from the archbishop. He might think twice if his nephew dies."

"Let me get this straight. You're giving up trying to kill my uncle and settling for me? Your employer's last attempt didn't fare too well."

"Presuming my employer was responsible, but there are always second chances—like me." Fawkes lifted the Ruger and pointed it at Daniel's head.

"I was wondering though," Fawkes said, "what you all were doing in the crypt this evening. Looking for something perhaps?

Bishop's bones, maybe? Or was it something else that pricked at your memory? Come, come, tell me now and I might spare your life."

"What a clown you are, to pick such a failed terrorist to mimic in this day and age. Why would I tell you anything?" said Daniel.

"I truly wasn't such a failure," said the man. "I may have lost my life, but I still manage to strike fear even in these modern times. Why look, my fine young priest. Even on this chilly night, the sweat of fear wets your brow. Perhaps you'll even yelp after I press the trigger."

Luca thought the man would never shut up, but when he did, Fawkes shot his friend.

But not before a grey shadow pierced through the darkness and slammed into Fawkes disrupting his aim. Grigio, the wolf-dog protector of Daniel, straddled the terrorist, baring his teeth to the masked man's neck.

Daniel stood stock still for a moment, his mouth open in surprise. Luca gasped but instinctively acted, smacking the gun out of Fawkes's hand before he could shoot again. He had every intention of pounding the killer's face into rubble, but Fawkes was exceedingly strong and was already pushing Grigio off himself.

"Don't touch me!" he said.

Luca saw he held something in his other hand. "It's a detonator, Dani," he said.

"Smart Swissy," said Fawkes. "In fact, it is connected to a bomb at the cardinal's residence at Westminster Cathedral, London. Have to even things out, you know—a Protestant archbishop, dead, on the one hand; a Catholic cardinal on the other ... Ah, the news will be spectacular tomorrow."

"No!" cried Daniel and Luca together, as Fawkes punched the detonator.

Fawkes was up and running before either Daniel or Luca could respond.

"Get him, Grigio!" cried Daniel.

The dog's teeth snagged an ankle, and Fawkes went down, smashing his face on the ground and knocking off his mask. Daniel knelt and picked up the plastic mask, glancing at Fawkes who turned and looked at him. Daniel gasped in surprise. He expected a face, perhaps even the real face of Guy Fawkes, but that is not what he got.

A melted visage confronted both Luca and Daniel. Even Grigio was surprised and backed away whining. The face was grey and corpse-like with weeping pustules excreting some kind of yellow fluid. In fact, liquid was now dripping all over the face. The figure's cavalier hat had been knocked off as well, revealing a bald head suppurating with sores. Yet, the man with the stricken visage was fast, leaping to his feet and running off into the darkness. Grigio made to follow, but Daniel held him back.

A further rustling rattled the bushes as Rebecca and two agents from MI5 showed up. They had heard the cries and came quickly. His face bleak and devastated, Daniel looked up at them and said, "I'm afraid your work is not done tonight. The assassins have struck again. The cardinal of Westminster is dead."

A BABYLONIAN INTERLUDE

Thursday, March 18, 11:30 PM, Hotel Conference Room, Canterbury Castle

IT WASN'T SOMETHING Daniel or Luca wanted to do. Being debriefed the second time in the evening was a pain in the ass. Daniel got Grigio some water once they made it to the hotel conference room, and they made themselves as comfortable as possible, answering the questions MI5 put to them without revealing much of what the Guy Fawkes character had said. They dwelt instead on the possible assassination of the cardinal, asking the agents to confirm that had happened. Word came back swiftly that an explosion had occurred at the residence of the cardinal, though no body as yet had been found. Authorities feared the worst.

Once MI5 had left, Rebecca looked at the two men in silence. She came to some agreement with herself and spoke, "Based on what you said this Fawkes figure looked like, I think you should see this now. I was going to wait until the morning but …"

"What?" said Daniel. "Show us what?"

"Ranbir has something." She took off her brooch pin and set it on the table, tapping it twice. The Ranbir avatar, the one Bart Finch from the Historical Antiquities Department of the CIA had developed, flashed into existence.

"Good evening, Msgr. Daniel and Capt. Luca," said the hologram. "As always, it is good to see you." The Sikh avatar was dressed in the ceremonial red turban of his people and camos with a sharp knife at his side.

"Tell them what you discovered," said Rebecca.

"Of course, Becky-san," said Ranbir with a smile. Rebecca gritted her teeth at Ranbir's ceaseless garbling of her name. "What you are about to hear and see is a conversation between Daniel's mother and father, recorded by one of our dragonfly drones, the evening after you left Babylon."

"You spied on my parents?" said Daniel, outraged.

"We're the CIA," said Ranbir. "We spy on everybody, even little old grandmas in walkers on oxygen."

"It was for their protection," said Rebecca. "We couldn't be sure that all the danger was gone from their camp. Put the outrage aside and listen to what they said. It's more important now in the light of what has just happened."

"You are going to see this in movie mode," said Ranbir. "All you have to do is make contact with me, and the images will appear in your mind."

Rebecca and Daniel each grabbed one of Ranbir's hands, and Luca took a firm hold of the avatar's very tangible shoulder. Even Grigio padded forward and placed a paw on Ranbir's foot.

Daniel's eyes went blank for a moment, and, then, the familiar landscape of the Babylon archeological dig took shape. It was near sunset, and the dragonfly drone was hidden amongst hundreds of other real insects capitalizing on the scrumptious mosquito delicacies presenting themselves this evening. It was leisurely flying towards two people who were standing at the edge of the dig looking at the developing sunset. The drone got close enough so Daniel could hear his parents talking.

Frannie Azar's arm was entwined with her husband Markoz's. "It's a beautiful evening," she said. "Even after twenty years on this dig, it never gets old."

"You're right you know," said Markoz, the evening breeze lifting the black curls on his head and cooling off the sweat-drenched wrinkles in his sun-tanned face. "It's this time of the day when I realize how old this place is. I swear that if I look out of the corner of my eye I can see the shades of the Babylonians of millennia past walking through these ruins, their colorful robes and echoes of haunting laughter reminding me of what a glorious people they were."

"Sometimes," said Frannie, "in the shadows of the evening, I think I see the ghosts of families around outdoor cooking fires, children playing, old men and women gossiping. The ruins don't look like ruins anymore. Instead, there are buildings all around and they are majestic."

"It was only our imagination—at least I thought it was," said Markoz, "until the events of the last few days. Something is happening here, where everything began long ago. The pope is right. This is a thin place, perhaps the first and most powerful thin place, where this reality and something deeper are meeting together and strange and wonderful things are happening."

"Bad things, too," said Frannie, shivering. Markoz put his arm around Frannie's waist, bringing her closer.

"Bad things, yes, but good things too, like those three brothers."

Frannie smiled. "You're right, of course, but it's the bad things that put our son in danger."

"It's the bad things that put the world in peril," said Markoz. "In fact, when you just shivered, I felt like something dead just walked over my soul. I thought I saw something out west, there in the darkness, near where that Marduk thing let loose his pack of sirrusha. Something's coming. There, out near those small ruins. Something is skittering back and forth. Do you see it?"

"Yes," said Frannie, "yes, I do. And we are pretty vulnerable out here. All the staff has gone back to their quarters. I'd feel better if we did the same."

"If it's something more than an animal," said Markoz, "I'd feel better if we took refuge down near the tomb. It's a place of power, good power. We'll be safer there."

They didn't exactly run. But they hurried. They didn't have far to go and the drone dragonfly followed them easily. It flew through the Esagila—the Temple of Marduk, and down the stairs with the archeologists to the newly discovered original Temple of Marduk. Its little computer realized that dragonflies don't visit underground temples often so it unobtrusively parked itself on the ear of the 10-foot gold statue of Marduk facing the tomb.

Empty of its three inhabitants, the tomb was still full of clay tablets and other cultural items from the Neo-Babylonian Empire, c. 600 BCE. After Markoz had turned on the wall sconces and lit the room up, their fear lessened a bit as the warm light was enhanced by its reflection off the golden walls of the temple. They stood close to the tomb and waited.

Frannie reached down and clutched a clay pot full of sand. "We don't exactly have many weapons here."

"Nope," said Markoz, "let's hope any visitors we have aren't particularly hostile."

They heard the skittering again in the temple above them, and saw a shadow creeping down the steps. It was tall, straight, and humanoid. Markoz didn't know what he expected. From the sound, he thought it might be some kind of Gollum creature from the movies, but the shadow moved like Babylonian royalty. The skittering sound came from under the robed figure where its feet would be. Wherever it walked, it rattled and rippled like water over pebbles, and, indeed, both Frannie and Markoz could see that it left watery tracks in its wake.

They moved to the far side of the tomb, and asked the figure what it wanted. Its features were shadowed so they really couldn't make out many details. It croaked at them as if it was trying to talk or try out a new language. Again, Frannie spoke, "What do you want? We mean you no harm."

"What do you want? What do you want? What do you want?" it repeated back to them. It paused for a moment and they saw it cock what passed for its head.

"Want flesh," it said, and reached out its arms.

Frannie just wasn't going to let it get any closer. Without really thinking, she flung the clay jar in her hands at the creature and struck it squarely on its head; whereupon, the pot shattered spilling sand over the figure's shadowed face. A horrible scream erupted as each grain of sand blazed like sparks from a fire. The light the sparks cast showed a face being eaten by the sand, consuming hair and burning skin.

"It's a water creature," cried Markoz, "and the silica is drying it out."

The figure clutched its face with its hands and skittered back up the stairs leaving its watery tracks behind. Both scientists gaped at the retreating specter.

"Not having experienced the previous few days, I wouldn't have a clue at what we just saw, but I think I can figure it out now," said Markoz. "There's a thing out there thinking itself to be Marduk, chief of the Babylonian gods, and now tonight, we have a new visitor with all the characteristics of Marduk's dad. I think that was Enki, the Babylonian trickster god of water and mischief. And that, my beautiful wife, does not bode well."

Daniel and the others came back to themselves as the drone's broadcast ceased. Ranbir blinked out of existence, but the rest looked at each other in wonder.

"You've got to be kidding," said Luca. "Guy Fawkes is a Babylonian god?"

"Or something pretending to be," said Daniel.

"I thought you should see this right away once you described what this terrorist leader's face looked like," said Rebecca.

"So, it wasn't just the Bedouin that was following us back to Rome," said Daniel. "We've got some supernatural freak from another reality coming after us here. But whatever talked to us this evening was quite understandable, civilized really. What we saw in Babylon was a ghoul."

"Obviously," said Luca, "there's been a swift learning curve. But even with that, is it possible that in such a short time such a creature could put together a terrorist group?"

"No," said Rebecca, "someone else is calling the shots, putting this thing as the visible head of the group, but pulling the strings behind the scene. We need to find out who that is."

"Let's get a few hours sleep and get together in the morning and talk some more," said Daniel. "It's bad enough that there's a new terrorist group functioning, but it seems to have some added heft on its side from another reality."

MISS JENNY WREN

Thursday Evening, March 18, Gemelli Hospital, Rome

POLICLINICO GEMELLI HOSPITAL never slept. It was like a modern biblical Pool of Bethesda with hundreds of people crying out to be healed and a talented but hassled medical community trying to bring healing out of suffering. It was barely controlled chaos. And that's how the pontiff found the place of healing at 10 PM when he and the two Swiss Guard, Mattias and Josiah, entered the reception area. He had given no notice that he was coming, for he did not want the aggravation of the press to hinder him from meeting with the woman who had almost killed him the day before.

The startled receptionist, used to the chaos that was the hospital, quickly recovered and said, "How may I help Your Holiness?"

"Miss Jenny Wren's room please," said the pope.

Armed with the number, he had Mattias and Josiah lead the way to the elevators up to the fourth floor where he found only one *carabiniere* guarding the room.

The pope went in alone and found the young woman sleeping, hooked up to a variety of machines and intravenous drips. She seemed so peaceful there, so different from the other day. But she was sick. He could see that. Life on the street had aged her prematurely, and her deformed left shoulder left her looking fragile. Her mousy hair hung lank to her shoulders, dark half-circles dangling under her closed eyes. Her skin was almost translucent. Her thin arms ended in claw-like fingers, one of them tapping aimlessly on the pristine sheet covering her body. Yet, she was tiny, like a frail little bird. No wonder Luca had named her so.

The pope did not want to bother her, but a voice behind him said, "The malady, forgive my wording, that possessed her the other day seems to be gone, but she has many other health problems."

The pontiff turned and saw a young hospitalist standing at the door. "I'm Dr. Nathaniel Rappini," said the man. "I've been tending the patient. I both heard and saw what happened yesterday, and you were lucky to have escaped injury."

"Some might say it was the luck of the Irish," smiled the pope, "but I prefer to think that my guardian angel helped out the Swiss Guard in keeping me from harm."

"So how did you do it?" asked Rappini. "I mean, I saw it on television. One moment, she was enraged and ready to kill you. The next, she melted into your arms. You said something to her. What was it, if I may ask?"

The pope looked closely at the young doctor. He was like so many of the young professionals he had met throughout Ireland and Rome, brusque, confident of themselves, sure in the knowledge that they had the universe in the palms of their hands. What the doctor had seen on TV must have puzzled his soul as much as an incurable disease puzzled his intellect.

"I said the words, 'Leave her,'" said the pope.

The doctor snorted and stifled a laugh. "Pardon me, but to whom did you say those words?"

The pontiff, stung by the cynicism of the doctor snapped back, "Why to the thing that had laid hands on her, violated her soul, possessed her."

"You mean the devil, or a demon."

"You know exactly what I mean. Are you Catholic?"

"Once, but no more."

"Then this must truly be a medical mystery to you," said the pontiff, slightly ashamed of his Irish temper, always hard to control. He leveled the grey gaze of his eyes once again upon the young doctor. "I'm sorry. It's just that now that I'm pope, I don't see such expressions of disbelief like yours so much anymore. I think some of the people I meet hide it better than you do."

"I'm not a man of faith, if that is what you mean," said the doctor. "I see enough evil just from what nature can do to the human body."

"I understand," sighed the pope. "I would imagine that seeing as much suffering as you do could harden the gentlest person, thinking that God doesn't care. I do not see as much suffering directly as you experience every day, but I must tell you, when this woman jumped from the barricades towards me—in that space between us, I saw the most haunted soul, gripped in a grasp of terror by something totally other than herself. The words just leapt out of my mouth. They were the same as our Lord said when he confronted a demon-possessed boy in Capernaum, his home town."

"You told whatever it was to leave and it left?" said the doctor, an eyebrow cocked quizzically.

"I did," said the pontiff. "Now tell me what else is wrong with her."

"Well," he said, "like many of the homeless, she is weak and malnourished, but that she could recover from. It's the stage four bone cancer that's going to kill her."

The pope sighed. So much suffering in the world. He leaned down and took the young woman's hand. "Miss Jenny Wren, wake up," he said.

The woman's eyes fluttered open and the pontiff smiled at her. "Ah, you answered to your name," he said.

"I ... I don't know my name," she said. Her eyes danced around the room. "Where am I?" she said.

"The hospital," said the pope. "You've had a rough time of it, but all will be better now."

"I know your face," she said. "I remember you smiling at me. I was so cold before, but when you smiled, I felt warmer than I have in a long time."

"Miss Jenny Wren," said the pope. "We hope to have you up and healthy soon, but you are sick, and this wonderful doctor—Dr. Rappini is his name—is here to help make you well. Now let me give you the Sacrament of the Sick, and let you get some rest."

The pope laid his hands upon her head, anointed her with holy oil, and watched her tired eyes close back to sleep.

The doctor stepped up to his side and whispered vehemently, "She will not get well. You should not make promises that you cannot keep."

Pope Patrick turned his handsome craggy face to the young man and snapped, "The pope doesn't lie. Looks like you have your work cut out for you, doctor. Keep me apprised of her condition. Miss Jenny Wren is special to me, and she will be special to you as well. Perhaps in the middle of all this mess we call the suffering human condition, you and I will find the healing power of God between us."

The pope turned and walked out of the room, leaving the doctor with his mouth open in incredulity.

THE POOR OF THE WORLD

Thursday Evening, March 18, Gemelli Hospital, Rome

MATTIAS AND JOSIAH flanked the pope as they headed down the elevator. When they reached the first floor, they found that word of the pontiff's presence had spread through the hospital, and, even at this late hour, people were gathered to catch a glimpse of the leader of the world's largest organization.

Pope Patrick obliged. He smiled and greeted and allowed a few 'selfies' to be taken. But as he and the Guard casually strolled toward the entrance, he caught sight of three homeless people in the waiting room, dressed as poorly as Miss Jenny Wren had been. For some reason, he felt compelled to stop and speak to them.

All three stood up to greet him, and a young man, no more than twenty, spoke, "Sir," he said, "did you happen to visit a young woman—the young woman who attacked you yesterday?"

"I did," said the pope with a smile. "And I can tell you she is feeling much better."

The young man and the two slightly younger women with him all spoke at once, "We were so worried about her. We all live around

Termini Station, and she was acting strangely yesterday morning, disappearing on us. We had no idea she would try to hurt you."

"Do you know who she is?" asked the pope.

The young man frowned. "No, not really. She's new to us and never gave us her name. We could see that she hadn't been eating and was quite sick."

"You can call her Miss Jenny Wren," said the pontiff. "That's what the captain of my Swiss Guard christened her."

One of the women smiled and said, "Fits her well. She's just a bird of a thing."

"You look troubled, my son," said the pope with concern.

"Well, it's just ... my name's Benjamin Capito, and I have to tell you that strange things have been happening down by the station. I mean, Miss Jenny Wren isn't the only one who seemed to be afflicted, what people of your religion call 'possessed'. Lately, homeless folks have been showing up mostly out of their minds, violent even. The regulars have started hiding from them. Jenny wasn't too bad when she came to us last week, but over the past few days, she got much worse, talking to people that weren't even there, spitting at the tourists, having fits, throwing herself to the ground, and all that. Something bad is happening," said Benjamin.

"Frankly," said one of the women, mousy hair hiding much of her face, "we're scared. I've never seen nothin' like this. Someone's going to get killed soon enough." Then she blushed to realize that someone had already been attacked the day before.

The pope laid his hand on her shoulder, "It's alright," he said. "We weathered that storm just fine yesterday. But you are correct. Whatever has taken possession of these people, whether it's bad drugs or something else, is going to cause great trouble and harm to Rome if more people are overcome."

Pope Patrick, like his predecessors before him, had a special spot in his heart for Rome's poor, and these three were obviously distressed over their friend's condition. If others were seeing what he saw in the face of Miss Jenny Wren the day before, then there truly was an incipient horror growing in the Eternal City.

Spontaneously, he reached out to them and covered them like a mother hen in his embrace. He remembered a song he especially loved which had Jesus saying:

> *"The poor of the world are my body," he said.*
> *"To the end of the world, they shall be.*
> *"The bread and the blankets*
> *"You give to the poor,*
> *"You'll know you have given to me," he said.*
> *"You'll know you have given to me."*

"I've got an idea," said the pope to the three, discretely passing some euros to Benjamin. "I'm going to send these two fine guardsmen down to the station tomorrow to take a look around."

"We don't want the *carabinieri* around," said Benjamin. "They'll just harass us."

"Noted," said the pontiff, "but these gentlemen are not the police. They're my Swiss Guard, and I'd like them to do some unofficial investigating. They'll be dressed in plainclothes, so you might not even notice them."

"Thanks," said one of the women. "That birdie girl … Miss Jenny Wren … do you think she will be alright?"

The pope looked sadly at her. "She's very ill. The doctors are doing everything they can for her." He looked at them for a moment and said, "Come with me." He took them to the reception desk and told one of the nurses present, "Please let these three up to see Miss Jenny Wren. They are her friends, and it's what she needs right now."

He watched them go towards the elevators, then turned to Mattias and Josiah saying, "Tomorrow, you need to look into their concerns. You know what we saw yesterday. I want you to find out if there are any others like that girl, what they are doing, and whether they pose a danger. Don't interfere. I don't want to upset the civil authorities, but I have a feeling that what we are dealing with is not the usual vagrancy or random violence that sometimes breaks out among the desperate. Something smells foul, and I want the both of you to ferret it out."

The Guard nodded as they escorted the pontiff to his automobile. The short drive back to the Vatican was made in silence, but once they pulled around to the Apostolic Palace, they found several clergy milling nervously about. It was already after midnight.

"This can't be good," muttered the pope, stepping out to greet the Cardinal Secretary of State.

"Your Holiness," said the cardinal, "there's been a terrible tragedy. The Archbishop of Westminster—Cardinal Vincent Traling—as well as the Anglican Archbishop of Canterbury, Peter Pomeroy—have been murdered this night."

The pope said nothing as he crossed himself. He couldn't help thinking that the events of the past two days and this night were connected. Evil was abroad and was striking at God's house.

WHAT THE FAWKES IS GOING ON?

Friday Morning, Early, Canterbury Hotel

BY THE TIME they returned to Daniel's room, both of the young men had worked themselves into a mighty anger. Rebecca could well understand their rage.

"Whoever or whatever he is," said Daniel, "he's no costumed clown. He just murdered a cardinal of the Church, an international incident that will be all over the morning's papers."

"Not to mention, he seems to be the brains behind the assassination of Archbishop Pomeroy," said Luca, pounding his fist on the hotel room's desk.

Daniel looked at Luca. "We need the three brothers. We have to figure out what's going on."

"I'll get them immediately," said Rebecca, rushing out the door.

It took them five minutes tops, and the three brothers popped into the room looking as refreshed as if they had had eight hours of sleep.

"What's wrong?" they asked in unison. "Something else has happened, hasn't it?"

It took Daniel just a few moments to bring them all up to speed. The three brothers didn't react except for scowls on their faces letting Daniel know that they knew what a garbage dump of trouble they were in.

"I've been thinking," said Rebecca hoping to tamp down on the male anger. "We've got to bring the Director in on this right away. Something bigger than the murder of two clerics is going on."

Daniel nodded, and Rebecca again pulled off a pin on her coat, activated it, and, in a moment, the hologram, Ranbir Singh reappeared. This time, he was wearing his characteristic turban but was clad in a late evening maroon patterned dressing gown with distinctive Indian slippers.

"Ah, Miss Becky, it's a good thing I was up with a good book late into the night. What can I do for you?"

Grimacing, Rebecca said, "Get us synced with the Director, please. It's an emergency."

Ranbir looked distracted for a moment, but then, with a flourish of his hands that any magician would compliment, he wove a screen into existence and, presto, the Director of the CIA, Leslie Richardson, appeared sitting on the side of her bed in a bathrobe.

"This better be good," she growled.

Leslie was a pretty good poker player. She even played with President Putnam and his cronies on Saturday nights. But even the Director of the CIA could not keep the horror from her face as Daniel explained what had happened with the archbishop and the cardinal.

"Not to mention," he said, "the very strange appearance of this Guy Fawkes character. I can't figure out what's going on or who he really is."

"Perhaps we can be of some assistance," said Shadrach. "My brothers and I have spent the evening putting our heads together concerning the origin of the murderous cell which attacked us earlier.

While we have only limited access to your computers, which are truly marvelous inventions your culture has created, we each have tremendous memory storage and many years of stasis to process the verities of human experience."

Abednego stepped forward and said to those in the room, "We are aware of what you call the *Memento Mori* terrorist group that matches the evidence presented to us today. The key is the tattoo their members wear. Rebecca was right to notice it. This particular group has only been in existence for several months, and not much is known about it.

"The tattoo worn by the assassin today on his right hand was an outline of a waterfowl, a drake actually, with the initials 'JJ' interposed on the breast of the bird. The group obviously is a secretive sort, and Daniel and Luca came in contact with its purported leader a matter of hours ago. The initials, 'JJ', stand for 'John Johnson', the *nom de plume* of one Guy Fawkes, a Catholic terrorist who was part of the cabal that planned the Gunpowder Plot in England against Parliament and King James in 1605. The group met in a pub, called *'The Duck and the Drake'*, hence the shape of the tattoo its modern members wear."

Meshach, much blunter than the other two brothers, interrupted, "The fact that John Johnson identified himself to you two as Guy Fawkes meant he did not intend for you to live. You have a saying in your time that a cat has nine lives. I would say, Daniel and Luca, that you are using up your allotment very swiftly."

Daniel dismissed the comment with his hand, "Yeah, maybe, but why would he identify himself with a man and group dead these past five hundred years?"

"If I may interject," said Ranbir, "while these three men have been talking, I have been scanning the web as well as various government sites for information about this group. There is virtually nothing on it except some articles written in obscure military journals and soldier of fortune magazines by a John Johnson. The articles themselves, individually, deal with the usual dissatisfaction with the present world order common to these publications. But I have compared them all, and, interestingly enough, there is one paragraph in each of the six articles I found that match chronologically and informationally with a paragraph in one of the other opinion pieces. Put them together, and a new separate article appears."

"The contents?" asked Rebecca.

"Ah," said Ranbir with a scowl, "you are not going to be pleased."

"Spit it out Ranbir, clearly for all of us," ordered Rebecca.

"It is a manifesto of sorts," said the hologram. "Unlike the ravings of the separate six articles, it is a coherent plan to disrupt society by striking not at military sites or operations, nor the economy, but rather at governmental and religious areas of society. In short, the group seeks to destabilize the societal structures that give meaning to the populace and a framework to the culture."

Daniel said, "Destabilize the belief systems and no economy or military will be able to hold society together. That's what happened in ancient Babylon."

"Indeed," said the three brothers together.

Shadrach continued, "When the Persians conquered our empire, there was very little destruction of the military or the economy. They simply brought in an entirely new belief system and sowed doubt into the people's minds about the credibility of their thousands of years old religion.

"You have found that in your own culture as well. The introduction of diversity and pluralism can often be inspiring and cause a new renaissance in human thinking, but used in another way, it can create doubt in the truth of any belief system, sowing the seeds of despair and nihilism within a culture, making people think that belief or faith is simply an add on to society and that the type of belief has no importance. That is what this particular terrorist group is trying to do."

Luca said, "And because such a method does not directly strike at military targets or economic centers, those in government will act too slowly to recognize the danger."

"What a clusterfuck," whispered Rebecca.

"Language," said Leslie, speaking for the first time, "but you are right Ms. Perez. It will be hard to get nations riled up about this until it is too late. The deaths of these churchmen are striking and will result in major headlines, but I doubt if many will see the rationale behind the deaths. My bigger concern is who is funding this group. The actions taken today are breathtaking in their complexity. It was fortuitous that Rebecca happened upon your dinner party when she did, or the Vatican would be mourning your death, Msgr. Azar."

"As we demonstrated in Babylon," said Daniel with a smile, "VERITAS members make a pretty good team, and it is not so easy to wipe us out."

"If I may," said Ranbir, "this group is not done with its shenanigans. The deaths of the archbishop and the cardinal are just the opening salvo. It is imperative that we brainstorm what the next move will be of this group. Obviously, this Guy Fawkes character knows about the attempt to restore the shrine of St. Thomas Becket, but, Msgr. Daniel, does he have any clue of what you discovered this evening in the crypt? Does he know about The Regale?"

"He didn't say," said Daniel. "But he must have known we were looking for something. He and his group will be watching us."

"What will you do next?" said Leslie.

"Find The Regale," said Daniel. "I want the archbishop's dream to become a reality. Finding this gem is our next priority."

"Before you do so," said Shadrach, "remember that this particular terrorist attack has connections with ancient Babylon and the way it was destroyed. My brothers and I surmise that though the

End Times Tablet threatens us with a worldwide peril, that same menace was once able to insert its tendrils into the destruction of Babylon, the greatest city in the world. The methods are too similar. My brothers and I posit that this Guy Fawkes character and the terrorist group are also connected somehow to ancient Babylon."

Leslie, wide awake now, added, "It seems clear to me that the crimes committed this evening have an international scope and may herald a cascading number of cultural and religious terroristic events. That means the United States and President Putnam, in particular, are going to want to be involved. I speak for him now as I ask you to consider adding Rebecca to your team as you did before. I'd give you Isaac as well, but as you know, Msgr. Azar, he is with your parents in Babylon. It's probably best he stays there since we may need to liaise with them. What can be more destabilizing than some heavenly object on course to intercept us? Perhaps this terrorist group is building upon the apocalyptic fervor. If so, the next few months will be a horrible burden to security organizations around the globe."

"What about MI5?" asked Rebecca. "Are we going to have them in the loop or not?"

"As you know," said Leslie, addressing the whole group, "MI5 is the FBI of the United Kingdom. They usually keep their own counsel. But I will tell my counterparts in MI6, their version of the CIA, about our involvement and agree in advance to keep them informed. That should satisfy them. Don't underestimate the king. He will want to be kept in the loop and, if decisions have to be made, share in that power."

"Well," said Daniel, "I don't think we'll be able to keep Sr. Cecelia from claiming a spot with us, particularly since our immediate search will be for The Regale."

BLOOD IN THE WATER

Friday Morning, March 19, Canterbury Hotel

DR. ABIGAIL DUCHON was piqued. She had been pacing her hotel room since the early hours of the morning. Unable to sleep, she allowed herself to tap into the anger well located deep in the Duchon psyche. Generations of that family in Brittany had literally terrorized any who crossed their path. She had their genes.

What upset her was the priest. Msgr. Daniel Azar, charismatic, good-looking, black curly hair fronting his olive-skinned angular face—he was just too good to be true. Smart, respectful, humorous, when necessary, he used every aspect of his personality to blunt her questions about the three strange companions that helped make up their team. And his bodyguard—she had heard the pope refer to Luca as Watson to Daniel's Holmes—did his best to make sure the conversation never returned to the three brothers.

But she was a mystery solver too. When she had cracked the blood code on the Shroud of Turin—the purported burial cloth of Jesus Christ—the so-called experts laughed at her and immediately questioned her praxis. Her methodology was sound; she knew that. She knew they sneered at the fact that she was a woman, even though her degrees matched theirs. She was young, though, and did not have as many successful feathers under her cap as did other researchers, but, within days, that all changed. No one could find fault with her discovery. How they had not come to the same conclusions as she did was a mystery to them.

But not to her. They were arrogant, secure in their belief that the Shroud of Turin was a forgery. But when she was able to actually isolate, not simply bloodstains, but intact hemoglobin structure on the Shroud, she was able to culture the cellular remains of what appeared to be the blood of Jesus Christ. At least, that is what she thought. The Nobel Prize committee thought the same.

Minimally, the evidence showed that the mitochondrial activity in the cellular remains had been energized far beyond its usual capability. Mitochondria were the little engines that activated the cells and allowed them to do their jobs. What Abby discovered was that the mitochondria, indeed, the whole body of the crucified man, had been exposed to a huge energy boost. This had been surmised for some time by scientists from America, but Abby's insight went much deeper. She saw that the energized mitochondria might actually have enhanced the normal cell structure of the blood. Though it was too early to be absolutely sure, she postulated that the boosted blood had capabilities to re-energize the body that it served, maybe even changing it to a higher form of human life, perhaps even resurrecting that body. Whether the energy first came from the mitochondria, or was imposed upon them remained to be investigated and discussed.

That's where the drift of her research was going, and she had discovered enough to make the most skeptical of critics take a new look at her evidence. The fact that there might be a scientific explanation for the resurrection of Christ did not shake her devout faith in the least. God created the human body after all. The miracle of resurrection took place within history, within a real human body. There were bound to be observable phenomena. Where that burst of energy came from would be a matter of faith to people. 'God caused it' wouldn't satisfy some, but Abby would deal with the facts as they came to her. What was most important is that the evidence showed something extraordinary had happened to the man in the Shroud. Suddenly, it was ok again to identify him as Jesus Christ. Even the skeptics reluctantly agreed.

Abby wasn't all that sure why the pope had included her in VERITAS. The Tunicle of St. Thomas Becket was a no-brainer for her. She would subject it to the same tests as she did the Shroud. After what she saw yesterday evening in the cathedral, she was intrigued whether there was a connection between the blood-spattered Tunicle and the presence in the church that she saw and felt. Could something similar have happened to the saint as happened to the man in the Shroud? On the surface, that's why the pope had asked for her help.

But that couldn't have been the only reason. There were those three young men named Shadrach, Meshach, and Abednego, entombed for millennia, looking like they were sophomores on the college football team. What was the nature of the stasis that kept them alive? Was it possible that something had altered their physiognomy as well? They seemed to have an affinity with the presence in the cathedral. A blood test on them would be of great help in figuring out who or what they were. Maybe that's what the pope was hoping for.

If so, she wasn't going to get much help from his adopted nephew. Msgr. Daniel seemed amazingly close-lipped. This VERITAS team the pope had put together had different levels of confidentiality. As far as Abby was concerned, that was going to stop now.

She barged out of her room, went down the hall, saw the light under the priest's door, heard some conversation, and decided just to walk in.

Daniel turned in surprise as the door swept open and saw a veritable tsunami of anger coalescing on Abby's face. Before he could even speak, she pounced.

"I've had it," she fumed. "I've been up all night bending my brain over what we are actually doing here, trying to figure out what happened in the cathedral this past evening, and here you are, the inner sanctum of our group, already moving on to the next part of the plan. A plan that not all of VERITAS is privy to."

"It's not like that," protested Daniel.

"Yes, it is," said Abby, not to be deterred. Taking a fast breath and pushing onward, she said, "You've got your right-hand man, Luca here, and your brain trust—the 'the three wise men'—and the international muscle, Ms. Perez, as well as this avatar thing ..."

"I beg your pardon," tsked Ranbir, "I'm much more than ..."

"Enough!" said Daniel, "Really, Abby, we didn't mean to exclude you or Fr. Salvatore."

"But you did," she said. "And I'd like to think we can be of help to you. But I won't stand for any more secrets, do you hear me?"

"I think she means it," said Luca *sotto voce* with a smile on his face. "Hell hath no fury like a Sindonologist scorned."

"Right you are," said Abby, "and I've already figured out that I may be of more assistance than even the pope thought. You three," she said pointing at the brothers, "reacted in a special way to the presence in the cathedral. We're going to find out why. I need your blood, and I'm going to compare it with Becket's on the Tunicle. My hunch is that there is something present in your blood and his that draws you together."

"You are perceptive, indeed," said Shadrach. "In fact, I would suggest you compare the blood of Daniel, the pope, and us with the Tunicle. There is much about us that you do not yet know, and much we ourselves wish to understand. The answers won't so much enlighten my brothers and me about who we are, for we know why we are here and where we come from, but Daniel and the pope will surely benefit as will you all. Together—and you make a good point Abby about us all truly being of one mind and one heart—we will figure out what we all should do about the dangers facing us."

"I didn't mean to go all secretive," said Daniel. "With what else happened this evening I just didn't want fear to grip us all."

"What else happened?" said Abby.

"Luca," said Daniel, "could you please go get Fr. Salvatore, and I'll call Sr. Cecilia. Everybody might as well know about the second assassination attempt and the death of London's cardinal. The sun will be rising soon. No more sleep for anyone this night."

WHAT'S THIS GUY DOING?

Friday Morning, March 19, Fowey, South Cornwall, England

JOHN NANCE HAD moored his 200-foot yacht, *Restless*, the previous week at the lovely seaside village of Fowey in southern Cornwall. Pronounced, 'Foy', it was an old town, older than the Norman invasion, and was a beautiful concoction of cottages, pubs, seaside life, and a relaxed ambiance.

After his audience with the pope the day before, he had flown into Cornwall Airport and taken the short drive to Fowey. This morning, he was awaiting his expected visitor at the Old Quay House, a popular hotel and breakfast place on the water. He was snacking on some smoked salmon and reading the *Times of London* when his guest appeared.

"John Johnson," he said with a smile, "you look like you slept the sleep of the angels instead of having to drive five and a half hours from Canterbury."

The man, who if he had dressed in a seventeenth-century period piece, would be a dead ringer for the terrorist Guy Fawkes, smiled and sat down at the table. He wore no mask, though his features vaguely resembled the features of the old Guy Fawkes terrorist, mustache and Van Dyke beard included. He was nattily dressed in a twenty-first-century business suit, however, and he deftly unfolded a cloth napkin and placed it on his lap.

"I never drive," said Johnson.

"How did business go?" said Nance, ignoring the strange statement.

Johnson pointed to the paper saying, "You see it right there. My associates took care of both the archbishop and cardinal. Chaos has ensued as you wished."

"Indeed," said Nance. "My meeting with Archbishop Peter last week was a good one. He was most impressed that I decided to fully fund the Becket Shrine."

"I don't get it," said Johnson. "You fund the archbishop's crazy proposal, and then you mark him for elimination. Sounds like cross purposes to me. Same thing with the Catholic cardinal of Westminster. You snuggle up to the pope and then kill his representative."

"Well, I've tried to kill the pontiff as well," said Nance with a smile. "He's just a little more bulletproof."

"My point is that you are good at causing pandemonium, but to what end? I don't get what your game plan is."

"You don't have to get it," said Nance, "so long as you and your associates carry out my wishes. But I will let you in on a little secret."

Nance paused a moment while the server brought tea for the two of them, and then resumed. "More than half the people in America no longer belong to a church, and the religious intensity of Europeans has fallen off the map. It would seem that trying to destabilize Christianity even more would be giving a nihilistic population just another push towards despair. But the West was founded on the bedrock of Christian principles. That ideology is stronger than you think. By funding crucial parts of the enterprises of the Church, I make it look like a renaissance is blooming for the faith. By taking out its leaders and monuments, I rock the West's very foundations and inject paranoia and worry into a populace that might not like Christianity so much but isn't quite sure it really wants it to fade from the world."

"Ok," said the Guy Fawkes mimic, "but you have your fingers in Islam and some of the Eastern religions as well. You support this new Mahdi."

"Yes, and for the same reasons. Historians and war planners have made it clear that the conflicts of the twenty-first century have been and will be primarily religious ones. It's a paradox. Waning religious fervor, but growing religious wars. By lifting up the religions, I cause them to be more hopeful about spreading their beliefs. By terrorizing the same religions, I destabilize countries."

"And your end game?" said Johnson.

"You mentioned that you suspected me of loving chaos," said Nance. "But I look for what comes after anarchy. The soul of humanity will always crave order. I intend it to be an order that I create. The West is done and dying. Its religion is on the wane. The perks that I am giving to Christianity will raise some hope in a cynical populace, but it will be the Indian summer of a dying way of thinking and believing. In the aftermath of the bloodshed that will result, something new will emerge."

"Then what's approaching from space will only help you sow chaos," said Johnson.

"It's all part of the plan," said Nance with a smile.

"What?" said Johnson with a sneer. "You can't possibly have known that we were coming."

"Don't be so sure. You truly do not know me as well as you think."

For a moment, Johnson was speechless. "Have it your way. You may think me just a minion, but others, better than you, have underestimated me as well. You should know that Azar and his friends were searching for something in the cathedral last night. They spent a lot of time in the crypt. Know anything about that?"

"Perhaps. They may be seeking a jewel, a bauble that carries great power. It's only a legend to be sure, but Azar is attracted to things like that. You should check it out, and you should finish what you failed to do last night. You didn't kill the Azar boy, and he is a threat to us."

"He was wearing that ring, as you said he would," said Johnson. "If it's similar to the rings the three interlopers from Babylon wear, then it protects him."

"I know, and I think my hunch about The Regale of France, for that is what the gem is called, gives me hope. It seems to be something similar to that ring. I want its power, so your task is to follow Azar, for I am sure he will search for it. Capture the jewel; kill the priest. He is precious to the pope.

"In the meantime, I have other operations that I must attend to. Keep me informed. All that you need will be at your disposal. You may take my associates, the *Memento Mori*, but tell them nothing of this conversation or the importance of The Regale. It remains for them just a valuable jewel."

"As you wish," said Johnson, standing up from the table. "What do you want done with the team the Azar boy has collected?"

"They are of no use to me," said Nance. "Dispose of them as you wish."

John Johnson walked out of the restaurant, looked back, and sneered as he walked up the street, muttering in a low voice, "I'm so much more than you think. In the old days, I would rip out your heart for your arrogance. But we are not yet as strong as once we were. Not yet, but soon."

BETTER TO REIGN IN HELL THAN SERVE IN HEAVEN

Friday Morning, March 19, Fowey, South Cornwall

IT TOOK ONLY minutes for John Nance to walk back to where his yacht, was moored. The captain and crew must still have been gone to breakfast because he had the ship to himself.

His palatial rooms were on the second level of the tri-deck yacht. The wood-paneled study welcomed him, dimming the sunny day outside on the observation platform. He was mostly pleased with what his messenger had told him, so he was a little bemused by the twinge of anxiety that accosted him as he sat behind his desk. Nance had formed the terrorist group, *Memento Mori*, and given control of it to the Guy Fawkes creature. He suspected it was not human because Marduk had whispered in his mind that he was sending him an associate. So far, so good.

Both the archbishop and cardinal had ceased to walk the human plane of existence. That was the good news. The minds and hearts of the English populace might be hardened against talk of divinity or religion, but Nance had great faith in the nascent superstition present in every human, religious though they were or not. The deaths would certainly cause wonderment and no little bit of worry as to why they occurred. Best case scenario—both the government and people would see them as the results of an attack on the spirit of the realm and the soul of the people.

So why the aching in the pit of his stomach? Of course, he wished the Azar brat had been eliminated by his messenger, but that could always happen later. So that couldn't be the cause of the acid reflux scraping his esophagus.

He turned to the large terrarium behind the desk and looked for his living talisman. And there it was. The *sirrush* he had created—the dragon from the myths of Babylon. It was only as big as a small dog, but it would grow to be as large as the biggest horse, with the back legs ending in the claws of an eagle and the front ones padding with the paws of a lion. Its neck was serpentine, ending in a scaly spine with a short tail. Massive teeth in a snake-like head. Cryptids were cool, he thought

The creature loved him and purred as he took it out of its habitat and set it in front of him on the desk. He remembered how he came to create it. The dream had come to him in the darkest of all nights just a year ago. Nance was a trillionaire which allowed him to dabble in sketchy things. Brilliant and trained in several medical fields, he styled himself as a cryptobiologist, dicing and splicing genomes, chromosomes, and other carbon-based material trying to concoct new forms of life.

He hit the jackpot with the *sirrush,* and it was all because of that strange dream. Someone or something spoke to him that night in symbols and myth. It wasn't from his imagination, no, indeed. A chanting almost, certainly a cadence he could easily repeat, insistent in its intense desire to be remembered. Its name was Marduk, and that's how Nance got introduced to the things that called themselves the Sumerian gods.

Then the most remarkable event happened. The symbols and myths conjured pictures of ancient creatures and things that walked the earth long ago, but Nance's mind translated all that into formulas and elements, organs and muscle. What might cause a dragon to have poisonous fumes or even fire—can mitochondria hold that energy? What sort of cellular regeneration would have to happen for a creature to be nearly impervious to modern weapons? How vibrant must the telomeres be to extend the life-span of a reptilian-mammalian hybrid that should really not be able to survive more than a few minutes outside of a womb or an egg?

He woke from that dream grateful to whomever or whatever sent it to him and he began to write, and after that, experiment, and then to create. He knew he was brilliant, but what happened after that most impressive dream was above genius level. And he never told anyone about it. An unmarked package soon arrived for him, however. It was a clutch of fossilized eggs from Iraq of unknown reptilian origin. If he could extract the DNA, he just might make that cryptid.

That's how the *sirrush* became his original and only creation—so far. But it would be the first of many. It was a brilliant achievement as were his other plans for societal change. So, again, why the anxiety?

He petted the cryptid for a while, but for the first time, doing so did not calm his nerves. Putting the little dragon back into its habitat, he began to pace around the room, becoming more agitated every moment. He felt his blood pressure rise, his heartbeat increase, and his breathing become more labored.

He thought he might be having a heart attack. He reached for the phone but was slammed to the floor by a powerful voice echoing throughout his mind. *Slave!* it thundered through the twisted grey matter of his brain.

When his mind cleared, he found himself on his hands and knees, almost kissing the carpet, his cheek wet with vomit. As he tried to stand, he was knocked down again. *Fool!* said the mind voice again.

"You!" said Nance out loud, recognizing the same voice from his dream. "I am no slave and I am no fool. I do not serve you as some chattel, and my intellect is at least the equal to whatever passes for yours."

He had never groveled to the voice in the dream, realizing that whatever entity it was needed his scientific expertise as much as he needed its knowledge to make those dreams a reality. Over the past year, he had cast his nets wide for potent religious myths that might have resonance in today's society. Archeology was an obvious choice to find hints, so when he came across the Azar dig in Babylon, he stopped to take notice. He hired the brothers whom he called the Bedouins to spy on the dig and report to him. He was amazed when they also discovered something else in that Babylonian wasteland, something he could only call a portal to another time, another place. As soon as Walid Badawi, the middle brother of the three Bedouins, discovered a real, live *sirrush* in that oasis from another dimension, another time, Nance knew he had also found the source of his dreams. He had tentative contact with that being that sheltered the Bedouins back in Babylon, and he had forged an uneasy alliance with it until now. Now, it was screaming into his mind, trying to make him a thrall like it did the three Bedouins, two of whom had already lost their lives to the cause.

Nance would have none of it. This thing that styled itself a Babylonian god named Marduk was powerful to be sure, but it had been shut away from the world for a long time. It was simply out of its depth in the twenty-first century. In short, it needed Nance.

A fact that Nance now re-presented to the entity occupying his thoughts. "You will not speak to me in that way," he said, as he climbed to his feet. He knew now where the anxiety had come from. Frustrated with its failure in Babylon to destroy the dig and capture whatever was of value in the tomb, the entity thought to punish the only other human that had helped set into motion those plans that failed.

Images of Marduk crushing Nance, drowning him in the oasis lagoon, rending him to shreds in the Babylonian wasteland came crashing into Nance's head, but this time Nance did not fall. The pain was great, but he had not become the richest man in the world or a noted scientist by wimping out at the first sign of a struggle. Marduk's reach was long but nowhere near as potent as if Nance was in Babylon itself. Realizing this gave Nance courage and he tempered his voice, talking reasonably to this strange creature. Walid had called it a *djinn*, a being from beyond the Thin places, very powerful, mercurial, but possibly, on a good day, helpful to humans.

"I thought we were allies," said Nance, "partners in this journey we take to release chaos upon the earth. In fact, perhaps it's time to stretch your influence beyond the Fertile Crescent and let humanity feel the touch of the ancient gods again."

At those words, laughter rang in Nance's mind, and he was surprised to see in pictorial form that Marduk had already attempted such contact. And Nance smiled as well, saying, "I think we can strengthen that troubled touch you gave to humanity, but only if you treat me as an equal partner. I'll be happy to dance with the devil, but I'll never simply twirl to your tune."

For a moment, silence reigned supreme in his mind, and then a sibilant hiss was heard. He almost mistook it for the sound the *sirrush* made when it slept, but then he realized that the entity in his mind was speaking a word, a susurrating, *Yes!*, which Nance decided was enough of an agreement to give him peace of mind.

THE CATS OF CARACALLA

Friday Morning, March 19, 9 am, Statzione Termini, *Rome*

MATTIAS AND JOSIAH were newly minted Swiss Guard, so they were young, but their training had given them a gravitas that belied their years. Nonetheless, they were excited to be tasked with discovering what was going on with the homeless and the beggars down at the Termini Station. Dressed in comfortable civilian clothes, they would blend in perfectly with the populace.

By the time they arrived, the station was already bustling with thousands of people trying to get to various destinations throughout Italy and Europe. The noise from the traffic in the area as well as the myriad conversations among people was horrendous. But they were not the young men's concern. The ubiquitous beggars were. People seldom noticed the homeless. They blended in with the atmosphere of the station and unless individuals were accosted by them for money, they simply melted into the surroundings.

But Mattias and Josiah were looking exclusively for them. They had never done that before, and they were surprised how many were present in the shadows and corners of the station. As the guardians to the pope, they had been taught, in what passed for boot camp to be very solicitous to the poor who came to the Vatican State. Whatever prejudices they had were exorcised during their training. So, it was with much compassion that they noted the suffering all around them. Just below the drone of excited conversations among the travelers, they heard the coughing, sneezing, and sniffling of people too poor to be healthy, too destitute for a ticket to anywhere but hopelessness.

"I've not a clue where to start first," said Mattias. "We can't just go asking them if they've seen any demonic activity lately. They'll run from us for sure."

"Noted," said Josiah, the more introverted of the two. "Let's just take a look around first and see what we discover."

They found nothing unusual. After a time, the press of the people became oppressive, so they thought they'd widen their observation to environs around the station.

Of course, the first thing that caught their eye was the imposing ruins of the Baths of Caracalla. A cruel tyrant in most other things, Emperor Caracalla had created an architectural wonder that stood the tests of time. Parts of it had been renovated through the centuries.

Even though it no longer served as the ancient Roman baths, it had many art displays and of course Michelangelo's amazing Basilica of St. Mary of the Angels and Martyrs. The entrance to the church looked like one of the little doorways into the baths themselves, but its unimpressive façade quickly opened into a magnificent worship space. The famous artist had incorporated the arching style of the baths into the lofty ceilings of the basilica and the church was full of beautiful mosaics and artwork. It was all part of the Renaissance's attempt to Christianize the ancient world's achievements.

Mattias and Josiah were familiar with all of that. What most interested them was what was beneath the baths. Back in the day when they were operational, tunnels ran underneath the acres of buildings allowing slaves to service the various pools of water, the libraries and gymnasiums and meeting places present within the complex. There were even the ruins of an ancient *Mithraeum*, a pagan temple, in the bowels of the baths.

Most of those tunnels were out of service, but as Mattias and Josiah walked around the perimeter they kept their eyes open for any anomaly which stood out. They quickly discovered they were not alone. This was a famous area for feral cats. Ruins always seemed to attract them. In fact, the city boasted over 300,000 of the felines, honored by the populace over the centuries for their yeoman's work of destroying vermin and keeping the plague at bay. Now the two Guard found themselves followed by a big tomcat, black with a white star on its forehead. Trailing him were at least a dozen other felines silently slinking around bushes and broken pottery.

"Look," said Josiah, "we have company and they are inquisitive. So much for our secrecy."

"Cats or not, it's good to look at these ruins. My hunch," said Mattias, "is that not much happens out in the open in the Termini. The *carabinieri* would only be too quick to notice. I wonder if the destitute in Rome have discovered new ways to get into the tunnels underneath these baths. It's just a short walk to the Termini from here. Maybe this big tomcat and his friends can help us find a hidden tunnel."

"Well, the poor who make this place a home are not going to be in any of the places we and the officials know about," said Josiah. "Let's look for the unexpected."

It was a long search, and they broke up their time with lunch at the Capitello, a fine place to dine not far from the Termini. The cats didn't join in, but Josiah snagged some scraps to give them later during their afternoon search. The *trattoria* was not in the price range of a guardsman, but Josiah had a grandmother in town who insisted he wasn't eating enough and slipped him money from time to time to get a decent meal. Who was he to protest that?

They talked over their meal about the assassination attempt on the pontiff and what they saw at the hospital.

"The pope thinks there is real evil operating here." Mattias crunched a buttered piece of toasted bread between his teeth.

"He may be right," said Josiah, "but we've seen nothing in a whole morning's search of the area."

"I still think the answer lies in those tunnels," said Mattias.

"You mean the ones we couldn't find," smiled his friend.

"We're not doing this right. We've got to look for the hidden and the unexpected."

"What do you suggest?" said Josiah.

"I suggest," said Mattias, "that we work off this lunch by walking the perimeter of the baths again, let the cats get a little closer to us to see what we are doing, and hope they can help us find any hidey-hole there might be."

That's exactly what they did, cats included, and though they found their clothes snagged and torn a bit from the vegetation and garbage present between the Termini and the baths, they had time to stop and feed the group of cats following them. It was like magic. Josiah gave a tasty bit of lunch leftovers to the big black tom and he was off in a flash toward the walls of the baths. Following him, they finally found an opening covered with a dead tree and discarded tent. Its black entrance beckoned them for further discovery.

"I didn't bring my flashlight," said Mattias. He scrunched up his freckled face in disappointment.

Josiah just laughed and pulled out a small LED military flashlight. "Never go anywhere without one," he said. "I'm noting your lack of preparation. Capt. Rohner won't be pleased."

The two took deep breaths and plunged into the tunnel, the tomcat running before them. Within seconds as they wound their way underneath the baths, they were in total darkness except for the light Josiah held. It was obvious this tunnel had not been used for much of anything in centuries.

After five minutes, Mattias said, "This looks absolutely hopeless. There's nothing here."

"Except for a faint light up ahead," said Josiah. "Might be something." A tiny meow from the black cat signaled feline agreement. Whatever was the source of light, it was flickering faintly.

"How far away do you think it is?" said Mattias.

"Let's find out."

The two Guard and the companion cat walked five more minutes with the faint glow getting brighter. Once Josiah could see Mattias's red hair in the ambient light, he turned off his own flash.

"It's got to be somebody's fire, but I don't hear anybody," said Josiah. The tunnel was not straight. It curved a little so it was a surprise to the two Guard when they turned into an open area and saw the flame. It wasn't much, just a garbage fire really, but no one was around. The tunnel had opened up into a circular gathering space.

"Probably for storage, originally," suggested Josiah.

"But again," said Mattias, "no one around now. Do you think they heard us?"

"They didn't hear me," said Josiah. "Maybe your sloppy footwork." He grinned in the shadows.

"Quiet," said Mattias, "someone's coming." The cat came running back and leapt into Josiah's arms.

They looked for a place to hide, but the smooth walls of the tunnel and even its gently curving nature didn't hold out much hope for them.

Josiah saw a malformation in the wall, and pointed to it. "I think it's some kind of nook." In fact, it was more than that. It was a carved-out section of the wall that gave them just enough space to hide.

Fortunately, they slid into the hidey-hole just as people showed up from the other direction.

There were six of them, pushing a seventh, hands tied and mouth bound ahead of them. They made their captive kneel in front of the fire.

Mattias and Josiah couldn't see much from their hiding place, but they heard the gruff voice of the leader, a male, say, "This was one of them. I was watching the hospital last night, and I saw him with two other women go into the clinic."

The Guard heard him slap the head of their captive. "Tell me what I want to know. What were you doing there? Were you trying to see her? Did you? Did that prick of a pope talk to you and let you see her? Open your mouth and speak to me."

The Guard heard another male clear his throat and say, "Rupert, he can't talk with the gag in his mouth."

Rupert snarled, "He's not trying to say anything." Yet, Rupert ripped the gag off and waited expectantly.

"I've got nothing to say," said Ben. It was clear to the Guard that the captive was the man the pope spoke to the night before.

Mattias and Josiah heard a fist smash into the face of Ben. The man cried out in agony. They regretted not bringing their firearms along, but the pope had insisted they just observe. None the less, Josiah reached out and held Mattias down who seemed to be ready to break cover and take on Rupert.

"We need to find out what he knows, what he told the pope. We need to find out how she is," said Rupert. "Bring the witch. She'll know what to do."

Mattias and Josiah heard a runner sprint down the tunnel.

"Isn't that a little extreme?" said a woman's voice. "Rupert, the witch is so unpredictable, and she acts like she's taking charge of everything."

"She knows a lot," said Rupert. "We've got to trust her. Everything depends on our secrecy. We don't have enough followers yet. She can fix that."

There was silence for a few minutes, and then the two guardsmen heard feet approaching again, more than one person.

"I am here," whispered a voice.

"We need you, Tia," said Rupert. "Ben, here, betrayed us and is just not being cooperative. We need to know what he knows and what he said to the pope."

"We wouldn't be in this predicament," purred Tia, "if your operative had done what she was told to do and killed the pontiff."

"She tried her best," said Rupert. "He was too well guarded."

"It shouldn't have mattered," said Tia. "What I put in her should have conquered everything in its path."

"Speaking of which," said Rupert, "just what did you do to her? I saw the attack on the news. She was too sick to have that strength and speed. How did you accomplish that?"

Laughter in the tunnel. "I gave her a friend. She couldn't resist. I have many more friends like that to give our followers. This was a test and even though it failed in its ultimate goal, I proved that it could work. Think of what hundreds of people like her could do if they were released among the citizens of Rome, or any of the major cities of Europe."

"Is that your plan?" said Rupert. "We take over the city with the possessed?"

"Don't be stupid," said Tia. "We do what we do to cause chaos and upheaval. It is for others to take control. We simply bring the darkness."

"Well, what about Ben here?" said Rupert. "He obviously told the pope something, but he's not been too cooperative. Can you make him talk?"

"I can do more than that," said Tia.

Mattias and Josiah heard her walking towards the fire and the bound captive. Mattias couldn't help himself. He needed to see, so he lifted his head to take a look. Fortunately, he was in enough shadow to keep him from revealing himself.

He saw Tia draw a long, pointed fingernail across Ben's cheek. Blood flowed in the tiny rivulet she carved. Ben's whole body convulsed and he began shaking. Terrified, he obviously knew who she was and what she was capable of.

"Tell me what you saw, and this shall go much easier on you," she cooed. "Otherwise, you will have to experience my master. I've brought him with me."

Ben sobbed openly. "Please don't hurt me. I didn't tell the pope anything. He knows nothing of what you are doing."

"You know," said Tia, with her fingers caressing her lips. "I'd like to believe you, but I'm having a difficult time of it. Let's see if we can give you some encouragement."

She had a backpack on. Mattias could see that clearly. She reached into it and pulled out a glass globe. In the firelight, he could see that whatever was inside was swirling with dark colors, as though a fire raged within its confines.

Amazingly, she took hold of the back of Benjamin's neck and easily twisted him around so he was facing the garbage fire. She bent his head toward the flames and said in a low voice loud enough for both Mattias and Josiah to hear, "Now we come to it, my friend. Something to loosen your tongue. Someone to fill up those lonely holes in your spirit. A force to make you into more than what you are and less. Come, don't be afraid. It only hurts a little, and then you will feel so powerful and be capable of so much."

She tossed the glass globe into the flames where it broke apart on contact. The fire swirled high and a high-pitched wail sounded bringing even Josiah to look at what was happening.

There was a thing in the flames or something that seemed to have a life of its own. It wasn't very big, but both the Guard felt the essential wrongness of it. Rupert and his companions fell to their knees and began keening, worshipping whatever it was.

While they cringed and bowed, the fire thing swirled out of the flames and popped down the screaming mouth of Benjamin Capito. His howl of terror immediately cut off and he fell to the ground unmoving.

"There," said Tia, "it is done. Observe."

For a moment there was nothing. Then, Ben began to spasm as if he was going into a seizure. In fact, he levitated off the ground, twitching all the way. In a moment, he stood before the flames, every joint of his body moving in frenetic activity. The keening of Rupert and his comrades made the entire area seem a hell hole of terror. The bonds fell off of the unfortunate young man and the twitching lessened. Whatever walked through the soul of Benjamin shone out from his eyes.

"This one is perfect," it spoke. "Most impressive, my Tiamat. You have done well."

"Thank you, my master," she said. She was the only one in the circle who was not cowed. "Can you find out if he told the pontiff anything?"

"I already have," it said. "Nothing of great import. Nothing that will stop our plans." Suddenly, the being inhabiting Ben began to sniff. "Someone else is here," it said.

Josiah and Mattias tensed, but it was the black tomcat that acted first. He jumped out of Josiah's arms and ran out towards the fire, leaping at Ben's face. With one of his big paws, he swatted at Ben and the pain from his claws brought momentary sanity to the boy's eyes.

"Get out of me!" he shouted, as the cat rushed the boy again and hissed and growled loudly in his ear. It appeared that Ben fainted, but before he hit the ground, the fire thing leapt out of the boy and back into the flames. It coalesced into a large figure, this time with an ancient masked warrior bearing a shattered eye hole. In fact, it looked like an ancient king or god.

"Babylon," whispered Mattias.

"Yeah," said Josiah. "Marduk to be exact. I remember how Luca described it."

"Beast," hissed the apparition at the cat. "You will burn for that." The figure threw a flame that would have incinerated the feline had he not jumped away.

The two Guard were momentarily too stunned to move, but then the cat turned its huge head toward them. The six-pointed star, white on its black head, shone out brightly for just a moment. The cat growled low and ran toward them. They got the message.

"Time for us to go," said Josiah. "Run!"

They took off down the tunnel and heard Tia's voice cry, "After them! They must not escape."

The ghost of the godling in the flames threw out spits of fire from his hands. When they landed on the floor, they turned into capering flame *sirrusha*, the dragon servants of the god-king Marduk. Their snake-like heads flickered over feline bodies with front talons like an eagle and rear paws like a lion. Following Tia's bidding, they quickly chased after the interlopers. They weren't any bigger than the cat who led the humans, but they were fast and dangerous.

Fortunately, Mattias and Josiah were in tremendous physical shape. Coupled with their athletic ability, the fear driving them on made them uncatchable. They burst through the opening in the tunnel into the bright afternoon sunlight. The screaming meows of the tomcat brought the rest of the nearby cats to the opening.

Mattias stopped to catch a breath, but Josiah grabbed his arm. "This isn't some horror novel. They're not afraid of sunlight. They'll keep coming!"

"Where to, then?" said Mattias.

"The basilica. Hurry!"

But they were too late. The *sirrusha* burst out into the sunlight, and, for a moment, everything came to a standstill. Then, the tomcat screamed again, and dozens of cats fell upon the flaming dragons, trying their best to dispatch them. It was a terrible standoff. Many of the felines were simply burned to death as the dragon vermin jumped them. But the black tomcat had obviously dealt with them before. He showed the others that if they snapped them in the back of their long necks, the fires died immediately without harming the felines. Once shown, the cats did a remarkable job of mopping up the *sirrusha*.

Josiah felt bad about leaving the felines to what might turn out to be a true catastrophe for them. Yet one more look at the tomcat convinced him that the big feline was urging them to escape. They ran along the base of the wall until they came to an opening that let them up into the baths proper. It wasn't far to the Basilica of St. Mary of the Angels and Martyrs, and a good thing too. Both of them looked back and saw some of the humans from the tunnel leaping through brush and garbage and climbing the wall to get into the baths. The little coven was chasing them with a fury they had never seen before.

Josiah and Mattias grabbed the door that marked the entrance to the basilica. There were tourists around, but not many. They quickly got out of the way of the chase, and the two guardsmen slipped into the basilica just as the coven reached the entrance.

Benjamin was with the evil group, and he appeared to be possessed again. The spirit of the god-king must have needed a ride. The thing in Benjamin snarled and smacked his hand against the opening as if he was encountering an invisible barrier. Both Tia and Rupert tried to enter as well but were unsuccessful in their effort. The unimpressive façade of the basilica was a mighty wall to the evil that attempted to enter.

Mattias began to laugh and Josiah with him. "I guess," said Mattias, "that this part of the horror novel is right. They can't enter consecrated ground."

"Thank God," said Josiah. Before he gently closed the door in the faces of those who sought their deaths, he let the big, black tomcat with the white star on his head saunter through into the church. The cat turned and sat regally looking at those who could not enter. He hissed as the doors clicked shut.

"Apparently," said Josiah, "we have found the corruption the pope was worried about. That witch talked about followers. Do you think the demon intends to corrupt all the homeless?"

"I don't think," said Mattias. "I know. What I don't know is how far along the process is. You heard that thing in the flames. It seeks to unleash this evil upon the whole of Rome and perhaps other cities. When, I don't know, but we're going to have to find a way to stop it. And we're going to have to try to save Ben."

ONE JEWEL TO RULE THEM ALL

Friday, March 19, Mid-afternoon, Apostolic Palace

THE PLANE FIGHT back to Rome was short but rather quiet. Daniel still had his hands full with a restive group. Sr. Cecilia hadn't been happy about being left behind in Canterbury, but she did agree someone with knowledge had to be on-site in case anything else developed.

By the time they arrived back in Rome and had a late lunch at the cafeteria in Casa Sancta Marta, the hotel for clergy and other Vatican guests, it was time for a mid-afternoon meeting with the pope in the Apostolic Palace to bring him up to speed on what happened.

Coming into his uncle's sitting room, Daniel noticed that the pope was attended by Josiah and Mattias. He wondered what the pontiff had tasked them to do while he and the rest of the team were in Canterbury.

"All right," said Pope Patrick, "let's hear it. All the news I know is terrible and bad. The deaths of the archbishop and the cardinal are major stories around the world, but nobody seems to see any rationale behind the assassinations. As you know, the terrorist group that caused this has named itself *Memento Mori*—Latin for 'Remember Your Death!' A little over the top dramatically speaking, but well in line for what they have already accomplished. Daniel filled me in on the satellite phone of the terrorist connection with this Guy Fawkes figure, but I want to hear from all of you everything that happened, how it all fits together."

They all gave their impressions of what had occurred, and Abby was still adamant about the importance of the blood spatter on the Tunicle and its connection to all the ring bearers. So adamant, in fact, that she had brought blood collection kits with her to the meeting and managed to get even the pope to agree to a sample.

"You have to understand, Your Holiness," she said, "you asked me to be part of this team to figure out the blood connection of the Tunicle with St. Thomas Becket. Little did you know that it would involve not only you but your nephew and the three brothers as well. But we have to go where the evidence takes us. My gut tells me that what we find will be significant to the success of this team's endeavor."

The pope smiled. "That's why I have you here, Abby. That's why you are on the team. My godson and nephew tells me you argue a persuasive case."

"Just doing my job," said Abby grimly. "This terrorist group takes us very seriously, and sees your nephew as grave threat. Whatever I can do to get to the bottom of the mystery, I want to do."

"I want to apologize again to all of you," said Daniel. "No more secrets between us. We're a team, and we've got to work together. But I'm intrigued, uncle. What have you had the other two members of our group doing?"

The pope nodded to Josiah and Mattias, and the two took turns telling the story of what they uncovered about the plot to kill the pope the previous Wednesday.

Mattias shook his red hair and said, "Something dark and evil is going on among the homeless of Rome. They are being abducted, turned into something awful, and used as tools to accomplish an agenda that neither I nor Josiah has completely figured out."

"It seems," said Josiah, "that the attack on the Holy Father was simply the first blow to what will become a bigger terrorizing of the populace of this city. I serve the pope, but I'm pretty basic and down to earth in my faith, and I've got to tell you, what we saw in the tunnels under the Caracalla Baths was no garden variety lawlessness. There was a supernatural element to it. The only problem is just making the people afraid doesn't seem worth the effort to actually involve demonic powers, if such a thing is possible."

Daniel stopped him, "Believe me, it's possible. Are you sure you heard the name 'Marduk' mentioned?"

"Yes," said Josiah. "That thing in the flames answered to that name."

"And you are sure," continued Daniel, "that whatever was in the flames called the witch 'Tia'?"

"Yes."

"Uncle," said Daniel, "that woman or witch has a name that is shortened from 'Tiamat', the Babylonian mother goddess. What in the world are demons from Babylonian mythology doing here in Rome's underground?"

Before the pope could answer, Abednego said, "There is a nexus here. The danger to your culture, to your very civilization, has its roots in the Middle East. You should not be surprised. That area has been the bane of the West for many centuries. We come from the cradle of civilization, and there are things there that are very old, older than humanity itself. Be less astonished that they are Babylonian in origin and more aware that where we come from represents a weak spot on your earth, a bad 'thin place', if you like, which has allowed a great evil to seep into your reality."

"I agree," said the pope, "and I have advised the same to your parents, Dani. Thin places exist for good or ill. We should not be surprised that there is a big one at the cradle of civilization."

Meshach strode forward. "The attack on us, the deaths of the archbishop and cardinal, the events in the tunnels of Rome are connected. They represent this evil's outreach to cause chaos and confusion in your world, to soften it up for the disaster that is coming upon us from the heavens. It seeks death and destruction, so the fact that we thwarted its attempt on Daniel's life in Babylon, Rome, and Canterbury is good for Daniel but does not mean much to this evil. It will try again or take another route."

"It's overwhelming," said Fr. Salvatore. "How will we ever combat this terrible malevolence?"

"It's not overwhelming," said the pope in a firm but soft voice. "It is the way of a fallen world. Humanity has faced such evil before. Don't forget, the last major battle, and the biggest so far, took place in tiny Judea where one divine human faced off evil and defeated it. Great deeds are often done in ordinary places and times.

"What we need to do," said the pope, "is not be overwhelmed. We will fight this evil step by step. Josiah and Mattias have told us of their wish to rescue Ben, to help the homeless of Rome, and there we will start to combat the supernatural force arrayed against us, whatever its plans for this city, or the other metropolitan areas.

"What Daniel and team have found in Canterbury tells me that one of the greatest weapons we can have is the healing power of God that so energized the medieval world through the intercession of St. Thomas Becket. Healing gives hope and banishes fear. That involves The Regale of France, and we know where that is, and our enemies do not."

"You cracked the clue from the parchment!" exclaimed Daniel.

The pontiff smiled, "I had to do something while I waited for your return. Thanks, by the way, for forwarding the contents of the parchment to me. It really wasn't that hard to figure out, particularly once I deciphered who wrote it."

"RCP, the initials said," whispered Fr. Salvatore. "Your Holiness is ever the archivist at heart."

"RCP," said the pope, "are the initials of Reginald Cardinal Pole, the last Catholic Archbishop of Canterbury. He, like Queen Mary, died from an influenza epidemic within hours of each other back in 1558. Did you know that Pole was the last of the Plantagenets to have a rightful claim to the throne of England? He must have been a thorn in Henry's side all the years he was a cardinal and a worry to that paranoid monarch. So, it's no surprise the clue is rather easy to solve once you know who wrote it.

"*Three lions rampant on the red,* stands for the Plantagenet coat of arms. *Lead you to the mournful dead* seems to me to indicate a grave or graves of said rulers. It's reasonable to assume that he means the Plantagenet rulers at the time of Becket. Those would be King Henry II and his queen, Eleanor of Aquitaine. Amazingly, their sarcophagi are intact at the Abbey of Fontevraud in France.

"*Pluck the jewel from where it lays; bring it to its proper place,* has to mean The Regale is with whatever is left of King Henry II's tomb. That's going to be a slight problem since the sarcophagi are clearly there but the graves were long ago despoiled by French Revolutionary anarchists and the bones scattered or destroyed."

"No, no!" said Luca with exasperation, "No more hunting for scattered bones. Please!"

"Luca," said the pope in mock criticism, "have a little faith in the cardinal who was the last Plantagenet. Eleanor of Aquitaine had the sarcophagi for the royal tombs sculpted out of stone. Stone lasts; bodies don't. Cardinal Pole would have put his faith in stone not bones, so we should look to the sarcophagi for possible answers."

"You found out something else while we were gone, didn't you?" asked Daniel. "Something in the archives that no one else has ever seen."

"Indeed, I did!" said the delighted pope. "I found a letter, sent by the cardinal to his courier, bodyguard, and spy, Michael Throckmorton. They were young then, and he was newly a cardinal. Both were adventuresome, and a final break had not yet come between Pole and King Henry VIII."

"I'll never keep all these Henrys straight," muttered Luca.

"Well," said Daniel, "you have my sympathies. Their lust for power and callous regard for life do make it easy to confuse them."

"Be that as it may," said the pope, "young Pole and Throckmorton were of the same age and ready to punish Henry in some way for his wish to bring down the Catholic Church in England. Pole knew that the many shrines in that country were being despoiled by Henry. Even Henry knew that the destruction of Becket's shrine was problematic so he waited till he felt strong enough in his version of the Reformation to attempt the deed.

"But Pole had his eyes set on the greatest prize at the shrine besides the bones of the saint himself. He knew he could not steal those—the attempt would take too long and probably would not succeed. Instead, he knew The Regale of France was cemented at the highest point of the shrine where it shone out brilliantly to every pilgrim present. It was also rumored to have great healing powers. Whoever possessed it, possessed the power of the saint. Pole thought to deprive Henry of his greatest prize."

"So, he gave the task to his courier?" said Daniel.

"Exactly," said the pope. "Throckmorton was not as recognizable or famous as he would soon become, so he made an excellent choice to be the one to abscond with the jewel."

"What did the letter say?" asked Rebecca, intrigued by what a government would consider a capital crime.

"I have the letter here," said the pope, and he reached into a file and brought out a fragile piece of parchment. It was covered by transparent archival plastic. "Written in Latin, it instructs Michael to go to Canterbury and with the help of a certain friar—not named, but obviously identified to Michael in some other way—appropriate the jewel just before the shrine closed for the evening and the wooden cover was lowered over the shrine. The monk would make sure the cathedral was empty, and the theft should only take minutes.

"Pole then commands his courier to return to him in Rome with the jewel post haste. All this has to happen before the king despoils the shrine. I am struck by the last lines of the letter:

'Michael, my friend, this is not grave robbing or theft. The presence in the cathedral—you will be aware of him as I have been; I am sure of it—is now about to be deprived of the shrine through which he acts as God's healer. I believe that presence is the saint, himself. His body will surely be despoiled and bones burnt or scattered. We cannot stop that. But if we hide the jewel, there may come a time to reunite it with him who has served as a bright light of God's healing for so many centuries. Return, successful and safe.'

"Now, I could not find Throckmorton's answer to the cardinal, or whether he was successful. Yet, The Regale was never mentioned in the list of the jewels and gold taken from the shrine by Henry's agents. Some say, Henry made a thumb ring out of it, but The Regale was too big for that. The fact is, the jewel never made another appearance. That's why I highly suspect that Throckmorton's journey and task were successful. But it will take VERITAS to confirm that theory. Your group needs to examine what's left of the tombs of Henry and Eleanor. The parchment clue left in Becket's skull by Pole is the surest evidence that Pole succeeded somehow in hiding the jewel with the Henry that first caused all this tragedy to begin. I think Pole would not have thought to hide the jewel in the decayed remains of either king or queen, but rather somewhere within the stone sarcophagi themselves.

"And now for a great ironic historical occurrence. Did you know that Pole and Michelangelo were close friends? I don't put it past the clever cardinal to have tasked the famous sculptor and stonemason to find a way to place the jewel within Henry's sarcophagi. Pole made a trip to Fontevraud Abbey in July of 1538. Curiously, it seems as if Michelangelo took that same month as a short sabbatical from painting *The Last Judgment* in the Sistine Chapel. What if he went with Pole to secrete The Regale within Henry's sarcophagi? He could disguise its presence there so that no one could find it. Even the French Revolutionaries centuries later could not have discovered it. How the abbey personnel ever kept the stone sarcophagi from getting smashed by those cretins is a miracle in itself."

"What about the second verse in the parchment clue?" said Luca, griping a bit about tomb robbing again, but, still, mesmerized by the mystery.

"You stretch my powers of research," smiled the pope, "but I'll make a go at it. *Then the one who weeps in shade, Shall place the jewel in pendant made,* has to refer to the saint himself. I am not sure of the nature of the being you encountered in the cathedral—perhaps it is the saint himself—but its ghostly presence is not new. Others have encountered it, including Cardinal Pole. Perhaps a reconnection with the jewel will cause the nexus of healing I was hoping for. We have the oculus which once enclosed the gem. My hunch is that pendant is made from the same meteoric material as the brothers' tomb."

The three brothers nodded their heads in agreement.

"Then shall the last two lines of the prophecy have a chance to come true: *Purpose fulfilled, peace shall come, Thus, the healing of the world begun.* And it is on this we must place our hope.

"I also believe The Regale is related to the rings some of us here wear, and we are going to find out what all this means. So, I ask you, Daniel, leave Josiah and Mattias with me, and take VERITAS to France and retrieve The Regale. Then we will see what it can do to help us fight this evil we face in Rome and throughout the world."

Pope Patrick stood up and went to his window overlooking the Square of St. Peter as the afternoon sun shed its weakening light. As the shadows grew long, he lifted his arms as if to embrace the city laying before him. "It will do no good to defeat the darkness in the streets and hidden places above and below this city if we have nothing left to offer the people. I am convinced that we will strike a blow against the disaster that approaches if we can offer hope and healing once again to the people of this world. That's our task, and that's my wish for you. Find The Regale; bring it back here along with yourselves, all safe and well."

ELEANORA REGINA ANGLORUM, SALUS ET VITA

*To Eleanor, Queen of the English,
Health and Life!*

Saturday Morning, March 20, On the Way to Fontevraud Abbey, France

EARLY ON SATURDAY morning, Luca picked Daniel up at the Irish College. He was surprised to find him all alone.

"Where's the hound?" said Luca. "Ghosting somewhere else perhaps?"

"Never around when you need him," said Daniel, also wondering where the fey dog had gone.

"And speaking of being alone," said Luca, "weren't Fr. Salvatore and Dr. Duchon supposed to be here as well? I spoke to Rebecca this morning. She was taking the three brothers to the airport early. They were fascinated by the jet and wanted a better look at its mechanics. By the way, I sent the weapons with them."

"You really think we're going to need that much firepower?"

"Pistols won't do it," said Luca. "I have no intention of damaging the abbey, but the forces against us seem well-armed and aim to stop at nothing whether that be killing us, or, if they already know about it, getting The Regale. I prefer to have a few more tricks up my sleeve."

Daniel grimaced as the car took a sharp turn. "We have to anticipate they know about the jewel, particularly if the so-called 'gods of Babylon' are the ones after us."

"What do you think about all that?" said Luca. "I got my degree in mainstream anthropology, not late-night ZOOM meetings on the ancient Anunnaki. Read a little about them last night. The Anunnaki were supposedly the ancient Mesopotamian gods who created a long-lost civilization far superior even to modern times."

"I know what you mean," said Daniel. "Ancient astronauts and alien conspiracy theories are foreign to me too. The idea that the gods of the Fertile Crescent are just a mirage covering up a more ancient civilization than we have yet discovered makes for dodgy best sellers, but I'm beginning to think there's an element of truth in that theory. I think my dad and mom and Uncle Liam are right, as are the brothers. Babylon is a powerful thin place that connects us with another dimensional reality. There was commerce once between us and whatever is over there. I think that's happening again. I just don't know why.

"Plus, we have the 'Oumuamua comet, asteroid, or spaceship coming our way and the brothers think it was here once before. I'm like you—not given to crazy stuff. But Marduk, or whatever it was that tormented us in Babylon, is definitely real. If there is truly a connection between that Guy Fawkes character and the thing my parents believe to be Enki, the Babylonian god of water and mischief, then we have to take seriously that Babylon is going to be the nexus of strange and dangerous events, at least for the next few months."

"Like I said," grimaced Luca, "pistols aren't going to be enough, and I'm not sure that what I have will kill a god."

"Let's hope we don't have to find out."

"You're worried though," said Luca. "That's why you left Dr. Duchon in Rome."

"Not really. Last night, I took the decision to ask Fr. Salvatore and Abby to stay behind. She wanted some fast results on the blood work and Fr. Salvatore said he'd help."

"Oh," said Luca, "it's Abby now, is it?"

"That's what she told us to call her," said Daniel, nonplussed.

"I don't suppose that familiarity has anything to do with her being beautiful."

"She is beautiful," he admitted.

"And smart."

"Smart."

"And about your age."

"Our age," laughed Daniel. "Don't be tempting my celibacy. It's not going to work."

"Just yanking your chain," said Luca. "And maybe seeing if I have a chance."

"O my God," said Daniel, "the world might be coming to an end and here you are checking out the possibilities for a love life."

"Checking my options, if you must know."

Daniel turned serious. "You know there is only one person I would have married if I hadn't become a priest."

Luca stopped his joking. "I know. Maria. Wished I could have known her. I met you long after that tragic accident happened. Her family treats you like their son."

"Yeah, they've been great to me. When we were in high school, we used to meet at their *trattoria* after class. She was ... amazing."

"I'm glad you kept up the relationship with her family."

"Right," laughed Daniel, throwing off the brief bout of melancholy. "You just like to tag along for a free meal whenever I decide to stop by."

"Hey, they love me too, especially once I told them it was my job to protect you."

"Don't worry, Luca. I'm not about to fall for Abby. She's smart, talented, crucial for our team …"

"And beautiful," said Luca.

"You never stop," said Daniel.

Luca did stop because he got to thinking that the grief in Daniel was deeper than he had suspected. He had met Daniel years later when the future priest was climbing mountains one August vacation. Just new to the Swiss Guard, Luca had decided to tag along to keep an eye on the pope's prize adopted nephew. He was astounded at the energy Daniel had and the risks he was willing to take to conquer the heights of the Tyrol mountains. The young man had an eye for danger. Luca didn't know why then, but in sudden inspiration, just as they were coming into the airport, he wondered if Daniel's lust for extreme sports wasn't just his way of exorcising or just plain handling his grief. He was about to say something when his friend chimed in.

"There they are, the brothers three, getting the down-low on the engines from Franco and Tony."

"And Rebecca," said Luca, "looking bored as could be. Look, Grigio is there, and even he can't seem to interest her in the ball he's carrying."

Conversation at the plane stopped as they drove up. Luca jumped out of the car and yelled at the brothers, "Heath, Nick, Jarod! There's a fire in the barn!"

The brothers looked uncomprehendingly at the Swiss Guard and Luca laughed. "Guess you guys didn't watch the old Western series I gave you—you know, 'The Big Valley'. Barbara Stanwyck, Richard Long, Lee Majors …"

"Luca," sighed Daniel.

"Oh, all right," said Luca. "Guys, it's just TV talk for stop what you're doing and get on board the plane. We're leaving as soon as the luggage is stowed."

It took only a few minutes to board the jet after putting the last of the baggage in the cargo hold.

As soon as they were airborne, Daniel gathered them around the conference table in the well-appointed jet and told them of his plans.

"I don't know what we are going to face at Fontevraud Abbey. For the benefit of Rebecca and the brothers, let me just summarize the layout of the place. We are going to be staying at the Abbey Hotel which will give us access to the monastery and the adjacent grounds both day and night. You might be interested to know that this huge abbey was Eleanor of Aquitaine's favorite place to be as she aged. She died a professed nun. The monastery was unique in that it was made up of both men and women, housed separately of course, and the whole thing was ruled over by an abbess instead of an abbot."

"Smartest thing the Church has done in two thousand years," muttered Rebecca.

Daniel gave her a stern glance and said, "That made it progressive, a source for new ideas, and an excellent retirement community for the most powerful queen of the Middle Ages. Eleanor was a force of nature, and even King Henry couldn't control her. Their love was a stormy one, but once he died, she interred his body there in the abbey, and the place became the Plantagenet burial ground.

"She lived another 15 years after his death, so she had plenty of time to devise some way to wreak her revenge on her oft wandering husband. He was a philanderer like so many kings, but he was discreet until he met the true love of his life, Rosamund, many decades his junior. He exhibited her like she was a trophy, and that, Eleanor could not stand. Rosamund died too young, but Eleanor never forgot and perhaps never forgave her husband. She had two sarcophagi carved out of stone for herself and Henry. Like the pope said, though their bodies were disposed of during the French Revolution, the stone sculptures remain in excellent condition. She made sure that in death Henry wasn't going to run off to any other woman. He would be covered by an effigy of stone. To make sure he remembered his place, she made her sarcophagus higher than his."

"But how does that help us?" said Rebecca. "Wouldn't Cardinal Pole have hidden The Regale in the tomb? That grave is long gone."

"Maybe," said Daniel, "but on the way over to the airport, Luca and I were talking about a hunch I had. Pole would have known how fragile bodies are and how eternal stone is. I think Cardinal Pole talked his buddy Michelangelo into coming to Fontevraud and hiding The Regale in Henry's sarcophagus. Pole could be quite a persuasive man and probably charmed the older artist into accompanying him."

"So, what's the plan?" said Rebecca.

"We are going to find the secret compartment, and retrieve the jewel."

"How are we ever going to move that stone around without anyone seeing us?" asked Rebecca.

"We'll do it at night, when no one is around. And as for moving the sarcophagus ..." At this, he looked over at the three brothers, then back to Rebecca ... "you really have to ask?"

"Don't forget the weapons," reminded Luca.

"Oh yeah," said Daniel. "Plan on having to neutralize some enemies. I don't know if the *Memento Mori* terrorist group will be waiting for us, but we have to assume they will. Most of the members will be your garden variety terrorists—that means really dangerous—but their leader, Guy Fawkes, is not human. That's why we have so much firepower. Shadrach, Meshach, and Abednego, we will need your understanding of this entity to help fight it. In the end, you three may be the only ones able to defeat it and save this mission. I feel confident that Luca and Rebecca can handle any of the ordinary terrorists."

"What will you be doing while all this is going on?" asked Rebecca.

"I'll be solving the riddle of the sarcophagus and finding The Regale, I hope—unless we all get killed in the process."

AN ABBEY WITHOUT A SOUL

Saturday Morning, March 20, Fontevraud Abbey, France

AS SOON AS the meeting broke up, the passengers glued themselves to the window as the jet flew over the beautiful Loire valley. It was a glorious spring day, and the land was responding to the generous sunshine. No wonder Queen Eleanor loved this area, thought Rebecca. She harbored a soft spot for the old queen whose no-nonsense nature and love of the arts gave birth to the troubadour tradition and the many myths of chivalry. The land almost literally sang its welcome to the swift plane flying over it.

They were due to land at Tours Airport shortly, Rebecca's mind quickly shifted to security concerns. Tours actually had a CIA posting, and Rebecca had called her contact the night before, asking him to scope out security arrangements at the airport. She didn't want to be taken unawares if the assassins had gotten wind of their plans. Her contact had just texted her that all was fine, and she breathed a sigh of relief.

After a gentle landing, they all piled into a rented Mercedes GLS 63 SUV.

"Sweet wheels," said Luca, getting behind the steering wheel.

"Be gentle with it, big guy," said Rebecca. "It cost my boss an unbalanced budget to rent it, but she figured its amped up engine would give us speed and maneuverability should we need it."

"It's only about a 45-minute drive to the abbey," said Daniel.

"Ah ... much more like 30 minutes at my speed," said Luca.

Grigio barked in happy anticipation. The brothers just slipped on their seatbelts, something they had gotten quickly used to in traveling with the team.

Soon, the Fontevraud Abbey rose before them, a huge complex set in the fantastic landscape of the Loire Valley. Gently rolling hills, woodland and farmland showed the pastoral location that the Abbey was known for. The renovations done during the last decades made the white face of the abbey gleam in the sunlight.

"No monks or nuns here anymore?" said Rebecca.

"Nope," said Daniel. "It's a secular vehicle now for an art museum and a venue for concerts and such. The renovations have made the façade and interior architecture look as of old, but there's little of religious decoration. A shame really. For a thousand years it was one of the premier abbeys of the world and a center for European spiritual life. Now it's just a beautiful, soulless shell. Magnificent in its own way, but I have a hunch it was truly spectacular in ancient days."

As they drove up to the Abbey Hotel, which was once the hospital for the poor and for lepers, they were amazed at its transformation into a chic and trendy guesthouse. It managed to look monastic and luxurious all at the same time. Their reservations as Vatican guests opened wide the hospitality arms of the staff, and they each were ensconced quickly into their separate rooms.

Daniel had given them all free time until lunch just to get a sense of the abbey and its environs. His room was what he called spartan luxurious. It kept its monastic trimmings but the room was filled with a bed, chairs, and desk that would put an aristocrat at ease. Daniel couldn't believe how comfortable the bed was. He really didn't mean to close his eyes, but close them he did and soon found himself in one of those dream visions the brothers had assured him was part of his prophetic destiny.

His inward gaze opened up to sweep the view of the abbey, only as it appeared centuries ago. He saw two men riding up in an open-air carriage, the driver depositing them at what could only be the ancient abbey's guesthouse.

For Daniel, it was like walking in a real-life hologram. He could actually touch whatever he wished, feeling textures, smelling the morning air with its rather pleasant mishmash of flowers and farm animals. No one, not even the ever-watchful chickens could see him, but he was careful not to bump into anything living.

He drew closer to the two men and immediately knew them as the young Cardinal Pole and the senior Michelangelo. Far from being elderly, the artist still possessed his hale strength and limber physique. It would be decades before he showed the weathering effects of age. Daniel guessed it was spring of 1539, that year when the future was carved into place by the will of a cardinal and the genius of a master sculptor.

"You've kept me in suspense long enough, Michelo," said Pole. "How can we hide The Regale from the assassins of Henry who surely know I took it and keep it for the time when it shall be revealed again?"

"We break into a grave," said the artist, "just like you planned."

"And watch King Henry turn over, rattling his bones."

Michelangelo laughed. "Nothing so dramatic. What I want is the sarcophagus effigy. We will hide the jewel within. It will take several nights' work but the stone shall melt away and where Henry's heart would be if the stone were flesh, The Regale shall rest."

"We're just going to put the gem inside that rock? It will be damaged?"

"Not at all," smiled Michelangelo. "The king, even in his anger at the sainted bishop, kept a place in his heart for his old friend. Such passing emotions

as wrath could not destroy the love he had for Thomas. So, I thought I would give the effigy of the king a heart worthy of that friendship, and encase The Regale within."

Michelangelo reached into his cloak and pulled out a leather bag from which he carefully took an exact replica of a human heart carved from marble and polished to the purity of snow. To Cardinal Pole's surprise, he saw that the artist had engineered a hinge on the heart which allowed it to open, and, in the cavity revealed, a place for The Regale to nestle in warm, sable fur.

"Extraordinary," marveled Pole. "However did you manage it?"

"It was nothing," blushed the sculptor, "the least I could do for a jewel that has brought healing to so many and stood for the honor and courage of the saint. The fact that it will now rest near Henry might bring the departed monarch some peace wherever his soul abides."

Pole handed The Regale to Michelangelo who took it and placed it within the marble heart. He closed it tight, and, for a moment, they were astounded as the red glow of the jewel suffused the heart with a lifelike appearance.

"Tonight, we start," said the sculptor. "I shall carve the cavity in the sarcophagus and you shall bribe the abbess so that no one disturbs us for several nights."

Mouth agape, Daniel could not believe what he was hearing, but then, like the morning mist which often covers the Loire valley in the springtime, his view was clouded over and his eyes opened once more onto his room in the modern Abbey Hotel.

Luca was talking to him from the doorway. "C'mon, you slacker, Rebecca and the brothers want a tour and you can do a better job than me."

Daniel ignored his words and said, "You won't believe what I just saw. More than that, you won't believe what we're going to find this evening."

"All right, spill it."

"Nope," said Daniel with a grin. "Let it be a surprise like it was to me. Trust me, it will make a heartfelt impression upon you."

Daniel snagged one of the ubiquitous tour guides around the abbey and got him to give them a private tour of the abbey and the grounds. Despite Daniel's previous warning to the group not to look for a lot of spiritual stuff at the museum-like abbey, he saw that the magnificently structured Romanesque church, rather sterile in its bright white stone renovation, had been considerably decorated with medieval tapestries, candles, and even torches. No chairs were in evidence, but as the little group walked up the nave, long as a football field, toward the Plantagenet sarcophagi effigies, the tour guide oozed excitement.

"You have come at an exceptional time," said the guide. "Tonight, the Loire Valley Medieval and Renaissance Society is hosting an evening festival of song and story honoring the abbey's long history with the Plantagenet kings and queens."

Daniel had already explained that they were from the Vatican, and a quick communication over a cell phone with the tour guide and the Abbey overseer settled plans for the night.

"You must come for the evening. We insist. It is a costumed affair but my supervisor has assured me that after this tour you can be outfitted from our rather extensive collection. We have these affairs fairly often so it's always good to have some on hand for guests who have come unprepared."

"You are too gracious," said Daniel. "Of course, we accept." He actually looked forward to the evening, even more so since it would give them the opportunity to stay late into the night and retrieve The Regale.

Rebecca and Luca looked astonished and the brothers mystified, but Daniel just said, "You'll all look fetching in hose and doublets, and especially you, Rebecca, in a medieval wimple. It will be fun."

The tour guide led them onward but as soon as he got ahead of the group, Daniel said in a lower voice to them all, "Besides, it gives us a reason to hang around the effigies and do what we must later on."

"I don't care what anyone else says," spoke Luca. "I'm wearing my Swiss Guard ceremonial outfit. It's Renaissance anyway."

"You brought it with you?" said Rebecca.

"Helmet and collapsible halberd, too," said Luca blushing. "I mean, Dani said we were going to a medieval abbey. I thought it might come in handy."

"It might just," said Daniel, laughing. "More than you might imagine."

After the tour, their guide dropped them off at the abbey's event planning center. A grandmotherly matron approached them, sized them all up, and then stared for several moments at the brothers. She snapped her fingers and an old man appeared with *pince-nez* on his nose.

"Jacques, these tall ones will need their costumes stretched a bit. Outfit them as musketeers. And you, my dear," she said with a smile at Rebecca, "shall be garbed as the greatest abbess Fontevraud ever had—Gabrielle de Rochechouart, the abbess that dazzled the great Sun King himself, Louis XIV. As for the priest, we'll make you into the visiting Pope Alexander III. And for this strapping young man," she pointed to Luca …

"I have my own, thank you," said Luca, as the matron pursed her lips.

"Very well," she said, "Let's get to it."

MASQUERADE

Saturday Evening, March 20, Fontevraud Abbey, France

EVEN THOUGH THE costuming for the evening's events took the greater part of the early afternoon, Daniel thought it was worth it. They had the perfect entry to the abbey church for the evening. He would make sure that they would be the last to leave. He had no idea, however, how long it would take to retrieve The Regale from the effigy. He was counting on the brothers to have something up their sleeve that would let them access the interior of King Henry's effigy without destroying the sarcophagus. Daniel had been very precise and felt reassured that Shadrach, Meshach, and Abednego understood very clearly how swiftly and without destruction the retrieval must be done.

The costumed group gathered just inside the abbey cloister where the guests had gathered and food was being served. Daniel noted that, of his team, only Luca seemed at ease in his Swiss Guard ceremonial outfit.

That was not true of the gathered guests. They were thoroughly enjoying themselves in their period costumes.

"C'mon you guys," said Daniel. "Loosen up a bit. We need to fit in at least somewhat amongst the gentry here. Look at them all. We have the entire Medieval, Renaissance, and Baroque eras with us this evening."

As they walked along the cloister among the 300 other guests, they all noticed the spring flowers in various bouquets that graced the courtyard, exquisitely perfuming the beautiful scene. Daniel pointed out to the team some of the characters the guests were cosplaying. There were kings and queens, priests and popes, but Daniel made sure to point out that Rebecca was the most gracious and beautiful abbess to grace the company.

"The woman whose part you play this evening stole King Louis XIV's, the Sun King's, heart, not for love of her physical attributes but for her mind. She was beautiful but she knew many languages, translated the 'Iliad', and made this place a cultural and intellectual center all the while being very holy herself. All in all," he said with a smile, "I couldn't think of anyone here more suited to play the part."

Rebecca wasn't sure whether to curtsey or not, but she did anyway.

"Just act natural," said Daniel, "and people will think you're the real deal." He said it so graciously that Rebecca blushed with pride.

They shied away from introducing themselves to other guests while they enjoyed the food and the medieval English madrigal being performed by equally exquisitely costumed singers. They were singing one of the madrigals from 'The Triumphs of Oriana', (Oriana being Queen Elizabeth I). Her costumed namesake was close to the little group, fanning her pockmarked face—hopefully, simply made of makeup—in swooning ecstasy, particularly when the musical piece ended as all of the triumphs did with the words, "Thus sang the shepherds and nymphs of Diana: long live fair Oriana."

A little bit of champagne, some filling hors d'oeuvres, and the VERITAS team began to relax. Soon the guests began filing into the church for music by the French National Orchestra with the Claye Vocale Choir. The orchestra seldom ventured from Paris, but here they and the choir were to play and sing Gounod's 'Mass of St. Cecilia' for the assembled guests.

The musical composition was less than an hour-long presentation so the venue was set up to keep the guests mingling, appreciating the colorful medieval tapestries hung especially for the event, as well as enjoying each other's costumes. There were benches placed discretely throughout the huge church for people to rest, but most chose to stand for the music, view the effigies of the Plantagenet rulers placed in the center of the nave, and basically become part of the abbey church itself.

"Amazing," said Daniel to Luca and Rebecca. "This church is, of course, decommissioned and doesn't function as a worship space anymore, but I was worried that this event would not be worthy of what this place once was. But those who designed this evening have kept the magnificence of the abbey church in mind and chosen a piece of music to hallow these halls. I'm impressed."

"No bacchanal tonight," laughed Luca. "I was worried as well. The French can be so unpredictable. All will be serene, I hope."

"Right," said Rebecca. "After the French savaged this place during the Revolution, then turned it into prison, only after that did they get religion again and restore this church. We have nothing like this in our Jewish faith. Since the Romans sacked and destroyed the Jerusalem Temple," she grimaced, "our places tend to be much smaller."

Shadrach spoke for the first time and said, "I am overwhelmed. Even in Babylon, this edifice would be honored as a great achievement of engineering. I foolishly thought only St. Peter's in Rome could be so inspiring, but it seems there are many such places of worship. You've taken us to Rome, Canterbury and, now, here. My brothers and I all agree that the centuries that came after us have created masterpieces in stone and metal. But from what you say, this place is no longer used to worship any god."

Daniel said, "You are too polite. You know well what our age faces. These buildings have fewer and fewer people visiting them for their original purpose. This is a museum and a cultural venue, nothing more, despite how beautiful it has been made to look tonight. The people here and those who maintain this place are not even aware of the magnificent jewel that resides here, one of the most powerful reminders of the connection of this world to the ultimate reality."

"I meant no disrespect, little brother", said Shadrach. "But I can still appreciate beauty even if its majesty has faded through the years."

Abednego added his soft voice in between orchestral pieces. "The music tonight is exquisite. You have not heard our Babylonian compositions which are quite different. Perhaps another time. But for now, this is music that would summon angels."

"Not a bad compliment," said Luca. "After all, you people are the ones who named the beings we call angels."

Meshach smiled and said, "We are not so different, even though we come from different times and realities. Beauty connects us all, for it transcends the ages."

None of them could counter that statement as the magnificent strains of Gounod's 'Sanctus' filled the church. It could have been the music of the angels, especially as the choir soared heavenward with the last strains of the hymn. But then a tremendous sound was heard at the entrance to the church, as the doors swung open and smashed against the stone. The music immediately ceased and all eyes flew to the figure that stood in shadow.

It walked forward into the light and revealed itself as a tall man in a long black cloak with a red satin inset, white leather breeches, black boots on his feet, and topping his head a cavalier hat with a white ostrich plume. A rapier was at his side, and a white mask covered his face with lips, nose, and eyes highlighted in black. A trickle of red was painted down one side of his lips.

"Guy Fawkes!" said Luca.

Daniel turned to Rebecca. "Did you bring the Ranbir avatar?"

"Sorry," she said. "I left him in my room, pinned to my jacket."

"Well, that's a pity," said Luca. "I think we could use him about now. I've got a feeling this is going to get messy."

Guy Fawkes strode through the assembly, and, when some tried to block his way, drew his sword. So ghastly did he look that most made way for him. Those that did not, he cuffed with his gloved hand. One security guard made a foolish attempt to grab him. Fawkes neatly carved some flesh from his arm. He walked up to the woman cosplaying Queen Elizabeth I and said, "As ugly as I remember you to be, you hedge-born whore."

Not to be outdone, the cosplaying gentlelady slapped the figure's face with her hand and struck back with one of the queen's famous quotes, "I have the heart of a man, not a woman, and I am not afraid of anything."

It was unfortunate she was so bold because Fawkes decided then and there to rid himself of the masquerading monarch. This he did with a swift slice of his rapier across her neck. There was stunned silence as the woman slipped to the floor of the nave, blood streaming from her severed carotid artery.

Before anyone could scream, Fawkes shouted, "Now get out of here! All of you!" They ran, and then they screamed—most of the guests.

"Not you five," said Fawkes to Daniel and his team. "You stay." He turned to the fast fleeing crowd and shouted, "Lock the doors on your way out. No one is to be let in or it will be the death of my hostages. My men, the *Memento Mori*, are outside and will see to your behavior."

It took only minutes to empty the church, and Daniel and friends found themselves standing alone alongside the Plantagenet effigies, while Guy Fawkes strode down the nave toward them.

"We meet again, priest," said Fawkes, "though I see you've been upgraded to a pontiff for the evening. And you," he pointed his sword at Luca, "at least you are now dressed as the clown you are."

"Don't go pointing that stick at me, you freak, or my halberd will smash your mask and your face into a million pieces." Luca was in a fury at the murder of the faux Queen Elizabeth I and was half-minded to strike Fawkes anyway.

"Enough," said Daniel. "What is it you want?"

"I want what you are looking for—The Regale."

"We don't have it," said Daniel.

"Not yet you don't," said Fawkes. "But it's here, isn't it, else you wouldn't be."

He leapt to the side of Daniel and snatched Rebecca in a headlock, pulling her back towards the entrance. She tried to free herself, but the man was superhuman in strength. She ceased her struggles as she felt the point of his rapier on her neck.

"Move just a little, abbess, and I'll slit your pretty throat like I did the other doxy." He saw the three brothers and Daniel raise their hands. "Oh, and don't try the rings on me. I know what they are now. I may not be able to hurt you who wear them, but I can hurt the ones you care for."

Luca reached for his sidearm, but as he did, Fawkes freed his own hand, throwing a dagger into Luca's chest. It pierced his right lung and a great whoosh of breath went out of him as he fell to his knees.

"Luca!" cried Daniel as he went to grab his friend.

"Oh, that hurts like a bitch," said Luca on his knees gritting his teeth. "But you should have tried for the other side you filthy bastard," he said to Fawkes.

"I never miss. I didn't aim for your heart; I just wanted you to suffer. You will serve as a visible reminder to those who wear the Star Sapphire Rings that I am still deadly. The woman and the man are dead if any of you try to harm me."

"All right," said Daniel, "we don't have the jewel but we can get it. It's in the effigy of King Henry II, right over there."

"You have no maces, hammers or axes. Just how did you propose to retrieve it?"

"Daniel has us," said Abednego. "And if you are truly aware of the power of our rings, then you know retrieving The Regale is well within our ability. We won't use any force for fear of damaging the jewel."

"Get on with it then. I have the authorities outside cowed enough for now. But we have not much time. My sword arm aches for the blood of this woman, and the useless hunk of flesh on the ground will bleed out soon."

The effigies of Eleanor and Henry along with Isabella and Richard the Lionheart, lay peacefully silent, staring up at the Romanesque ceiling of the church. Daniel couldn't help the wandering thought that these monarchs, had they been alive, would be at this moment carving up Guy Fawkes into miniature pieces. But their days of whacking and thwacking, whoring and ruling were long over.

"Here," said Meshach, taking charge. "Shadrach, Abednego, place these discs on the corners of Henry's sarcophagus. They will slide right under the stone." Shadrach took the front, Abednego the back and they slid palm-sized discs made of some unknown substance beneath the corners of the effigy. Daniel thought he saw the discs liquify for a moment as they slid under the stone. Immediately, the effigy began to rise in the air.

"Anti-gravity discs," exclaimed Daniel.

"We have another word for them," said Meshach, "but we know about gravity. The name is appropriate for what the discs do."

By now the sarcophagus had risen six feet above the floor.

"Take this," said Meshach, handing Daniel a similar looking disc but a little larger, this one not solid but having a donut hole. "Place it on the stone beneath where you think the king's heart would be."

Daniel looked at the effigy of King Henry II, dressed in blue and red painted stone robes and guessed. He looked underneath and figured about where the heart would be and placed the disc directly on the stone. He felt it vibrate and quickly drew away his hand.

"Not an anti-gravity disc, I take it," said Daniel.

"No," said Meshach, "it transmutes matter. It will liquify the stone, allowing any separate object to fall through its lesser density."

Luca gasped, "You've got all sorts of cool things in that ditty bag you packed from your Babylonian tomb."

"Don't speak," said Daniel. "Just rest."

"Rest?" snarked Guy Fawkes, "If you don't get on with it, it will be eternal rest for him."

Meshach directed Daniel, "Hold both your hands underneath the disc and catch whatever drops out."

Everyone looked expectantly at Daniel's hands, until with the tiniest of sounds, a human heart dropped into his grasp. Well, not a human heart exactly, but a marble version of it carved exquisitely by Michelangelo himself.

Daniel marveled that his dream vision had been so exact. He watched the stone solidify above him, and moved out from under the effigy. Shadrach and Abednego touched the other discs, gently lowering the sarcophagus to the floor of the church.

"Where's the stone?" gasped Luca.

"It's here," said Daniel, "encased inside the heart."

"There," said Fawkes, "that wasn't so difficult, was it? Now give it to me."

Suddenly, Daniel felt the heart begin to pulse in his hand. He stood up looking at the marble heart as it began to glow red.

"What's it doing?" snarled Fawkes. "What sleight of hand is this?"

"I don't know what it's doing," said Daniel. "Nobody has seen this since Cardinal Pole and Michelangelo put it here five hundred years ago."

The heart pulsed warmly in his cupped hands, but then something strange happened as he thought he heard a whispering sound and, then, felt two hands on his arms, lifting him up and helping him to show the heart to Fawkes.

"Stop it!" shouted Fawkes.

"I can't!" said Daniel. As invisible arms helped him hold up the sculpture, red rays came from the marble heart as it rose from his hands, striking the floor by the effigy of King Henry.

In the flash and the mist The Regale created, a figure could be seen dressed as a bishop with a crozier in hand.

"Holy Return of the Jedi, Batman!" gasped Luca.

Daniel fell back down to cradle Luca. "You can't help yourself can you my friend? That's a mixing up of movies and tv shows don't you think?"

"Yeah, but it's the best I can do when I've been stabbed," grimaced Luca, falling silent.

But the figure conjured from the pulsing marble heart was not quiet. "What is this place?" it said. "The jewel calls me from my sleep in Canterbury." The figure paused a moment and then said, "You, Guy Fawkes, are not who you seem."

As Daniel stood up, just below the heart glowing with the encased Regale, the bishop strode forward, reached suddenly, and tore the sword from Fawkes's hand. Rebecca threw herself out of the terrorist's way. The bishop continued, "You are masked as the man from history, but you are not him. You are far older than that." The robed bishop smashed his crozier on Fawkes' mask and shattered it. Water gushed out from beneath the broken visage.

There was no human face beneath. Instead, it was the slime of the swamp, moving with the worms of the marsh. There were eyes, and there was a snapping fish-like mouth and the stench of decaying matter.

"Enki!" said the three brothers together.

"It cannot be, but it is!" said Shadrach.

"It is the trickster god of the Babylonians," said Meshach, "or something pretending to be."

"Where's all the water coming from?" said Rebecca.

"Enki is a water deity," said Abednego. "Some say it is Marduk's father."

The figure began to laugh and great gouts of water sprayed from his mouth. "That red stone can't hurt me any more than your Star Sapphires. I will have what I seek."

"No," said the bishop, thrusting his crozier in front of the thing that once mimicked Guy Fawkes. "The stone may not hurt you, but I can. Depart now, or be destroyed."

The entity howled in anger and threw itself at the bishop who simply opened wide his arms and clutched the god-thing within his vestments. With a flash of red and a thunderous clap, both disappeared.

Daniel barely noticed as he threw himself on the floor towards his friend. "Luca, Luca! Don't die on me!" said Daniel.

"Not if I can help it," gasped the Swiss Guard.

"Do you think that thing destroyed the bishop?" asked Rebecca. "If not, maybe he could help."

"That vision," said Abednego, "has gone to take care of a great evil. He is otherwise occupied, but not destroyed. Look, The Regale still pulses. Whoever the holy man is, he is still synced with the stone. Both still live."

Daniel gently laid Luca down and stood up. "This marble heart holds The Regale. Look, Michelangelo had it constructed so that it can open."

As Daniel took the pulsing sculpture, he opened the heart. The Regale blazed forth in the shape of a six-pointed star.

"It's beautiful!" said Rebecca.

"Magnificent!" said Daniel.

But the brothers fell to their knees. "It is as we thought," said Shadrach. "It is the Star Ruby. Only one exists, and we thought it lost."

"What does that mean," said Daniel. "Can it help Luca?"

"Indeed, it can," said Meshach. "You have noted the Star Sapphires have healing powers, and under normal circumstances, they work well. But that is not their primary purpose. Besides, Luca was struck by a greater evil than even the Star Sapphires could counter. The Star Ruby, however, was made to be a vehicle of healing when paired with the right person.

"Apparently, the one we met in the Canterbury Cathedral was or is such a one. What you saw tonight was a type of avatar like Rebecca's Ranbir. The being in the cathedral had imparted his persona to the jewel. By itself, the jewel could not have defeated Enki. This is not magic, or a miracle as you might think. It is the property of this gem and the person to whom it is united. It is a technology those who came before us had perfected, and from what we have seen of the Ranbir avatar, you people are well on your way to perfecting the same."

Daniel disagreed but kept the thought to himself. No avatar touched his arm and hand to activate the jewel. Someone was with him this evening independent of The Regale, and it was more miracle than some ancient Anunnaki technology.

Daniel lifted the jewel and placed it on Luca's chest. Gently, he pulled out the dagger, poisoned and corrupted no doubt by Guy

Fawkes's hand. Rather than gasping in pain, Luca breathed a sigh of relief, as all watched in amazement as the wound healed and closed under the red light of the jewel.

"Man, I like rubies," said Luca, sitting up with no effort and seemingly healed.

"The Regale is truly one of a kind," said Meshach. "It has been lost to time, but it must have been passed down quietly through the ages until it came to Canterbury and the one who haunts the cathedral."

Truly, the party had come to a definite end. As Daniel and his team burst out of the cathedral doors, they swept through the confused crowd, relieved that no one else was seriously hurt and the terrorists had suddenly departed. Daniel thought for sure he heard Luca whistling one of the guardsman's old favorites—an ancient Kenny Rogers song, 'Ruby Don't Take Your Love To Town'. Not a bad ballad to accompany the escape of The Regale from France.

THE BLOOD IS LIFE

Saturday Evening, March 20, VERITAS Headquarters, Vatican Archives

WHILST DANIEL AND team were masquerading at Fontevraud Abbey, Fr. Salvatore and Dr. Duchon had spent the entire day analyzing the blood samples from the Tunicle, the pope, Daniel, and the three brothers. The lights were bright in VERITAS's new underground lab.

"So, what do we have?" said Fr. Salvatore. "I haven't been much help to you today."

"On the contrary," said Abby, "your ability to take these results down so they will make sense to all of us later is amazing. You've even helped me clarify my hypothesis."

"Which is …?"

Abby took off her glasses and stared at him over the electron microscope. "The blood that we've taken is, in itself, absolutely amazing. It is type AB, and even though that is rare in itself, it has qualities no other AB blood has. First of all, AB is a naturally receptive blood type. If you have it and you are injured, any blood type will work for you if you need a transfusion. It is accepting of the energy any fresh red blood cell will give it.

"Second, this AB blood from the samples is extraordinarily receptive because, from everything I have been able to determine, each cell of this blood possesses mitochondria."

"Ah," said Fr. Salvatore, "the energy-producing dynamo of a cell. But what's so special about that?"

"Because, my good reverend father, human red blood cells don't possess mitochondria. Some other animals do, like birds and reptiles. But human red blood cells don't. It's possible for me to posit that the Shroud of Turin samples of blood from the crucified man also contain red blood cells with mitochondria, but the Shroud is far older and the organic material much more difficult to analyze for me to be sure. But I am confident in the samples of blood taken from Becket's Tunicle and the actual blood samples from the pope, Daniel, and the three brothers."

"Okay," said Fr. Salvatore, "let me play devil's advocate for a moment. So what? So, what if there is mitochondria in the red blood cells; what's the practical effect?"

"That brings me to the third part of my hypothesis," said Abby, with wonder growing in her eyes. "Mitochondria in a human red blood cell would mean that cell is capable of absorbing outside energy and transforming it for use in the body. What you would have is an augmented human, able to absorb energy and do things that no other humans could."

Fr. Salvatore scrunched up his bushy eyebrows. "You mean like a superman?"

"Not quite. Superman, as the myth goes, is Kryptonian, not human. A human with mitochondria in his red blood cells would have greater endurance, strength, health, ability to heal from injury, and better mental acuity—but still be human."

"Sounds like Superman to me," said a quiet voice behind them.

"Your Holiness," stuttered Fr. Salvatore, "we did not hear you come in."

"Peace, my friend," said the pope. "No need to stand on ceremony. We are in this research together. Abby, I heard some of what you said, and I think I can help lift the mystery a little.

"When Daniel first put on the ring so many years ago, he was just a child. We could never take the ring off him. It was if it had affixed itself to him, become part of him. It changed him. He never suffered a sniffle afterward, and he always found himself attracted to extreme sports, never managing to get an injury in any of them. He was the smartest seminarian in his class, amazingly facile with languages, yet he didn't have the attitude of a savant or the ego of an intellectual. That 'smartness' of his was just natural, so it seemed. I often thought the ring might have some effect on him, but, now, I'm sure. It did not give him new abilities but enhanced those he already possessed.

"You see, it has had the same effect on me. The same type of ring is on my hand, and I already have felt its effects. We who bear a ring are able to heal at least some ills. I know I think more clearly, but the best evidence is the news the doctor gave me today. I never told Daniel, but late last year, I was diagnosed with a lung tumor. Only my physician and I knew. It was small, but it would eventually have to be taken care of by this summer. I knew I was waiting too long. I had a CAT scan today—routine, I told everyone—but the results were not routine. There was no sign of cancer. It was as if my body had healed itself. But now we know better, don't we? It was the ring and the energy it provides, specifically formulated to enhance the human genome. Am I right, Abby?"

"Amazing!" said Abby, "and I'm grateful to God that you are healed, but I think you are correct. The rings enhance the human genome, even turning on some genes that have always been dormant. And, I think it is safe to safe that they enable red blood cells to produce mitochondria. That means that Shadrach, Meshach, and

Abednego are human as well because I wondered about that. Their height, their somewhat alien appearance …"

"They have borne their rings for many ages," said the pope.

"But it's changed them!" said Fr. Salvatore. "Will you become like them?"

"Well," said the pontiff, "if I get to be seven feet tall, it will enhance my status when I play pickup basketball with the Swiss Guard."

"You know what I mean," scowled the priest.

"It took many years for them to become like they are now," said Abby. "But I'm becoming surer of the fourth part of my hypothesis, and that is this: the rings were gifted to humans for a reason. They enhance human abilities, give the energy for unused DNA to be activated, and enable a human to become what he or she was meant to be. The changes the rings have induced have pushed the evolution envelope ahead by several tens or hundreds of thousands of years."

"I also think at one time Becket possessed a Star Sapphire Ring, though not when he was murdered," said the pope. "It would have protected him. We have yet to figure out why he had a ring during his lifetime, though he was surely one of the leading lights of his era," said the pope. "Since this is an evening for hunches, let me place one in play. I think the ring I wear was worn by Becket, was lost then found by St. Anthony of Padua, and eventually made its way to the Vatican Archives. There are only supposed to be six Star Sapphires and one is still missing. This is a guess on my part, but one I somehow feel sure of."

"Maybe the ring you wear is good for substantiating hunches," said Fr. Salvatore. "Maybe you should take this year's Peter's Pence Collection for the Church and go to Monte Carlo, and try the ring's luck with gambling."

The pope laughed out loud. "I think not. We've had enough scandals, but points to you for creative thinking on ways to balance the Vatican budget," said the pontiff.

Abby was in no mood for joking. "Back to the issue at hand. The results of these tests mean we have an idea of what the three brothers are capable of and what you and Daniel will be able to do. I suggest we get the brothers to start training the two of you because if a crisis as big as the one you predict is coming, I think we're going to need the five of you at peak strength. Remember though, the changes in your physiognomy enhance your humanness. What you can do might seem superhuman to others, but, when push comes to shove, you can be hurt, bleed, and die like every other human being.

"I want to give you the fifth part of my hypothesis; namely, that these rings were given to humanity for a purpose, to show us what we can become and perhaps give us a path to moving our evolutionary development more rapidly than Mother Nature was planning. Why? Because humanity is about to face another major crisis, one which it has faced before and overcome. We have much to investigate."

"Indeed," said the pontiff. "If everything goes alright at Fontevraud, the team will be back here tomorrow afternoon, and we will convene a meeting of VERITAS to trace our next steps. But this information is to be kept totally confidential. I invoke the Pontifical Secret upon it. There are enemies, I fear, who would use this in the coming crisis to humanity's detriment. My address to the United Nations is on Tuesday, and we shall have to see how your discoveries today, and the results of the trip to the abbey affect what I'm planning to say."

As the pope left, Abby turned to Fr. Salvatore with a quizzical eye and said, "What's the Pontifical Secret?"

Fr. Salvatore looked at her and said, "It means you really, really can't tell anybody what you know."

"Or what?" said Abby.

Fr. Salvatore said with a gleam in his eye, "Or we'll have to kill you."

She gasped and he quickly added, "Not really, but close to it."

BETRAYERS

Saturday evening, March 20, Near Midnight, Fowey, England, Yacht Restless

JOHN NANCE'S YACHT, *Restless*, was still berthed in Fowey's harbor Saturday evening. He was all alone in his stateroom, enjoying an 18-year-old Macallan scotch before retiring for the night when his satellite phone rang.

"This better be good," said Nance.

"It is," said the voice. "The blood tests have been done, and it is as you suspected. The rings you wanted so badly do change the humans who wear them. This poses a complication to your plans. The ones who wear the rings are equipped to challenge the forces you are about to set in motion. They could imperil the results."

"Nonsense," laughed Nance. "It's not just Rome that will experience my next wave that will instill fear in humanity. Several other population centers in Europe and America will have their citizens experience the anarchy I hope will touch off other cities around the world. It only takes a spark to get a fire going. The pope and his friends will be able to do little to stop me."

"What about the CIA? Leslie Richardson, the director, has a member on Team VERITAS. The agent is dangerous enough, but if

Richardson takes seriously Rebecca's warnings, the might of the USA will be used against you."

"Doubtful," said Nance. "What I'm doing has never been done before. I am harnessing myth and legend, things the world's governments give little credence to, and using them to bring down civilization. They won't know what hit them, and it will be impossible for them to prepare."

"You know best, of course, but I still fear what will happen if the governments of the world take the threat seriously."

"I understand the pope will make his address to the United Nations on Tuesday. That will give us an inkling on how seriously they will take his warning."

"He's very persuasive."

"That he is, my dear priest. That is why you will keep me informed on whatever he plans. I'm certainly paying you enough."

"Why are you really doing this?" said Fr. Salvatore. He deliberately ignored the comment by Nance that he was betraying his pope for money.

"We've talked about this before," said Nance. "Something big is coming. That asteroid or ship or whatever it is will strike earth. It's been here before. Humanity survived its first encounter once before. It will again. I just prefer to be the one to pick up the pieces."

"The Anunnaki might have something to say about that."

"That's what you think this is all about—some ancient astronaut crazy conspiracy theory? Chariots of the Gods and all that?" Nance took a sip of his scotch before he broke out in uproarious laughter.

"You, yourself, said the ancient gods of Babylon were rearing their fearsome heads."

"I said that something manifesting itself as the ancient pantheon of Sumerian gods was making its presence felt. I don't quite understand everything, but whatever this is, it is not omniscient and its efforts have not always been successful."

"Whatever," said Fr. Salvatore. "You know I trust you and I will keep you well informed."

"See that you do," said Nance curtly and ended the call.

That's when he heard the sloshing sound slapping down the corridor nearest his stateroom. The sound paused outside the doorway.

"A night for visitors, I see," said Nance. "Come in, whatever you are."

The door opened slowly and a decaying webbed hand left its imprint. It was attached to something Nance could only liken to the monster from the *Creature of the Black Lagoon* films of his childhood. Or maybe *Swamp Thing*, he thought.

"John Johnson, your Guy Fawkes's visage isn't quite what it was." The figure remained silent. "Enki," he said, "I did not think you would be back so soon. Failed again I would guess?"

A hiss came from the creature standing before him. "I could unmake you, human," it said, "for your irreverence and lack of worship. Millions used to bow before me."

"Don't flatter yourself," said Nance. "It wasn't you they bowed to. You are just an incarnate memory—dangerous enough, but nowhere near the original you were modeled after."

Like wind through marsh grass, the creature hissed a laugh. "For now," it said. "But when the host comes again, I shall truly be restored."

"We shall see," said Nance, his eyes narrowing. "Now tell me what happened in Fontevraud. I take it your Guy Fawkes's cosplay didn't work out as you thought."

When Enki finished telling the tale, Nance was still for a long time. Then, suddenly, he whipped his glass of scotch into the crackling flames of the fireplace before him. "Damn that Azar. He thwarts me again." The brittle gaze of his black eyes landed on Enki once more. "He is only a man, even though enhanced by that damnable ring. All you had to do was recover The Regale. It is crucial to our plans. Was that so difficult?"

"I was not expecting the shade from the temple in Canterbury to interfere. It is powerful and swept me away back to this island."

"Hmm," meditated Nance, "I did not expect the ghost of Becket to disturb us either. I thought it was confined to the cathedral. Yet, we should not be surprised that there is resistance to what we want to occur. This failure of yours will not impact the next stage. The entity that is Marduk is currently in Rome setting the seeds for what will be perceived as a great demonic uprising. Confer with Marduk in Rome and see that our plans for the disruptions in other cities of Europe and America will not be interfered with. Without the softening up of the populace, the return of the vessel you put so much hope in will be compromised. I am sure you want to succeed where you failed thousands of years ago."

"Yesss," whispered Enki. "It shall be as you wish. For a human, you are particularly suited to what we have in mind."

"Never forget it," said Nance. "There's a reason you failed last time. People like me are rare, and it is well you treat me as an equal if you wish to be triumphant over humanity. I've never been to your Otherworld. Some say that it is beautiful, but you only paint me pictures of horror. Do you exaggerate?"

"No, and yes," said Enki. "Much of what was once beautiful in that land is ours now—we have made it a desert or fetid swamp. Its beauty is but a passing thing. This world has much potential for us and is why we come."

"I'm not sure you are telling me the whole truth. I hear things from other places in the world where other beings as powerful as you but on the side of good, as it were, are also breaking through. You are carrying an ancient war to our shores, perhaps?"

"Perhaps," said Enki, "but that would be none of your affair. Keep your eyes on the prize we have described for you and there will be nothing anyone can do to stop the rise of the Anunnaki."

"Stop with the Chariots of the Gods crap," snapped Nance.

"I only seek to frame things within your reference," said Enki.

"I'm not some superstitious peasant," said Nance. "Whatever you are, the ancient gods are not you. Don't you have some minions or whatever to help with Rome and the other cities? I thought so. Use them. Now get out of my sight. Your failure tonight disappoints me."

As if it was never there, Enki disappeared. Nance walked to the door and saw the wet swamp slop the creature had left behind. Ancient god or no, he thought, that thing was a nightmare. He'd have to get housekeeping to clean up the mess.

A SUPERPOWER FLEXES

Saturday Evening, March 20, The White House, Washington D.C.

LESLIE RICHARDSON, DIRECTOR of the CIA, was pitching a fit. She had just sat down with the President and the First Lady for a quiet dinner in the Family Dining Room where a crackling fire made for a cozy atmosphere for the chef's dinner of Steak Oscar. Then Leslie's phone rang. Excusing herself, she took the call in the hallway, irate that Bart Finch, from the Antiquities Division, was calling. Damn him, he never seemed to take a night off. She'd have to do something about that.

"What is it?" she snapped.

Unfazed, Bart asked, "Have you seen CNN or FOX News?"

"How could I?" she said. "I'm trying to have a nice dinner with the President and First Lady."

"So sorry," he said, not sounding sorry at all. "There appears to be some sort of riot among the homeless in New York City this evening."

"So?" said Leslie, not surprised that another riot was forming. New York was getting good at this.

"I wouldn't have bothered you, but reports have the transients tearing everything apart and attacking passers-by. But that's not the big thing. Law enforcement is handling it. There are also reports of these people acting like they are possessed, having great strength, losing their personalities, and acting almost bestial. I hope you see the connection between what the Vatican Swiss Guard found on the streets of Rome and what's happening in New York. It seems coordinated and centered on causing all kinds of chaos and anarchy."

The director had been briefed earlier on the strange occurrences in Rome. "Any reports of this happening elsewhere?" asked Leslie.

"No ma'am," said Bart, "but Ranbir says there is definitely a connection. Something is being let loose in these two cities whether medical or spiritual—depending on your ideology I guess—and it bodes ill for the upcoming session of the United Nations where both President Putnam and Pope Patrick are scheduled to speak."

Leslie was silent for a moment. "Sorry for snapping at you. You were right to call. I'll brief the president immediately, but I need you to call Dulles Airport and get my jet ready to fly this evening to Rome. Things are moving faster than I expected and I need to see the pope. If he and the president are going to speak on Tuesday, we have to have a plan and security will have to be tight."

"I'll get on it immediately. Now get back to your dinner and enjoy what you can of the evening. You can plan on an 11 PM take-off. That will put you in Rome shortly after 12 noon. Hope that will work."

"It's the best we can do," she said. "By the way, you're coming with me. And bring the newest Ranbir avatar. I want the pope to have the resources we have. He's going to need it. Get Tom Bentley, the CIA attaché at the embassy, to drive us to the Vatican when we land. Not a word to anyone else about my trip, especially the sycophants at our embassy who think the papacy is some relic of the past best consigned to the ash heap of history. Bart, I want in and out of Rome in just a few hours. We have much to do to prepare for the pope's arrival. Now let me get back to dinner. At least I have something to share that will keep the conversation going."

She re-entered the dining room, sitting back down as if nothing had happened. Taking a spoonful of clam chowder—Putnam's chef made an excellent New England version—she nearly choked when the president nonchalantly said, "So how are things at the Vatican this evening?"

"How did you know?" said Leslie, dabbing her mouth with her napkin.

"Oliver was on the phone with the pope earlier this afternoon," said Harriet Putnam, enjoying far too much the discomfort her friend was in.

"That's true," laughed the president. "I've only talked to him a few times since he was made pope, but this Pope Patrick grows on me. If he golfs, we might well become friends."

"So, you know about the Rome disturbance?" asked Leslie.

"I do, and, normally, I would have passed it off as just the populace's penchant to dramatize ordinary weird behavior, but the pope called me and asked me if we had any similar occurrences. I told him no."

"Prematurely, I'm afraid," said Leslie, and quickly brought him up on the New York riots.

"You know, I'm more inclined to think it is some kind of poisoning or drug-induced furor," said the president. "I saw the movie, *The Exorcist*, when I was a boy, and it scared the bejesus out of me, but I've never come across anything like it in real life."

"Neither have I," said Leslie; "although it is similar to that plague outbreak in Tralee, Ireland last fall."

"So, why are you two giving these accounts such credence?" said Harriet.

"Because the pope has some cred, dear," said the president. "He wouldn't have called me if he didn't think there was a danger to us."

"He thinks it is spreading to cities around the world, doesn't he?" said Leslie.

"He does, indeed," said the president. "I'm not sure he's wrong. We've been talking, he and I, about our upcoming speeches to the UN on Tuesday. He's trying to convince me to make a joint address. He's got this idea that this thing from outer space that's heading our way and this rise in some sort of demonic possession are connected. I told him I hadn't heard such a cockamamie story since my Aunt Rue thought the grim reaper was trying to take her third husband from her. She had lost two to sudden death before." He paused.

"Well," said Leslie, "don't keep us in suspense. Was there some ghostly monster after your uncle?"

"No," laughed the president. "That worry happened during their third year of marriage. Thirty years later she was praying the guy with the scythe would come sooner rather than later and harvest that no-good husband of hers."

They all laughed but the director brought them back to earth. "So, what made you believe the pope besides his credibility?"

"I've never heard someone sound so serious and ominous in my life," said the president. "He said the two events are connected. That golden tablet Msgr. Daniel Azar and his parents translated in Babylon last month intimates a nexus between a dark evil on earth and the object in the heavens. I don't know how the ancient Babylonians could have possibly known about all this, but there's something in my gut that tells me to pay attention."

Leslie said, "When science, religion, and politics start merging—well, let's just say if it's not the truth we're getting, it's at least a reality we are going to have to deal with. Something's happening here, and it's going to present an entirely new problem to the world."

"That's exactly what the pontiff said, and why I believe him. I shouldn't have become president, Leslie. I was the last person they expected to win those debates and primaries. Only you and Harriet never doubted. I felt it in my gut that this was the time to make a difference. Didn't know what I was going to make a difference in. Oh, I had my economic plan and my foreign policy ideas, but my intuition told me I was supposed to run for another reason. Maybe this is it. I'm taking a guess that it is, so when the pope called me and asked me to team up with him at the UN, I agreed."

"Did you tell anyone?" asked Leslie.

"Not a soul but the pope, you, and, of course, Harriet. We've got to keep it that way; otherwise, the leaders of the nations will think we're crazy. These two speeches will have to convince them differently. There also is a chance that one other will join us on Tuesday—someone who will surprise the world."

"Someone I know?" asked Leslie.

The president just smiled. Leslie looked at him and said, "I'm flying to Rome tonight."

"After dessert, I hope," said the First Lady.

"Of course, but I need to go. I need to find out more than just the idea that events in Rome, and New York, and that object in space are connected. I need to know if there are threats able to manifest themselves on Tuesday when both the president and the pontiff speak."

"Wouldn't a phone call do?" asked the president.

"No sir," said the director, suddenly becoming very formal. "There's someone else I have to see there, someone I trust with my life, the pope's, and yours. His name is Capt. Luca Rohner of the Swiss Guard. He's in charge of security for Msgr. Daniel Azar, the wunderkind of the Vatican. That young priest has more mystery in him than those Babylonian tombs he was excavating with his parents. He was capable of amazing deeds while in Babylon. In fact, that whole expedition would have gone south if not for him and his friend, Capt. Luca. If Daniel Azar is part of the papal entourage to New York, then Capt. Luca will be coming along. He and one of my operatives, Rebecca Perez, can head up Vatican security while liaising with our own Secret Service to keep you, Mr. President, safe at the United Nations. I'm going to Rome to make sure the Vatican sends us all the help it can."

"Surely, our Secret Service is more than capable of handling security, even helping out the pope, if necessary," said Harriet.

"Yes," said Leslie, "they are, if the threat is just mundane from your everyday, average assassins. But something happened in Babylon that was not simply earthly. Things walked the night that should have stayed in the time of the dinosaurs. An entity worshipped as a god made its presence felt. Long dead priests and royal advisors were said to trod the dust of Babylon again. So the rumors say. I'm not particularly credulous or superstitious, but neither Msgr. Daniel Azar, Capt. Luca Rohner, nor members of my team who were there denied what I've just said. If it was just the *Memento Mori* terrorists we had to worry about, we would be fine. But my gut says whatever the enemy is will bring more exotic weapons."

"We live in interesting times," said the president.

"Don't we, sir," said Leslie. "And don't forget wishing their enemies to live in interesting times was one of the worst curses the Chinese could give anyone. Let's hope it's not true for us."

A QUICK TRIP TO ROME

Sunday Afternoon, March 21, 1 PM, Apostolic Palace, Vatican City

LESLIE LANDED IN Rome exactly at 11:30 AM. She was in her limo and being driven towards the Vatican just as Pope Patrick was finishing the Angelus, the weekly prayer with the people on St. Peter's Square.

"I forgot about the Angelus and the crowds," she said to no one in particular in the limo. "Still, we should be fine. We don't have the 85-vehicle convoy that the previous president had when he visited the pope last year. What a pompous ass!"

Leslie was quiet for a moment and then said, "Of course, now we are just one limo and we're going to get caught in tourist traffic from the tourists coming from St. Peter's Square. Tom," she said to the CIA driver tasked from the embassy to drive her, "I was stuck with cans of Mountain Dew on the flight. Vile stuff. Veer off into the Borgo neighborhood and let's stop at the McDonalds on the Borgo Pio. I'm thirsting for a diet Coke like the Chinese are itching for the results of our last killer satellite test."

"Yes, ma'am," said Tom, crossing the Tiber and taking the fastest way to McDonald's.

"No wine, no sparkling water?" smirked Bart from the front seat.

"Quiet, you flower child throwback," said Leslie. "I'm not Catholic, but doing without diet Coke for the entire flight is worth a Lent's penance, I bet. I'll ask His Holiness when I see him."

The black limo smoothed up to the curb outside of Mickey D's. Bart didn't even have to be asked. He knew he was tasked to go in and fill the director's order. While he did that, Leslie looked at the quaint neighborhood full of side streets and alleys. It was just after noon and there were people out. After all, it was a Sunday, but the buildings still cast dark shadows down those side streets and alleys. She was looking down at one of them when she saw the strangest thing.

It seemed like someone had fallen right in the middle of the side street. The view was shadowed but someone or something else was standing over the prostrate person. It would have looked like an ordinary assault and robbery if it was in the United States, but something was just a little bit off. Then Leslie had it. The standing figure had no weapon, but was hunching over the fallen person and reaching out, grasping the victim's head with its hand, its oversize hand with long, super-extended fingers.

Leslie tapped a pin on her black coat—nothing but the finest black for the Vatican, for that's what ladies in official capacities had to wear. Immediately, Ranbir, the holographic avatar Bart had created, appeared on the seat beside her.

He looked out at her with dark eyes, his Sikh turban a dark red color. "Madam Director," he said, "how may I be of service?"

"See those two down the alley? I need to know what's happening."

"Of course," he said. "Immediately."

Ranbir was a hologram, but he did have dignity. He could have just walked through the limo's side door, but instead, he showed off a little and solidified himself enough to have to open the door and get out. Less awkward in case anyone was paying attention.

Leslie watched him move swiftly down the alley. She put on a rather attractive pair of glasses that Bart had given her for just such a situation. Ranbir was broadcasting from his ocular implants to the visi-screens embedded in her eyewear. She was seeing what he was seeing, and she gasped.

Close up as she saw through Ranbir's vision, she could see the prone victim shaking as the attacker grasped the man's head. That was weird enough, but then Ranbir came close enough to attract the attacker's attention. The head turned and it was monstrous. It may have been human once, but its face was twisted and snarling. Leslie thought that if it had horns it would have looked exactly like how Satan was depicted in the artwork she had seen in the Vatican museums the last time she had visited. Only this visage was draped with what looked like seaweed—a sort of Rastafarian underwater look, she thought.

Ranbir didn't hesitate the minute he processed the scene. He rushed the attacker and tackled him to the cobblestones. Bart had upped the avatar's offensive capabilities and the avatar's hands sent thousands of volts into the demonic beast—with no effect. The thing simply cast Ranbir across the alley to smash against the opposite wall of buildings.

It's pretty difficult to impact a hologram to any degree, even a solid one, without some serious electronic weaponry. Bart had assured Leslie that the avatar was virtually indestructible. But the demon had something special that appeared to neutralize Ranbir. It let go of its victim's head, stretched out its distorted hand with the long, twisted fingers and sent tendrils of blue flame across the alley into the face of the avatar.

Leslie screamed as the bright light burned across her corneas and she ripped off the glasses as fast as she could. For a moment she was flash blinded, but there seemed to be no permanent damage as her sight quickly returned. Must have been a fail-safe built-in by Bart just in case something like this ever happened.

When she could see again, she saw the demon thing pick up its victim with one arm and carry him down the alley, disappearing into the shadows. Ranbir's holographic image lay still on the cobblestones. People must have heard the commotion because they were beginning to look down the side street. Leslie quickly tapped the pin on her lapel and the Ranbir avatar disappeared.

Just then, Bart jumped into the car with a diet Coke. "Here you go, boss," he said.

Leslie just took the drink and sucked down a mouthful. "We've got a problem. Ranbir is either dead or hurt."

After she told Bart what had happened, he muttered, "Impossible. He can't be hurt that way. For lack of a better word, you're saying he was hit with some kind of eldritch energy—magic if you will. I don't believe in that stuff."

"Well, that's clear," snarked Leslie, "because whatever hit him, he wasn't prepared for."

Bart grimaced. "Point taken. I've got my laptop. As soon as we get to the Vatican, I'll do a diagnostic. I'm sure he'll be alright. In real life, it takes more than a demonic entity to kill a Sikh warrior. I made this avatar tough. He'll be okay."

"I hope so," said Leslie, sucking down the drink and feeling the caffeine take hold. "I've grown rather fond of him."

They were only a few hundred yards from the Vatican City State, and in minutes they had driven around the Leonine Wall and St. Peter's Square to enter the Courtyard of San Damaso, the private receiving area the pope used to welcome guests. They had called ahead, and there he was, waiting for them as the limo pulled up, two Swiss Guard by his side.

"Good trip, I hope?" said the pontiff.

"Till we got here," said Leslie. Bart Finch stepped out of the limo, shocked with a little celebrity awe at the pope. "This is my techno-geek, for lack of a better term, Your Holiness. And he has some disturbing video for you to look at. It seems that the dark side has come to the walls of the Vatican again." Leslie looked at Pope Patrick knowingly and then slurped her diet Coke for further emphasis.

A SUNDAY BRUNCH AT THE VATICAN

Sunday Afternoon, March 21, Apostolic Palace, Vatican City

LESLIE WAS SURPRISED to see an ambitious brunch going on in the pope's apartments. Msgr. Daniel and the team were all assembled, stuffing their faces with prosciutto canapes and glasses of Chardonnay.

"Back from wine country so soon?" she said, arching one eyebrow.

"How did you know we were there?" said Daniel and then looked over at Rebecca. "Ah, yes, your spy."

"I am not!" said a pseudo-shocked Rebecca giving a quick smile. "I'm a useful and valued colleague."

"And a spy," said Luca. "But a very valuable colleague and necessary part of our team," he quickly added.

"Thank you, Luca," said Rebecca. "It's so nice to be appreciated. Tell her what we found, Daniel."

"Don't worry, Daniel," said Leslie. "She doesn't tell me everything, just that she had a surprise waiting when we met again."

Daniel gathered everyone around. Even his uncle and godfather, the pope, wasn't exactly sure what was going to happen.

"We found it," said Daniel, "though I rather think it found us. The Regale is as beautiful as we thought and possesses an unknown power. Look!"

He reached into his backpack and took out Michelangelo's carved marble heart containing the jewel that had lain in the effigy for so many centuries. As he opened it, the red gem floated up and hovered in mid-air.

Even the pope gasped in awe. "It's absolutely beautiful. I can hardly believe that King Louis originally gifted it to Thomas Becket's shrine."

"The king was generous but not that generous," said Daniel. "The story goes that The Regale leapt from Louis's hands and affixed itself to the shrine. I've got a feeling this stone is used to traveling, making up its own mind where to go. It seems that it had traveled for many centuries before it ended up in Louis's possession."

Then, as if it believed it had revealed itself properly, The Regale lowered itself back into its marble heart and Daniel closed the receptacle.

Abednego stepped forward. "My brothers and I have a theory. Even though we have never seen this stone before, we hypothesize that it is similar in kind to the blue sapphires we wear. The ancients who made them developed the crystals to hold information and the power necessary to perform the tasks woven throughout the crystal substrate. The Star Sapphire Rings have some healing power but are more effective in causing forceful change in the environment as we have seen—weapons if you will. We do not think The Regale is a weapon as such, though from our experience with Enki in France, it has the ability to be so should it be necessary."

"Enki?" said Leslie.

"Yes," said the pontiff. "It seems our team ran into one of the wandering Babylonians—a powerful one at that. It does not work alone. Though the *Memento Mori* terrorist organization that it uses is made up of humans, apparently, this revenant is also surrounded by its own demon heavyweights. That's important to know because, curiously, it seems to be shedding its Guy Fawkes's persona, at least some times, and deciding to walk in the form of the Babylonian god of water and mischief. While the team was making its way back from France, I did a little checking and concur with the brothers that these demon spawn that attend it are called *gallu*—the ancient wet workers of Enki."

"Let me guess," said Leslie, "hunchback-like, large hands, claws on fingers, face like a werewolf devil, and dreadlock hair?"

"How did you know?" asked Abednego.

"Met one just about an hour ago on a side street by the Borgo Pio McDonald's."

They looked at her strangely. "I needed a diet Coke, but that doesn't matter now. It had attacked someone when Ranbir went to the rescue and got zapped for his efforts. The thing carried its victim away."

"And Ranbir?" said Rebecca. "Is he okay?"

"It stopped him cold," said Bart who pressed a button on a remote. Immediately a prone Ranbir appeared on a couch, his left arm crossed over his eyes, with a white handkerchief in his hand.

Rebecca came to his side and said, "Is he okay?"

"I'm not deaf," said Ranbir weakly. "You can address me directly, Miss Becky."

"He's not up to snuff," said Bart. "That *gallus*, or whatever you call it, disrupted his electromagnetic field. I didn't think anything could do that. I'll have to make adjustments so that doesn't happen again."

"But what's most important," said Leslie, "is that this Enki now has henchman in this city. Perhaps this godling is behind the demonic possessions you've mentioned to us, perhaps even the ones in New York. This spreading menace is one of the reasons I wanted to come. Ranbir needs to become the communication link that holds us all together, so Holy Father, I'm giving you a pin like I have with the requisite command codes so that you can summon the avatar whenever necessary, communicate with us, and otherwise increase your knowledge base."

"I'm honored with your government's trust in me," said the pope. "I will take good care of him."

"I'm sure you will," said Leslie. "I am afraid, though, that this arrangement is purely a personal one. The United States may not have this close connection to the Vatican in the future."

"Let's hope that's not true," smiled the pontiff. "I'll try to make a good impression."

For a moment there was a brief silence and then, Josiah, the Swiss Guard, said, "I don't believe Enki is the only mastermind behind the possessions here. Marduk is as well if the manifestation we saw in the flames down at the baths is a true one. What would be worse is if the two are joining up somehow."

"The fact," said Daniel, "that people are being violently possessed in at least two cities means some kind of plan has been implemented. We can expect more reports from other urban areas, I think. I'm surprised that these things, the Babylonian godlings as you call them Uncle Liam, can plan like this. Infecting the populace in this way shows an operation that has a clear end."

"I don't see it," said Rebecca.

"Nor I," said Leslie, "but you have me hooked. Go on."

"When I was a child," said Daniel, "I was taken to see Saddam Hussein one night. That's where he gave me his Star Sapphire Ring. It was the night the Americans began their bombardment of Baghdad. They called it 'Shock and Awe.' And believe me, it was. Its purpose was not only to destroy certain sites but to cow the military and people into inaction by fear and chaos. I think that is what is happening here. These beings are intelligent—for monsters. I'm beginning to think of them as rational weapons. Something or someone else is in league with them though. I suspect a human hand in this. An alliance has been made, and we have to figure out why and how to stop it. In the meantime, I think our world is going to experience a demonic expression of 'Shock and Awe.' What we have seen in Rome, and what Leslie has told of us of the strange riots in New York are a prelude of what's to come. The question is, how will we fight this? No one will believe what's happening."

"Precisely," said the pontiff. "That's why the United Nations meeting is so important. I'll need to raise this issue in such a way that I won't be laughed off the dais. What we are seeing is the first move of the action foretold by the End Times Tablet. It's as clear as day to me, but outside this room, to few else. People expect religious figures to talk apocalyptically. Most dismiss such chatter as idle claptrap, and usually they are right. But not this time. I can't just simply tell the United Nations the world may be about to end, so I've been arranging my own allies to help me out."

Leslie smiled, "You know, President Putnam will be there."

"Indeed, I do," said the pope. "I'm the one that asked him to come."

"Then, if you don't mind," she said, "I'd like to briefly speak to Luca. The Captain of the Swiss Guard and I have some security planning to do. We are foolish to think that last night's riots in New York are anything but an overture to some attack at the United Nations. I'm not sure we can stop such an intrusion, but maybe we can shield persons from harm and use the event as exhibit one of what's coming for us in the months ahead."

INTERLUDE

Sunday Evening, March 21, 9 PM, Vatican, Apostolic Palace, Papal Apartments, Vatican City

"COME IN," SAID Pope Patrick to the gentle knock on his apartment door.

Daniel poked his head in saying, "Got a moment?"

The pope smiled and said, "For my one and only favorite nephew and godson? Of course!" He set a notepad and pen down on the coffee table before him.

"A little retrograde, don't you think?" said Daniel looking at the scrawl on the paper.

"Just working on my address to the United Nations. Cardinal Stefano gave me the Secretariat of State's version of what I should say. A good man, but he hasn't got a clue as to what I'm actually going to do. His draft is this vague reference to signs of the times and how we all have to work together as one community of humanity. True as far as it goes, but it's not going to uplift the cynical delegates that will be attending or calm down the people of the world. For me, getting down and dirty with pen and paper seems to be the best way to concretize my thoughts."

"Do you think it will make any difference?" asked Daniel. "I mean, no one has ever gotten the world to act together with one accord."

"No, you're right, but we have never faced a world threat like this before."

"Luca thinks we should be watching old movies like *Independence Day* and *The Day the Earth Stood Still* for hints on how to fight a non-terrestrial enemy. He's just kidding, but …"

"The Captain of my Swiss Guard never ceases to amaze," said the pope. "He's not all that wrong though. Let's see if Ranbir agrees with him. I haven't had the chance to activate the hologram."

The pope was in black pants and a white shirt, but the pin the director had given him was right above his left shirt pocket. He pressed it and Ranbir appeared standing before them.

"All better, I see," said the pope.

"Indeed, Your Holiness," said Ranbir. "Bart has made a few upgrades. I'm a better version than the last."

"Ah, don't you get tormented with multiple personalities when Bart does that?" said Daniel.

"Oh, no, Reverend Monsignor, not at all. I erase my previous incarnations for my own peace of mind and consistency. Who wants old memories of what I was knocking around the circuitry? Always upward and onward; that's what I say."

"What's your take on the Babylonian incursion?" said the pope. "My astronomers and other scientists posit an extra-terrestrial origin, even if these entities have been here before. The scientists don't seem to like my Irish mythological hypothesis; namely, that this is an incursion from a parallel universe, or, as I like to say, a break-in of the Otherworld through the Thin Place that is Old Babylon, into our reality."

"Actually," said Ranbir, "your hypothesis makes more sense with one caveat. I believe whatever is coming our way is not simply a natural meteorite but a vessel of some kind. Its origins may come from a parallel universe. Bart has programmed me with the skepticism of scientists who doubt the proliferation of intelligent life throughout the cosmos. That's the Fermi Paradox as you know."

"Right," said Daniel. "The paradox states that if there is intelligent life in the universe it should have contacted us by now. The 'Where is everybody?' question has seemed pretty convincing to me."

"Correct," Ranbir continued. "His Holiness's contention that there is a parallel universe, or a Thin Place, where these entities come from is at least as probable as the alien theory."

"Don't damn me with faint praise," said the pope sarcastically. "These Babylonian entities have great knowledge of us, more so than they would if they were just occasional visitors from light-years away. Besides, there are the other intrusions."

"What do you mean?" asked Daniel.

"Dani, before I sent Director Richardson on her way back to the United States this evening, I asked her to widen her perspective even more than connecting the New York riots with the Rome demonic possessions. I have had rumors for nearly the past year of other places on earth that are hosting some kind of active Thin Places. There is a spot in Wisconsin that is troubling, a tiny village called Tinker's Grove, but the one that gets my most attention is the Ireland pandemic of last fall."

"I know," said Daniel. "If it was just the sickness, we could accept it as a pandemic like Covid-19, but the reports of strange creatures …"

"You think the Irish imagination is going overboard," laughed the pope.

"A little maybe, but it was clear that something caused more destruction there than the pandemic. Besides, it isn't often that even the credulous Irish mention sighting St. Michael the Archangel ranging across the skies on his valiant steed."

"At least not in the 21st century," said the pope.

"I have checked into those apparitions," said Ranbir. "It is impossible to confirm anything other than a radar signature for the supposed angelic appearance, but something did occur in the skies last fall in your homeland, Your Holiness."

"You can call me, Patrick," said the pope. "I have no need to stand on ceremony when I'm with my avatar."

"Okay, Paddy."

"Paddy?" said the pope with an arched eyebrow.

"Isn't that the familiar Irish term for your name?" said Ranbir.

"I hate it," said the pope.

"I'm sorry … Paddy," said Ranbir apologetically.

The pope sighed, "Why not stick with 'Your Holiness'."

"As you wish, Paddy," said the avatar.

Daniel was in hysterics on the sofa, but when he regained his composure, he said, between gulps of air, "Okay, Uncle Liam, back to the speech. Did you get your special guests to back you up on what you have to really say?"

"Yes, and they will be there. No secrecy. They were expected to come, but the delegates will be surprised when they mount the dais with me. Don't forget, I'm going to give you a chance to say a few words, expert archeologist that you are."

"You sure you want me to speak? It will be a great breach of protocol."

"I've already cleared it with the Secretary-General of the UN. I'm grateful that Rabindranath Basu from India was elected Secretary-General last year. I can't imagine that dour Presbyterian from Scotland who is the General Assembly President giving me a chance like this. As it stands, the General Assembly may throw Basu out for arranging our little conspiracy. Nonetheless, it has to be done."

"I have checked the communications office of the United Nations. No rumors exist about what you are planning to do," said Ranbir with a satisfied smile.

The pope looked indignant. "You don't even know what I plan to do."

"Not exactly," said Ranbir, "but the probabilities are few. You will attempt to unite the nations in a world collective to challenge the incursion the Anunnaki, or Babylonian godlings, represent."

"Sounds a little communist to me, but, basically, that's true," said the pope.

"It will not be primarily a military alliance," said Ranbir.

"No," answered Daniel. "We will need military technology, but this war will be fought on a different type of battlefield."

Ranbir cocked his head quizzically so much so that Daniel and the pope thought he might lose his turban. "I am having a difficult time understanding."

"Well," said the pope, "free a few circuits and process this. The Church has basically no military weapons with which to wage a conventional war. I am under no illusion that millions are going to die in the coming conflict. Our enemies will have battlefield weapons of which we know little about."

"Yes," said Daniel. "Shadrach, Meshach, and Abednego all confirm that the mythology behind the last incursion so many thousands of years ago spoke of earth destroyers and city annihilators. Damn near eradicated all of civilization. There will be warfare of that sort this time as well."

"That's why we will need the superpower nations to help," said the pope. "And they will have to work together."

"If the nations choose to work together," said Ranbir, "I do not see the problem. The combined military power of the earth is enormous and should prove to be a worthy opponent of whatever is coming our way."

"You'd think so," said Daniel, "but like my uncle said, that will be just a sideshow. The battle is really between light and darkness, and the main battlefield where that war is waged is always on the inner, spiritual plain. The End Times Tablet clearly reflects that. Faith, belief in a higher power, the ability to turn human consciousness into a moral weapon against evil—this will be the virgin and primary territory this war will be fought on. Did I get that right, Uncle Liam?"

"Yes, and that's where the Vatican and the pope come in. I am the leader of 1.5 billion Catholics, the largest religious denomination in the world. Though humans have many beliefs, almost all are dedicated to the Light, however, they define it. I am taking it upon myself to bring all believers into a united front against our enemy."

"Without weapons? Fond as I am of Capt. Luca, how many armed men do you have?" said Ranbir sarcastically.

"For an avatar, you have a particularly nasty and snarky side," said Daniel.

Ranbir looked hurt as he said, "That is how I challenge illogical thought."

"Well, get this," said the pope. "Your historical chips ought to remind you of Pope St. John Paul the Great's martialing of the forces of freedom in eastern Europe last century. The communist powers that existed at that time ridiculed him with Stalin's oft-quoted saying, 'How many armed divisions does the pope have?' Turns out that uniting the hearts and minds of people into a force for freedom was all that was needed to cut the legs off the communist oppressors. He galvanized millions. The pope's actions, in concert with the Western powers, ripped the Iron Curtain into shreds. We have to accomplish the same sort of thing. It's our only hope."

Ranbir had the good grace to look chastened. "I will factor that into my projections." He paused for a second and then said, "I have done so and it still does not look promising."

"That's because you deal in cold hard facts, Ranbir," said the pope, "while I deal with faith, the belief in things unseen. Factor in the faith, and I think you'll find us a challenge for what is coming."

"As you wish, Your Holiness," said Ranbir as the avatar disappeared.

"Got a bit of convincing to do there," said Daniel.

The pope sighed, "The avatar is the least of our worries. Now go get some sleep and let me get back to work. I've got to convince the Holy Spirit to inspire me a little more in my address if we are to pull this off."

INTO THE THICK OF IT

Monday, March 22, Rome to New York

AS PER PROTOCOL, Pope Patrick departed on a late morning *Alitalia* flight to New York's JFK Airport. Daniel and Luca were among the contingent that saw him off.

Daniel said as the plane taxied away, "You'd think he'd use the jets that Nance gave us."

"The pope seems to have some ambivalence towards things where Nance is concerned," said Luca.

"Yeah," said Daniel, "I get that, but as long as there are no strings attached, I think it's okay to use them. After all, we're using them today."

"So we are," said Luca. "Speaking of which, we best be on our way as well. We can fly a bit faster than the pope and I want to be on the ground to meet with the security contingent of the Secret Service that will coordinate the pope's and president's security."

"I thought they wouldn't want to cooperate much," said Daniel.

"Well, not usually, but the pope and president made it clear both to the Guard and the Secret Service that security would have to be coordinated not only between the two but also with the king of Great Britain's bodyguards."

"I can't believe he got King Henry to go along with all of this," said Daniel. "And the fact that we've kept it secret is just amazing."

"It's a strong triumvirate. The president, pope, and king each have charismatic personalities, and, thank God, they get along. If it was otherwise, there wouldn't be room in one space for all three egos," said Luca.

"You're right, there," laughed Daniel. "By the way, Rebecca said Leslie Richardson would meet us at JFK Airport as well. She wants us to take a practice run without the major actors through the streets of New York and to the UN complex."

It only took a few moments for Luca and Daniel to reach their jet, and they found Rebecca waiting on the tarmac for them. The brothers had already boarded, and the pilots were all ready to take off, so in moments they were airborne.

The plane had just leveled off when Daniel turned to Luca and said, "I hope I didn't insult Salvatore and Abby by leaving them behind again, but they need to keep investigating the Tunicle relics and the possible connection to the Shroud of Turin. Besides, to tell the truth, I didn't want to fill them in entirely on what is going to happen in New York. They are the newest on our team and, even though we have vetted them, I don't want to leave them alone with information about what's really going to happen. We can't afford a leak."

"Well," said Luca, "they aren't the only ones you left behind."

Just then, there was a chuffing back towards the tail of the jet where the chapel was. The door opened, and out pounced Grigio, tail wagging with a smile on his face.

"Speak of the devil," said Luca. "I was mistaken."

Grigio barked sharply.

"Don't think he likes being compared to the infernal one," laughed Rebecca.

The dog turned his head away from the three and decided to nose up to the brothers who enthusiastically petted the creature. Shadrach even gave Grigio a few treats.

"What are those?" said Luca, "Babylonian biscuits? I thought you Middle Easterners didn't like dogs much."

"Not true," said Meshach. "Our Daniel, before he passed, had a beautiful dog that used to follow him around Babylon. It's not surprising that our Daniel of today is also attracted to a beast of this nature. Long ago, Daniel was very convincing when he taught us to see the wisdom of having a canine friend around." Meshach affectionately rubbed Grigio's ears.

"I for one am glad he's here," said Rebecca. "The streets of New York have been getting crazier over the past few years, and though security will be tight, there's enough strangeness around that having Grigio might be the extra help we need. Particularly if those demon familiars show up there."

"There's that," Daniel said. "I asked Leslie to check on reports of strange happenings near the UN. If the Anunnaki are going to make an appearance there, ordinary security won't be able to handle that problem. Grigio will be helpful, as will the brothers. And that, my friends," said Daniel to the brothers, "is why I brought you. You will be introduced at the UN for what you are, honored visitors from the past. I will tell the truth about you, but, in actuality, you are here in case the bad guys show up. We can't afford to have the delegates hurt just when we need everyone's cooperation and help."

"We understand," said Abednego. "What about the End Times Tablet? Will it be there as well?"

"Yes," said Daniel, "even though my father felt the original needed to stay in Babylon, my mother believes it important that the world leaders see the real thing. The Prime Minister of Iraq is having it flown over here in his own jet."

"Well," said Rebecca, "that doesn't feel very wise or safe."

"I know," said Daniel, "but the tablet has lasted this long through empires that would have loved to destroy it. It will probably make the trip just fine. Besides, it's the only tangible proof we have, other than astronomical observations, that what we said is coming will actually appear. People have a right to see it. Now get some sleep, all of you. I doubt we will be sleeping much tonight, and tomorrow is going to bring some amazing excitement."

Daniel dowsed the lights and everyone settled in for the long trip.

PUTTING ON THE RITZ

Monday, March 22, Ritz Carlton Hotel, New York

JOHN NANCE WOKE up in the Ritz Carlton suite after a wonderful night of uninterrupted sleep. He had arrived in New York late Sunday afternoon after being advised by Fr. Salvatore of the pope's traveling plans.

He loved this suite and the Ritz Carlton hotel itself. He had stayed there many times. The night before, he quaffed a tumbler of Macallan 18 yr. old scotch while gazing over Central Park to the beautiful New York skyline until he had grown tired. He went to bed at 10 PM, which was early for him, not worrying particularly about the pope's plans for the UN. Fr. Salvatore had been sketchy about them, and Nance decided that Monday would be the day to ferret out any new info. Nance found the Judas trait valuable, and one never knew who might possess it. However, Fr. Salvatore had befriended him in the previous pontificate. It took only a little push and a modern-day equivalent of 30 pieces of silver to convince the priest to be a spy. It was enough to know that the pope intended to tell the world leaders something about the coming crisis. The fact that Fr.

Salvatore was not on the trip was a hiccup, but Nance had other means to get information.

In the morning, over a catered breakfast of steak and eggs and a little tipple of scotch, Nance read the New York Times and saw the articles briefing the meeting of the UN. It was unusual for the organization to have a spring meeting but the crisis fast approaching the world was worth the confab. Not that the delegates would solve anything. They rarely did, but Nance was intrigued by the continually growing list of world leaders that planned to attend. President Putnam and the pope, of course, but King Henry IX of Great Britain was a surprise—he apparently was already in town.

Heavyweights all three, indicating to Nance that the original purpose of the meeting had been raised from mere discussion to the possible formulation of a proposal. Other world leaders had decided to attend as well, including the President of France and Sung Kai, the Deputy Chinese Premier. Even the Russian prime minister was coming, though the nation was still somewhat a pariah for what it had done to Ukraine. What was that pontiff up to? Not for the first time, Nance berated the dead Benito Mussolini for allowing the pontiff to keep Vatican City as a state unto itself when the dictator concluded the Concordat between Italy and the Holy See back in 1929. That meant the UN had to recognize the Vatican's sovereignty, giving the pope equal standing with any world leader.

Nance swirled his morning scotch in his tumbler. Dithering around with churchmen, he thought. What a waste of time—except that it wasn't. This pope had ambitions on the world stage with the talent and intention to make a difference. Nance's scotch hand swirled left, then right. What to do, what to do? He felt his gut was correct that the pope should be eliminated, but he had failed the first and second time before he even knew the pontiff had a new plan. To off him now would be too soon. Until he knew what Patrick was up to, he'd have to let him live a little longer.

Then there were the so-called Anunnaki. The wild card in all his attempts to bring the secular governments under his control. Again, he remembered the first contact those things had made with him. The being named Marduk was, at first, amazingly diplomatic and seductive. They had similar goals, said Marduk, and could work together. And so, they had, even though Nance realized he was a convenient pawn in the Anunnaki's grasp. So Marduk thought.

Nance had pieced together enough of past history to figure out that the last time the Anunnaki tried the domination of humanity, the attempt ended in failure. It was, however, a pyrrhic victory for humanity which was almost destroyed.

Now, these things, for that's what they were, murky, inhuman things—aliens really—thought Nance with disdain—desired to use him to hedge their bets. Two sides could play that game. While Nance entered into a partnership with Marduk and Enki, the only Anunnaki he had met, Nance searched for weaknesses he could exploit. He laughed to himself because he was more than willing to help the pope, in the short term, fight these bastards if it weakened both Church and alien just a little bit. And who knows, he thought, the Anunnaki might take care of the pope for him. Then his own path would be clear.

His domination of the world powers would be done with a velvet hand. He sought to control, not rule. That was the problem with potentates of the past. They tried too hard and were incapable of handling all the exigencies of leadership. He was content to be behind the scenes, as long as he had the final say. First, take care of the pope, and then follow up with the Anunnaki. Humans had defeated them before. Nance was sure that, with himself at the helm, they could do it again.

The sun was lifting high above Central Park when Nance heard a slapping on the outer casement walls. Next to one of the windows was a small buttress with a hanging Corinthian column cap that could have handled a gargoyle perched on it. Now, just a shadow was there, but Nance could see it was moving, creeping like slime over the stone towards his window.

This would be a dramatic entrance, he thought, not the least bit fearful. The oozing shadow slid over the window until it found a slight separation in the window and the casement. Like a puddle of black oil, it poured through the space onto the Persian carpet beneath the window.

"Enki," said Nance, "that better not cause a stain. Pull yourself together and let me see you."

The puddle obliged and formed itself into the humanoid water monster with its long frog-like hands, dreadlocks of seaweed, and the fish lips on its mouth burping little streams of water.

Yet, in a clear voice, it said, "Greetings, John Nance. I bring you, as you wished, our plans for this unexpected meeting between the human rulers here in this city."

Nance grimaced, "I've heard of the chaos you are causing in some of the European cities, particularly Rome, and there are whispers that some of the weekend's disturbances here in New York were also caused by you. Is this the best you can do? Simply trying to frighten the delegates won't stop their plans."

"Correct," said Enki, sloshing from one foot to another. "But it will keep the authorities of the city busy, while I and my accomplices slaughter the delegates in the hall. Never underestimate the power of fear."

"Going as yourself?" quizzed Nance.

"No," said Enki. "Fear, as I say, will have its place in this attack, but for these delegates, what they fear most is terrorism. It's time for Guy Fawkes and his team of terrorists to make another appearance. So universal is the Fawkes mask that just seeing its face should still a few hearts, and me and my merry men will stop the rest. Just leave it to us."

Nance was amazed that when Enki employed the human persona of Guy Fawkes its human speech was no longer garbled and it spoke more like some Shakespearean actor.

"Oh," said Enki, as he began to puddle into a liquid again, "do you have your *sirrush* we helped you create?"

"No," said Nance, "it is back in Europe on the yacht."

"Good, it is too young to take part in what we have planned, though it would wish to. Watch and learn, and most of all," said Enki with a smirk as his head liquified, "respect what we can do."

Then, the pool slipped out the window and was gone.

Nance swirled his scotch again thinking how insufferable these interlopers were. No wonder we got rid of them 11 thousand years ago, he thought to himself, drinking off the last of the Macallan.

THE STREETS OF NEW YORK

Monday Afternoon, March 22, Turtle Bay Neighborhood, New York

LESLIE RICHARDSON HAD the driver pull the Secret Service limo up to the Ritz Carlton and watched from the back seat as Daniel, Luca, and Rebecca climbed in beside her.

"The Ritz is a little ritzy for the Vatican, don't you think?" she said with an eyebrow arching.

Daniel smiled and said, "My uncle gets a discount at all their hotels. Something about getting them into the Dublin St. Patrick's Parade a long time ago. Besides, we're on the lowly seventh floor in ordinary rooms. We left the brothers watching movies."

"Yeah," said Luca. "They wanted to see the *Left Behind* films, the ones starring Michael York, who is the only good thing about those movies—weird, Rapture crap."

"I thought Catholics believed in the Rapture," said Rebecca, referring to the doctrine that before the end times Christ would snatch up true believers to the heavens so they did not have to go through the end times tribulation.

"Wrong denomination, Rebecca," said Daniel. "That doctrine was invented in the 19th century by evangelicals, who had a very literal idea about what the end of the world was going to look like with the antichrist and all that."

"Don't know if they were right," said Leslie, "but what's coming sounds like a lot of tribulation that people would be thankful to escape."

"Right you are," said Daniel. "So, what's the plan here?"

"Just to take you around the Turtle Bay neighborhood abutting the United Nations complex so you can see our security precautions. We've got the area locked down tightly, and there was no repeat of the strange rioting and beatings of last week," said Leslie. "We've got a co-operative complement of Secret Service and New York's finest along with UN security forces providing peacekeeping activities and personal security for the delegates. It should be enough."

"If we were facing just an ordinary, earthly, terrorist threat," muttered Luca.

"Now, you're the one sounding rapturous," joked Daniel.

"Don't laugh," said Luca, "just because there was a bad film made about the supposed end times, doesn't mean part of it can't be true. I don't trust the peaceful night you guys had last evening in the city."

"Believe me," said Leslie, "neither do I, but our show of force must have caused at least a cautious reappraisal by whoever is behind the disturbances."

"Do any of you have ideas on the instigators?" asked Luca to Leslie.

"No, but that doesn't mean I'm putting any credence, and I mean any credence whatsoever in Daniel's Anunnaki hypothesis."

"Don't weigh me down with discredited conspiracy theories," said Daniel. "I said that parts of the original Anunnaki theory, wild as it is, may have hit the jackpot on pinpointing a time when visitors, aliens, whatever, or just plain advanced humans tried to take over what was then the known world and make it go in a different direction than it ultimately took. For God's sake, Leslie, you've seen enough in the past few months to at least suspend a little of your disbelief."

Leslie stared at Daniel in silence for a few moments. "You're right. I was a bit too dismissive, just like you're a bit too credulous, End Times Tablet notwithstanding. What I'm telling you is that, no matter what, everyone should be safe tomorrow."

"Think so?" said Luca. "Look at that."

The limo was cruising the side streets near the UN complex when Luca pointed out a small gathering of homeless.

"What about them?" said Rebecca. "I don't mean to sound callous, but they look like the usual poor that inhabit the city."

"That's just it," said Luca, "they seem to look like the usual poor, but they're not. No busking, no panhandling, no setting up shelter for the coming night. They're just standing there together, watching—waiting."

"Hey, look!" said Daniel. "It's Grigio. I wondered where he got to."

Leslie said, "That crazy dog appears and disappears. How did he ever get this far from the hotel on his own?"

Grigio was sauntering down the street, a seeming stray and a big one at that, but sucking up to passers-by and getting lots of attention. Until he turned his own laser gaze to the group Luca had pointed out. The dog stopped his walking and stared straight at them. Then he turned his head and looked at the nearby limo. For a moment, Luca thought the dog gazed straight into his soul.

"Something's wrong," Luca said.

"I agree," said Daniel. "Grigio is trying to tell us something."

The dog approached the group of vagrants. Daniel sincerely hoped the beast wasn't going to hurt them. The homeless always got a bad rap, being blamed for the countless woes that plagued modern cities.

He needn't have worried, because it didn't come down that way. Instead, the group turned as one toward the dog. Most canines would have run at the overly curious attention the dog was getting, but not Grigio. He still approached, but cautiously. When he was about five feet from the group, the cluster of individuals acted simultaneously, each lifting an arm and pointing at the dog with an index finger.

For a moment, all movement on the street seemed to stop. Walkers and other passers-by paused and turned to watch the strange group. Time stood still as each one in the group pointed in silent accusation at the dog. Then came the scream, a sound as one from the homeless group—shrill, piercing, invasive, penetrating even the bullet-proof limousine. The passengers clapped their hands over their ears, as did anyone on the street within hearing distance. Daniel felt his head might explode, but even in his pain, he lifted his gaze to find Grigio, who was bent low to the ground in obvious distress.

As if lifting some great weight, the dog struggled to his feet again, took two paces toward the frightful group, lifted up his muzzle and howled for all he was worth. It was a melancholy sound, of years past and loneliness lived, of the challenge given and battles won. It was the song sung by all canines who ever lived, a haunting music to dispel the dark. Strangely, it covered the screams of the homeless, and as the howl died away, it dampened the atmosphere around the street like a blanket of snow falling in the wilderness after the pack had hunted, and the group, whose voices threatened to tear out the heart of Grigio, fell silent.

Daniel heard the next sound but wasn't sure anyone else did. He saw Grigio bare his teeth and heard the low growl issued at the zombie-like people. They seemed to come to themselves. Each shook their heads as if emerging out of some kind of stupor, looked at one another quizzically and went their way. With nothing to see anymore, everyone on the street resumed their business. Even Grigio, after watching the homeless disperse, panted with his tongue out and made his way to the limo. Daniel opened the door and let him in.

"You okay, Grey One?" he asked. The dog gave his wolfish smile and licked Daniel's face.

"Yeah," said Luca, petting the dog, "they went all *Invasion of the Body Snatchers* on you—zombies pointing at you like you were the problem. Even I was a bit worried." Grigio chuffed and ducked his head against Luca's chest.

"What are we going to do if that happens tomorrow?" said Rebecca. "We can't use force against them. Visibly, they did nothing wrong, but I have never felt such evil. That scream they let loose was terrifying. I just knew that bad things were going to happen."

"But nothing bad did happen," said Leslie, "and that's because this great big grey hulk confronted them with courage. He showed no fear. We'll have our weapons if we need them, but I'm going to send out a memo to the security forces to be aware that if there are troublemakers about tomorrow, they will seek to play on our fears and superstitions. We can't let them cause us to back down."

"Good luck with that," said Daniel. "People's fears are almost impossible to defeat unless a person is aware of how the fear mongers work. But send the memo, anyway. Couldn't hurt. Grigio, is this area safe now?"

The dog chuffed what everyone took for a yes. That's when Leslie decided to do a tour of all the side streets once again, and ask for an all clear from the dog who happily obliged.

"I'm getting you a K-9 vest for tomorrow," said the director. "We're going to deputize this dog and use his skills. I've got a feeling he'll be a help in keeping things safe."

Grigio sat up straighter on the seat and made himself look as noble as possible. Everybody burst out laughing.

Grigio whined, but Luca put his arm around the dog's neck. "Laughing with you, buddy; never at you. Always laughing with you."

BOOK OF DANIEL CHAPTER 7

Monday Evening, March 22, The United Nations Complex, Blackwell's Pub, New York,

LESLIE INSISTED ON buying dinner after the security check of the surrounding neighborhood. Nobody wanted Italian from the ubiquitous bistros and ristorantes surrounding the area, so she suggested Blackwell's, a pub and restaurant noted for Irish and American food as well as killer pizza. It was just the kind of place Daniel loved, and the proprietors even let Grigio come in and lay underneath the table. For the first time since getting to New York, Daniel relaxed. Chaldean he might be, but his uncle, the pope, had schooled him in all things Irish, and he found himself adopting a brogue as clear as if it had been uttered by an Irish speaker himself.

The restaurant was half full, which was not unusual for a Monday night, but it even provided music from a three-piece band. Daniel felt he was in heaven because it was a quintessential Irish trio who sang and played with the lead being taken by an Irish lass with a wicked glint to her eye. Luca was enchanted as well.

They ate their dinner, Daniel insisting that Luca try the Irish stew, and all ordered an after dinner Guinness. Leslie was a great conversationalist, not surprising, thought Luca, for a CIA spook, and she got Rebecca to talk at length about her time as a part-time archeologist and full-time Mossad spy. The alcohol didn't make Rebecca spill any state secrets, but she told enough to enthrall everyone else in her tales of Middle-eastern mysteries.

The band knew what it was doing. It played a mixture of upbeat trad Irish pub songs and ballads, getting the customers to clap or sway as the song demanded, but then the Irish lass said they had one song left before the break. It was the melancholy, but beautiful ballad, *The Rare 'Ould Times*, one of Daniel's favorite songs. It was about all the changes that came about in Dublin city at the turn of the nineteenth century, and about love lost and growing old. And yet there was a beauty to it that was somehow uplifting.

Just like most Irish music, thought Daniel, where all the women are beautiful and all the songs are sad. As the band started to play the ballad, Daniel caught sight of a plaque above the bar. Inscribed on it were the words,

> *"Who knows where we go when we hear Irish music,*
> *and we are left a little while alone?"*

He let the woman's clear and lovely voice carry the beautiful tune throughout the pub and into his soul. He thought his heart would break at the lyrics:

> *Raised on songs & stories, heroes of renown,*
> *The passing tales & glories, that once was Dublin town,*
> *The hallowed halls & houses, the haunting children's rhymes,*
> *That once was Dublin city, in the rare 'ould times.*
> *Ring a ring a' Rosie,*
> *As the light declines,*
> *I remember Dublin city,*
> *In the rare, 'ould times.*

Daniel had chosen archeology because he saw great beauty in the past. His uncle had placed in his heart a sentimental feeling that someone should mourn what once was, and preserve the wisdom that once had been. Daniel thought the modern age too quick to dispense with the knowledge of the past. For a moment he felt a tinge of sadness for the Babylonian brothers, who gave up the past to warn the future. He vowed to make their presence as comfortable as possible. They were a treasure the world needed to preserve.

As the verses spun out from the Irish group's ballad, he felt Grigio's head upon his lap, and he closed his eyes to be transported by the music and he found himself segueing into a dream state.

First, he thought he was back at the Ritz-Carlton Hotel, because for a moment he saw the three brothers, watching the movie. As one, they lifted up their heads and seemed to stare at him, worry in their gaze. Then they were gone. Instead, he found himself at the Visitor's Plaza at the UN. He had never been there before, but he knew he was looking at it as if he were standing there in the middle of the complex.

Only things weren't exactly right. A setting sun shed its blood-red rays across a decayed city, and its violent light fell across the plaza. The huge iconic UN building, the Secretariat skyscraper, looked like several cruise missiles had given it a brutal beating, for hundreds of windows were broken and large pieces of metal and broken glass littered the ground. He could hear the wind howling through gaping holes. What had happened here?

Daniel saw, too, the General Assembly Hall, its roof caved in. Paper and garbage blew freely around the plaza, and he realized that he was all alone. Disturbed as he was by the sight, what really captured his eye was a statue, and it looked familiar to him. Then he remembered. It was a controversial sculpture. Artists from Mexico had crafted a multi-colored animal hybrid dragon-looking thing. Daniel immediately thought of the sirrusha *from Babylon, the dragons that had plagued him and the entire archeological team not more than two months* ago, but this sculpture was not of a sirrush. Instead, it was a fusion of a jaguar and eagle, the statue having the body of the cat and the wings of the bird. There was a sign beneath it saying, 'The Guardian of International Peace and Security.'

Immediately, his memory jogged, and he remembered why it was so controversial. Some of the evangelical Christians and conspiracy theorists felt it was very close to the lion and eagle beast described in the Bible's Book of Daniel, chapter 7. It also seemed to hearken to a beast of the Apocalypse from the Book of Revelation with the body of a leopard, the mouth of a lion, and the feet of a bear. Daniel often criticized the far-right loons of his religion who saw the antichrist and the end times in everything, but even he felt a shiver down his spine. He remembered his dream from Babylon and the dictum that he must fear the terrible beast whose mouth was fire, whose breath was death.

This statue was a little too close for comfort, but no matter how he tried, deep dread filled his soul. Then it got worse. The sculpture turned its head, looked at Daniel and spoke:

> "You, again, little man.
> Think you to forestall me once more?
> This is not Babylon,
> The City of the Dead.
> This is the heart of humanity.
> The City at the center of the world.
> You petty humans seek to unite
> To oppose what you do not even understand.
> But I am coming,
> I, whose mouth is fire,
> Whose breath is death,
> Whose will is woe.
> Through the heavens, I soar,
> And soon you shall see me.
> But first come the ones who serve,

The gallu, the demons of the underworld.
Nothing you do can stop them.
From the waters they come,
To make a ruin of what you call
This place of peace.
See what they have done?
The winds of decay
Whisper through the rubble,
Sweeping away what little hope remains.

Dreamer, behold your doom,
A ruined city, a glory shattered,
A people lost in the valley of the shadow of death."

Despair gripped Daniel's soul, but then he felt a presence beside him. He looked and there stood Grigio who leaned against Daniel's side. He looked back at the statue, whose colors luminesced in the dying twilight, and the priest spoke one word,

"Never!"

The so-called 'Guardian of International Peace and Security' belched flame as Grigio leaped for its throat. The wings of the beast flapped to intensify the conflagration, and the hot breath appeared as almost a solid shield of fire. It struck Grigio full-on, and enveloped him in smoke and brimstone. But it did not stop him. The dog crashed into the neck of the sculpture and so terrible was the meeting that the head of the hybrid snapped at the throat. The marble effigy crashed to the ground, shattering into thousands of pieces. Grigio landed on top of the pedestal, and seized a flapping wing breaking it off as well.

Daniel looked at Grigio and smiled. Then his brow furrowed in anger, he looked at the broken guardian and once again said, "Never!"

The dog came back to his side and together they beheld the ruined plaza. The mournful wind spoke of what was once truly a hope of peace and security, namely, the gathering of the nations of the world, and the harsh whispers of the *paper and garbage, scraping on the stone pavement murmured the false promises of harmony and protection when uttered by a voice from the past, whose mouth was fire, whose breath was death, whose will was woe.*

Daniel's eyes snapped suddenly open, and he heard the words sung plaintively through the pub:

> *Ring a ring a' Rosie,*
> *As the light declines,*
> *I remember Dublin City,*
> *In the rare, 'ould times.*

He looked to see the Irish lass finish her ballad. She no longer gazed at him with a wicked glint in her eye, but instead shed a tear down her face, as if she beheld a terrible sorrow.

Rebecca narrowed her own eyes. "Where have you been? You zoned out on us during that song."

Daniel smiled ruefully, "It's just like that plaque says up there, *Who knows where we go when we listen to Irish music, and we are left a little while alone?*"

MEETING THE ALLIES

Tuesday, March 23, Morning, United Nations Complex, New York

ON A DEEPLY foggy Tuesday morning, the pope's limo and security detail arrived precisely at 9 AM at the General Assembly Hall. There was no rush since the pontiff's speech was not scheduled until 10:30 AM. As Pope Patrick and Daniel exited the vehicle, Daniel pulled his uncle aside for a quick word.

"I'm so worried, Uncle Liam. The dream I had in the pub—this whole place was in ruins."

The pope smiled, "Dreams are what might be, and the Weaver of the Loom may not have set the threads yet."

"Is that some Irish pagan myth breaking through your orthodox soul?" smiled his nephew. "Weaver of the Loom?" Then Daniel turned serious again. "I feel a terrible danger all around us. Even the murk and fog today lend themselves to evil things waiting in the mist."

"Now, who's sounding like an ancient superstitious Irishman? I always thought there was a little bit of the green in that Chaldean soul of yours."

"Seriously, uncle," said Daniel, "don't discount what I saw. Look at my ring—and yours. I can see the faint blue glow, and that means something momentous is afoot."

The pope put his big hand around the neck of the priest and pulled him close to his chest. "That's why I love you, Daniel. Your heart is pure and clear, and you have a passion to see the Light triumph above all things. I am so proud of who you have become. But we cannot live in fear. Rest assured, something will happen today, whether for good or ill or both I do not know. But if we do not make this attempt, I fear that what is coming will destroy all that humanity has built."

"How did you ever get the President of the United States and the King of Great Britain to stand at the podium with you today?"

"I'm an Irishman," laughed the pontiff. "I got them to agree by telling them just enough to stroke their egos and whet their curiosity. They are most essential for this plan to work. Nothing like this has ever been tried since medieval times. Church and state have barely been on speaking terms for centuries. It's time for that to change, at least for a little while. I may be old school, but I still think the proper alliance of Church and State, where neither ruled the other but each worked for the betterment of humanity, brought out the best of our civilization.

"By the way, Daniel, I'm not sure how all of this will shake down, so I had my secretary volunteer you to be our media liaison with Sky News and the BBC. Lionel Mergen, the urbane, and if you'll pardon my language, somewhat bitchy commentator from Sky News along with Sandra Blessing from the BBC, sense a bigger story than the other media outlets. The fact that they are here, apparently, is already making the media think it's overlooking something. I'll expect you to answer their questions forthrightly following the meeting. Imagine it—the king, the president, and the pope trying to give the world back its spine! Should be historic."

Daniel just looked at the pope, speechless. The pontiff had been very busy in the last few days. There were not going to be just some random talks, but, instead, a closely choreographed event between three of the world's great leaders.

Luca broke up the little *soiree*, opening the General Assembly door, saying, "Holy Father, they have arranged a green room where you and your guests can prepare for the address to the General Assembly. Follow me, please." Cpt. Luca, dressed this time in an understated black suit, strode through the hallway, populated by security forces, Rebecca silently bringing up the rear of the papal entourage. However, when they got to the green room, the pope only motioned for Daniel, Luca and Rebecca to enter with him. He asked his other attendants to wait in an adjacent area.

Daniel stifled a gasp as he walked into the rather large space. There were just a few other security officials present, but that wasn't what caught his eye. Leslie Richardson, he saw immediately and nodded to her, but it was the sight of President Oliver Putnam and King Henry IX that threatened to take his breath away. There should have been no way for the pope to have convinced these two to back his proposal so openly, but the relaxed demeanor of the leader of the free world and the best-known royal on earth belied his unbelief.

It was the king that most interested Daniel. He already knew a lot about President Putnam, a basically conservative politician in world affairs and moderate in his social agenda. He was popular at home and was seen as a strong leader who didn't shrink from challenging the other major powers to behave themselves.

The king, Daniel did not know, except for two facts. A young royal, still in his late twenties, he was extremely controversial. He had a wish to rule, not simply reign. As head of state, he still possessed, in theory, many of the powers of a ruling monarch, powers seldom used in over a century and a half. He had acted in two areas that previous modern-day royals had never trod.

First, he took seriously the fact that he was the head of the nation's armed forces and was making direct decisions affecting defense and national security. All quite legal, if never really acted on before.

Second, and on much more shaky ground, he asserted his independence from Parliament by abrogating Parliament's law that the monarch must be a member of the Church of England. With a flair for the dramatic, King Henry had revealed a year earlier that he had converted to Catholicism and intended to be the secular protector of both the Anglican and Catholic churches in the realm. Most people in the kingdom were not that much inclined to spiritual matters anymore and didn't think much of it, but Parliament was initially incensed.

"Times change," he told them. Besides, he was an only child of the previous ruler and the nation was not ready for the crisis a change in dynasty would bring. Surprisingly, after some grumbling, Parliament issued a law saving face and allowing the monarch to convert. They not only reaffirmed his authority over the Anglican Church but also recognized the important role he would play among the Kingdom's Catholics. The pope had so far remained silent on this matter.

This was not as controversial as it would seem, for relations were already very good between pope and king with the Catholics in the realm who had grown to a sizable minority. Indeed, they represented the largest practicing religion in the country, even surpassing the national Anglican Church.

The young, aggressive king was very good at keeping Parliament off balance and had not just suggested but had also appointed a Prime Minister of his choosing. Popular with the people, King Henry was revitalizing a moribund British society and energizing a monarchy that had grown increasingly stagnant over the past century.

The young king, only slightly older than Daniel, caught the priest's eye and motioned him forward. "Msgr. Daniel Azar, I am privileged to meet you. Your uncle has recently chatted with me about your exploits in Babylon and the fascinating finds and friends you have discovered there among the ancient tombs. It seems you have a penchant for causing trouble and surfacing enigmas. Tell me one thing. Is the End Times Tablet to be taken seriously?"

"It is, Your Majesty," Daniel said, extremely surprised that his voice was steady without a trace of nervousness. "It represents the most dangerous threat our global civilization has had to face in thousands of years."

The king smiled in excitement. He was dressed in black morning dress with a yellow waistcoat, but what really set him apart was the thin, gold crown he wore on his head. He had it made, and it was so light that it appeared woven into his red hair. He was considered extremely good looking and there was no lack of ladies wishing to be his queen. His blue eyes flashed at Daniel.

"As you know, Daniel—may I call you that? Of course, you may call me Harry for we shall, I think, be fast friends—I have crossed the Tiber, and once again, the monarchy is Roman Catholic. They should have tossed me from the throne when I did that, but Parliament has no spine. What we do today will be vastly more important and earth-shattering. Parliament will forget my offenses against it.

"I think you know what I mean. Sr. Cecilia Campbell has updated me on what you found in Canterbury. The ghost of Becket perhaps—who knew? And of course, the pope has filled me in on The Regale. When this is all done, I have plans for that. I think you will approve. Now come, let me introduce you to President Putnam. He's not as fun as I am, but he's a good chap anyway."

Daniel allowed himself to be led along and had hardly to utter a word as the king introduced the priest to the leader of the free world.

The president looked at Daniel and said with a smile, "I would patter about and ask you about yourself, but I already know more about you than you do. Leslie has filled me in on what you have accomplished so far. We are going to be depending on you greatly in the days to come."

"Indeed, we will," said the pope, coming over to join them. "Now, I must take these two esteemed leaders away from you, Dani. We have only an hour left of planning and much still needs to be done."

Daniel breathed a sigh of relief as a president and potentates retired to a table at the end of the room. Luca and Beth approached him sympathetically, their eyes asking how the introductions went.

"I'm not a politician," said Daniel, "but it doesn't matter. I don't think I met politicians just now. These guys seem like true world leaders."

Rebecca snorted and said, "That's because the crap is about to hit the fan, and there won't be time for silly posturing, campaigning, or endless compromising. We are about to be attacked by who knows what, and the world is hardly prepared for it. Do you really think these three are going to be able to convince the General Assembly of the threat and gain their cooperation?"

"Not totally," said Luca. "Russia will bitch and complain but that's where the pope comes in. He's on great terms with the new Russian patriarch who has done much to heal divisions among the Orthodox from the Ukrainian war. If the patriarch agrees humanity is at risk, the president of the Russian Republic will side with us if for no other reason than to gain face again with the allied powers.

"Not so with China. She doesn't have many allies, but she's big and atheistic. There's really no spiritual side to appeal to since the state fulfills both the political and spiritual roles. Their president is so old now, but he still insists on his picture in the front of every house of worship no matter what religion in that country. I don't think we'll get any cooperation from them and that's going to be our greatest weakness. If I were our enemies, I'd use that country as the base of operations."

"We don't even know what our enemies look like," sighed Rebecca.

"Well, actually," said Daniel, "we do, or we have a pretty good idea. Marduk, the being that unleashed all that hell in Babylon, and Enki, that thing that's both an *avant-garde* Guy Fawkes terrorist and some slimy piece of kelp that crawled out of the nearest swamp are entities from a parallel universe. We've already talked about how physicists have determined such a universe is a possibility.

"I like my uncle's more poetic description: they're from the Otherworld, a place both like and unlike ours. Through the Thin places on earth, they have been able, at times to cross over into our realm and wreak mischief. The last time they did so with any great strength or numbers was thousands of years ago. That's going to be hard for some to believe, but if the nations follow the opinions of the scientists and the other religions recognize the possibility of other dimensions within their spiritual reality, we might actually come together in some sort of alliance to fight this threat. All we have to prove is that the threat is real. Those we fear have been here before and nearly destroyed humanity."

Daniel paused in thought for a moment and then continued. "In Judeo-Christian religious literature, they are called the Nephilim, often wrongly translated as 'giants.' Scholars like to consign them to the dustbin of mythology, but archeology is beginning to bring to light civilizations that existed thousands of years ago that were more advanced than they should be. I think that once we strip away all the mythology, we will still be left with an almost unbelievable hypothesis that there were once Nephilim or Anunnaki, as the Babylonians called them—beings who worked in concert with humanity at times and against us at other times. They sound peculiarly like the entities we are dealing with now. Legend says that they turned against humanity once, and we defeated them at great cost. We were wiser then and recognized our peril. I wonder if we will do the same now."

Daniel fell silent, and then Luca spoke, "Well, we're about to find out. The triumvirate has broken up and looks ready to go out and face the General Assembly. We've got places on the floor for security and I've saved a place for you, Dani, and the Babylon boys. Let's get ourselves out there and settled."

PRELUDE TO THE APOCALYPSE

Tuesday, March 23, Morning, The General Assembly Hall, United Nations, New York

THE DELEGATES OF the General Assembly were all milling about the floor when Daniel, Luca, and Rebecca came out a side entrance and took their places at the security desk to the left of the rostrum. The Babylon contingent of VERITAS was already seated. Leslie Richardson, the Director of the CIA, had shown up and reserved their seats. The delegates, themselves, only slowly took their places as Pope Patrick, King Henry, and President Putnam strode up the steps to their ceremonial chairs behind the rostrum amidst the noise. Though everyone saw, few pretended to notice. Nobody granted precedence to anyone in the hall of the General Assembly. Too many egos.

However, the President of the UN for the year, James McCoy of Canada, seemed to hold some sway as he gaveled the hall into a semblance of order. He occupied the middle position on the dais. To his left and the delegates right sat Rabindranath Basu, the Secretary-General. He was a charismatic scholar from India and very pro-western.

Daniel didn't watch the delegates take their seats. Instead, he looked past the rostrum and saw to its right a large easel covered with a white cloth. That must be the End Times Tablet, he thought.

Luca and Rebecca swept their eyes over the floor and the exits, looking for anything out of the ordinary. Both were pleased that their suggestion of armed guards around the hall as well as within the assembly body were implemented. The delegates could not have been happy, but this was an extraordinary meeting. Many other world leaders had shown up to sit with their delegations, making the hall a ripe target for anyone to cause instant chaos throughout the globe.

Luca and Rebecca also realized there was a heavy security presence outside the General Assembly and throughout the UN complex. The delegates were as safe as safe could be. Luca took a long look at the VIP section for spectators. It was full as well, but the only one he spotted worth his attention was John Nance. The white-haired patrician was making his way to a seat reserved for him, and for a moment Luca entertained the thought wondering why the trillionaire had come. Then again, thought Luca, Nance probably saw the papacy as important since he had donated so much money, so maybe he was here to watch over his investment.

Of course, there was always the ubiquitous media. That's who Rebecca was scoping out. UN President McCoy had to devise a lottery to handle the larger than normal media presence. Major networks from throughout the world were present as well. So little official news had been released about the asteroid, destined to visit earth, that all sensed great news would be made this morning at the General Assembly. The media had eagerly taken up the notion that a world-wide plan for confronting the crisis was absolutely necessary. Rebecca made a mental note of where Sky News and the BBC had set up shop. She'd be the one taking Daniel over to begin his interview after the morning's festivities were done.

Within moments, Daniel's attention was riveted onto UN President McCoy as he, again, gaveled the meeting to order, and without much ceremony, introduced the pontiff and invited him to speak.

A hush fell over the General Assembly. Popes had spoken before, but rarely, to the delegates. Most of their speeches had been formal takes on the stability of the world and the prospects for a stronger peace. But they were not Pope Patrick. Everyone already knew the mercurial pontiff was known to throw a surprise or two. Expectations were high for what he was going to say.

Without preamble or notes, the pope looked at the delegates and spoke. "Now is the time for the people of the world to unite to preserve our very existence and the cultures which have given birth to humanity. You may ask why it is I who am speaking to you. The answer is simple. It was the scientists of the Vatican Observatory at Castel Gandolfo and the Vatican Observatory in Arizona that discovered the 'Oumuamua Asteroid was not simply a random rock from somewhere outside our solar system but was instead a vehicle, not made by nature, aimed at our planet, and destined to arrive in our vicinity sometime this year.

"An archeological dig in Babylon, partially funded by the Vatican and headed by the world famous archeologists, Drs. Markoz and Frances Azar, dug up a tablet attached to an ancient tomb. The son of these scientists is my nephew, Msgr. Daniel Azar, himself a noted archeologist and expert of ancient languages. He is the one who translated the End Times Tablet, and that translation revealed to us the danger that has brought us here today.

"The unnatural asteroid approaching us and the End Times Tablet are connected by the date of November 1. Modern science and ancient prophecy concur with this, and that connection proclaims doom for the world."

The General Assembly erupted in an outpouring of questions and dismay.

The pope, who had spoken to hundreds of thousands many times in his travels, could be heard easily above the outcry. "Unless we act together!"

The voices died down and the pope repeated more softly, "Unless we act together. I know that many of you have trouble believing the danger we are in. That is why I have asked Dr. Markoz Azar to present the End Times Tablet to you, for you to see and witness what some of us already know."

The pope backed away from the podium and from a side door to the right of the dais stepped up the famed archeologist. Dr. Azar silently walked over to the covered tablet and whipped off the white sheet. The crowd gasped again, for the real End Times Tablet was made of gold, and it shone like fire within the hall.

"Come up here, my son," said the archeologist, "for if anyone should tell them about the tablet it is you who translated it."

Daniel had given many sermons to church crowds but had never spoken, literally, before the world. He was nervous, his black cassock, trimmed in scarlet piping and magenta sash rustling softly as he made his way to his father. Dr. Azar nodded encouragingly, and Daniel turned to face the crowd.

His voice was somber as he spoke, "The words are written in the ancient language of Akkadian, except for the last line which is carved in English. Remarkably, that last sentence is as old as the End Times Tablet—nearly 2600 years of age. That, in itself, was enough to send chills up my spine when I first saw it. Amazing as that is, the message is even more troubling, for it recounts the coming of something inhuman, something which has been here before.

"We know from the archeological ruins, recently discovered throughout the Middle East, that advanced human civilization is far older than we thought. The discovery of Gobelki Tepe in modern day Turkey, dated to 10,000 BCE, was our first hint. Other sites have confirmed that advanced societies flourished and died thousands of years before what has been previously known as the beginning of civilization. The recent discoveries in Babylon make us posit that something beyond the natural order destroyed these communities. The End Times Tablet and the tablets we have found in the tomb assert that a powerful force had visited these ancient civilized areas with destructive intent. This alien thing that haunts the outer regions of our solar system promises to return and destroy everything that we know." Daniel's hand reached up and pointed. "The Tablet starts with these words:

> *By the rivers of Babylon,*
> *We dreamed the dream—*
> *The night visions of terrible power.*
> *A Beast from shadows between the stars—*

At that moment, Daniel appeared to stumble backward and lean against his father who caught him with both hands. Lights flickered in the Assembly Hall and then went out, but the End Times Tablet still let out a golden glow. A high-pitched shriek swept through the room like the sands beating against the stones in a desert storm, and two golden rays of light shot out of the top of the tablet and fell upon the green marble wall behind the rostrum. In golden letters upon the wall, the rays carved out three phrases:

> *Whose mouth is fire.*
> *Whose breath is death.*
> *Whose will is woe.*

The shrieking ended in a wail of sorrow, and as that came to an end there came another sound as of a rushing wind. As the delegates' attention was drawn once more to the front of the room, they could see that both Daniel and his father were no longer alone. Standing with them were three shadowy figures dressed in ancient Babylonian royal robes, a sapphire ring glowing on the ring finger of each of them. Tall with curled black beards and mitered hats, they reached out their arms and together pulled Daniel close to them. Behind them, the golden phrases carved on the wall grew brighter.

"Speak little friend," said one, "and tell them as once you told an ancient king what the phrases say."

Daniel's face was empty of emotion as if he was in a trance. He did not need to look at the phrases carved in the wall or gaze at the tablet, but instead stared out at the crowd in the dark. He used his ring to magnify his voice and spoke loudly enough for everyone to hear, his speech in the cadence of the poets and storytellers of old, and even the most skeptical of the delegates were entranced by what he said:

> *"I walk in the dark by the rivers of Babylon,*
> *Falling into sleep by its gentle shores.*
> *I see in the night, visions of terrible power,*
> *A Beast coming from the shadows between the stars.*
> *It speaks in the empty spaces where no light shines.*
> *It is the one—whose mouth is fire.*
> > *This means it comes to burn all life.*
>
> *It is the one—whose breath is death.*
> > *This means it comes to whisper enmity between all things and peoples.*
>
> *It is the one—whose will is woe.*
> > *This means it comes as the destroyer of the world."*

The Chinese delegation rose as one. Only their shadows could be seen. They screamed at Daniel, "Myths and fears! Stories and weakness to cover the West's duplicity. You simply seek hegemony over us all!"

For a moment, it seemed as if the mutterings of other delegations would join in the chorus, but the three men by the End Times Tablet seemed to grow even greater in stature as did Daniel who stepped forward from the embrace of the strangers, his trance broken. The priest raised his arms and thundered, "Enough! You have seen. The End Times Tablet has engraved the message. It has been explained to you. Nothing more needs to be said except to decide what to do."

At that moment, the lights tripped back on. The three men were gone, though Daniel noticed that Shadrach, Meshach, and Abednego, dressed in normal clothes, were seated placidly behind Luca and Rebecca back at the security desk. As the assembly adjusted their eyes to the light, Daniel led his father off the dais and through the side door.

"Are you alright?" said Markoz to his son.

"I am, though it felt like I was walking in a dream."

"The carvings are real," said Markoz. "They're still engraved on the wall, and you explained what they revealed to the world. That's what prophets do. Perhaps it is right that our three visitors from the past connect you with their friend, the original Daniel."

"Dad, please," said Daniel, pleading with his father.

The elder Azar embraced his son, whispering in his ear, "The world is changing and strange things are happening. I don't think your part is done yet."

Confused and a little upset, Daniel made his way back to the security table where Luca and Rebecca looked at him worriedly.

His head was down, but he said softly, "I'm okay, really."

A hand reached out and fell on his shoulder. It was Abednego's, and the young man spoke to Daniel saying, "Now you begin to know what we have known for so long. It is a terrible burden to bear, but we will help you do so."

Daniel said nothing. King Henry was speaking and once he started paying attention to the monarch's words, he began hearing amazing things, though he wasn't sure if the delegates, so secular in their world view, would recognize how extraordinary the king's words were.

Canterbury was to be turned back over to the Catholic Church with its own archbishop, and the Bishop of York would now lead the Anglicans as the Primate of All England. The tall king, with his close-cropped red beard, stared intensely with his blue eyes at the crowd.

"This may sound insignificant to many of you delegates," said the king, "but I assure you it is not so. Let me tell you a story. Canterbury once held a shrine honoring a great saint who had been martyred by my predecessor with my same name. The saint was a man who cared for all people, rich or poor, weak or powerful. The moment he was killed, miracles were done in his name and a shrine was established. The Shrine of St. Thomas Becket was not just a place of healing and hope for the world, but the place of such wonders for many centuries. Millions came from around the world seeking a promise of peace, a place where men and women could dispel the darkness of their lives and embrace the Light. They found it, and the world was better for it. But often, the dark rises again to destroy the good that has begun to flourish.

"Another predecessor of mine, also with my same name, long ago destroyed that hope, sacked the shrine, and helped divide the secular from the sacred. That action only served to weaken the west and divided our soul from our mind, our head from our heart. I, King Henry IX, in concert with the Holy Roman Pontiff, act to rectify that terrible decision so that it will be a sign to all of you that governments, philosophies, and religion must unite in a grand union to oppose the threat that is at hand. For it will seek to divide us, destroy our hope, and attack our people. A war for our existence is coming. We cannot win this coming conflict simply on the battlefield, for that is not the only theater it will be fought in. Hearts and minds will be battled for as well, and we will be fodder for the Beast if the secular and sacred cannot find a way to act together."

President Oliver Putnam then rose and approached the podium. His words were simple and direct. "As much as I appreciate his majesty's insistence on a new alliance between might and morals, I am here to represent the armed strength that must go against this force which attacks us. I am not a particularly religious man, but I recognize the poverty of the human spirit that affects our world, so count me in on this effort.

"However, I do understand that civilization cannot endure on faith, hope, and love alone. Weapons of war and men and women of valor must stand against an enemy that will use any method to destroy us. Under the aegis of the United Nations, I propose a union of the world's armed forces, no matter how large or small. Our sole purpose shall be to put aside our differences, unite, and fight the invader, wherever it shows itself and in whatever form. Already, it has attempted to infiltrate our cities, sowing destruction and fear. And I believe it will continue …"

At that moment, the exit doors flew open, and in strode the figure of Guy Fawkes. He strutted in like a peacock, black cape flaring, cavalier hat sporting a waving ostrich plume. Using his sword as a cane, he pirouetted down the center aisle, tapping a delegate here on the shoulder, there on the head. He would have looked like a jester had he facial contortions to match his clownish behavior. But his face did not move, for the white mask with painted black eyebrows, nose and mouth and thin goatee made the figure look like a macabre mime. Not clownish at all, but a threatening caricature of terror. The energy of impending doom that reeked from his presence mixed with the redolent fear beginning to sweat through the pores of the delegates. Security immediately backed President Putnam away from the podium, but the delegates' attention was all on the figure of Guy Fawkes.

Fawkes had stopped midway down the central aisle and stood tapping his rapier on the floor. A voice spoke from the mask, saying, "Ah, I came too late for the sound and light show. The prophecy has already been carved. Did the little priest decipher it for you?"

Fawkes pressed the point of his sword into the throat of the French president sitting with his delegation. "What? Cat got your tongue, Excellency? No matter and no need to answer. Prophecies about the end of the world can be disconcerting. Besides, I am sure that *Monsignore* Azar did a credible job of explaining.

"But," he said, moving across the aisle and kneeling on one knee to face the President of the Congo, "it is so hard to convince the skeptical. That's why I'm here. To assure you of your doom."

A flash of blue light beamed out of Shadrach's ring finger to strike down Fawkes, but the figure simply batted it down with his sword. Tsking, Fawkes said, "Now, now, you Babylonian freak, don't be starting a holocaust here." The figure turned and tapped the cheek of the Israeli ambassador with the sword, "We've had enough of that in ages past, haven't we? However, you all must be convinced of the tablet's truth. So, I am here to help you listen."

Fawkes stopped for a moment to let a heavy silence settle over the Assembly Hall. "There, you should be hearing it soon. It shall first sound like the call of a crow far away, or the hooting of an owl high on the wind. But as it approaches, it shall be a sound of roaring beasts, a prelude of what is to come, and you shall be afraid, very afraid."

Daniel heard it first, and it sounded just like Fawkes described. Far away the crows were calling with owls hooting high in the wind. The sounds garbled as they came closer, combining to roar like beasts in the jungle. All it took was for the noise to grow and the delegates began to scream in terror.

That was bad enough, but then the windows in the lobby outside the hall shattered.

THE *GALLU*

Tuesday, March 23, Mid-morning, General Assembly, United Nations Complex, New York City

ANTOINE PETRIE WAS fishing off a concrete walkway on the bank of the East River just a ways down from the East 51 pedestrian walkway. Not the greatest place to fish, but there was a bit of green space, and he was up for the urban angling challenge. Hadn't caught a thing, which was surprising since it was so darkly murky this morning, what with the fog hanging all over the place.

Things were pretty quiet except for the sound of the nearby traffic, but Antoine heard the burbling starting out there in the water. Something was swimming, and it was the size of a huge dog, or even larger. Antoine squinted, trying to get some clarity through the fog. Squeezing his eyes tighter, he saw something slipping smoothly through the water, splashing surprisingly lightly as it came to the surface, crawling on all fours up onto the walkway. It turned toward him, and Antoine found himself choking back a scream.

Bigger than a small pony, it looked like a humanoid hyena, dappled skin shining wetly in the murky light, East River water droplets smacking the ground beneath the grotesque body. Antoine saw the head and he immediately thought of that werewolf movie he liked so much, *An American Werewolf In London,* because the skull of this thing was partly humanoid and then hyena-like with its jaw all jutting forward, spit or river water dripping from it. It was giggling like a hyena too, and, for a moment, it stood on its hind legs. Antoine saw that its front feet were like muscled arms with huge pointy-clawed hands. Its piss-yellow eyes gleamed over Antoine for a spell, giving him the heebie-jeebies as he looked.

"Holy shit," he whispered to himself, "that damn thing is going to come and eat me." He couldn't move, and just as he thought Mr. Hybrid-Hyena Man was going to bound over and jump him, the monster tilted its head the other way as if it heard something else in the water. It had.

Antoine heard it too. More splashing, slithering, and smacking. He saw other monsters just like the first coming ashore. Seven of them in all. He counted them twice, but they paid no attention to him. Seemed like they had something else on their minds. Funny thing was, as they moved their limbs, their bones crackled. Sounded like the screeching and crackling sounds the crows that usually bothered the places by the river liked to make. Annoyed Antoine like hell, usually. But the birds weren't here, and the monsters did the snapping and clacking, cawing and screeching for them. In fact, their screeching sounded like crazy owls hooting at nighttime, a sort of haunting laughter on the wind.

They all stood on their hind legs looking south towards the United Nations complex. Then they went back down on all fours for just a little spell. Antoine thought, as they dripped-dried, that they grew in stature, much like that werewolf creature in the movie he liked so much. That was a mean motherfucker, but he had to admit that the movie monster would be toast if it met up with one of these hyena things. They were truly badass. Antoine considered it was about time to be slinking away himself, but he needn't have worried.

The seven weren't thinking about him. He heard them hooting and clacking together and then deciding to run downriver towards the United Nations.

Should he call 911? Nah, he knew no one would believe him. He had the morning paper beside him and he caught the headline, *World Leaders Meet This Morning At UN—Crisis Over End Times Tablet.*

He reckoned that if those monsters were heading to the UN, the delegates were going to have a lot more to do than talking about the crisis.

Antoine Petrie was right. The leader of the things that had crawled out of the river set a straight path towards the complex. They didn't come in secretly at all. Noisy all the way, they announced their presence to whoever was nearby. And those too near were not ignored as Antoine had been. They were dispatched.

The seven leapt into the United Nations Visitors Plaza bounding past the jaguar/eagle sculptured monstrosity known as *The Guardian for International Peace and Security*. They looked like distant relatives of the stone beast. As they made their way toward the General Assembly Hall, they interrupted their yipping and yowling to rip apart any spectators near them. And there were many. Hundreds of observers had gathered on the plaza to witness the results of the debate inside the hall. Screaming, the crowds parted like the Red Sea as they saw the seven monsters approach them.

The carnage was ancillary violence for the seven. If someone was in the way, they had no difficulty beheading them with a snap of their jaws or disemboweling them on the spot, but the monsters did not go out of their way to hunt.

Making enough noise to wake the dead they had just dispatched, the things from the river paused outside the General Assembly Hall facing the security forces that had quickly massed to meet them. The NYPD commander of the SWAT team was momentarily confounded. Shoot, and civilians could be hurt. Hold fire, and the delegates could be compromised. But seven inhuman looking monsters from hell could help anyone make a decision, and the commander ordered his men to fire. He needn't have bothered. The bullets seemed to have no effect as the seven gazed at the General Assembly lobby windows and then picked the ones they intended to crash through. They simply leapt over the massed SWAT teams and shattered the glass with their dappled bodies.

Even above the yelling of the delegates, the crashing of windows could be heard in the General Assembly Hall. Rebecca thought the time was right and she pressed the lapel pin on her blazer. Ranbir, the Sikh avatar, appeared in the empty seat next to her. Leslie Richardson had reserved the extra place just in case the hologram was needed. She arched an eyebrow at Rebecca who said to her, "We need info. I don't know what that noise means."

"It means, Miss Becky," said Ranbir, "that the heavyweights are here to put a real hurt on all the delegates. Mr. Fawkes just seems to be observing." In fact, Fawkes was simply standing there, but as Ranbir spoke, Fawkes turned his head and stared at the avatar. "Good hearing," whispered Ranbir to the table.

The center doors to the General Assembly Hall crashed inward, and on all fours stepped in the largest of the seven things that had crawled out of the East River.

"My God!" said Daniel, "it's a …"

"*Gallus*," said Ranbir, finishing Daniel's sentence. "Have I ever told you all, that a *gallus* is a demon from the Babylonian version of hell, a water demon really in league with Enki, or Guy Fawkes as he is appearing now? By the way, the Arabs took that name *gallus* and translated it *ghul* which is where we get our word for 'ghoul'."

"Great," said Luca, "thanks for the myth note. It looks like the hyena version of the beast in *An American Werewolf In London*," not knowing that he was in sync with Antoine Petrie who, at that moment, was busily skedaddling himself the opposite way up along the East River.

"Not really, Captain," said Ranbir in his most professorial way. "A *gallus* prefers to walk on all fours but is bi-pedal as well. Possessed of immense strength, it is a flesh eater and blood drinker. More of a shape-shifter than a werewolf."

"And a *gallus* never travels alone," said Daniel. "There are seven major *gallu*, and they work together. Their leader is named Asgalu."

The moment Daniel spoke, the beast turned and looked at him. "What?" said Daniel, "do all these entities have super hearing or something like that?"

"No," said Shadrach, "but it does sense your presence."

Guy Fawkes grinned at Daniel, and Asgalu hooted three short howls. In answer, his six compatriots came barging into the hall. All of them raised themselves up on their hind legs, snapping and clacking their forearms and paws. They were easily eight feet tall. Why they stopped, Daniel wasn't sure, but they stood there, opening and closing their claws while sweeping their gaze across the room, looking at the upcoming lunch.

Fawkes spoke, "So here we are, among the best of the best the world has to offer. True, the advent of real terror is months from now, but we thought we'd soften you all up; give you a taste, so to speak, of what is coming your way."

Daniel leaned over and whispered to Luca, "Get the pope, president, and king into the green room with my father. Get Leslie and Rebecca to take the UN VIPs with you as well. The pope has his ring and can use it to protect you all in case we fail here."

The security team in place inside the General Assembly Hall chose that moment to open fire on the seven *gallu*. Daniel saw the *gallu* shrug off the bullets and swarm into the delegates' seating. It was an immediate massacre. Bodies were thrown into the air, some with limbs severed. Daniel saw the German president perish as the jaws of one of the monsters settled around his neck. Dozens were already dying. The Russian prime minister and all his delegation fell to one *gallus* who cut a swath of destruction through them.

Then, Daniel had an idea. He had practiced with his ring lately and found that he could do more things with it. He used it now to amplify his voice as he did during his prophecy, but he added a force of compulsion with it. He shouted over the destruction, "Asgalu! I name you. Hear me now!"

The *gallu* were ancient entities, birthed and given names back when names had real power. The leader of the *gallu* looked up in surprise. He paused, knowing that someone knew his name and had called out a challenge. For a moment, all the *gallu* paused the carnage and looked to their leader.

"Who speaks my name?" said the demon. "Who challenges me?"

"I do," said Daniel. "I know you and what you are. You reek of murder, mayhem, and magic. You come crawling up from your watery grave to do the bidding of your master." Here, Daniel waved his hand at Guy Fawkes, who doffed his hat and grandly bowed.

"No more shall die here today," continued Daniel.

"You, little man? You will stop us?" The *gallu* hooted and howled, cracking their limbs together.

"Myself and my friends." Shadrach, Meshach, and Abednego stood up and moved toward Daniel.

"Four of you," hooted Asgalu, "against seven. Poor odds."

"Well," sniffed Ranbir, "standing up at that moment, they have me too." He thrust his palm at the smallest *gallus*, and a laser shot out, smashing into the beast and knocking him through an exit door.

"Guess you're recovered, huh?" said Luca to the avatar. "That's not going to go over well with the hounds of hell. I think now's a good time for Leslie, Rebecca, and me to get the guests of honor into the back room like Daniel said."

Guy Fawkes snapped his head around and saw his *gallus* flung through the doors. He turned to Daniel and his friends, pointed his rapier, saying, "You've interfered enough. Kill them," he said to Asgalu, "and then come back and kill the rest in this hall. The one whose mouth is fire, whose breath is death, whose will is woe, needs to make a statement. Let death reign here so that the world will know what is coming."

The seven *gallu* screamed and charged, leaping over delegates and stomping down the aisles toward Daniel, Ranbir, and the three brothers. A primal scream ripped through Daniel's mouth as he and his friends moved forward to meet the approaching monsters.

Daniel's ring blasted Asgalu in the torso, throwing him back fifteen feet. He knew he couldn't allow the thing to lay a hand on him. He'd be ripped to shreds. Ranbir had no such worry. Though he could have blasted a *gallus* with his laser again, he chose to smash into the nearest one and take him down. Thanks to the upgrades Bart had given him, he was able to dematerialize the parts of his holographic body the *gallus* tried to grasp while punching its snout with his fists. The three brothers engaged the other five as one, blasting them methodically with blue fire from their rings. They were surprisingly effective. Slowly, but surely, Daniel and his friends pushed the fiends back toward the exits.

The smell of blood from the carnage outside permeated the lobby gagging Daniel. Even as he used the force pent up in the ring to batter Asgalu, he was appalled at the damage the *gallu* had already done. He redoubled his efforts, shouting to the brothers and Ranbir to herd the demons out of the building.

By this time, the shocked and injured crowds of observers had been led away from the Visitors Plaza, so, that when the three brothers blasted five *gallu* back out of the General Assembly Hall, they were pretty much all alone with them, except for the dead bodies that littered the square.

Daniel's heart nearly stopped when he saw all the dead. A chill wind rippled his cassock in the air as the fog wisped around it. Asgalu had landed on his side from the blow Daniel had used to thrust him out of the building. The beast snarled and charged again on all fours, saliva whipping from his mouth, fangs seeming to grow longer.

In the few moments of the battle, Daniel had discovered something about the *gallu*. They worked on fear and terror, and though physically powerful, they had no particular supernatural gifts except for shape-shifting. On second thought, that was probably power enough. They were eaters of the dead, carrion hunters of the underworld, immensely strong and powerful. All they needed was terror to cower any foe they chanced upon.

He knew they were the servants of Enki. The mythology of Babylonia testified to that. For a moment, his gut churned as he wondered where Enki's Guy Fawkes creation was, and why the godling thought to veil himself in that guise on this day. But Daniel had to trust Luca, Rebecca, and Leslie. Protection of his uncle and the leaders of the free world rested totally with them at the moment.

His attention was arrested again by the charging Asgalu. It was microseconds in his mind, but he felt a rage building up in him and he found he could feed it into his ring. His finger and then his right hand pulsed, and he wondered if this was what it felt like to hold Thor's hammer, or Charlemagne's sword, or Arthur's Excalibur. Didn't really matter. He knew he was a weapon now. His sadness at all the death and destruction, his rage at the present and coming attack on humanity fed the cry that burst from his mouth as he blasted Asgalu with blue fire, again and again, pushing him back across the stone pavement. Concrete benches flew across the plaza as the demon smashed into them. So constant was Daniel's barrage that Asgalu could not counter-attack.

With a tremendous force of effort, the *gallus* stood up against the fire, roared his pain, and charged again. It hit Daniel hard but did not knock him down. This time Daniel grappled with the beast, and he felt the claws of the *gallus* rake across his back. He screamed in pain and willed the ring to fill his body with fire and destroy the demon. Daniel burst into flame, blue fire rippling throughout his body. Unburned, he watched the boiling blaze, almost like Greek fire, cling to the *gallus* and envelope it with the heat of a forge. Daniel, possessing a strength he didn't know he had, picked up the beast and threw him across the plaza.

Asgalu smashed into the sculptured *International Guardian of Peace and Security* and shattered the stone into splinters as the demon exploded in a conflagration of flame. Daniel fell on the ground, flickers of flame dying over his body. His cassock was intact except for the rips on his back where the claws of the *gallus* had pierced, but he felt no pain, figuring that the ring had already cauterized and healed his wounds.

Looking around, he saw his friends finishing off their own enemies. Ranbir had dispatched his demon similarly to Daniel by burning it to death with laser fire.

The brothers, however, clearly had fought such denizens of hell before. But they were outnumbered. They corralled their five opponents and circled them with a ring of fire, gradually closing it tighter and tighter. One of the larger *gallu*, risked severe burns by punching and pummeling his fists against the barrier. Either his strength worked, or the brothers faltered in their concentration. Daniel saw the largest *gallu* break outside the circle of fire and grab Shadrach by the neck. Hurtling across the plaza came Grigio. Where he had been until now, Daniel couldn't figure out. But he breathed a sigh of relief as the big dog tackled the demon, ripping out his throat. Shadrach stumbled to his feet and gave his strength to the faltering fire barrier. Anger at the presence of these monsters flared among the brothers, and they smacked the scorching circle closed, constricting it until the five *gallu* combusted in an explosion of flame.

Daniel looked around. He saw the shattered statue and, looking up, saw that many of the windows of the Secretariat skyscraper and the other nearby buildings of the complex had broken and crashed to the ground during the melee. Then, he remembered his dream of carnage in the complex. Only, now it had come true. So many dead; so many injured. The security forces were creeping back into the plaza, and the SWAT commander looked at the charred tile and battered bodies all around him.

"Are they gone?" he asked Daniel.

"For now," said Daniel.

"Did you send them back to hell?" questioned the commander.

"We did, and let's hope they stay there a long time."

Daniel suddenly remembered that they were hardly done with the danger. "Come on," he yelled to his friends. "Back to the green room."

Grigio whined and looked back from where he came. Clearly, thought Daniel, the dog had places to go and things to do. "Go on," he said. "Do what you need to do, but come back soon." The dog turned and went running in the opposite direction. In his mind, Daniel wished his companion well, but to the avatar and the brothers, he said, "We have to go. They are in trouble back there. Guy Fawkes is still alive."

WHY GUY?

Wednesday, Late Morning, March 23, General Assembly Hall, UN Complex

"WOULD YOU LOOK at that!" said Guy Fawkes, peering out the glass doors of the General Assembly. "Looks like I'm going to have to toughen up my henchmen just a little bit more. Ah, no matter," he sniffed, rubbing a gloved hand along his masked nose. He strode back to the center aisle and stopped.

"You're leaking," said a nervous delegate from the Netherlands, pointing to a puddle around Fawkes's boots.

"Ah, so I am, you cretin," snapped Fawkes, bringing back his sword to lop off the fool's head. But then he paused. "You are a waste, and your death will have to wait. When I come back as I truly am, you'll see water as you've never seen it, and your tiny little country will be under the sea where it truly belongs."

Fawkes sniffed loudly and strode away up toward the rostrum. Seeing that his quarry was gone, he detoured to the side door behind the gold wall with the huge UN symbol hanging from it.

"Now, where has that dreadful king gotten to?" he said.

Luca and Rebecca had placed the remaining security team in positions outside the Green Room, and they had barricaded the entrance from inside. Luca felt that Daniel, Ranbir, and the brothers would be able to handle the *gallu*, but he was dead sure that Guy Fawkes would try to break into the Green Room. President, king, and pope were irresistible bait to the fey creature from hell. Luca remembered Fontevraud and swallowed hard. Fawkes was not to be underestimated.

"Feckin' ghouls," muttered Luca.

Rebecca heard him clearly and cocked and eyebrow. "Feckin'? Feckin'! You can't even say the right word?" She laughed.

Luca blushed. "Heard the pope say that the other day when he couldn't get a door in the apartments open. He doesn't like to swear so I figure it was an Irish euphemism."

"Feckin'," said Rebecca. "It just doesn't have the same visceral feeling as the regular English word."

"You tell that to the pontiff," said Luca.

"Tell him what?" said the pope, coming into the conversation.

"Nothing, Your Holiness," said Luca, blushing again. "We can expect Guy Fawkes to try to break in here."

"Yes," said the king, joining the three. "Just exactly who is he, really?"

"Well," said the pope, "he's the one responsible for carrying out the assassinations of the Archbishop of Canterbury and the Cardinal of Westminster."

"But he can't be Fawkes, himself. I mean, the man has been dead for over 400 years."

"Nothing with the threat we face is ever what it seems," said the pope. "I know you understand this, Henry—if I may call you that. You can call me Patrick if you'd like, just not Paddy—always hated that moniker."

The king smiled.

"As I was saying," continued the pope, "dead though the real Fawkes may be, the power that is against us has thought it wise to have a simulacrum, a poseur, as it were, become him and take on all the connotations of the old Fawkes and the modern public's perception of him as a terrorist."

"I hardly think some old English disgruntled Catholic is going to strike fear in the hearts of the rest of the world," said the king.

"I don't know," said President Putnam from across the room. "He seems to have done a pretty good job just now out in the General Assembly Hall."

President of the General Assembly, James McCoy, the rabid Canadian socialist who had gotten himself elected to the post, snarled at Putnam. Fiery red cheeks blossomed even more in his anger. "You idiots have brought down disaster upon us. The things you said; the audacious plan you've invented. The Chinese and their allies in the third world are up in arms, and that terrorist fop that walked in threatening to kill people right and left … you know more than you are admitting, and whatever it is, it is leading us to the exact catastrophe of which you fear. Idiots!"

"We do know more," said the pontiff, "but your accusations aren't inspiring us to give you more information."

"Seriously, Your Holiness," said Secretary-General Rasu, "I thought it was a good idea to have you speak. I thought it would calm the world, but with what has happened …"

"You all have only made it worse," said McCoy.

"No," said Putnam, "we've just baited the bear and made him come out roaring. It's good for the delegates to see the horror that we are facing."

"If I may," said the pope, "King Henry raises an excellent question of why we have a Guy Fawkes imposter out there. Remember where this current threat began—in Canterbury, where, through the course of several centuries, a serious fight has occurred over the place of the sacred and the secular in public life. The two have seldom lived together in peace. They represent the constant war between the heart and mind of humanity, the soul and the intellect.

"There was a time," continued the pontiff, "when England ruled the world, and this particular fight was carried on throughout Europe and even into the countries that now make up the developing nations. It's an old conflict with a modern face. For instance, the president of China still refuses to let me visit because such a state affair would give legitimacy to the millions of Christians in his land and, in his view, set up alternate power positions. The battle between St. Thomas Becket and His Majesty's predecessor may have taken place upon England's pastures green centuries ago, but Becket's murder had worldwide meaning, and still does. The ancient struggle is constantly played out, again and again."

"I don't see how," said Basu. "A personality clash between a bishop and a king so long ago—you can't seriously think such a thing would still have repercussions today."

The pope placed his hand on the shoulder of the king as he passed by to stand before the Secretary-General and said, "The names have been forgotten by most, but the reality still exists. Is there room for the spiritual in modern life? All it takes is a little gunpowder to make that conflict real again. Guy Fawkes represents that flashpoint which has become more and more an anxious crisis present in the gut of human beings.

"Did you see how that thing dressed?" continued the pope. "Luca is the movie expert here, and I'm sure he could wax eloquent over how Fawkes's costume is iconic, thanks to the films of recent years that have used that persona to dredge up fear in people's hearts and minds. The mask that mimics the now dead face of a real person from long ago, strikes absolute terror into people's souls. Just witness what happened in the hall. Fawkes represents chaos, not one faction over the other, and seeks to exploit the ever-present tension between all that is worldly and all that is holy. His presence here today confirmed just that. The terrorist doesn't care which side wins as long as anarchy is the ultimate victor."

Turning his head to James McCoy, the pope said, "And you, sir, are a fool if you think you can placate such a force. That thing in the Guy Fawkes regalia will tear you apart as much as it would any of us."

The pope had hardly finished when screaming was heard beyond the door. Shots rang out, but the anguished cries of people in pain were louder. When all was silent, Leslie Richardson looked at the barricaded entrance to the room.

"Luca and Rebecca, get them back from the entrance! Now! Ranbir, front and center before the door." she cried.

"Yes, ma'am!" said the red-turbaned Sikh hologram. Rebecca and Luca grabbed the king and the pope whilst Leslie took Putnam by the arm and pulled him away. For a moment, they all stood silent in a seemingly infinite pause, waiting for something to happen.

With a bang, the door burst in, effortlessly, the piled-up furniture simply thrust aside. Guy Fawkes strolled through, laughing gently. "And here they are, the best of the leaders of the free world—the patronizingly pious pope, the pugnacious and almost Falstaffian king, and the power president ready to use the might of the world against what is coming. How convenient for me. And you," he said to Ranbir, "I have discovered which electrical grid powers you. I may not be able to hurt you, but I can cut off the force that gives you energy." Enki gently tapped his finger on Ranbir's shoulder and the avatar fell like a stone and winked out of existence. Enki looked over at the UN representatives. "Now, what shall I ever do with you?"

"We're not with them," said James McCoy. "The UN never takes just one side."

"Well, I'm with them," said Secretary-General Basu to Fawkes. "They represent the last best hope from the chaos that's approaching; the chaos that you seem intent on causing."

Fawkes began to clap his hands, "Most noble, most heartening, most challenging." Then, he paused. "Ah," he said, "where did I leave my sword?" A finger touched his eye as he bowed. "Don't go anywhere, I'll be right back."

He sauntered out the door. They heard a laugh as he cried, "There it is! I knew I left it somewhere." A scream echoed out in the hallway. Fawkes dashed back in. "I left it with one of your guards, or, rather, in one of your guards. Forgetful of me."

Then, Fawkes stepped forward and twirled the point of his rapier. "I need it now, because I don't need any of you. You have become ... inconvenient." He let out a long sigh.

Pope Patrick stretched out his hand and fired off his ring. A dome of blue surrounded everyone and projected a barrier between them and Fawkes.

Fawkes tsked. "I forgot the damnable ring you wear. One of those bested me not long ago, saving this wretched captain's life," he said, pointing at Luca. "I'm working a way around it though. Want to see?" He touched the tip of his sword to the barrier and a flash of fire shot up in the air. "Not that way, I suppose." He began walking around, playfully stretching out now one hand, then the other, almost touching the barrier.

All of them wondered when Fawkes would charge the force field and use some kind of power against it. It was a moot point, because at that moment, James McCoy, President of the UN General Assembly, chose to lose his composure. He still clutched in his hand the Assembly gavel, and now he rushed the pontiff, lifted up the gavel, and struck the pope on the head. At any other time, it would have been a killing blow. But Luca saw a subdued blue flash as the hammer struck the pope's skull. The pontiff crumpled to the floor, but Luca guessed he wasn't dead. The ring had somehow shielded him from a fatal strike.

None the less, the blue dome and barrier snapped off, the ring no longer controlled by the consciousness of the pontiff, leaving the group at the mercy of the terrorist.

James McCoy approached Fawkes, his arms wide. "Pay no attention to them. The world wants peace, not conflict. It was their fear that made them oppose you and speak today before the delegates. I can help you. I can speak to the world."

"You miserable fool," snapped the Secretary-General. "We need to stand as one. You betray humanity!"

McCoy stood, arms akimbo, pleading with Fawkes, and the terrorist looked at him blankly. Then, without a word, the terrorist ran the President of the UN General Assembly through with the sword. Like a deflated balloon, McCoy hissed out his last breath and collapsed at the feet of Fawkes.

"Nice try," said Fawkes, "but I don't want peace. I rather like the chaos I've caused. Now, where was I? Oh yes, about to dispatch the lot of you. Shall I take you one at a time enjoying the moment, or do you prefer I execute you like I did the guards, quickly and without remorse?"

The figure touched his mouth with a gloved hand as if deliberating. Luca and Rebecca readied themselves to leap at Fawkes, but just then, a blue fire flashed out from the pope's body and crashed into Fawkes. The pope raised himself up on his knees and blasted Fawkes again. Luca saw the pope gain his feet and then realized what the pontiff was going to do. Luca had boxed with the pontiff in the Swiss Guard gym. He had heard the stories of the pontiff's youth and how good he was in the ring. He experienced firsthand that the pope had not slowed down much in his middle years. Luca had been well-thrashed. But this was not going to be boxing. Instead, the pope stood and with his right fist, punched the air in front of Fawkes. A blue force—Luca thought it actually looked like a fist—smashed into the masked face of Fawkes. The mask flew off and smacked against the wall as Fawkes's body hit the ground.

"Stay back!" said the pope as he approached the prone figure, right hand blazing in blue fire. He knelt on the chest of Fawkes and placed the energy-pulsing hand on whatever beat in the place of Fawkes's heart. His kneeling figure obscured the true face of the terrorist and the pope whispered to it, "I know you, Enki, who you are, what you do, and what you are trying to accomplish. I cannot kill you, but maybe I can send you back to the hell from which you came."

The pope raised his hand to make the Sign of the Cross, but Enki threw the pontiff off and made for the door. Unfortunately for him, Daniel and his friends arrived at the same time. No words were wasted. The rings from Daniel and the brothers flared. But Enki didn't die. The fire surrounded him, but, unlike the *gallu*, the godling didn't combust or disappear. Instead, Enki stood, in obvious pain, his gills gasping, seaweed dreadlocks dripping, and his fish mouth gulping.

Enki managed to croak out a challenge. "Twice you have bested me. But it matters little. I am the Lord of Chaos, and I have succeeded this day in terrorizing the world if not killing you. When I return, we will resume what has been started, and your kind will be blotted from the face of the earth."

Suddenly, it was like all the air around the creature was sucked into itself and a blackness grew to encompass Enki. As if water was rushing in to fill an empty space, the darkness collapsed upon itself, taking Enki with it. With the sound of waves smashing against rocks, the Babylonian godling disappeared.

"He is a talker," said Luca, "and a twisted Shakespearean narcissist. Wished he just would've died. Although, I must admit the melting into the black hole was very Wicked Witch of the West-like. What a copy-cat. Can't even think of a new way to disappear."

"Wish you would've killed him, Your Holiness," said Rebecca.

"Ah," said the pontiff with a sly grin, "then I would have to go to confession. However, there's an old saying, 'Better to ask for forgiveness than permission.' Seriously though, the next time you see this thing, do not speak to it; do not hesitate. Try with all your might to destroy it. Because that's what the good guys do—and we are them."

A gasping sound was heard behind them, and they turned to see Secretary-General Basu clutching his heart. The stress and strain had been too much. Rebecca, in the absence of Isaac, was the go-to member of the team who knew CPR so she was at his side in moments, while Leslie called for an ambulance.

"It's been a dark day," said the king clasping the hand of the Secretary-General. "I fear many have died; don't you dare die on us as well." The king helped move Basu to a corner where Rebecca could continue her care of him.

"Many of the delegates perished," said Daniel, "but the loss of life among the guards and the spectators outside was greater. We took a beating here today. It's going to make the surviving delegates wonder if we can succeed in protecting the world."

"That's why we begin now," said President Putnam. "We need to get the Secretary-General through this health crisis. His loyalty here was extraordinary, and we will need him in the coming days. As for me, I'm not wasting any time. I'll be talking to governments tonight, twisting arms less than gently for their help."

"I believe I shall have great news for all of you tomorrow," said King Henry. "I fly back tonight and will have something to say to the world by mid-morning."

"I have a splitting headache," said the pontiff, wiping a smear of blood from his forehead. "First time anyone has managed to gavel me into silence. I'm going to have to get Shadrach, Meshach, and Abednego to give me a crash course in this ring. It stopped the death strike of that gavel, but, as you could see, I felt it and was … a little indisposed for a moment. Can't let that happen again."

Shadrach said, "Daniel has learned much in the past weeks on how the rings work. Your duties have kept you from learning his lessons. It is imperative that you give us time to teach you. You are fortunate you weren't killed."

"I'm lucky I was once a boxer and learned how to take a beating," smiled the pope. "But point taken. Starting tomorrow—lessons for the Irishman."

"It's got to be chaos out there in the Hall. And I've got an interview to do with Sky News and the BBC," said Daniel.

"Lucky you," laughed King Henry. "The only media that makes that Guy Fawkes character look like a pushover."

"Rebecca and I will go with you," said Luca, watching her approach. The paramedics had arrived and were attending the stricken Secretary-General.

"So will Ranbir," said Rebecca, "but invisibly, back in my lapel pin." The avatar had briefly re-appeared, his connection with the power grid re-established. Sitting up on the floor, he rubbed his head as if he had a concussion.

Hearing Rebecca, Ranbir grimaced at the thought of being deactivated again. "As you wish, Becky-san. I need some aspirin anyway." He obediently blinked out of existence.

They all checked on Secretary-General Basu. The paramedics had arrived and had stabilized him. The EMT in charge said his EKG looked good, that perhaps it was not a full heart attack after all. The Secretary-General was conscious and accepted the well-wishes of everyone. But as the pope leaned over to bless him, Basu grabbed his hand, "I am not of your faith, but what you have said and done here today will not be forgotten. I shall make sure the world remembers. All of you represent the last, best hope for humanity. I've seen 'Oumuamua arcing through the skies through our own telescopes. I agree with the need for total unity to defeat this threat. And I will fight against those of our own kind who seek to do the enemy's work by dividing us. You have my word."

"And you have my blessing," said the pope with a smile, "and my thanks."

***

The delegates had fled the hall as had the spectators in the guest seats. The media was mopping up with a few interviews, but in the shadows stood John Nance. For a moment, he watched Msgr. Daniel Azar begin his interview with Sky and the BBC News. He had seen most everything that had occurred, and as he walked out the doors, past the paramedics picking up the wounded and the dead, past the shattered anamorphic sculpture of *The International Guardian for Peace and Security*, now a mess of rubble on the ground, he was not impressed by Enki's actions this morning.

True, the godling had caused great terror which would certainly have a ripple effect over the coming days, but Enki's *gallu* had been defeated, and Enki, himself, checkmated at last, or so it seemed. The pope lived, as did the president and the king. Nance felt a little distance would be necessary for a while till his confidence in his associates was restored. Perhaps a yacht excursion to the South Pacific.

He needed to think about such loose cannons as Marduk and Enki. Nance was beginning to understand why whatever beings they actually were had failed to completely destroy humanity so long ago. They were impulsive and arrogant. He knew he was only dealing with the Junior Varsity team. Whatever was on 'Oumuamua was far more powerful. But he had expected more. These entities were mercurial and impatient. That led to serious mistakes and, perhaps, ultimate failure in their mission. He needed to do some thinking. A walk along the East River to where the *gallu* surfaced might clear his head. As he left the UN complex, he didn't notice a ghostly canine detach itself from the rubble of the plaza and follow him.

Meanwhile, at the very moment Enki disappeared, back in a hospital in Rome, Miss Jenny Wren sat up suddenly in her bed, screaming.

AN INFESTATION GROWS

Tuesday Late Morning, March 23, Gemelli Hospital, Rome

NURSING SUPERVISOR GEMMA Tortelli heard the scream from the patient in room 434. She had been making rounds and was sitting for a moment at the nursing station chatting with the main floor nurse. Gemma had heard about the elfin patient, barely 80 lbs., whose illness had garnered the attention of the pope. Whispers about exorcism were bandied about the hospital, but she didn't hold to that nonsense. Not that she wasn't a good Catholic. It was simply that years of nursing experience had caused her to always look for the natural explanation. Nonetheless, she hurried to the bedside of the patient everyone was calling Miss Jenny Wren.

The young woman was sitting straight up in her bed, clutching and wringing her hands. She stared at the upper corner of her room, and, when Gemma entered, the nurse could hear her repeating over and over, "They're coming! O God, they're coming!"

Gemma and the floor nurse tried to ease her back down onto her pillow, but Miss Jenny Wren was having none of that. With a strength that belied her size and condition, she grasped both Gemma's and the floor nurse's arms.

"You must believe me!" she said, gasping out the words. "Please, get the pope. He will know what to do."

Gemma was not a young woman anymore, and she was beginning to notice with her patients that her grandmotherly ways were very helpful at calming worried souls. She stroked Miss Jenny Wren's hair, and as she smoothed the tangled brown curls, she soothed, "There, there, my dear, we can't always bother the Holy Father now, can we?"

"But we must!" she said. "He needs to know."

"Know what, exactly?" said Gemma.

The young woman looked at her with hardened eyes, "I can't tell you that. He wouldn't want me to."

"Perhaps," interjected the floor nurse, "we could get your friend, Ben, up here and you could tell him. He left his number in case he was needed."

"No!" said the woman, fear like an electric current running through her face. "He's not himself anymore. He's not who he says he is. Please, don't bring him here."

"Miss Jenny," said Gemma, "he brought you here. I'm sure he would want to know you aren't feeling yourself."

"No! I told you! Bring him here and you will all die!" She said the words with such vehemence that both nurses took a step back.

Gemma's mind was moving rapidly. She needed to get Dr. Rappini back here. He wasn't due till afternoon rounds, but it was clear that this young lady was going to need treatment before that. Then she remembered a card she had stuck behind her lanyard identification badge. One of the nurses had given it to her the night Miss Jenny Wren had been brought in. Gemma had just missed the pope's visit, and the assisting nurse had brought her up to speed and given her the card.

She took it out and looked at it. Imprinted with the emblem of the Swiss Guard, it had the names of Corporal Mattias Kurz and

Corporal Josiah Hindermas on it, along with a telephone number. Written on the back was a signed note from the pope himself, "Call these men if her condition warrants it."

"Well," she thought, "at least I won't have to call the pope himself." She turned back to the young woman and said with all the matronly kindness she could muster, "If you lay back down and let this nurse sit with you, I will make a call. The pope has left word that his associates are to come immediately if you need them. Will that be satisfactory?"

Miss Jenny Wren flopped back down on her pillow and sighed, "Please call now. Tell them to hurry! They're coming."

Gemma nodded to the nurse who took the young woman's hand. She excused herself to make the call, thinking on her way back to the nurse's desk that Miss Jenny Wren was a hopeless case and she sure hoped the Swiss Guard knew what they were getting into.

The young woman bit her lips, darted her eyes, and started every time an unusual sound came from the hallway. The nurse kept stroking her hand and saying words of comfort to her.

Of course, none of the three could know that Ben was shuffling through the car park at that moment with the same homeless girls that had accompanied him when Miss Jenny Wren had been brought to the hospital the previous week. He and his compatriots were looking the worse for wear. Their scruffy homeless pants and shirts looked even more tattered and dirty. Their eyes weren't vacant, but the pupils were much larger. An intelligence was behind them, but it wasn't human. It was as if it needed more vision to see. People unconsciously veered away from them. Ordinary folks didn't want to react with the homeless anyway, but this new avoidance was visceral, not needing conscious intent. Something was wrong with Ben and his friends.

As Ben and company stopped for a moment and looked up at the Gemelli hospital toward the window behind which Miss Jenny

Wren lay, Josiah and Mattias were picking up Abby and Fr. Salvatore at the Vatican, bundling them into an unmarked car. It was Mattias' idea to take the two. The nurse supervisor had said the woman's doctor would not be available till the late afternoon, so Dr. Duchon would be a welcome addition. She might be primarily a scientist now, but Mattias knew her record as a physician was stellar. She could be useful. And, of course, Fr. Salvatore would be indispensable if the problem with the young woman had anything to do with the possession that had afflicted her the previous week.

It took only minutes for the four of them to arrive at the Gemelli Hospital, but it was minutes too long for Miss Jenny Wren and the nurse who sat by her side.

Ben and crew had already entered the hospital and signed in as guest visitors. The receptionist wrinkled her nose at the smell, but other than their shabby condition she could find no reason to prohibit them. She nodded at security to keep an eye on them, but Ben disarmed her with a smile. Had she looked more closely it would have appeared to her that the smile was simply pasted on, but the words were the right ones, "We'll be just a few minutes," he said. "I know that Miss Jenny Wren needs her rest."

Josiah, Mattias, Abby and the priest entered shortly after. They notified the receptionist who they were going to see. She said, "Well, that lady is most popular. She just had some friends come in to see her." She looked around and then whispered low so no one else could hear, "You know, some of those others that hang around the Termini Station." Though Abby and Fr. Salvatore did not know what that meant, a shudder of fear went through the Swiss Guard. If it should be Ben that was one of the guests, well, they thought, Ben wasn't really himself any more. The young woman could be in deep trouble.

Mattias took Abby's hand and rushed with her to the elevator while Josiah pushed the priest along.

"What's wrong?" said Abby. The Guard had not briefed the doctor or the priest on Miss Jenny Wren's friends. They simply hadn't thought to.

"The visitors," said Josiah, "I think there may be a problem with them. We told you what we saw in the underground tunnels beneath the Baths of Diocletian. Ben was there, and he is one of her friends. But Ben had been possessed by something. When we took refuge in the church, Ben and a bunch of crazy zombie-like associates were with him."

"Zombie-like?" said Fr. Salvatore who had heard the conversation. "What in the world do you mean?"

Mattias pushed the priest to go faster. When they got to the elevator, the doors opened immediately and the elevator was empty. Thank God, thought Mattias. Then, he answered the priest, "If Luca was here, he'd explain it better. He'd say they looked like the walking dead from that American television program. Have you ever seen it?" Both Abby and the priest shook their heads. "Well, I have and I've seen these guys as well. Scary as hell. Whatever people they once were, they aren't any more."

At that moment, the elevator doors opened and screams could be heard down the hall. Nurses were yelling and running to shut patient room doors, but Josiah could see that one door was open and a bare bloody arm was sticking out of the entry way. He and Mattias drew their pistols and began running.

Getting to the doorway, they each took in the horrible sight. The attending nurse had been dragged to the doorway. The sheet of blood from the bed to the body proved that. A cut across her neck plus the vacant eyes told them she was dead. Yet blood was still pumping from her severed throat. Whatever had happened had just occurred. Mattias looked to see Ben, with a knife raised high, standing over the prone figure of Miss Jenny Wren who was screaming loudly. They heard him say, "Jenny, Jenny, birdie fine, what have you told the pope this time?"

Like a perverted Greek chorus, the three girls with him on the other side of the bed leaned over and said in unison, "Jenny, Jenny, birdie sweet, shouldn't have talked to the pope last week."

Abby and Fr. Salvatore were at the doorway, stunned by what they saw and unable to make any sense of what they heard. They saw the knife flash downward toward the young woman's body, but it was Josiah's bullet that struck first, a clean torso shot that propelled Ben's body backward and caused the knife to clatter to the floor. The gun sounded like a canon within the confines of the room, and Abby and the priest shouted in pain, hands up to ears.

Mattias trained his gun on the girls while Josiah moved toward Ben. "Back against the wall, ladies," said Mattias, but the three only giggled, one of them wiping a bit of drool coming down the side of her mouth.

Mattias motioned for them to move and waved the pistol threateningly. They backed away towards the wall. "Good, good," said the Guard. "You may be something other than human, but those bodies that clothe you will not shield you from bullets. Just look at Ben there."

Josiah had reached Ben who had fallen to the floor. Blood was pumping out of his chest. The shot had been true. It had hit an artery close to the heart.

"Let me help him," said Abby. "Maybe we can still save him."

"Stay away," said Josiah, "he is not himself."

"I am myself," said whatever possessed Ben, "and I shall rip you all to pieces."

Josiah backed up, gun still pointed at Ben as the young man grabbed the bed rail and began to haul himself up. He paused and looked at Josiah, smiling as blood bubbled from his mouth. "All of you are too late," he said. "We came for this wretch but only to make her one of us again. I told the Master not to reward her like this, that she should be punished, but he wanted her. He wanted her from the first, and he shall have her." Ben raised himself higher onto his knees and said, "There is nothing you or that religious pontificator can do to stop us. We are too many. What was it one of my cousins, still burning merrily in hell, used to say? Ah yes, he used to say, 'We are legion.' And we are. Already we are on the move to the cities that remain uninfested."

"Is Ben still in there?" said Josiah quietly.

The man smiled, "Not much of him left. I've been devouring him slowly and, I might add, tastefully."

Ben climbed up to his feet and made to take a step forward.

"Come no closer, or I'll shoot you where you stand."

Ben gargled a laugh as blood spurted from his chest wound. "Seems like you've done enough damage already. I'll be gone, but there will be others. Take them girls."

As he fell in his death throes, the man who had been Ben looked across the bed and nodded to the three against the wall. His eyes closed as he slipped to the floor.

Fr. Salvatore had been blessing the body of the assisting nurse, but as Ben fell, he got up to go to his side. He never made it across the room. One of the girls leapt at Mattias, who fired his gun striking her in the shoulder. She still managed to crash into him.

The other two went for the doctor and the priest. Josiah managed to get Abby behind him and squared off to meet the rushing woman. However, the last girl also leapt and was able to put her hands around the priest's throat. Fr. Salvatore felt the nails cutting into his skin, but that was nothing compared to the pressure this girl was able to impress upon his neck. He felt like he was in a vice. She bent down to him, her red lips brushing his ear.

"I know who you are, Judas," she said.

The priest choked out, "What do you mean?"

She laughed and whispered again, flecks of spit against his ear. "You betray the one you serve, and the one I serve tells me to take you and make you one of us."

"Please," he said, "please don't do that." No one else could hear his words, she had so choked off his breath. Flecks of light were spinning in his eyes as consciousness threatened to leave him. Then he heard three shots. Immediately he felt something warm over his face, and he tasted blood. Josiah had shot the woman attacking the priest in the head, as well as the one that wanted Abby. At the same time, Mattias had thrown himself away from his attacker and headshot her as well.

For a moment, there was silence as the gunfire echoed away. Then Abby sobbed, "Did you have to kill them? They were just young women."

"Not anymore, they weren't," said Josiah, holstering his gun.

"I'm so sorry doctor," said Mattias, "but as we told you, we've come across things like this before. Any humanity they once had is gone. Had the pope not seen Miss Jenny Wren as early as he did, she would have permanently fallen into darkness as well."

At that moment, the young woman on the bed sat up, her eyes clear for the first time in days. She looked at the destruction around the room. "Are they … are they dead?"

"They are gone, Miss Jenny, said Mattias. "What you see here are not your friends. Your friends left long ago. These were things that sought to destroy you. I am so sorry."

Fr. Salvatore was rising off the floor, rubbing his neck. "They were demons, that's what they were."

"I guess you could call them that," said Josiah, "but they were demons with a purpose. What we saw beneath the Baths of Caracalla the other day has grown. They are like a hive now in the bowels of this city, and I fear they are the same in other cities as well. We need to tell the pope. He's due back here later this afternoon."

A strong knock sounded at the door. It was Gemma, the nursing supervisor. She had heard what was said. In fact, she had heard much of the altercation from outside in the hall. She had little time for supernatural explanations. These people were crazy, obsessed with Miss Jenny Wren. There would be a logical explanation. But she knew evil when she saw it, and it had been present in the room.

"I'll need to take the patient out of the room," she said in her most authoritative nursing voice.

"Of course," said Abby. "Let's you and I take her to another room where I can examine her."

Josiah and Mattias helped maneuver the bed around the blood and bodies as the two women took Miss Jenny Wren out of the room. Josiah expected her to go into hysterics, but she was calm and looked back at him and Mattias. "Thank you," was all she said, as she was wheeled out of the room.

Fr. Salvatore stumbled out as well, unhurt except for a sore neck, and followed Abby and the nurse, relieved that no one seemed to have heard what that crazy girl had attacked him had said.

"Are you hurt?" said Josiah to Mattias. "After all, you were assaulted by a woman, a very small woman."

"It was a demon, you misogynistic cretin," sniffed Mattias. "I had things perfectly under control. Even under that onslaught, I remained unharmed."

Josiah laughed and embraced his friend. Arm around Mattias's neck, he said, "Jesus, Mary, and Joseph, what a bitch of a day, and it's only morning."

THE ENCIRCLING GLOOM

Tuesday Afternoon, March 23, Rome and the Vatican

AS THE TWO Swiss Guard waited downstairs at Gemelli Hospital for Abby and the priest to come down from Miss Jenny Wren's new room, Josiah took a call from Daniel. For ten minutes, Josiah was quiet, listening to what Daniel had to say. Then, he spoke and told the priest what had just occurred at the hospital. The call ended shortly thereafter and Josiah looked up at his friend and said, "Disaster at the UN I'm afraid. The pope and the rest of them will be back late this afternoon."

"Everyone alright?" said Mattias, concerned.

"Yeah," said Josiah, "but Fawkes/Enki was there as well as some kind of new monsters, ghouls I guess we'd call them, but Daniel said their real name is *gallu*. They, apparently, are Enki's servants. They were sent back to wherever they came from and Enki disappeared. When I told Daniel what happened here, he said it looks like Enki's farewell and that young woman's scream happened about the same time. You think he's coming here for a visit next?"

"Wouldn't doubt it," said Mattias. "Let's drop the other two off back at the Vatican and go back down to the bus station and see if anything else is happening."

As the two Swiss Guard drove Abby and the priest back to the Vatican, the four were quiet, rather stunned into silence from what had happened. Mattias was driving and he rolled down his window and stuck his hand out. The cool of the morning had been replaced with the thick heaviness of a humid atmosphere.

"The temperature is rising," he said. "And the clouds are darkening. I think we are going to be in for the first spring thunderstorm."

Abby looked pensive, saying, "Fr. Salvatore and I have a little more work to do in the lab. The bloodwork that we've been studying correlates to the Star Sapphire Rings. I can't prove it yet, but I think the rings were created to have an almost parasitical effect on humans. What the ring gets out of the cooperative relationship, I'm not sure, but I believe it does do something to the body, allowing for the creation of mitochondria in the red blood cells."

"That's all Greek to me," said Josiah.

"She means," said the priest, "if I have to dumb it down that much to you, that the rings make superheroes out of their human hosts. The rings are energy enhancers."

"What about the Shroud of Turin?" said Mattias. "You spoke last time of the blood on the Shroud having the same kind of energy-enhancing mitochondria."

"I did," agreed Abby, "but I was wrong. There are subtle differences in the cellular structures. Those who wear the rings bear blood signatures that show the cellular material has been artificially enhanced. With the Shroud, it's different. It's as if that body was, from its conception, created with a genome that produced mitochondria in the bloodstream naturally."

"Be careful," said Fr. Salvatore, "you'll be giving us an alien Christ."

"Quite the contrary," said Abby. "If the Shroud held the body of Jesus, and my hypothesis is correct, then Jesus had a perfected human body from the start. He was as humans were meant to be, and the rest of us show a defect in our composition. How that happened I don't know—perhaps a biological effect of Original Sin—but I do think the rings were meant to remedy that somewhat. They are artificial enhancers and simply give humans the ability to become, at least while the rings are worn, what they were originally meant to be."

"Amazingly cool," said Josiah. "That would explain Jesus being able to do miracles."

"Only partially," said Abby. "Our faith tells us that Jesus is one hundred percent human and one hundred percent divine. I'm only talking about the part that deals with his human nature. I have no way of knowing how his divine nature built and expanded his perfected human powers."

Josiah said, "Well, I'm no great theologian, but it sounds like you've really expanded the understanding of who Christ is just from his bloodwork and given us an understanding of what humans were once capable of—and of how the rings make that capability possible again."

"We're going to need all the help we can get," said Mattias. "Josiah and I are going back to the Termini Station and see what's happening. That seems to be ground zero for whatever is happening to the homeless. What happened to Ben and his girlfriends may also be occurring to others."

"If I had a ring," said Abby ruefully, "I'd give it to you. Sounds like you might need it."

"We'll be fine," smiled Josiah. "We're tough enough to kick some demon ass now." He high-fived Mattias as they turned into the

Vatican. Letting the doctor and the priest out, they quickly went back the way they came.

It took them just a short time to reach the Termini Station, where, at first glance, all looked quiet.

Josiah suggested, "Let's take a quick trip around the Baths of Caracalla and see if we can spot any suspicious activity. Mattias drove slowly around the boundaries of the baths. The darkening clouds were scaring the people inside for an early lunch, so pedestrian traffic was minimal. In fact, both of the Swiss Guard felt creeping anxiety up their spines as they noticed the lack of vagrants and homeless in the area."

Mattias said, "When we were at the Termini a few days ago, the place was humming with people just loitering around. Now, no one."

"I know," said Josiah, absently biting his lip. They parked the car and went into the Termini. Rome's public works had recently built a koi pond on one side of the central area of the station. The thought had been that hassled passengers would be soothed by a bit of wildlife. In the middle of the pond was a tiny island for turtles and tortoises. Brightly colored, singing finches flitted through the small trees rooted on the island. It had taken the city a year to design the environment, but both Josiah and Mattias agreed with the populace of Rome that it was beautiful and made the Termini a tourist attraction as well.

The two Swiss Guard stood before the koi enclosure, not watching the wildlife but instead scoping out the travelers walking by them. Nothing was the least bit suspicious. Josiah's attention was interrupted by a soft tapping behind him. He turned and saw one of the underwater plants bumping gently against the glass.

"Look at that," he said to Mattias. "Ever seen anything like it, moving on its own?"

Mattias said, "Maybe, it's just caught in the flow of the water pump that keeps the lagoon fresh."

"Tapping pretty hard," said Josiah.

Mattias bent down to look at the green length of the plant tapping away. It was weird, he thought. He could swear the leafy extensions at the end of it looked like fingers. For a moment, the plant was swept away from view and Mattias moved closer and squinted more carefully.

He didn't really see the hurtling vegetation. His brain simply registered movement as the plant came back smashing and breaking the glass before him. It happened too fast for him to do anything, but Josiah cried out as water gushed over the two and the plant wrapped its appendages around the face and shoulders of Mattias, dragging him into the pond. They both disappeared immediately, and Josiah howled his anger, plunging through the opening, stepping on the floundering fish. He pushed his way through the flowing waters towards the island in the midst of the lagoon.

He was almost there when a bulbous green head, dread-locked with seaweed, surfaced and turned toward him. From the description his other VERITAS teammates had given, this was obviously Enki. Josiah stopped, but he couldn't even scream. His eyes were focused on the hideous fish mouth of the entity. Suddenly there were bubbles right next to the head, and Mattias surfaced, eyes wide, but mouth covered with plant material.

"If you ever hope to see him again," croaked Enki, "it would be best to stop this fruitless search for my servants, demon and human alike. You cannot stop what is coming, and if you attempt to find me or my nest, your friend here will be—how do you humans say it?—fish food."

Josiah reached for Mattias, but Enki pushed him back underwater. "Let him go," hissed the godling. "I may let him live after a fashion, but it will go worse for you if you pursue me."

Enki's head disappeared underneath the water. To his credit, Josiah immediately dived, trying to get his hands on Mattias, but Enki as well as Josiah's best friend had disappeared completely from the lagoon. Josiah surfaced screaming as the *carabinieri* rushed into the water, pistols drawn, to see if they could help him. Josiah's eyes were wide, and he was gasping for breath.

"He's gone!" shouted Josiah. "Mattias is gone!" He gripped the shoulders of the nearest *carabiniere*. "Get me back to the Vatican and assemble your SWAT team. We've got to hunt for its nest."

The *carabinieri* were the paramilitary police force of Italy, highly trained. And though they had only seen something green with what looked like teeth and eyes moving around Josiah, they were wise enough to realize that, though the threat was unknown to them, the Swiss Guard would not be hallucinating. Strange things had been happening in Rome the past few days. The officer who had his hand on Josiah's shoulder, guiding him out of the lagoon, was intuitive enough to know that something evil had been present in the water, kidnapping the Swiss Guard's partner, and posing a threat to the people of Rome. As he walked Josiah to the patrol car, he was already on the radio asking for reinforcements to meet at the Termini within the hour.

By the time they returned to the Guard barracks, Josiah had calmed down and said to the officer, "Go on back to your men. I'm going to get five of the Guard who have been briefed on this infestation problem and meet back at the Termini with you. Don't start the search without us."

"What infestation are you talking about?" said the officer.

"You saw what I saw in the lagoon?" said Josiah.

"I saw something. It was hideous."

"More than you could possibly know," said Josiah. "The disturbances in Rome and in other cities this past weekend up to today have to do with this entity you saw. It's deadly, dangerous, deceptive, and will stop at nothing to succeed with its plans."

The officer was quiet for a moment and then said, "What does it intend? What does it want to do?"

"It's taken the most vulnerable," said Josiah, "and turned them into weapons of chaos to terrorize this city. Fear is its goal, but it will not hesitate to use death and destruction in its wake. We've got to try to get Mattias back before he's totally turned."

"Turned?" questioned the officer.

"Possessed would be the better word," said Josiah.

The policeman chuffed in derision. "A little too much Hollywood don't you think?"

"Stay by my side, and by the time the afternoon is over, I'll ask your opinion again."

THE NEST

Tuesday, March 23, Early Evening, Baths of Caracalla, Rome

UNFORTUNATELY, IT TOOK most of the afternoon for Josiah to gather five Swiss Guard and the captain of the *carabinieri* to form the SWAT Team. Nonetheless, by early evening, both groups were able to meet at the entrance to the Baths of Caracalla. One of the things the *carabinieri* had been able to accomplish in the afternoon was the early closing of the tourist attraction. The place was deserted.

Josiah did the briefing. "This dirt road to the left of the entrance will lead us to the steps taking us down to the *Mithraeum*. You guys are soldiers so you know all about Mithras, right? No ... okay, just a little refresher then. Mithras was the soldiers' and poor people's god during the Roman era. He was an import from Persia and was associated with light and water. Mithraism was a secret religion and a real competitor with the young Christian Church. All its houses of worship, called *Mithraeum*, were underground. The one here is the largest ever discovered.

"They may have sacrificed bulls, but for sure they had feasts. Their holy places are set up like banquet halls. There is another underground chamber beneath this *Mithraeum* which may have been used for sacrifice. As a secret society, Mithraism had initiations and ranks."

"Were they violent?" said the captain of the SWAT team.

"We don't know, and it doesn't matter. Still, you have to know the background. It's the perfect place for a modern cult to gather. The people who are probably occupying the *Mithraeum* are some kind of demon cult, and their leader will probably take on aspects of Mithras."

"Take on?" said one of the *carabinieri*.

"I wasn't kidding when I said this was a demon cult," said Josiah. "The leader of this group most likely is not human."

Muffled guffaws could be heard among the SWAT team but the Swiss Guard stayed silent.

"You laugh," said Josiah, "but I speak the truth. Mattias and I have encountered an entity like this before. It is powerful, and when it possesses people, those possessed have great power as well."

"Shoot to kill?" asked the captain.

"Only, if necessary," replied Josiah. "These homeless didn't ask to be possessed. Hopefully, their humanity is tucked away in their bodies somewhere. We've got to try to save them. But our first priority is to rescue Mattias and take down their leader. With him, you may use deadly force the moment you see him. Any more questions?"

There were none.

Josiah led the five Swiss Guard and the SWAT team to the aboveground entrance to the *Mithraeum*. He and the captain checked their weapons. All were ready.

"Now remember," said Josiah. "This place has been closed off and on for the past decade. It is closed now for excavation and repair. Anyone you see shouldn't be there so count them as the enemy."

Silently, they proceeded underground to the tunnel that would lead them to the *Mithraeum*. It was the largest of the underground rooms, so the tunnel was fairly wide, its builders anticipating greater numbers.

They could hear muffled chanting ahead. Down the tunnel, they saw the entrance to the *Mithraeum* had been boarded up, but a flimsy door was in place. Josiah and the captain of the SWAT team glanced at each other. Bad news for the escape plan. There would have to be a calculated retreat with a slow egress. They only hoped their team members could escape with Mattias safely and not get bunched up by the doorway.

Getting in was easy. Josiah gently opened the door. There was a transept, empty of people, just before them. An ornate mosaic floor greeted their eyes, and torches throughout the room beyond illuminated the space.

Josiah stifled a gasp. He had expected ruins, but the *Mithraeum* looked like it must have appeared as of old. A high vaulted ceiling was overlaid with gold. Tapestries hung on the walls. Scenes from the life of Mithras decorated them. There was his birth from a stone, his sacrifice of the bull, his gaining water from a rock, and many other illustrations. In the front was an altar stone with the same bull sacrifice motif. At its base, a large censor wafted incense into the air, giving the whole place an otherworldly feel.

Reluctantly, Josiah admitted the room looked beautiful. He wondered if it was restored or if Enki was using his magic to create the illusion. The people who were chanting were on either side of the *Mithraeum* on long benches. They had not heard the soldiers enter.

Josiah held up a hand to the team and motioned them to walk forward up the center aisle. There was a large rectangular floor tile, different from the others, two-thirds of the way up the aisle. Josiah paused before it and spoke, "Silence!" he shouted.

The chanting immediately ceased, and dozens of blank faces turned towards them. None of them was Mattias. The possessed did not move or make any threatening gestures. But before Josiah could speak again, the rectangular slab began to descend into an underground pit.

He said softly to the captain, "That has to lead to the underground room where the bull was sacrificed." Josiah turned to the right and then to the left saying each time, "Where is Mattias? What have you done with him?"

A snickering began and rose to laughter from the possessed. It was only cut off when the slab of stone began to return from below. There was a figure upon it, dressed in a dark blue robe, covered with stars and planets of gold, that shimmered in the torchlight. The incense was thick, but Josiah caught a glimpse of the face. It was a mask. Not that again, thought Josiah. That water monster god had disguised himself, once more resembling the Fawkes figure, probably thinking that this face would scare even the possessed.

The figure's voice was mellifluous. "Ah, guests for the sacrifice."

"Where is Mattias?" asked Josiah. "Just give him to us and we will leave."

Enki laughed gently. "You never give up, do you? Even at the loss of your friend."

Josiah caught the tang of shed blood in the air, and he noticed that one hand of Enki's held a curved dagger. Worry crept up his spine, but he said, "I see no bull here to sacrifice. What kind of game are you playing with these innocent people?"

"Not so innocent in a few moments," said Enki. "For once they drink the blood of the sacrifice, they will truly be my servants forever."

Enki swept away his voluminous robe, but before he could even finish, Josiah's gorge rose up in his mouth. He instinctively knew what he would see. And then he saw. It was the figure of a man, prone at Enki's booted feet. He was clearly dead. The pool of blood around him testified to that. Horrified, Josiah caught a glimpse of the face he knew. Mattias' pale visage stared open-eyed in glassy death at his friend and comrade-in-arms. His throat had been slit, and a massive wound in his chest suggested his heart had been removed.

Josiah screamed in anger and hate, "Kill him!" Gunfire from all of SWAT and the five Swiss Guard pummeled into the body of Enki. His laughter only grew in volume as the bullets caused him to jerk spasmodically up towards the main altar. Once he reached that, the godling jumped up on the altar, whatever passed for blood in his body liberally coating the stone.

He wrapped his blue robe around himself, and once the soldiers had finished emptying their clips into him, he said, "Constantly diverting me from my purpose. That's what you do. No matter. You can take your friend. I have what I need from him—his very soul. But let's see if you can leave. They may not be my permanent servants yet, but they still do my will." He spoke in the language the homeless had been chanting, and they turned as one towards the soldiers. Enki jumped from the altar, went behind it, and disappeared, his laughter growing fainter as he exited the room to one of the secret passageways.

Josiah said to the captain of the SWAT team. "Help me get Mattias, and, then, let's get out of here." They grabbed the man's limp arms and began to drag him down the center aisle. The possessed began to follow, their movements choreographed as one, stretching out their hands to touch those who would dare rescue Enki's sacrifice.

"Don't shoot! Don't shoot!" cried Josiah. "Just get to the exit."

Those who were possessed moved slowly. Just like the zombies from the movies, thought Josiah. Luca and he had watched many iterations of the undead. He was amazed that they acted like that in real life. Suddenly, a possessed came unexpectedly from a side aisle and grasped Josiah's arm. The man, or at least it once was a man, went to bite the Swiss Guard's arm, but the captain of the SWAT team dropped Mattias for a moment and rushed to stab the possessed in the side of the head. The once homeless person collapsed soundlessly to the ground.

"I'm sorry," said the captain to Josiah, "he was going to kill you."

"Right," gasped Josiah. "Thanks for breaking the orders. I owe you."

They made it quickly down to the exit without any more incidents. The possessed were following, but they were slow.

The soldiers got through the doorway and helped Josiah and the captain carry Mattias through the door. Some two by four wooden beams were on the floor, and they used them to block the doorway, hopefully giving them a few extra minutes to escape.

Josiah let them take his friend, and as they hurried up the tunnel and to the stairs that would lead them safely outside, he turned to look at the *Mithraeum* and shook his fist at the evil present there.

"You've killed one of the best men I've ever known," shouted Josiah. "Even if you are really the devil, there will be hell to pay for this. I will hunt you wherever you are, Enki. Wherever you go, I will follow until you permanently crawl back to the muck from which you came!"

THE GRIEF OF THE GOOD

Late Tuesday Evening, March 23, Apostolic Palace, Vatican City

"I CAN DRIVE you to the Vatican," said the captain of the SWAT team. Josiah had already placed Mattias's body in the back seat and called the pope who had just arrived back at the Apostolic Palace.

"No," said Josiah to the captain. "This is between the pope and his Swiss Guard. Thank you for what you have already done. We will be in touch. This is not over yet."

Josiah knew he was in emotional turmoil, so he appreciated the escort the *carabinieri* gave him back to the Vatican. When he drove into the San Damaso Courtyard, the tears flowed freely. There was the Swiss Guard, his comrades, perhaps seventy of them, in their ceremonial uniforms, double-lined in front of an arch where waited Pope Patrick, Captain Luca Rohner, and Daniel.

Gently, Josiah removed Mattias's body from the back of the car and carried it to the front of the Swiss Guard line where he stopped.

"Who brings our fallen soldier to the gates of the Vatican?" said Colonel Mario Minitti, head of the Swiss Guard.

"I do. Corporal Josiah Hindermas. I bear the body of Corporal Mattias Kurz who gave his life in service to His Holiness."

The present pope had altered this tradition by having one of the Swiss Guard pipe softly, "The Flowers of the Forest," an old Irish lament for the dead. As the piper played, Josiah walked between the two lines of Swiss Guard, and as he passed, each saluted the body of the departed Mattias.

Over the music could be heard the lament of the pope chanting:

> *Who is the soldier, dead from the battle,*
> *Brought now before his comrades in arms?*
> *Who is the warrior whose wounds have consumed him;*
> *His body a witness to the vows that he bore?*
> *I am the one before whom he swore,*
> *Oaths to the Christ to keep evil away.*
> *Died though he did,*
> *And his passing is sorrow.*
> *Victory he won*
> *By the faith he has kept.*
> *Michael, Michael, Michael of the morning,*
> *Angel from heaven come rescue this soul.*
> *Take him to Christ, his struggle abated.*
> *Take him to heaven, to his eternal home.*
> *For now, he is tired,*
> *A stranger on earth,*
> *Lead him to the land of the angels,*
> *And everlasting rebirth.*

The music stopped and the pope spoke again, "Eternal rest grant unto Mattias, O Lord."

The Swiss Guard answered, "And let perpetual light shine upon him."

"May he rest in peace," said the pope.

Together the assembly in the courtyard said, "May his soul and the souls of all the faithful departed through the mercy of God, rest in peace. Amen."

The Swiss Guard turned to face the pope. They raised their right arms and held out their white-gloved hands in the characteristic salute, thumb and two forefingers extended, representing the Trinity.

The pope blessed the body of Mattias and then all the Swiss Guard. He backed into the shadows of the arch and a gurney came forward covered in the papal flag, and Mattias's body was gently laid on it. Josiah did not leave his side.

The pontiff, Luca and Daniel stayed until the courtyard was deserted. They waited until Josiah came back to join them.

"I know he was your great friend," said Daniel. "I am so sorry."

"As are we all," said the pope to Josiah. "But, for the time being, we must put our grief aside. We have much to share with you, Josiah, about what happened at the United Nations today. All of us need an update on everything that occurred at the *Mithraeum*. I did not expect our enemy to move this swiftly. We must strike back soon if we are to have any hope of defeating its power."

From out of the shadows trotted the grey wolf-dog, carrying something in his jaws. Daniel let out a cry of joy, but Luca said, "We left him at the United Nations. How did he get back here?"

"Grigio is not entirely of this world," said the pope.

Daniel agreed, "He walks roads that we could never find. I'm just glad he's back. Exactly what do you have in your mouth, boy?"

Grigio stopped before Daniel. The wolf-dog lowered his head and spat an object out of his mouth. The minute it hit the courtyard floor, images cascaded into Daniel's mind.

He saw a dog running, and a man fleeing down by the East River. The stranger turned around yelling in fear. Daniel recognized the face. The dog leaped, grabbing the hand of the man, and bit. A scream shot to the sky.

"What is it, Dani?" said Luca as his friend shuddered, clutching his arm. "What was it you saw?"

"Look," said Daniel, pointing at the severed finger on the ground.

"There's a Knight of St. Gregory ring on that finger," said the pope. "It is a papal gift and marks a warrior for the Church. It is rare to find one, but this is a ring I've seen before."

"Yes," said Daniel, "on the hand of John Nance."

"What a great 'warrior'," said Luca sarcastically.

"Why would Grigio have attacked him, and where?" said Josiah.

"Grigio took off after we rescued the team and the UN representatives. He must have known Nance was lurking about."

Daniel shuddered again as the dog looked at him and visions exploded in his mind—Nance at the UN hidden in the visitor's area, Nance looking over the bodies in the plaza, Nance down at the river searching, searching for something.

Coming to himself, Daniel said, "It's not a lot of evidence, but I think Grigio is trying to tell us that Nance is somehow implicated in all of this. Could he know about the Babylonian entities?"

"Possibly," said Luca. "He also has the wherewithal to clone the *sirrush* we saw in the desert. Maybe he's the human link to what's coming against us."

"Well," said Daniel, "he has a sore hand now."

Grigio smiled a wolfish smile and yelped with pleasure.

MIRACLE IN CANTERBURY

Wednesday Morning, March 24, Canterbury Cathedral, United Kingdom

SR. CECILIA CAMPBELL walked under brilliant morning sunshine towards the cathedral. The previous night she had received a copy of a high priority e-mail. She opened it and let out a little gasp. The cathedral and environs were to be closed on Wednesday, and she was to expect some major deliveries and an important, unnamed guest.

At this early hour of 8 AM, there were no tourists to turn away yet, the birds were singing, and she felt a hope burning in her natural, optimistic Jamaican spirit that she had not noticed previously. The news of the day before had been both startling and horrific, what with the slaughter at the United Nations. The news was still sketchy as to exactly what the violence entailed.

However, the amazing part of that day still stunned her. The United Nations was to act as one against whatever threat was approaching them from the outer edges of the solar system. This new alliance was going to be a military, cultural, and religious coalition in order to preserve humanity. Not everyone agreed, especially the Chinese and their allies, but Sr. Cecelia was great at reading tea leaves.

This good news was going to happen regardless of what the Chinese wanted.

Then of course, there was King Henry's announcement that Canterbury was to be turned over to the Roman Catholic Church. She figured that was going to cause quite a stir, but noted that the prime minister had called a special session of Parliament last night to vote in the king's recommendations. The power of the monarchy was reasserting itself, and she, for one was pleased. This particular king was well-loved and seemed to forecast a bright future for the United Kingdom and what was left of the Commonwealth.

She sighed a little as she opened the doors of the church. She supposed that she would be out of a job, now that things were Romanizing. She walked the empty cathedral and drank in the silence. She loved to be here in the early morning. The peace was so calming, and it truly got her centered for the day. She walked to the Trinity Chapel where once the Shrine of St. Thomas Becket stood. Now there was simply a Presence Candle in the middle of the empty floor. Whatever did the king have in mind, she mused.

She was lost in thought for a while until she heard soft metal clinking behind her. Her breath caught in her throat for a moment, and a dozen possibilities echoed through her mind. She turned, and there was the king.

"I hope I didn't startle you," smiled King Henry IX. "Your secretary mentioned that you might be here."

Speechless, for a moment, something very rare for her, she managed the requisite curtsy. She said, with her voice cracking, "Your Majesty."

He smiled broader. "Don't stand on etiquette, pomp, and circumstance. Call me Henry. We shall be seeing quite a bit of each other in the months to come."

"So, I'm not to be terminated." The words simply popped out of her mouth. She couldn't believe she said something more outrageous.

"Speaking of pomp and circumstance, you certainly have covered that well." She straightened herself and stared him in the eye.

He laughed heartily, dressed as he was in his full Irish Guard regalia, his scarlet coat sporting the gold braid and his well-earned medals. The beautiful sword at his side only accentuated the dashing appearance he had crafted through the years. The filigreed crown woven through his red hair sparkled in the morning sunlight shining through the Becket stained glass window up high in the chapel. He could be affectatious, and he wore the sprig of Irish shamrock twined in the crown above his right ear.

"They told me you spoke your mind, and I'm glad of it. We shall need your backbone in the days to come Sr. Cecelia. Not only are you not terminated but somewhere down the line, we will have a royal title for you to add to the enhanced position I have in mind for you. As for me, I have a speech to give right here this afternoon, and I'm afraid I must look the part. I prefer jeans and a sweatshirt, but this will have to do."

"I thought you were giving Canterbury to the Catholics," she said with just a hint of judgment in her voice.

"I am Catholic," he said, "so I don't intend to give it to anyone. What I said yesterday is that there will be a Catholic Archbishop of Canterbury, but the Pope and I have worked it out where this place will be a center for all who seek God. It's not going to be some watered-down mindfulness center. It will be vibrant. It will be holy. And it will be unabashedly Christian and Catholic.

"We both agreed, based on Msgr. Daniel Azar's recommendation, that you must stay on and hold the disparate elements together. Some will see it as my toss to soothe the Anglican feelings, but you are simply the best at this. There will be problems. However, it will never be as tumultuous as in Reformation times, but I'm sure there will be mountains to climb and pits to fall in.

"Did you know that Parliament, late last night formerly passed the succession law allowing me to reign and rule and my successors as well regardless of religion? It passed overwhelmingly, and even I was surprised. I think I scare them a little. It's been centuries since a monarch has taken back the prerogatives of what is essentially the monarchy's to possess."

"I'm surprised you got away with it," said Sr. Cecelia.

"So am I, but it wasn't a political thing. Unlike so many kings and queens before me, religion for me is not just a rag to clothe the office. I converted during my time at university. Last night, my Minister of Transportation whispered rather loudly in Parliament, 'The crazy king found his God at Oxford if you can believe it.' I called him this morning and before I sacked him, I told him, 'You could have made the insult stick if it had been Cambridge, your alma mater.' Then, I called him an offensive twit. I'll have to go to confession for that."

Sr. Cecilia cracked a smile and found herself laughing along with the king. "Your Majesty—Henry if you truly wish—aren't you worried about an eventual rebellion?"

"Absolutely not. What do you think is going to happen? Another War of the Roses? Another Jacobean rebellion although on the Protestant side? As I was thinking on all this, I realized an upside to the woeful decline of faith in our land. Most people don't care, so they won't have the energy to fight.

"Besides, Parliament is so fearful of November 1 that they were willing to invest me with the authority I needed. I had it bandied about that I would dissolve Parliament if they did not cooperate. Between you and me, I think they granted what I demanded so that they had someone else to blame should everything go awry. You see, Sr. Cecilia, they and the monarchy took a separate but equal risk. They are willing to see how I do. If I fail, all hell will break loose besides that which is coming for us. The monarchy bets on success as confirming the righteousness of reclaiming its ancient standing. I think it's a worthy risk."

"And you came here, today, to cement your achievement?" asked Sr. Cecilia.

"Not exactly. Even as we speak," said the king, "plans are afoot concerning the shrine that Archbishop Pomeroy has been building secretly for over a year in one of my holdings in Scotland. As you may know, John Nance, the wealthy philanthropist …"

"You mean the trillionaire," said Sr. Cecelia, disparagingly.

"Indeed," said the king. "He has funded the project. The archbishop, rest his soul, didn't trust the man's long-range plans, but the funding was upfront with no strings attached. I spoke with His Holiness this morning by phone, and he told me not to trust John Nance. Wise words. It seems the man is somewhat power-hungry and is trying to play both sides in this conflict against one another for his own gains. Is he evil? I don't know. What I do know is that he is not entirely on our side. So, we must be careful and not be entirely on his.

"I'm not sure it was wise for the archbishop to take the funds. But it was a lot of money, which would be needed to recreate the shrine to its medieval splendor. Maybe the archbishop was naïve, trusting too much in the good he still saw in the man. No matter. We will turn whatever Nance's reasons are into good.

"Even you, Sr. Cecelia, with all your knowledge of Canterbury and its history, cannot conceive of how much expensive beauty was bequeathed on this shrine. What's fascinating is that, though the pilgrims were in awe of the shrine's wealth, its worldly value meant nothing temporal to them. Over the centuries, its physical beauty began to stand for the longing for healing, for a touch of God, as it were, that each pilgrim prayed for. The beauty of the shrine represented the beauty in their souls that God himself surely saw. It was a glimpse of heaven here on earth, and stood as a monument to their faith. Its presence assured them that God was near, caring for them and loving them.

"My predecessor, Henry VIII, of not so revered memory, never understood that. He just wanted the money the shrine could provide when the gold was melted down and the baubles sold. He couldn't even see the beauty and the importance of The Regale which became lost to him and to the people for these past hundreds of years. But now your friend, Msgr. Azar, a young man possessed of many gifts, has found that jewel, and his team, of which you are a major part, has found the link between that gem and the spirit of St. Thomas Becket. There was real healing not only in this cathedral but in the whole Church when both were joined."

"You know," said Sr. Cecelia, "it is said by many of us here and many down through the years that Becket still haunts these halls. Do you believe such things?"

The king grimly smiled. "Someday, I will tell you of the conversion of an atheistic college boy to the faith of the ages. But until then, accept the fact that I do believe such things. Something strange happened here five centuries ago. When my most wretched and scrofulous ancestor plundered the place and the break somehow occurred between Becket and The Regale, the saint's presence remained trapped in here, unable to act, usually unable to manifest.

"The miracles ceased; the saint's power was neutered; the memories became recollections which then became tall tales. What was once the hope of millions sank into the dust of ruin. Until an archbishop had a vision and enlisted the wealthiest man in the world and an upstart king into his plans for a renewal of spirit and energy among the people. That's what this shrine is going to be. Now, because of his address to the United Nations yesterday, the pope has made it even more important as the signature example of the power of faith and culture against the entity that seeks to destroy us."

"You can't possibly build such a shrine before November," scoffed the nun.

"On the contrary, it is already built. The workers who are coming are not going to manufacture it here. They are simply going to put it together, starting this morning."

As if on cue, the cathedral doors banged open, and workmen started to arrive, carrying the crates that held the unassembled shrine.

"Surely, you don't believe a recreated medieval shrine could actually shake up this cynical and sarcastic world?" said Sr. Cecelia.

"Not by itself, no," said the king. "But let me let you in on a little secret. The shrine isn't the only thing that will be built. In time, the cathedral will be completely restored. Canterbury will remain the picturesque village it still is so that we will stay rooted in history, and a massive hospital and research complex will be built on the outskirts of town on land owned by the Crown. It's the least the monarchy can do to wipe the stain of its own sin away. There will be a union of science and faith here in this place. The West has suffered enough from the split between the two. With the help of the pope and the American president, we might just have the power to make this happen. That's my dream. That's my wish. And, as king, that's my command."

She looked at the young king, standing in the middle of the Trinity Chapel, the Presence Light burning beside him. The sun glinted off the gold crown, the red surcoat gleamed in the gloom of the cathedral, and his sword hinted of hidden power within the king. Sr. Cecelia wasn't a hopeless romantic, but she did love the tales of Arthur, King of the Britons, and she wondered at the electric fire that thrilled up her spine—was it similar to the feelings felt by those who saw the Once and Future King?

Maybe, it was just from the cathedral doors being opened by the workmen, but there suddenly came a swirling wind into the chapel that stirred the motes of dust high up in the cathedral ceiling and then swirled down to circle the young king. The dust motes, illumined by another burst of sunlight, surrounded the monarch in what looked for a moment like a glowing, golden tempest.

His hair lifted slightly. He looked around somewhat startled and said, "Do you hear that? It's music, an ancient tune I think, and monks ... singing."

Sr. Cecelia heard nothing, but she saw the king, for a moment larger than life, and lifting up behind him, a ghostly mitered head appeared with hands raised in benediction. The presence signed a cross over the king. For a moment, it seemed as if time stopped, and then the hands moved downward and rested on Henry's head.

"What was that?" He jumped, startled, but when he turned the presence was gone.

Sr. Cecelia said, her own voice shaking, "That, Your Majesty, was the benediction of a saint. It seems this is no longer only your idea. May God help us all."

A REVELATION OF SOME SECRETS

Wednesday, Late Morning, March 24, VERITAS Headquarters, Vatican City

"WELL, THANK GOD that, except for our poor Mattias, all of you are safe." Dr. Abby Duchon's words summed up the summary both Josiah and Daniel gave of the previous day.

"He is the first of the VERITAS team to sacrifice his life," said Daniel. "I knew our work would sometimes be dangerous, but in our short existence, almost all of us have been threatened directly with death. Uncle Liam," Daniel said to the pope, "perhaps this is too much to ask of all of them."

"Perhaps you are right, Dani," sighed the pope. "I, too, did not think we would be in so constant fear for our lives. There is no shame for anyone who deems it unnecessary to continue to put themselves in harm's way."

"Ridiculous," snapped Abby. "Before the Holy Father got here, I made the rounds with all of you. I see no weakening of our resolve. Look, no one is even making an attempt to leave."

Fr. Salvatore moved his right foot back in line with his left. Probably not the best time to go for coffee. But he was worried. He had tried to call John Nance this morning once he had seen the ring finger of the philanthropist on the lab table, and Nance was not picking up. Fr. Salvatore was now a Judas without a high priest to lead him.

"Before anyone else speaks," continued Abby, "I must tell you of the discoveries Fr. Salvatore and I have made concerning the rings, the gem, and the Tunicle. First of all, the Star Sapphire Rings are rings of force and power. They are meant to defend and protect. I know you knew this," she said looking directly at the three brothers, "and it would have been helpful for all of us to have known so as to save some time."

The brothers looked appropriately embarrassed, and the pope said firmly, "Exactly what I told them last night."

"Believe us," said Shadrach, "the meaning you people give to transparency is a totally new concept to us, but one, because of the circumstances we all have just been through, is absolutely necessary. We will keep you informed about what we know, and share our knowledge."

"Good," said Abby. "Then, I am sure you can confirm that the Star Ruby—The Regale—is primarily a healing stone. Just as the Star Sapphires have some ability to heal, so the Star Ruby has some ability to apply force and power, but its primary directive is to heal."

The brothers nodded in the affirmative.

"Now to the most stunning part," said Abby. "I took blood from the Holy Father, Dani, and the brothers—all those who wear a ring. Their blood cells all possess mitochondria that normal humans do not have, giving them the ability to do things ordinary humans cannot do. They are not supermen, but they are enhanced humans. Shadrach, Meshach, and Abednego, you must begin extensive training for Dani and the pope. It is absolutely necessary for them to know what they are able to do."

Abby looked at the other members of the team who had shock on their faces. "Don't get ahead of yourselves," she said. "That's not the most stunning part. This is: I compared their cellular structure to the Star Ruby and the Star Sapphire Rings, and, then, on a whim, I compared the cell structure of the blood on the Tunicle with the evidence as well. The crystal structure of the gems matches the blood cells I tested, meaning there is a symbiotic relationship between The Regale, the Star Sapphires, and the ring wearers.

"The rings and The Regale are not parasitical. I was wrong about that. When joined with a human, they operate in concert with their human counterpart. Much is given to the human, but the only thing the gem and the rings get back is the ability to manifest their inherent abilities. There is more to discover on this, but those tests can wait for later."

Abby was silent for a moment and then walked over to the Tunicle. "The blood of Becket matches the crystal structure of the rings as well, which means that at one time he wore a Star Sapphire Ring."

"It's as I told you, Dani," said the pope. Turning to the group he said, "From my own personal research, I surmised as much. I've been able to trace his ring, which he lost at some time, to the Vatican Archives. It is the ring I am wearing."

Abby smiled, "I thought as much. But there is more. The blood on the Tunicle is even more attuned to The Regale. I believe that any of the ring wearers could make it work, but Becket's blood has been modified even further on a cellular level. I don't yet know exactly how, but I hypothesize that The Regale has chosen Becket to be the main user of its power.

"Here's what I think has happened. Many of us witnessed Becket's presence in Canterbury Cathedral several days ago. The appearance was impressive but there was a lostness, a hopelessness present in that entity. Something had been left unfinished. I believe that when Throckmorton, the aide to Cardinal Pole, took The Regale to keep it from the king these many centuries ago, Becket's spirit, life force, whatever you want to call it was inadvertently trapped in the cathedral. He did not have the energy to leave. He had bequeathed to The Regale, a part of his personality, his spirit as it were. That's what made him able to manifest himself when Daniel held The Regale at Fontevraud Abbey. Becket was able to thwart Enki and save Luca. If we can reunite the presence in Canterbury Cathedral with The Regale, the pope's words at the United Nations will not be in vain. The mighty healing force of the shrine will be whole again, and humanity can only benefit."

"Spectacular, Abby!" said Daniel. "I knew my uncle was right to bring you aboard."

"But there is still one more thing," said Abby. "I know you are going to plan what to do about this demonic infestation thing that is going on, not only in Rome but in other cities of Europe and in New York. You must take The Regale with you. Although, not at full strength, it might still possess the ability to heal those possessed. Becket, or at least a part of him, will be with you as well. Think of him as like the spiritual version of Ranbir."

Rebecca grimaced and said, "As long as he at least calls me by my right name. You all should know that Ranbir is ready for duty again."

"Good to hear," said the pope, "because right after this meeting, we are going to the *Mithraeum* and root out the source of Rome's spiritual corruption, and nothing will stand in our way."

"You can't go," said Luca, shocked. "I can't allow it. I'm responsible for your safety, and if you go—well what if something would happen?"

"He's right, Uncle Liam," said Daniel. "We can't risk it."

A shadow of anger passed swiftly across the pope's craggy face, and then his visage softened. He saw the faces of the others with emotions of pleading flowing across them. Except for the brothers. They looked at him, measuring for the first time the mettle of the man. What they actually thought, they neither revealed by expression or iterated with words.

"I appreciate the concern, Luca. But I can't be a prisoner of the Vatican. This whole episode started when Miss Jenny Wren, possessed by an evil older than time, tried to kill me. That evil aimed for me. Do you think if I do not go, I will be safe here? I'm safer with you, my protectors. Alone, here, I am so much more vulnerable.

"Besides, it is tradition for the popes to sneak out of the Vatican once in a while. My predecessors did it often, and on the slim chance they were discovered, it made great news. We've had skiing popes, mountain climbing popes, hunting popes, and even warrior popes.

"I won't be going to a food kitchen or buying a piece of music. I won't be going to my favorite restaurant. I'll be going to confront an ancient evil with the best friends anyone could have."

"You'll look silly in your white cassock," grumbled Luca.

"Yes, I will," laughed the pope. "That's why you are going to find those cool tactical black pants the Guard wear and the black tactical vest. I'll even wear a helmet if you insist. Back in the day, oh, 1300 years ago, my predecessor, Pope John VIII, led the papal navy against infiltrating Islamic terrorists and won a great battle. So, this has been done before. And he was older than I am. I am one of the ring wearers so I have tangible power. But I also have something better. I have the Church's Rite of Exorcism. It worked a week ago. I have no doubt it will work again. We're in God's hands my friends, and the power of Christ is with us. Now kneel for my blessing, even you my unbaptized brothers—it will work with you as well."

He blessed them there, in the underground lab, and except for the brothers from Babylon, he gave each of them the Body of Christ in communion. He laid hands on their heads instead, whispering to the three, "When this is over, we must talk. You possess immense power, great knowledge, and ineffable wisdom, but your souls must be brightened by Christ. You have given us so many gifts. This is one we can give you." They bowed in acknowledgment of his offer.

When the pope had left and the group had dispersed, Daniel and Luca were left alone.

Daniel said, "I don't think Fr. Salvatore and Abby like being left behind again. I know they are not soldiers, but simply holding the fort down does seem kind of a letdown."

Luca said, "My favorite poet, John Milton, said, 'They also serve who stand and wait.'"

"Wow," said Daniel, "so eloquent on this day."

Luca smiled, "Warriors always wax eloquent on bashing and slashing day. After all, we might not return." He paused for a moment, looked away, and then brushed his eyes with his right hand. "Listen," he said, "we've already been through a lot together, but with your uncle and you risking your lives this afternoon, I just have to say …"

"No, you listen," said Daniel. "If it comes to that, save the pope. He's holding all this together. There hasn't been one like him since Pope St. John Paul the Great. The world needs him. Save him, please, if you have to choose."

Luca turned and sniffed his sinuses clear. He looked again at his friend saying, "Your uncle made me swear to always protect you. I will do as you ask, but I don't know what I'd do if I lost you. You befriended me when I first came here, a snot-nosed boy with an arrogant streak who was despised by the other guardsmen. You got me through that. We were friends long before I was your protector. Besides, you don't need much protecting now, magic ring and all."

Luca looked out to the underground garden and who should saunter in as if he had been running in the fields somewhere but Grigio. Luca started laughing, "Look at him. When needed, he's here. Come here, pup."

Grigio's tongue was out and he had his smiley face on, which, for a wolf-dog looked something between hilarious and sinister. He came and sat before Luca and Daniel.

"Now you listen to me, pup," said Luca. "I can't be everywhere this afternoon. Watch out for this guy, okay?" The dog yelped in agreement and wagged his tail. "And no fingers today," said Luca. "Go for the throat." Again, Grigio yelped with what seemed a little too much joy.

Luca looked at Daniel, "Do you know what my favorite musical is?"

"Musical?" smiled Daniel. "I thought you only liked old TV shows."

Luca laughed and said, "Come on, I just quoted John Milton to you. I'm a cultured guy. Anyway, it's the 'Scarlet Pimpernel.' It's the story of an English Lord during the French Revolution who disguises himself as the Scarlet Pimpernel and goes to France to rescue people who are going to be guillotined."

"Sounds like the good version of Guy Fawkes, doesn't it?" said Daniel.

"Yeah, I guess it does," said Luca. "Anyway, there's my favorite song in there. It's called 'Into the Fire', and don't worry, I'm not going to sing it for you, but there's this verse that goes,

> *Into terror, into valor,*
> *Charge ahead, no, never turn,*
> *Yes, it's into the fire we fly,*
> *And the devil will burn.*

"That's where we are going this afternoon, Dani—into terror. That thing has tried to kill me once. I don't intend to give it another chance. That's where the valor comes in. I'm so glad I'm a Swiss Guard, a member of the oldest standing army in the world, and all we are charged to do is guard the pope and stop evil. How cool is that! I'm so proud to be able to do this."

Daniel had never heard Luca share this much about what being a Guard meant. Moved, he said, "Luca, you're the best. That's why the pope made you captain."

"I don't know if I'm the best," he said. "But I love going into the fire, and it's even better with you at my side." He put his arm around Daniel's neck and said, "Come with me, Dani, and let's go burn the devil."

Not to be forgotten, Grigio barked again and muscled his way between the friends. Luca laughed and said, "Ok, pup, it's us three then, the Three Musketeers, 'All for one, and one for all'."

INTO FIRE, INTO HELL

Wednesday Afternoon, March 24, Mithraeum, Baths of Caracalla, Rome

EIGHT PEOPLE, A holographic avatar, and a huge ghostly wolf-dog assembled in the Courtyard San Damaso just before one o'clock PM. The three brothers were dressed in black upscale jogging suits, having eschewed wearing any tactical gear. They looked like normal, albeit very tall, supremely fit athletes. Grigio was by their side, though in the bright sunlight he looked to fade in and out of focus. Not for the first time, Daniel wondered just what Grigio really was. Nonetheless, he was happy to have him along.

Ranbir was there as well, activated again and chatty as always. Daniel, Rebecca, Josiah, and Luca were outfitted in tactical gear complete with helmets, gloves, and bulletproof vests. Each carried a Heckler and Koch Mp7 submachine gun with suppressor and was proficient in its use.

Daniel had The Regale with him tucked away for safekeeping. Luca had a few more armaments stuffed here and there in his vest. The last man in tactical garb took off his helmet, revealing himself to be Pope Patrick. There was a little gasp from some of the others because they were only used to seeing him in white. The form-fitting tactical gear revealed him to be in surprisingly good shape, though Luca had seen him often enough in the Swiss Guard gym to know that he was as fit as any 50-year-old could be.

Actually, thought Luca, the pope looked pretty dashing. He just hoped the man kept his helmet on. If any of the paparazzi recognized him and took pictures, it would be an international sensation. The pope had refused to carry any armaments, which was a good thing again, thought Luca, since a pope with a submachine gun would not only be a worldwide sensation but a scandal as well. Luca still wasn't sure having him tag along was a good idea, but he had to make it work.

"Listen to me carefully," said Josiah, whom Luca had chosen to give the last briefing. Just like yesterday, we asked to have the Baths of Caracalla closed down. Two days in a row was a stretch for the tourist board, but the captain of the SWAT team ran interference for us. There will be no *carabinieri* with us today, though. We are on our own. The Holy Father asked that it be so.

"I'm the only one of the group that's been in the *Mithraeum*. I swear the room is enchanted or something. It looks like it must have looked two thousand years ago. The thing to watch is the hole in the main aisle. It has a tile that raises and lowers down into another room where sacrifices occur."

He paused for a moment, then swallowed. "That's where that thing killed Mattias. Speaking of the Babylonian godlings, you brothers are in charge of corralling Enki and disabling or killing him, and handling any other creatures he brings. I figured you had more experience with things of its kind since you were around them once upon a time."

Meshach gave a feral smile and said, "It will be our pleasure. We have yet to determine whether they are the same deities as the ones the Babylonians worshipped. At least we know, that whatever they are they take those deities' form and function. If it is in our power, we will dispatch them."

"The rest of us," said Josiah, are basically backup. Ranbir, I'm asking you to tag along with the Babylonian brothers and be part of the power quartet. You four are our firepower. The rest of us will fill in where needed and keep the possessed from causing too much trouble. They are slow. Daniel and the Holy Father have rings they can use to stun any who try to attack them. Luca, Rebecca, and I have tasers to knock them out, and, if necessary, guns to shoot those who appear too deadly. We will try to save as many as we can. And the dog? Well, the dog will do anything he wants to do. Any questions?

There were none. Josiah had provided one of the Swiss Guard's unmarked armored vans which easily accommodated them. The drive to the baths was pretty silent until Luca looked over and saw the pope looking pensively out one of the tinted windows.

"You look like an armored spy, Your Holiness," said Luca.

The pope gave a slight grin.

That was when Luca said, "And with your helmet on you look like ... and he broke into the Johnny Rivers song from the old TV show *Secret Agent Man* ...

> *Secret Agent Man,*
> *Secret Agent Man,*
> *They've given you a number,*
> *And taken away your name.*

Everyone on the van broke up laughing, and even Grigio gave forth with a couple of yelping howls. Luca was a pretty good singer. It was the incongruity of it all that made even the Babylonian brothers laugh. They weren't the only strange ones now.

DISINFECTION

Wednesday Afternoon, March 24, Baths of Caracalla, Rome

JOSIAH PULLED THE van up to the exact spot as the day before outside of the Baths of Caracalla. The place, as expected was deserted. Departing the van, their boots clicked on the asphalt, but once they hit the dirt road, their steps muffled. Birds could be heard singing, and the cats of Caracalla peaked from behind bushes and stones at what they considered a small, invading army.

"It is a beautiful place," said Rebecca. "It feels its age."

"Yes," said Josiah, "but it is rotten at its core. Just wait. You'll see."

They were quiet, then, walking silently down the steps toward the tunnel that would lead them to the *Mithraeum*. Daniel felt the atmosphere shiver like falling water does when one passes through it.

"Ah," said the pope, "did you all sense that? A thin place, manufactured most likely by the enemy, that allows it and his henchmen, along with us, to pass to and from the Otherworld. I think we find ourselves in its domain now."

"Must be so," said Daniel quietly. "I doubt that the staff of this place refreshes these ancient torches along the tunnel walls. There's no dust either as if the place has been kept immaculately clean."

Once again, Josiah could hear chanting up ahead. "There will be a barrier up here and a wooden door that signals the entrance to the *Mithraeum*."

Except there wasn't. The tunnel took a right curve and descended more steeply. As they came around the corner, they saw no debris or flimsy door. Several tunnels met here in this space. Instead, a bas relief of bronze with the two carved torchbearers of Mithras on either side of a heavy iron door greeted them.

"Listen to me carefully," said the pope. "This is not our world or reality, but everything you see and experience here will be real to you. You can be hurt or killed. This is the *Mithraeum* as it once was. Perhaps it is even more splendid than it existed in our reality, for this is the Otherworld. There will be things here that are not human. Some may be on our side, but I would not bet on it. Trust only each other and do not pay attention to anything Enki or the possessed say. Lies are in the air they breathe."

"Josiah," said Luca, "how do we get through this door?"

"I don't know, captain," he said. "It was just a flimsy, ply-wood door before. Looks like it's made of solid brass."

"Let me try," said Ranbir, stepping forward. The avatar ran his hand over the exterior, finding nothing. "There is no keyhole or latch here. This door was meant to be opened only from the inside."

"There is another entrance behind the altar," said Josiah, "but I have no idea which of these tunnels would take us to it."

"No matter," said Ranbir. "What good is an avatar if he can't handle a little brass door?"

Everyone, except Rebecca who truly knew the hologram's capabilities, watched in amazement as Ranbir simply stuck his hand through the brass door to the other side.

"It's not magic, but rather, technology," she said. "Bart has given Ranbir the ability to dematerialize parts of his form and materialize it elsewhere. Just a matter of protons, electrons, and energy. It's no different than when he entirely dematerializes when he is deactivated."

"Shush, Miss Becky, you old schoolmarm. How can I work with all this babbling going on?" tsked Ranbir.

Becky laughed but grew quiet as they all recognized that Ranbir's arm, on the other side of the door, was searching for something.

"Ah!" he said, "here it is. A simple latch is all." He grunted and pulled his arm back. The brass door came open with him on expertly oiled hinges. It did not make a sound. They entered the transept area and stared.

Josiah wasn't surprised, but the others were. What he saw the day before, the others were now experiencing for the first time, and they could not believe the beauty before them. The tapestries glittered in the blazing candlelight in all their pagan glory, their gold threads reflecting light from the golden tiles of the ceiling. The atmosphere was bright and warm, a whispered current of air filtering through some ancient vents and gently moving the tapestries so that the figures on them seemed to come alive.

Daniel was surprised that The Regale, recumbent in a pouch within his Kevlar vest, begin pulsing. He couldn't be sure, but the stone seemed to transmit some sort of excitement. Daniel whispered, "Not yet, Archbishop. Enki can't know you are here. You're the fallback plan."

"We have studied this religion," said Abednego, "since we first heard about it several days ago. Clearly, it is no wonder that Mithraism rivaled Christianity for dominance in your religion's early days. This is a warm and inviting place with mysteries and secrets attractive to any searcher of the unknown."

"It was a boy's club," said Rebecca, breaking the mood. "I can feel it. Women were not welcome here."

"It's true," said Daniel. "They weren't. This place, this cult, was for the disaffected males of the empire—the poor, the homeless, the veterans cut off by wounds or retirement from their fellow soldiers. To them, it represented life and hope. But it was not. The promises the cult made could not ultimately be kept, and what looked like an equal battle between faiths withered through the years. Christianity crushed this cult. The hope Mithraism preached was false."

A burst of soft laughter lilted through the *Mithraeum*. It took them all a moment to realize it was coming from the hole in the center aisle, just yards from where they stood.

Luca said, "I presume that leads down to the room of sacrifice?"

"Yes," said Josiah, "there is a moveable tile that raises up anything below and lowers anything here down to there."

Grigio, who had been hanging back behind the team, now cautiously approached the hole. He looked over the edge and saw fire deep below. His sensitive nose recoiled, and his lips pulled back as he smelled brimstone sulfur mixed with cloying incense. He leapt back with a little yelp and shook his head.

"Maybe not the room of sacrifice," said the pope. "Perhaps, instead, the pits of hell."

A quavering, wavering voice drifted up from the depths, chanting, "Out of the depths, I cry to you O Lord; Lord, hear my voice! Let your ears be attentive to the voice of my pleading."

"Pay no attention to that," snapped the pontiff. "It is the devil quoting Scripture, twisting the Psalms to his own dark uses. It will not be the last time Enki tries such a thing."

"Enki!" breathed out the three brothers in a whisper. But they were heard.

"Ah," said the voice from below, "once again, I hear those who refused to worship me from of old. How I have anxiously yearned to renew our friendship."

The voice was getting stronger now, as something was rising from below. Josiah recognized Enki immediately, dressed in the same dark blue robe with golden planets and stars embroidered on the fabric, glittering in the candlelight. Yet, the face looked different. No mask this time, just a morphing visage. One moment there were glimmers of the Guy Fawkes face and at other times, the dreadful countenance of the Babylonian water deity showed forth. Only the hands never changed, and they were not human. Elongated fingers with what looked like octopus suckers adorned each hand. The better to grip you with my dear thought the Swiss Guard.

"Do not look at its face," cried Daniel. "It moves and shifts to trap your vision and ensnare your consciousness. If you must look, stare only at the robe—it is not part of the demon."

The brothers opened fire immediately with their rings, but the sapphire flames were repelled by an invisible force around Enki. The godling laughed, drifting several feet above the floor towards the altar in the front of the room.

"I have tired of the beating you have given me with those Star Sapphire Rings. I admit they gave you an advantage, but today, at least, you will not be able to harm me with them. I have taken certain measures to protect myself."

The entity reached the altar, and as it had done the day before, stood on top of it and faced the VERITAS team. "I think I'm supposed to say," it chuckled, "'You are probably wondering why I called you all here.' Well, let me be frank. I called you to kill you. You have disrupted our plans enough in the past few days. But no longer. Even as we speak, my puppets are filtering through several of your European cities, and, as you know, the great metropolis of New York. They are directed by my human associates, terrorists of

Memento Mori. Have I told you how much New York reminds me of Babylon? Cosmopolitan, ethnically diverse, religiously varied, but with a vibrant inner corruption. It will be a pleasure to take it apart piece by piece until only those that worship the One Who Is Coming will be left."

"We are honored," said the pope with a sneer, "to have delayed and obstructed your plans. But to be honest, we do not know much about them. Who is this One Who Is Coming?"

Daniel inwardly smiled. In all the pagan literature he had studied, it was a *fait accompli* deities could not resist bragging about themselves or their accomplishments. The pope was giving the team its best chance yet to figure out why November 1 was so dangerous to humanity.

"I am so glad you asked," said Enki. "The One Who is Coming currently resides in the object you have called 'Oumuamua, this asteroid of sorts making its way to rendezvous with earth. The One whose mouth is fire, whose breath is death, whose will is woe, has sent the Babylonian gods to earth as once it did before, to prepare its way."

"You lost the last time you were here," said Abednego.

"A mere setback," laughed Enki. "Humanity was more talented and vigorous than we believed. In a way, it was what you call a good learning experience for us."

"What makes you think anything has changed?" said Meshach.

"Look around Babylon boys," said the entity. "The world is even more divided than when that idiot king of yours built that tower to reach the heavens. More than language splits the nations now."

"You're worried though," said Daniel. "Otherwise, you would not have attempted the slaughter of the delegates at the United Nations."

"Concerned, not worried," smiled Enki, briefly allowing the Fawkes image to grace his face. "You have seen that my imposition of chaos there was just as effective as murder."

"Still," said Daniel, "you are not entirely sure."

Anger flared across Enki's visage. "Ah, you are the brat who defeated the best of my *gallu*. Asgalu is currently resting far below. But I have brought his offspring. Perhaps you all would like to meet them."

He looked toward the pit and squawked like a vulture.

"The dead call to the dead," muttered Luca.

"Shut up," said Enki. "I killed you once and can do it again. You don't have your ghostly guardian angel with you this time."

A warning glance from Daniel silenced Luca's response. Even the jewel seemed to pulse less as if it sensed Daniel's concern for too early a reveal.

As the godling was speaking, the team heard a rattling from the pit. Soon, deformed and elongated appendages appeared at the lip of the pit as a smaller version of *gallu* began to haul themselves up from the depths.

Enki cried, "Behold, the children of Asgalu, here to revenge their father's injuries."

"In ancient Babylon," cried Shadrach, "they were known as the 'ankle-biters.' Small but deadly. We must beware."

Daniel saw they would barely reach up to his waist, but their clawed hands and feet and their dagger-toothed mouths clearly transmitted their threat. In the golden light, they shone green as if the muck of the ages clung to their deformed bodies.

Luca pulled out his Mp7 and shot the closest one, blowing its chest apart. "It seems that Enki has chosen not to protect his little ones with any kind of force shield. Perhaps he can't." Luca blew another into eternity that dared to approach its brother's corpse.

Enki screamed, "Destroy them!"

The *gallu* responded, hopping and prancing toward Daniel and his companions. Each of the team opened fire on the approaching horde. Some of the *gallu* were smart, choosing to split off from the group and make for the tapestries where their sharp claws could find purchase to climb. They would attack from above.

Ranbir quickly walked toward the altar, using his finger lasers to plow a path towards Enki. Daniel had instructed him not to let the godling slip away. Bart had recalibrated the hologram's energy field so that it could not be disrupted by either a force shield or an energy blast from the enemy.

Ranbir, however, had a flair for the dramatic. He flashed his ceremonial dagger high over his turbaned head and slashed Enki's energy field to shreds. He slammed it into the shield causing a cacophonous blow to ring throughout the room and spark out the energy barrier.

He did not have as much luck with Enki. All members of the team had been given *carte blanche* to execute the godling if they could, and Ranbir saw his chance. Yet, his dagger shattered when he tried to pierce the cloak that Enki wore. His cybernetic brain processed that the robe was like some ancient Kevlar that also protected the entity from harm. Yet, the existence of the robe proved the Babylonian gods were powerful, but they were not indestructible. They could be killed or at least sent back to some shadowy sort of existence. Ranbir was anxious to find out which. He went for the throat of Enki, and the two grappled on the altar.

The rest of the team formed two groups. The brothers went forward to try to destroy the main cluster of the *gallu* while the other four backed down the aisle, raised their heads and started shooting at those climbing the tapestries and launching themselves from their perches toward the team.

The pope and Daniel fired their rings, easily disposing of those that threw themselves through the air. Likewise, the guns used by

Luca and Rebecca did the same. But there were too many. They neglected those that lurked among the benches, reaching out to grab their legs. Daniel felt one latch onto his calf and sink his teeth into his leg. The material of his uniform was made of Cordera which was impervious to tearing or being penetrated by sharp objects, but the bite pressure was immense. Daniel couldn't help crying out, knowing that there would be a great bruise on his shin soon. He reached down and picked up the *gallu* by the neck, and with his ring flaring, twisted the creature's head till a satisfying crack was heard.

Daniel loved extreme sports, and he now felt the adrenaline rushing through him as if he was doing one of the dangerous pastimes he often found himself enjoying. In a way, this was as exciting as rock climbing or parasailing. Luca looked over and saw the gleam in his friend's eye and shouted, "Now you've got them! Let's send these bastards back to hell!"

Even Rebecca joined in the shouting and they all redoubled their efforts to exterminate the infernal vermin.

Except for the pope. He nodded at Daniel and moved alone up toward the pit, pausing only to dispatch the *gallu* who tried to wrestle him to the ground. They hung on his legs but he was strong. His ring blasted them back into the pit, but there was no excitement in his heart. He wondered if these creatures had always been twisted, or had the entity known as Enki warped and tortured them into what they had become.

The pontiff moved quickly around the hole in the floor and set his eyes on Ranbir and the godling, fighting on the altar. He knew he didn't have to protect the avatar, so he moved in until he was beside the two.

"Ranbir," shouted the pope, "can you disable the demon?"

"I've tried my best, Paddy," said Ranbir. "Perhaps you'd like a run at it. Just do what you have to do before Enki reconstitutes his energy field."

The pope grabbed Enki's robe and threw the monster down onto the altar. The pontiff's ring flared and tendrils of blue flame covered the robe and punched into the altar, holding Enki down. The godling screamed in defiance.

"You think you can defeat me this easily? Look who comes."

The team had dispatched the *gallu* and heard Enki clearly. They looked all around the room but saw nothing. Then Daniel screamed, "The tunnels! They'll come from the tunnels!"

"Who or what?" shouted Luca.

"The possessed," said Daniel. "I can hear them already. Quickly, get everyone up to the altar."

Enki saw this as a moment for his escape, but the pope had other ideas. He strengthened the sapphire flame bonds as his attention was drawn to movement in the back of the room.

They came like the quiet dead, shuffling forward, blank expressions on their faces. The homeless, the poor, the disaffected—all those who wandered the streets of Rome, lost and forgotten. In their hands, they each held a vial, and the glass objects glowed green. Daniel didn't think they looked particularly dangerous this time. Nonetheless, Grigio leapt down the aisle and stood before them, growling a warning. Daniel wondered what Enki was up to.

The demon began to laugh softly. "You thought I could only defeat you by force, but you are wrong. I can defeat you through pity and despair. Look at them. Each one gave me their allegiance, and if they resisted, I took it. Just as much as the *gallu*, they are my servants. I could have them attack you. That's what their brothers and sisters are doing up above in the streets of Rome, the cities of Europe, and New York even as we speak.

"However," said Enki. "I have a better plan. See their leader? That tall strong handsome boy who should be out wooing his girlfriend? He has been so helpful, but he is expendable. Watch."

The pope had neglected to bind Enki's hands. Daniel saw the demon's fingers twitch. The tall man down the aisle moved his hands apart, one empty hand and arm held high, while the other hand clutched a vial. The human thrall dropped his flask. It shattered on the tile floor, and, for a moment, the young man's eyes cleared; his awareness returned; and then he screamed, falling dead on the floor. The green vapor, released now from the shattered glass, hovered in the air for a moment and then dissipated.

"Oh, what a pity," said Enki, "his soul is gone. I had intended feeding on their souls down through the ages, but I can let them go just as swiftly if I wish. Let me rise. Free me, or I shall kill them all."

To demonstrate that he was not lying, Enki felled another five with just a flick of his fingers, until the pope, at the top of the altar, reached out over Enki's shoulders and covered up the demon's hands with his own.

"Quickly, Dani," said the pope, "do what you must."

Daniel took a breath, reached into his Kevlar vest to the special pouch he had sown in, and took out The Regale. If this didn't work, then the final attempt would rest with the plan he and the pope had devised. The Regale, over the centuries, had become a religious object, a holy thing, able to dispel sin, sickness, and even, sometimes, death. But it had not been used in centuries and had been separate for as long from the relics of St. Thomas Becket. Nonetheless, the attempt had to be made.

Daniel held the jewel high above Enki, who squealed in horror, clenching his eyes closed as the Red Sapphire flared out a warming glow.

"Get that thing away from me!" snarled Enki.

"Will you let the possessed go? Will you give them back their souls?"

"Never!" cried the demon. "They are mine, my delectable delicacies, the fruits of my labor. You can never have them."

"Use it!" cried the pope to Daniel. "Use it now!"

Daniel lifted The Regale higher and then plunged it down towards Enki, pressing it upon the demon's chest.

Enki screamed as The Regale burned down through the robe into its skin. But then, Enki began gasping out some kind of chant in Akkadian. The most Daniel could decipher was that it was some demonic ward of protection against all that is good. As the entity chanted, its breathing became more regular, and it began laughing.

"It is too weak," Enki said. "I knew it could not conquer me."

"Uncle Liam," shouted Daniel, "the gem is not at full strength. It's going to have to be you."

The pope looked over Enki's head into Daniel's eyes. "Whatever happens," he said, "stay strong my beloved nephew."

Daniel stifled a sob as the pontiff moved around the altar and pushed Daniel aside. He laid his hand on The Regale and pressed it again into the demon's chest.

"You cannot harm me, priest," said the demon. "And even if by some chance you defeat me, one is coming who is mightier than I, whose sandal straps …"

"Silence, devil!" cried the pope. "You shall not mock the Word of God."

Then, bracing his arm on The Regale, the pope rose up to his full height, and with his right arm signed the Cross over the prone figure saying:

> *By the living God,*
> *By the true God,*
> *By the holy God,*
> *I exorcize you,*
> *Most unclean spirit, adversary of faith,*
> *Enemy of the human race, purveyor of death,*
> *Father of Lies, root of evils.*

I command you, accursed dragon,
In the name of our Lord Jesus Christ:
Be uprooted and be put to flight.
Christ himself commands you,
He who ordered you and your companions
To be cast down from the heights of heaven
Into the depths of the earth.
Christ himself commands you,
He who commanded wind, sea, and storm.
Christ himself commands you,
He the eternal Word of God made flesh.
Be humbled beneath the mighty hand of God;
Tremble and flee
As we call upon the holy name of Jesus.
Before whom hell quakes,
And to whom the blessed angels cry
With unceasing voices,
'Holy, Holy, Holy Lord God of hosts.'
Depart, therefore,
In the name of the Father +, and of the + Son,
And of the Holy + Spirit.

A booming crack was heard above and masonry cascaded down from the ceiling narrowly missing those near the altar.

Above the screaming of the demon, whose cries grew ever more panicked and terrified, could be heard the loud AMEN of the VERITAS team. As the pope took his hand off The Regale, it floated up and over to Daniel who grasped it in his hand. Enki sat up, some kind of dark dribble pouring from his fleshy mouth, and screamed, "You cannot do this!"

"Too late!" cried Daniel. He was breathless now. He had felt The Regale draw upon his strength. It took his uncle to utter the ancient words of exorcism to bring Enki to defeat. To seal the moment, Daniel knew what he had to do.

Everyone thought that exorcism was nice and dainty, a throwback to the parlor tricks that mediums used back in the previous centuries. But Daniel's knowledge went back farther, and he knew that exorcists often had to wrestle with the demon to get the souls apart from them. This was no different. Time for part two.

A wrenching howl swept through the *Mithraeum* as Enki screamed again, and a strong wind swept up the aisle shaking the tapestries. Some were torn in two and fell upon the benches below. The possessed never moved, but neither did they let go of any of their vials.

Taking a deep breath, Daniel raised The Regale high and said, "The power of Christ commands you!"

There was a sound as of thunder over the dry plains, lightning crackling through the sky from east to west, its flashes splitting asunder the heavens, and for a moment, the very earth shook under them and golden dust drifted down from the vaulted ceilings of the *Mithraeum*.

Daniel plunged the gem down with all his might, and such was the power of the blow that it pierced the blue robe and gnarled, amphibious skin of Enki, plunging into whatever passed for its heart. There was a blinding red flash causing Daniel to let go of the jewel and instinctively cover his eyes. They all did, and when they looked again, Enki had stopped moving. He was not dead. He had fallen back on the altar and his eyes flicked to and fro, but steam was coming up from his chest.

At least that's what Daniel thought it was until it started coalescing above Enki's body. The ghostly figure of the bishop appeared. "You have done well, Holy Father, as has your nephew. This is one of the worst of the demons of hell. It goes by many names," he said in a hollow voice, gesturing at Enki. "Allow me to finish," said the apparition. Daniel looked to the pope who nodded his approval and the ghostly archbishop said, "*Fiat, Fiat, Fiat lux!* Let there be, let there be, let there be light!"

The bishop's hands burst into cleansing fire. Enki screamed in agony, while the figure, who appeared to be Thomas Becket, sometime Archbishop of Canterbury and saint, lifted the demon, carrying him down the aisle, bound in his burning hands. The apparition stood over the opening to the pit and without ceremony dropped Enki in, wrenching out The Regale as the figure fell. Becket held the glowing jewel high over the pit. The demon fell screaming, and Daniel thought the entity shrieked far longer than the pit was deep.

The archbishop looked at him and smiled the first soft smile Daniel had ever seen on that face and said, "For one so evil, the fall is mighty. For this one, hell is far away and the journey horrific and deadly. It shall be long before it bothers anyone again."

Then, the apparition walked over to the possessed and held up The Regale. He said these words which echoed throughout the hall,

> *Deliver, O God, these servants*
> *From every hostile power,*
> *And keep them safe,*
> *So that*
> *They may love you from their hearts,*
> *Serve you by their works,*
> *And extol you with their praise.*
> *Restore again their life O Lord!*

The vials shattered. The VERITAS team members, including the pope, gasped in horror, but they need not have worried. The green mist within them turned to gold as the souls were absorbed into the hearts of each one of the men and women standing before them.

Their faces cleared, their eyes took on new life, and as consciousness returned, they began to sob and clutch one another.

Some said later that they remembered the spectral figure dressed in a bishop's robe holding up a radiant jewel, but all remembered the dignified man with salt and pepper hair who approached them, blessed them, and said, "My name is Patrick and we are here to help. Do not be afraid."

CONSIDERATIONS

Wednesday Afternoon, March 24, Oval Office, White House, Washington, D. C.

LESLIE RICHARDSON WAS ushered into the Oval Office at 12:30 P. M. Once the door was shut Leslie immediately said, "Oliver, there have been developments."

"Good ones, I hope," said the president, sitting back in his reclining desk chair.

"I believe so. I have just heard from Captain Luca Rohner of the Swiss Guard. He'll give a longer briefing tomorrow to me, but the short of it is that the Enki entity has been neutralized, and those that were possessed or under thrall, however you want to look at it, have had their humanity restored and are fine."

"How did that happen?" asked the president. "Wait, tell me later. If it involves the pope and his nephew you are probably going to add in a lot of supernatural horseshit, and I just finished lunch. Don't think I'm up to that yet."

Leslie smiled tautly and drily said, "That horseshit probably saved your life yesterday."

"I'm well aware of that," he said ruefully. "It's just a lot to take in at once."

"Well, there's more, I'm afraid," said Leslie, "though if you can tolerate a little paranormal stuff, you'll be pleased." At Putnam's head nod, she continued, "There were no outbreaks of riots by the possessed in New York, or in any other of the major cities of Europe. It seems that whatever the VERITAS team did in Rome neutralized the threat and restored the possessed to health. The appropriate authorities have arrested all members of the *Memento Mori* terrorist organization who were coordinating the worldwide operation. Rebecca is downloading her report to Ranbir even as we speak. I can have the avatar debrief us within the hour."

"That will be fine," sighed Putnam. "I, too, have some good news, though more on the practical front. I was able to get NATO to agree on our November 1 alliance, and I think I might just have Russia convinced as well. They seem willing to put off conquering any of the surrounding principalities and republics for the time being until we get this crisis solved."

"Well, that is good news," said Leslie. "Heard anything from the Islamic nations?"

"Not yet," said the president. "They are meeting later this week to take up the issue of the Mahdi. The Babylon incident last month brought Dr. Nabil Kassar to the front of the line for that position. Any new intel on him?"

Leslie frowned as she said, "Kassar is an enigma. From what Rebecca and Isaac report, he entertains the notion of being the Mahdi, but eschews the usual radicalism that goes with that title. I had a chance to talk to Daniel a bit about him. They have had several conversations. Daniel is wary of him, but says if he proclaims himself as Mahdi we will have to take him very seriously. Having been a first-hand witness of all the events surrounding the End Times Tablet in

Babylon, he is a believer. Daniel thinks Kassar will aid our cause. Rebecca and Isaac concur."

"There is one other problem," said Oliver. "Here, let me pour you a scotch. We're going to need a drink."

"You're speaking about the king."

"Exactly," said the president. "We don't just have a monarch on our hands anymore; we have an actual ruling king. Not only did he slip the religion thing over on the Parliament, but more importantly, at least to my eyes, he got them to let him actually command the United Kingdom's armed forces."

"But wasn't the monarch always commander-in-chief?" said Leslie.

"Only theoretically. The monarchy hasn't much used that power in two hundred years. But it never gave it up, and that's why Parliament had to go along with the king's desire to assume direct control—national emergency and all that."

"He's an engaging personality," said Leslie. "We should have paid closer attention to his rise to the throne. In all honesty, however, he will be a help and not a hindrance."

"I sure hope so," said Putnam. "I watched his afternoon conference from Canterbury earlier this morning. Not only does he seem to be able to rule, but he's also a good politician as well. He showed workmen beginning to assemble the shrine and expects to have the project completed in a couple of weeks. We are invited to the consecration of the new shrine. We'll have to go, you know."

"Well," said Leslie, "you wouldn't want to miss the possibility of some more 'supernatural horseshit.'"

"A poor choice of words," said the president, "which I think you will never let me forget."

***

Just as Director of the CIA and the President of the United States were talking, the door to the underground VERITAS headquarters opened, and a man strode up the aisle toward the laboratory display table at the far end of the room.

Dr. Abigail Duchon and Fr. Salvatore were again looking at the various blood samples through the electron microscope. Images were projected onto screens behind them and Abby was just pointing out a new anomaly. She heard footsteps, turned, and saw John Nance approaching. His right hand was bandaged where Grigio had amputated his ring finger. Cold sweat broke out on her forehead.

"Mr. Nance," she said with a hesitant smile on her face. "I hear we have you to thank for this magnificent headquarters."

He never said a word to her. He simply took out a gun and shot Fr. Salvatore in the forehead, who proceeded to drop dead on the floor.

Abby clutched the table and felt her world spin. Before she passed out, she saw Nance look dispassionately at the body and said, "I loved the treason, but hated the traitor."

Before she lost consciousness, she heard herself saying, "Plutarch? Did he quote Plutarch? Why in God's name did he do that?"

A TIME FOR MIRACLES

Sunday Evening, May 20, Canterbury Cathedral, Canterbury, England

THE DAY HAD been a smashing success, a triumph of faith and freedom. Daniel and Luca walked up the road from the village of Canterbury proper, all of whose citizens along with thousands of guests were still in a festive mood. The medieval village had been spruced up and decorated with outdoor stalls selling food and the inevitable shrine souvenirs. For this was the day of the consecration of the restored Becket Shrine.

"Amazing day," said Luca. "I think Josiah was happy for the task of escorting the pope back home. The rest of the team still seems to be enjoying themselves in town."

"Except for Fr. Salvatore," said Daniel softly.

"Except for him," said Luca, neutrally.

"I know what you think of him," said Daniel. "And it's true. He was a traitor."

"He was a veritable Judas."

"But I can't believe he was all bad. In fact, I don't know why he took that role."

Luca said, "Because John Nance can be very persuasive when he wants to be. He promised him something Fr. Salvatore truly wanted—money, fame, power, whatever. Fr. Salvatore bit like a bass on a hot summer day."

"Then Nance killed him."

"In Nance's world," said Luca, "he probably thought he was doing us a favor. Fr. Salvatore had to threaten him somehow for Nance to act that way. The balls of that guy, walking into our headquarters and plugging him in the forehead. If I see Nance again, it will be the last time he sees anything."

"Fr. Salvatore was the leak to Nance. Who knows how many years that had been going on? He had to convince himself that what he was doing was right; otherwise, his conscience would not have let him continue."

"I can't be so kind," said Luca. "He nearly got us all killed, and I'm surprised he didn't kill Abby after he unalived the old priest."

"You know I had to really persuade her to stay with us. She was very traumatized, but we need her. Her research into the Shroud of Turin led to her discovery of the changes in those who bear the Star Sapphire Rings. That will be valuable in the coming months, and she may discover more."

"She'll be fine. It's Nance I can't figure out," said Luca. "He gets rid of a traitor that hurts us, but still, he is against us."

"Or is he?" said Daniel. "He travels to the beat of a different drum."

"Ah," said Luca, "Linda Ronstadt. Didn't know you liked her music."

Daniel smiled. It had been months since Luca joked like he used to. Perhaps he too was coming around.

They came to the entry of the cathedral and the one they were waiting for stood leaning against the massive doors.

"Were you going to spend all day eating sticky buns?" said Sr. Cecelia with a smile. The new Director of the Canterbury Cathedral Ecumenical Center was happy to see them. She told them the new shrine had one last surprise for them.

"It was a glorious day," said Daniel. "The pope, the king, the new Archbishop of Canterbury—a Catholic cheered by a mixed crowd of Protestants, Catholics, and Anglicans. Haven't seen that in centuries."

"Everyone senses a new hope with the shrine. Having so many major world leaders here today didn't hurt. Even if they don't know exactly how the shrine is going to play a role in defeating the enemy that is coming, people are believing what you, your father and mother, and your uncle are saying."

Luca beamed at the nun. "You did a marvelous job in keeping the workmen on task. Let's take a closer look."

They went inside, up through the Quire, and into Trinity Chapel. There it was, in all its glory. Erasmus, who, hundreds of years before, described its predecessor in detail would have been astounded. The reconstituted shrine looked almost the same. It was built on a platform of smoothly cut granite. Its base, which was ten feet high and 40 feet long was made of rose marble, just like the original and from the same quarry. On one end was the altar where Mass was celebrated that day by the pope when he consecrated the shrine. Then came the three ten-foot arches. On top of them rested a slab of marble. Then came the golden casket which looked like a mini-cathedral. Sr. Cecelia had been busy the past months seeking contributions from all the countries of the world. The casket, which now held the few remaining bone relics of the saint as well as the Tunicle, was shining and glimmering in the candlelight from the jewels donated by a hopeful world and fastened onto the sides and top of the casket. The artists had done an amazing job of integrating the jewels into the reliquary. Above, was an intricately carved oaken cover which would be lowered over the casket when no services were scheduled and no pilgrims present. It had colorful medieval woven tapestries on its sides and was a piece of extraordinary artwork in itself.

But there was something new, something Daniel wanted a closer look at. No one was sure what was originally in the space between the arches back in the medieval era. Perhaps it was simply offerings from pious people and burning candles. That was not the case now.

"Ok," said Daniel. "Spill it, Sr. Cecelia. The real story on how there comes to be a fountain of fresh water in the middle of a cathedral at the base of a reliquary."

"You know the essentials," said the nun. "I was alone here the day after the workmen completed the shrine. It was so peaceful here, and everything was beautiful. Remember what we saw here the first time you visited? Well, that happened again. A breeze gently blew through the Quire and into the chapel, making the candles flicker. You could barely feel it, but, immediately, I knew someone was with me. I looked all around but could find no one. Then from around the corner of the shrine walked a bishop."

"Did he look like Richard Burton from the movie, *Becket*?" smiled Luca.

"He was tall, good looking, and had immense presence. I knew who he was."

"Usually, this is the spot in miraculous sightings where the vision tells you to build a beautiful chapel. But there's already one here," said Daniel.

"Quiet" clipped Sr. Cecelia, a little miffed that the two were interrupting her story. "The bishop moved with a crozier in his hand and pointed to the area between the arches, underneath the reliquary. His voice was pleasant enough, but it was firm. He said, 'Dig and make it flow.'"

"It's amazing what you did," said Daniel. "You called the workmen back, took them to the lower level immediately beneath the shrine, and had them dig. Twenty feet down you hit a spring of water. Thank God for modern engineering. Those guys figured out how to get the water to the shrine proper and the fountain is beautiful."

"The water runs off to spigots outside the shrine so that the faithful can take some home. What most people forget," said Sr. Cecelia, "is that in the early days of the original shrine, the peasants scooped up the blood of the martyr, mixed it with water, and that became the source of many of the early cures."

"Of course," said Daniel, "Abby would say it was because of the special blood type Becket had because he once bore one of the Star Sapphire Rings. His blood had healing properties. I prefer a more divine interpretation."

"So do I," said the usually skeptical nun. "This holy water from the spring blessed by the pope today will be what pilgrims can take home from here. Perhaps it will bring them some solace, perhaps even some healing."

"A doubting world is going to mock this," said Luca. "We're not in the medieval era anymore and Christendom is long gone."

"No doubt you are right, Captain," said the nun. "But they will only mock if healings do not happen. You must admit we have been guided to reconstitute the shrine on the recommendation of a saint above our pay grade."

The three of them smiled and laughed a little at themselves. That's when they heard a soft yip behind them.

Daniel looked and there was Grigio, amazingly solid this evening after a full day playing with the kids of Canterbury. But he wasn't alone. Alongside him strode the figure of an archbishop. As the apparition came to a stop before the three, Daniel said, "We are honored, Your Grace. We hope you approve what has been remade."

The figure was not quite solid but was no longer the ghostly form from before. His white vestments were trimmed in gold, as was his miter. One gloved hand carried a crozier, and he looked healthy and well. His voice had a subtle echo as if it was not quite completely present in the church.

He said, "It is more beautiful than it once was. And you have made a special place above the altar of the shrine for The Regale." His free hand pointed to the beautiful ruby glowing brightly in its special spot mounted on the gold façade.

"Even as the Holy Father enshrined it today, I felt its power flow into me, now that it was back in its true home. I know you are worried that the opulence of this shrine will offend people, but the whisperings I have heard around the world do not bear that fear out. Why? Because it is no longer seen as wealth. The king who destroyed the shrine so long ago thought it was only worth money, and look what it bought him. Nothing but sadness, violence, and division. No, people see the shining shrine as a light in the darkness, as a testimony to the Christ who, filled with the Holy Spirit, came to bring good news to the poor, release to the captives, recovery of sight to the blind, to let the oppressed go free, to proclaim that God has not yet forgotten the people of the world."

"Perhaps," said Luca, "all the money spent here could have been used for the poor."

The apparition walked up to the arches and looked in at the flowing fountain. "There is a place for beauty in this world. Money is spent but once. Beauty endures, inspires, and gives hope. Pilgrims always want something to take back with them. This water will suffice. It is not magical, but it is holy, and to those whose hearts are open to hear the voice of God and feel his presence, the water will remind them that healing is possible. Within weeks it will be all over the world, and serve as a sign that we will not be victims of the darkness that returns."

"So, you will help us?" said Daniel.

"My place is here. But I will help. Call on me in your need, and I and The Regale will make our presence felt throughout the world. Farewell, my new friends. You have awakened me from the sleep of ages to a new era of hope."

Daniel watched the bishop turn and walk down the aisle, Grigio by his side.

"What is that pup doing?" said Luca.

"What all dogs do—get into mischief," sniffed Sr. Cecilia, but with a grin on her face.

"Actually," said Daniel, "I think I know why he's here and what he's supposed to do, and I know a little more of what he is. He is a psychopomp, a strange name for an exalted position. He is a soul guide, the traveler between the worlds, a connection between both life and death, bearing both messages and power. But," he said with a wistful smile, "mostly, he's my dog, and I'm glad that he's with me."

The archbishop had disappeared into the unlighted portions of the cathedral, and Grigio came bounding back, tongue lolling, ready for a new adventure.

"Don't worry, pup," said Luca smiling and ruffling the hair on the wolf-dog's head. "We'll be in the thick of it again soon enough."

THE END

END NOTES

The Conorverse

My novels take place in the Conorverse. It's my writing world and it is based on the first of my fantasy novels, *ROAN: The Tales of Conor Archer, vol. 1*. Fantasy novels and paranormal thriller novels often take place in our normal world but with a few changes. So, for instance, in the Conorverse, there are such things multiple universes. In my world system, there are only two universes. In both sets of novels, they are called This World and the Otherworld. There are certain sites on the globe, called Thin Places, where the walls between the worlds get very thin, so thin that beings can cross between the two universes. Interestingly, modern physicists posit the existence of many multiple universes. I'm just a little shy of doing that.

In my fantasy novels, there is a great conflict between the two realms. In fact, they once were together, then split, and now are coming together again. Much history has passed, and much fear is engendered because neither side knows how this will work. In my paranormal thriller stories, things are a little clearer. The Otherworld is trying to elevate what passed as the Babylonian gods to their previous importance on earth. Nothing good is forecast from this. The End Times Tablet foretells a crushing defeat of humanity.

Eventually, both sets of stories will intersect, but not for a while. There are tales to tell and secrets yet to be revealed.

The Anunnaki

The Anunnaki are a set of seven or eight gods in the Sumerian, Assyrian, Babylonian and Hittite cultures. Mid-eastern cosmology is convoluted so let me try to keep it simple.

These gods gave birth to the other gods. By the time, Babylon rises to its second empire, two of these gods become pre-eminent—Marduk and Enki. Marduk is seen as the chief god overall, and Enki is primarily a god of water and of the earth.

Here's where theology, science, and conspiracy theory meet. In the late 1960's several books came out that postulated that the Anunnaki were aliens from another planet, come to earth to provide humanity with special knowledge. They appeared before recorded history and stayed through the early parts of history such as the pyramid building of the Egyptians. The authors of these books felt that humanity had made great leaps forward in knowledge that could only be accounted for by outside help. Most scientists discount these theories as crypto-archeology.

Yet, the new finds in southeast Turkey at Gobelki Tepe crack some holes in the critiques. Gobelki Tepe is dated to 9000 BCE, almost four thousand years before recorded history. And this site shows great advancement. It should not have the complexity it does. Other sites in the area show the same and may be even older. A human society, whom we do not know, was able to construct things that should have been out of their league.

Now Genesis 6: 1–7 comes in with the story of the Nephilim, the sons of God, the fallen angels who came to earth and gave humanity knowledge long before recorded history. So much has been made of very scanty information about the Nephilim. The myth of the Nephilim gives rise to the idea that great civilizations, long lost, existed before what we know as the written record of humanity's history. For the most part, archeologists have sniffed at the idea of lost civilizations. They think they have discovered almost all that there were.

Yet, I believe that stories hold a modicum of truth. Stories simply do not come from nothing. Even now, skeptical biblical archeologists are having to take back their belief that much of the history recorded in the Bible is false. Why? Those same archeologists are finding remnants of battles fought, documents written, and cities built that were all thought to be flights of human imagination. I think there is some wiggle room for an open mind to still operate in the hopes of finding out the truth about ancient history and the possibility of lost civilizations. Hence, my take on the theories in my paranormal thrillers.

Archbishop St. Thomas Becket

Thomas Becket (1119–1170) is arguably the best-known churchman, politician, and influential figure of the Medieval Period. Becket was born in London, the son of a merchant. He was well educated but because of financial reverses in his family, he had to earn his living as a clerk when he reached the age of 20. Fortuitously, Thomas got a position as a clerk in the Archbishop of Canterbury's retinue. He was well-liked by the archbishop who gave him important missions in Europe and insisted he further his education.

Becket was extremely talented—one of those people whose personality sucks the air out of the room, so competent does he seem. The archbishop made him Archdeacon of Canterbury—a very important ecclesiastical position. This happened in 1154, and from there, Thomas' rise was meteoric. In 1155, the archbishop recommended the young man to young King Henry II and suggested he be made Lord Chancellor. This happened immediately because Henry truly liked Thomas. They became best friends.

Thomas was a secular man of his time. He was religious and did not engage in any particularly bad behavior. He liked nice things and would dress sumptuously. He could be gruff, but his friendship with Henry was real. He was the star of Henry's court. So close did they become, that in 1162, Thomas became Archbishop of Canterbury. Not yet a priest, he was immediately ordained. Henry placed his hopes on Thomas' friendship that his close friend would help him sway the balance of power between Church and State that always simmered in the Medieval period. No such luck.

Thomas had a conversion experience. Touched by God with the responsibility given to him, he changed his lifestyle and became an ascetic. He grew to have a love for the poor and was determined to protect the Church against the State. Thus began a conflict between King Henry and Archbishop Thomas over the rights of the Church. Henry felt betrayed and over the years, the friendship waned and bad blood increased. On Christmas Day in 1170, Henry said something at a banquet like, "Would no one rid me of this meddlesome priest?" Four knights took this statement as an order and carried out the murder of Becket on December 29, in Canterbury Cathedral.

Immediately, that very night, miracles involving the archbishop began to occur. In fact, Canterbury Abbey recorded 700 miracles within ten years, some very high profile, including the King of France's son.

The Medieval world was rocked by this murder and King Henry paid a high price. He had to do public penance and was scourged by the monks of the abbey. He was appalled at what the knights had done and grieved the loss of his friend. Europe rallied around the new martyr and Pope Alexander III canonized Thomas Becket as a saint in 1173, just a little more than two short years after Becket's martyrdom. Throughout Europe, churches were named after him, and many miracles, not simply at the Shrine, were recorded.

The best biography of the saint is *Thomas Becket, Defender of the Church (Our Sunday Visitor, 2020)*. The 1964 movie, 'Becket', starring Peter O'Toole and Richard Burton is a fine portrayal of the personages and the conflict between them

The Shrine of St. Thomas Becket

Immediately after Becket's death, pilgrimages began to Canterbury. Because of the plethora of miracles, the saint became quite popular, seen as the protector of the poor and the rights of the common person. Pilgrimages continued to grow until a massive shrine was constructed in 1220. The translation of his relics to the new shrine in the main part of the cathedral was a world event at the time. Dignitaries from everywhere attended as did thousands of people. They were not disappointed.

The shrine was an incredible work of artistic magnificence. To mark the 850th anniversary of Becket's death, scholars recreated a virtual shrine so that people today can see what the people of the past saw when they came to visit Canterbury.

To get a true image of its beauty, please Google the various articles that show its digital reconstruction.

For nearly, 400 years, the Shrine of Thomas Becket was the third most popular pilgrimage destination in Europe. Only the Holy Land and Rome were more visited. What's more, the record of miracles kept growing. The Shrine proved to be one of those Thin places where people might truly come into contact with the divine. St. Thomas Becket was a great intercessor. Geoffrey Chaucer wrote the famous *Canterbury Tales* about a pilgrimage to this shrine.

When King Henry VIII broke with the Catholic Church, he ordered the destruction of the monasteries and shrines. The Shrine of

St. Thomas Becket was completely destroyed, and Becket's bones were lost, in 1538.

The memory of Thomas never died, though the miracles came to a halt after the Shrine's destruction. In the never-ending struggle between Church and State, the loss of this center of pilgrimage was terrible.

Mithras and His Cult

Mithras was a Persian god that got imported into the Roman Empire. We are not going to be concerned about what he meant to the Zoroastrians, because the concept of him changed when the Romans adopted him.

Soldiers were particularly attracted to him, as were the downtrodden. As a mystery religion, Mithraism had several stages one had to pass through. To commemorate his life, followers would build their *mithraeum,* their places of worship, underground. The interior was set up like a banquet hall with an altar at the front. Because their rites were secret, we know little about their worship.

What we do know for certain is that Mithraism was a strong competitor with Christianity for the hearts and minds of the people of the Roman Empire. In fact, Christianity competed heavily against this religion and finally suppressed it by the end of the 4th century, though remnants continued for hundreds of years afterward.

The Shroud of Turin

The Shroud of Turin is a large piece of linen cloth purported to be the burial wrappings of Jesus Christ. They were left behind in the tomb after the Resurrection. It is found in the Cathedral of Turin,

Italy. What is amazing about the cloth is that it contains a negative image of a crucified man. When photographed with modern techniques a reverse image appears with photographic likeness. People who are experts on the Shroud are called Sindonologists from the Italian word for the shroud, *Sindone*. It appears out of the mists of history in 1354, but rumors of its existence can be traced back centuries.

It was denounced as a fake by some, but over the centuries, Catholics have accepted it as true. The Church takes no stand over the authenticity of the Shroud. Officially, it neither affirms nor rejects it. Unofficially, popes, bishops, priests, and other Church leaders have embraced it as real.

In the second half of the 20th century and into the 21st, scientific tests have been conducted on the Shroud with conflicting results. Sometimes the tests veer towards authenticity, sometimes not. Part of the problem is that the Church will only allow an infinitesimal sample of the cloth to be tested. Without a larger sample, the discussion as to authenticity will go on.

This is a large subject matter about which many books have been written. I've studied this matter thoroughly and my opinion leans strongly towards authenticity. The books are easily found on Amazon and make my case better than I could. Be sure to get the latest copyrighted ones. The Shroud is an amazing relic and has brought many people to believe in the Resurrection of Jesus Christ.

Guy Fawkes and the Gunpowder Plot

Most people are familiar with Guy Fawkes from the caricature mask of him used in the movie, 'V for Vendetta'. Most people, however, really don't know who he was. His name is inextricably woven into the November 5, 1605 Gunpowder Plot which saw a group of Catholic terrorists plot and almost succeed in blowing up Parliament and the Protestant King James I. Their purpose was to install a Catholic monarch. Only the dampness of the cellar where the gunpowder was stored thwarted what surely would have been a catastrophic explosion.

Guy Fawkes (1570–1606) has been described by his contemporaries as a man whom people would instinctively like. He was a Catholic convert and his Jesuit friend, Oswald Tesimond, said he was "pleasant of approach and cheerful of manner, opposed to quarrels and strife ... loyal to his friends." He was, says Tesimond, "a man highly skilled in matters of war." Competent and pious, he easily endeared himself to his fellow conspirators. Fawkes has been described by the author, Antonia Fraser, as "a tall, powerfully built man, with thick reddish-brown hair, a flowing mustache in the tradition of the time, and a bushy reddish-brown beard." Fraser notes that he was "a man of action ... capable of intelligent argument as well as physical endurance, somewhat to the surprise of his enemies." So, in short, he was a charming, intelligent, swashbuckler.

Though Fawkes was not the leader of the conspirators, he is the most well-known. It was he who was in charge of the gunpowder, and it was he who was caught by soldiers in the cellar where the explosives were kept. He was sentenced to die on January 31, 1606, but on the scaffold, he fell and broke his neck, thus delivering himself from being hanged, drawn, and quartered.

For centuries afterward, Guy Fawkes Day is celebrated on November 5 by the British. Effigies of Fawkes are burnt. The cry that day is "Remember, remember, the 5th of November." Obviously, it is said so that such a plot never occurs again.

In the novel, the Guy Fawkes persona remains a figure of mystery and terror tinged with a religious twist. This works well in the world's struggle to once again see a partnership between secularism and belief.

(Wikipedia has gathered a great deal of source material, including sourcing Tesimond and Fraser's quotes. The article is sound and I highly recommend it for more information.)

'Oumuamua

This is an actual space object, in fact, the first interstellar space object noted in our solar system. It was discovered on October 19, 2017. Its maximum size is estimated at 3000 feet long and 548 feet wide. I make it larger in the story. After all, even the astronomers are really only guessing at its size. We know it is not a comet, and it truly remains a mystery. Reputable astronomers do muse over whether it is of natural or alien origin, so it becomes an excellent talking point for the events of November 1 in the novel.

OTHER BOOKS BY E. R. BARR

I hope you enjoyed this second novel in the new series called the VATICAN ARCHIVES. You'll be hearing about more adventures that involve Msgr. Daniel Azar and his best friend, the Swiss Guard Luca Rohner. These new stories take place in the Conorverse—that world inhabited by Conor Archer and his friends. Conor Archer is the protagonist of two, soon to be three, urban fantasy novels. Someday, these stories will intersect. And now, you are a part of that family as well. We are a tight knit group of people looking for adventures that ennoble and celebrate humanity.

THE TALES OF CONOR ARCHER

ROAN

SKELLIG

THE VATICAN ARCHIVES

GODS IN THE RUINS

(Available from all popular Internet book retailers)

DRIFTLESS
(coming 2023)

Series, like the VATICAN ARCHIVES and THE TALES OF CONOR ARCHER, depend on the support of readers like you. One of the ways to guarantee more stories like these is to leave a book review on the Amazon or Barnes and Noble websites. If you enjoyed *BENEATH THE BISHOP'S BONES*, please take a moment and write a review. It's the best way you can thank an author.

E. R. Barr

ABOUT THE AUTHOR

E. R. Barr spent his youth wandering around "Conor Country" known better as the "Driftless Area" of the southwest corner of the state of Wisconsin. The Mississippi and Wisconsin Rivers and the lands around them, dotted with Indian mounds and filled with stories and legends, fueled his imagination. Not till he started traveling world-wide did he truly begin to see connections between Ireland, Scotland, Wales and the lands where he was born. His forebears came from those ancient nations and settled there in Wisconsin. Always wondering why, he kept searching for answers. A Catholic Priest, a university professor, high school teacher and administrator, a popular speaker on all things Celtic and Tolkienesque, E. R. Barr makes his home in northwest Illinois. He is the author of the urban fantasy series, THE TALES OF CONOR ARCHER including the novels *ROAN* and *SKELLIG*. This is his fourth novel. Find out more about him and Conor's world by checking out the following website:

www.talesofconorarcher.com

From the author of the VATICAN ARCHIVES series comes:

An orphaned young man with mysterious power, his friends and a faithful dog combine their strengths to fight an ancient evil that seeks to conquer the world.

Available from all popular Internet book retailers.

Also from E.R. Barr

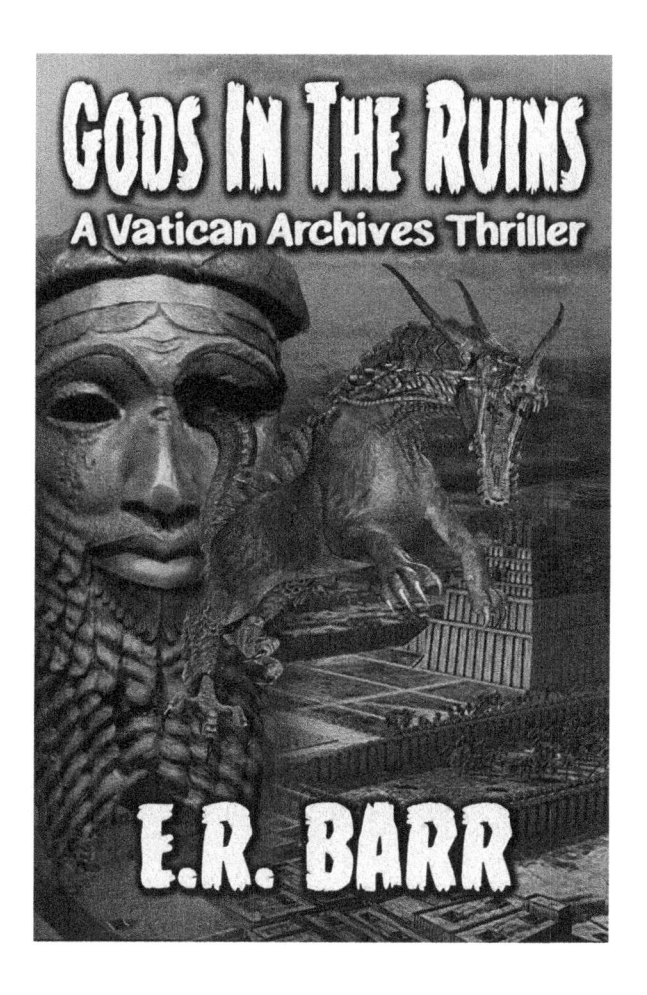

An ancient tomb is discovered in the ruins of Babylon. The Pope sends Vatican archeologist Fr. Daniel Azar and his best friend, Swiss Guard Luca Rohner to Iraq to investigate the tomb's warning of the end of the world and the terrible beast that will usher in the coming apocalypse. But who or what is in the tomb? And does it promise hope or threaten extinction for a waiting human race?

Available from all popular Internet book retailers.

Made in the USA
Monee, IL
06 October 2022